THE CARLOS CHADWICK MYSTERY

BOOKS BY GENE H. BELL-VILLADA

fiction
The Carlos Chadwick Mystery
A Novel Of College Life And Political Terror

The Pianist Who Liked Ayn Rand
A Novella & 13 Stories

memoir
Overseas American
Growing Up Gringo in the Tropics

literary criticism
On Nabokov, Ayn Rand and the Libertarian Mind
What the Russian-American Odd Pair Can Tell Us about
Some Values, Myths and Manias Widely Held Most Dear

Art For Art's Sake And Literary Life
How Politics and Markets Helped Shape the Ideology and
Culture of Aestheticism, 1970-1990

Borges And His Fiction; A Guide To His Mind And Art

Garcia Marquez: The Man And His Work

Writing Out of Limbo
The International Childhood Experience of Global Nomads
and Third-Culture Kids by Gene H. Bell-Villada and Nina
Sichel with Faith Eidse and Elaine Neil Orr

▫◻◻◻▫

THE CARLOS CHADWICK MYSTERY

A Novel of College Life and Political Terror

Gene H. Bell-Villada

▫◻◻◻▫

Printed in the United States of America
First Printing, 1990
Second Printing, 2020
ISBN:978-0-938513-06-3
Library of Congress Control Number: 89-85380

AMADOR PUBLISHERS, LLC
Albuquerque, New Mexico, USA
www.amadorbooks.com

Acknowledgments

With special thanks to: Marjorie Agosin, Ronald Christ, Patricia Corkerton, Linda Danielson, Barbara Foley, Mary Lusky Friedman, Janice Hirota, Robert Jackall, Katherine Singer Kovács (in memoriam 1946-1989), and Steven Kovács, Rachel Kranz, Carol McGuirk, Eugene Moretta, Thomas Smiley, and Harry Willson.

PUBLISHER'S PREFACE

by Adela Amador

The earnest young pastor was berated unmercifully at the church door one Sunday morning in the mid-1960s for suggesting in his sermon that North American involvement in Indochina was immoral as well as unconstitutional. "You mean you think you understand world history and U.S. foreign policy in Southeast Asia better than the Secretary of State?" he was asked.

"Oh, Lord, yes! Yes!!" he replied.

At another church door encounter the same pastor was told that he consistently presented a one-sided view of the war in Vietnam. "You should learn to give the Devil his due," he was told. It was meant more metaphorically than mythologically, probably.

"The Devil gets his due in every Pentagon release, every issue of both morning and evening newspapers, every television broadcast of the world news tonight, and every letter mailed free of charge to all constituents by both local Senators and our Congressional Representative," the young idealist replied. He thought he was obligated to try to provide "balance," with his maximum of twenty minutes a week, not counting other matters that needed attention in sermons. Needless to say, he did not succeed.

That young man is older now, if not wiser, and now he dares to presume that there are questions which do not have two sides to them, in spite of proverbial wisdom to the contrary. "What is the second side of nuclear waste with a half-life longer than the history of civilization?" he asks. "What is the second side to annihilation of the Biosphere itself?" he asks again. These are good questions.

Now we come with Gene's remarkable novel, and the theme is "balance," as the word is still used in the opinion-forming media. This book can be read on two levels. On the one hand, it is a straightforward account of the radicalization of its callow protagonist. On a deeper level, the novel is a not-so-subtle sendoff of the manipulations of the storytelling media and a comment on the way the orthodox American mind works, or doesn't work.

Neither of these two ways of reading this novel should be overlooked. Stretch, and enjoy!

□

TABLE OF CONTENTS

Foreword to the British Edition

by George O.R. Newell

[An earlier version of this essay appeared in
The New Statesman, 15 August 1980.]

Strange place, America. There's no industrialised country with
such a tiny left, and yet no place on earth with such seamless and
intense anti-leftism. During my travels between coasts I've
encountered some amazing notions entertained by our transatlantic
cousins as to what "socialism" is. I remember a bright young
waitress in a Utah college town, who, after commiserating with me
about how "things are pretty primitive over there" in London,
asked why we let "those socialists" wreck our economy. She's not
the first American friend to have told this roving reporter that
National Health Service is a total flop. Recently a clerk in a good
Chicago shoe store informed me that, in Russia, you're allowed
just one pair of shoes. One. So it goes.

For those who populate the minimal U.S. left, it's not easy.
Just finding a suitable role and style poses a difficult enough task
for them. Some reasonable and apologetic sorts work hard within
the Democratic Party fold (now the Republicans' moderating
wing). Others try keeping alive a 1930s Popular Frontism,
mimicking certain stereotypical American quirks and mannerisms.
Or they mouth a simplistic Maoism and Third Worldism, as many

1

New Left types did in the 1960s. And then you have the extreme cases, youths mostly—Weatherman-this, Symbionese-that, and the more recent Carlos Chadwick of Richards College—who, turning angry, completely reject Americanism and its whole high-tech caboodle. One can understand the fury of these young leftists. From the day of their birth it has been constantly hammered into them that theirs is "the greatest country in the world." Then come wars in Vietnam and Peru, and other such hints that American Greatness may not necessarily be the case. Their discovering another America can be, in the language of the Freudianised, "traumatic" in the extreme, a shock greater than, say, realising that White Man's Burden was just a bit of sanctimonious drivel.

Nobody has really figured out what role Chadwick played in those bombings. Though media people high and low like to speculate, none of their theories show much substance. But the question that seemingly both baffles and fascinates many Americans is: Why would Carlos do it at all (assuming he did)? What forces would possess a privileged student at an élite New England college either to resort to such tactics or express such glee at the results? This was the aim of Fred Jennings, veteran staff writer for *Manhattan* magazine.

The Carlos Chadwick Mystery was Jennings' idea. Editor-gatherer Jennings also did its Part 1, a report on his search for Carlos and the fullest investigation so far into the background to that bizarre episode. In addition, being aware that legendary Richards College beauty Livie Kingsley had once known Carlos romantically, he asked her for some personal remembrances. What we get in her memoir is not just a *very* close look at her sometime boy friend, but also a rare glimpse into a bright young American coed's heart and mind. Her life-and-loves story surpasses anything the best heartstrings-press romancers might think of. Along the way we're treated to an intimate account of American small-college exotica, with its diverse architectures, first-rate gymnasiums, monumental libraries, overheated rooms, sexual mysteries, clubby hooliganisms and curious mix of brutal workload with philistine anti-intellectualism. And yet this isn't the America of *Animal House*. One sees the numerous attractions and genuine advantages of its way of life. It's no wonder that Ms. Kingsley wrote an earlier, warmly nostalgic book about her *alma mater*.

Mr. Jennings also generously includes Chadwick's "ideological closet farce" entitled *"Perspectives Industries, Ltd.,"* a kind of updated Orwellian spoof in which mind control is exercised not by State and Party brainwashing but via frenetic consumerism and a phantasmagorical free market. Under a huge eponymous idea-manufacturing firm's expert guidance, confusion and cacophony reign supreme in the land, and prove far more delectable instruments of control than were Big Brother and the Thought Police for Airstrip One. The play combines 1920s vaudevilliana, the ubiquitous telly talk-shows of our time, and a reimagined history: the South, with British help, have risen again sometime after 1865 and imposed themselves, even putting a king in power somewhere. Bond slavery persists while Abolitionists are regularly blasted for their fanatical "dogmatism;" and some militants (whose personal styles will spark not a few jolts of recognition) live by the ideas of one "Marcus Karl," rudely defying bland CEO sloganry in the process. Revealing, if talky and prolix, Chadwick's farce gives fantastical shape to the rampant relativism—shall we say *perspectivism*—that permeates much of U.S. life today. I've heard many a clever Yank pronouncing the very same lines that a crudely hyperbolic Carlos has assigned to his cartoon-like characters!

Jennings and Kingsley do an admirable job of bringing the Chadwick mystery into focus. My sole caveat is that in the end the figure of Carlos is as elusive as it was at the start. The mystery remains unsolved, and a prime reason, I think, is that neither gumshoe Fred nor memoirist Livie shows much sympathy for their subject's evolving leftism. It never seems to enter their thoroughly tolerant, modern minds that such thinking might have some meat to it. After all, the notions a wide-eyed Carlos Chadwick picked up in France are fairly commonplace across the globe, but in the U.S. they're branded "far left." Still, we should be thankful to an

American editor and the two writers for having included Chadwick's thoughts, if only to refute or dismiss them. Life imitates art: we see Carlos from both and many sides, and just as in his closet play, all those sides are equal. Only in America.

"Divided by a common language" was how the witty Irishman on his American lecture tour described U.S.-U.K. ties. But the rift extends to our respective political languages as well. There isn't so much as a Labour Party in the States, a void that makes for the eerie unreality of U.S. political life. There are topics that most Americans simply cannot confront without their good old Pavlovian juices frothing up. They get plenty of laughs at the ease with which Trotsky *et alii* disappear down the Soviet memory hole—but just try mentioning, say, Haymarket or Mayday or Joe Hill to them and the words draw a bewildered blank. A young Pakistani writer whom I know once characterized Americans as "Martians." He may be right. And yet if you're in America the curious thing is that it's the *rest* of our globe that seems peopled by multi-racial Martians and Marxians alike. Carlos Chadwick does come across as something of an extraterrestrial in much of Jennings' and Kingsley's pages.

Well, if America is the world, and this her Century, then I suppose Carlos might as well be an *E.T.*

□ □ □

PART 1

Who Is Carlos Chadwick?

by Fred Jennings

Chapter 1

Everyone knows how the fabled '60s came to their end: with an ugly bang. That bang also ushered in our uglier Age of Terrorism. Before then, it looked as if the Symbionese Liberationists had pushed leftist violence to the outermost limits. But the Richards College bombings took things much further. The deadly explosions and their aftermath gave us Americans an all-too-vivid glimpse into the dark recesses of Marxist fanaticism and Third World hate.

I may as well refresh readers' memories.

April 8, 1975 was an unusually warm evening for the New England Berkshires. Babcock House residents were finishing off some ice-cold drinks with their invited faculty members and friends. It was a semi-formal affair in the tradition of "guest meals" held on alternate Thursdays at every Richards dorm. Men sported their best plaids, women their brightest silk dresses. They had just put aside their cocktails and were filing leisurely in for dinner. Through the large picture-window you could see Richards College's privately-owned ski slopes, streaked with recent snows

5

that took on a low sun's deep hues. Male and female voices oohed and aahed. Babcock residents snaked their way in between the round cherrywood tables, seeking preferred company. Faculty people stuck with their individual hosts.

They were sitting around waiting for salads when suddenly there was a dull thud. Much louder were the sounds of shattering glass and terrified human cries. Here and there someone helped prop up a shocked neighbor or injured girl friend. Mostly it was every man for himself and head for Babcock Quad. The actual incident lasted just minutes. Eleven out of 165 people were to be found dead, including a Black chef and a Chinese-American waiter. Forty-two were wounded badly enough to be taken to nearby South Adams Hospital.

Next we shift to Chapman House, at the farthest corner of the campus. In the venerable old wood-panelled lounge a small group of student-faculty guests is sipping drinks and making pre-dinner small talk. They hear distant sounds but think it the thunder of a possible rainstorm. "Oh, oh, the PMF," a blasé female voice says lightly; her roommate giggles. Sixty seconds later the New England row house is shaken by a deafening noise. A surprised football player is catapulted several yards from the porch onto the highest branch of a nearby oak tree, and suffers only a chipped front tooth and a scratch on his face. Chapman meanwhile flares up like a box of kitchen matches. Some, shocked by the detonation, freeze like scared rabbits. Eighteen out of forty-nine people are quickly enveloped by fire or falling beams. Later, a fireman discovers, along with the remnants of a clock-activated bomb, the mangled body of Puerto Rican senior and campus radical Marta Cristina Colón tossed on the lawn. The thumb and index finger of her severed left hand are gripping the time button of the clock, evidently trying to tamper with the mechanism in some way. She becomes a temporary suspect.

The firemen would have their own hands full that night. The bass horn boomed through the power plant smokestack, resounding again and again, signalling to volunteers and making their tired bones tremble. A rescue squad rushed in from South Adams to assist at both disasters. Coat-and-tie meals ended abruptly as students, professors, employees and ordinary townsfolk ran out and allayed their curiosity. At Babcock or at Chapman they stood silently horrified as bodies were dug out and carted off on stretchers.

Within the hour a Pittsfield TV crew was on the scene. By 2 A.M. Roberta Waters and her United Broadcasting staff were all over the college town, taking disaster footage and interviewing anybody still alert enough to talk coherently. Beginning next morning the quiet, hilly, now-scarred campus would become a familiar sight on network news, just as Ole Miss, Columbia, or Kent State had once been. Until then few Americans—outside of "Little Ivy Four" students, genteel Republicans, or the educational elite—had so much as heard of Richards College. Now it was the Year of Richards.

The official number of dead, including wounded who didn't survive, would eventually be reported at thirty-two, including five faculty members (two from Athletics, two from Political Science, and a woman economist from Chicago), and also that Black chef, a 62-year-old grandfather whose own origins in Richards-New Ashford went back to the 1860s. And of course the remainder were Richards students, most of them the children of well-to-do parents from Northeastern and Southern suburbs, with a sprinkling from Texas and Illinois. The two college buildings—one aged and stately, the other sleek and geometric—had been utterly destroyed.

Chapter 2

For hours there was chaos on campus. Filets went uneaten, textbooks unopened, silverware unwashed as everybody stood around discussing the events. Library employees did little more than talk frenziedly about "what happened" though no one really understood what had happened or why. And other than contact the authorities, no one much knew what was to be done. The wildcat is the college emblem but, owing to phonetic coincidence, Richards students are known by the punning nickname "Richies," and a strange sight it must have been, these affluent youths—robust, healthy, and at ease with both status quo and cosmos—now confronted with so much unexplained death and destruction on their turf. One blonde woman sophomore from Greenwich later admitted to me that not since kindergarden had she known what it is to cry. "All that suffering, it just didn't seem right," she said, wiping a tear from her rosy cheek.

At the time most all Richies were grief-stricken, even hysterical. This wasn't some remote natural disaster in a Third World village but a gruesome tragedy undergone by their own classmates and friends, their brothers and sisters and themselves. One reason for the shared agony of those first ninety minutes—aside from anxiety as to who was dead—was sheer confusion as to the steps to be taken.

Finally, at 8:25 P.M., several Richards cars topped with loudspeakers began cruising about the school grounds and its surroundings. With great urgency the amplified voices announced an extraordinary all-College meeting for 10 o'clock at Putney Auditorium. At radio station WRCR-FM a soft-spoken disc jockey with the unlikely name of Crystal Sweet interrupted Beethoven's *Eroica* several times so as to advise Richards listeners. The radio and the school paper staffs divvied up the alphabet among themselves, rang up Richies and faculty people, and informed them of the President's announcement.

Putney Auditorium is a long, massive red brick rectangle with a portico propped up by thick Roman columns. Inside there are two rows of oaken pews, two layers of balcony, and a famous baroque organ, brought over from Weimar by a 19th-century benefactor. E. Power Biggs recorded some Bach here in the mid-50s. The building is the arena for major Richards events and "big-name" speakers, such as Governor Reagan in '68. Never had the place appeared as full as it did that evening, however. People stood even in the choir lofts. Sobs could be heard.

At 10:15 a visibly pale President Hastings strutted out onto the stage, papers in hand. An eerie silence settled over the crowded hall, followed by the sound of rustling papers. From his lectern the President recapitulated in brief what had transpired. He then reassured everyone that the proper authorities had been notified and would be arriving shortly.

He slowed down, folded the papers, and now spoke vigorously. He urged all members of the Richards "family" to adhere to their best traditions. "In the name of the trustees, I appeal to you to avoid panicky reactions, to remain calm and rational as you continue with your routines." He reminded his listeners that they were mature human beings and asked them to report any suspicious-looking activities to Security or the Police. "And finally, I exhort all students to attend classes tomorrow Friday. I believe it in everyone's best interest that Richards remain in full academic operations to the extent that such is possible."

A clap of distant thunder finalized those words, eliciting scattered shrieks and nervous laughter. Hastings shared in the momentary levity, his long taut face loosening up somewhat. He smiled and then reiterated that, until officially announced otherwise, classes would meet as usual.

Then he moderated the evening program. Two deans and two student leaders took their respective turns stating comforting words. "I love Richards, I love it so much I want us to stay cool," said the Senior Class President. There were also brief statements from diverse political groups, with spokespeople from the Left nervously deploring all political violence, and the Libertarians condemning violence as "typical Communist tactics."

Things wound up bit by bit. A star member of three athletic teams, his face still ruddy from the Florida sun, got up and expressed the hope that this dastardly deed wouldn't hurt the big weekend swimming meet up at Williams College. There were hisses. (In fact the meet was cancelled next day by both schools.) From the audience came statements of concern and requests for help, and the blonde female sophomore tearfully reminded them that many of their classmates were now dead and gone.

"They're dead! They're dead!"

Her boy friend reached up, sat her down, and calmed her. President Hastings adjourned the meeting. In the cool outside air, some 1,600 Richies shuddered as they headed home.

Chapter 3

Few of the students sat down with their books that night. Library employees reported eight users, two of them an elderly couple, obviously retired townsfolk, and a conscientious soul rushing in to return her overdue Reserve books. Few Richies got much sleep either, and the reason wasn't loud stereos or Frisbee games. Far into the night they gathered at one heap or another, watched the workmen dig into the rubble, and talked to reporters or other Richies. Some sat anxiously in their rooms phoning family. Everywhere there was speculation as to who had done it.

For besides the grief and hysteria there was an uneasy curiosity, a hunger to find out who, what, why. Hyped-up imaginations ran wild in search for possible culprits. A rumored Berkshire branch of the Symbionese Liberationists. Local fundamentalists who objected every Spring to Chapman House screenings of X-rated films. But also the anti-porn feminists, why not? A radical-lesbian commune 25 minutes south in Lenox (notorious for their angry Letters to the Editor). And then those marginal leftists on Radcliff Road. Or maybe the Black Students Group. Babcock and Chapman were ultra-conservative houses, so suspicion fell inevitably on the dissident sects. After all, news had leaked out of Marta Colón's mangled body.

Meanwhile, WRCR held night-long talk and commentary. Spokespeople from vulnerable and suspect groups either repeated earlier statements or sent first-time declarations of their own. The president of the Republican Club dwelled at length on the possibility that the Kremlin may have been testing a deadly new space-age weapon at Richards, their aim being "to destroy America's next generation of leaders." More deans came by and used the air waves to soothe the bereaved and allay student fears. Firemen, patrolmen, rescue workers, and media people compared this experience to past ones. The Sheriff of Richards-New Ashford virtually wept as he read his short sentence of commiseration.

Next morning most students went to class, though many a course never materialized. Rings around their eyes, the Richies congregated on still-brown lawns or in well-furnished hallways talking or asking questions. American Studies courses were particularly thinned out since Babcock and Chapman housed a high proportion of A.S. majors. On the other hand every Richie who could did quietly show up at certain Poli Sci and Econ courses. The chairmen of those departments made repeated hushed entrances, stood immobile, in a near-whisper tersely announced the faculty deaths, said that substitutes would be assigned shortly and, with spectral resignation, dismissed the groups.

Students at larger lectures spent the full fifty minutes whispering back and forth. Some in the back rows listened to WRCR through small earphones. Others stayed outside to share radios for an extra minute or two. Younger profs put their poetry or philosophy assignments aside and opened things up to discussion about "what happened." Most Richies, however, felt as ill-disposed to intellectualizing the events as they were to debating Descartes or T.S. Eliot. What they really wanted to know was, Has anyone else died? Has my brother come to? Did I really survive Babcock? and, Who did it?

Chapter 4

Student mail at Richards arrives about 11:30 A.M. Beginning around that time the Richies gravitate toward Cooper Hall, an early 1900s Gothic structure. Ivy-blanketed from its angular front vaults to its soaring bell tower, at its core is a spacious, high-vaulted dining commons, where solemn portraits of all former Richards presidents alternate with gracefully-pointed and abstract stained-glass windows. The building, made to last, now serves as Freshman Union and student Post Office. Congestion reigns late in the mornings, when freshmen line up for lunch and general human traffic amasses in the corridors to check postal boxes or watch for the "MAIL IS IN" sign. All the shared horror and consternation couldn't disrupt that morning's routines. Freshmen were hungry, as on any other day. Richies wanted their morning mail, and soon.

Among those standing about was Kit Wills, hockey player and second in command at WRCR. Hands in his Pendleton coat pockets, he paced the Cooper Hall foyer, smiling at passersby and greeting them by name, but nervously hoping for something, just anything to arrive from his girl friend of five years, currently studying in Madrid. He tried reviewing his Spanish grammar, but slammed the book shut on seeing the past subjunctive. Through the distant P.O. wire mesh he caught sight of the religiously-awaited sign being placed on high by a mechanical pole. Along with several others he rushed over to the mailboxes. He needed a full four tries at his combination dial and griped petulantly at the lock. Seeing neither familiar stationery nor the desired hand, he felt his entire insides sink. The one item he did find was a plain brown envelope, slightly larger than standard U.S. size, with blue Air Mail stickers in two languages, postmarked Montreal, at 20:30 hours, April 8. There was no return address.

Inside there was a neatly typed note, with none of the formalities—date, salutation, etc.—of letter-writing. It said:

Glad to see you folks getting a taste of what it's like in Vietnam and Peru these days! Hope you can laugh it off as a fun joke and not take yourselves too seriously! Laugh, Richies, laugh at yourselves, dammit! (I'm laughing at yourselves too.) And shun all simplistic value judgments, do. Who's to say what's right or wrong, eh? Who's to say it ever happened? Gotta remain open-minded, since everything's subjective, after all. From one perspective the results are, well, smashing! (Excuse pun.)

While deploring the loss of innocent Richie lives, every bit as much as Richies deplore the loss of innocent Vietnamese and Peruvian lives, I am nonetheless ecstatic. Here's to more such successful returns, and Long Live the NLF and the Peruvian Marxist Front!

Kit Wills read it once, twice, read it again and again, feeling amazement at the hot item he had in his hands and confusion as to what to do with it. Madrid was far from his mind. For a moment he stared blankly through the Gothic window, then rushed out. At a fast clip he cut across a slushy knoll, getting water in his moccasins. At the ever-deserted library he xeroxed the document ten times, leaving behind thirty cents accumulated change in the coin-return slot. In one portion of his Spanish book he carefully placed the original; in another, the photo copies. Heart pounding fast, he scurried back to Cooper annex and WRCR.

At first he considered delivering the mystery note either to the President or Security. He also thought of consulting WRCR staff first, but temptation prevailed. The broadcasting booth was conveniently empty. Side 1 of Bach's *St. Matthew* had just begun. Crystal Sweet was out briefly.

He faded the music, lifted the tone arm, and put on the mike. His voice trembled slightly. "This is Kit Wills. We interrupt this program in order to make a special announcement." He cleared his throat, excused himself. "I have just received in my mail an anonymous note, postmarked Montreal. It reads thusly:"

Slowly he stumbled over it, mentioning the punctuation along the way, then read it once more. Kit Wills' reading quickly electrified Richards. In each and every dining hall there was at least one radio going. When Kit pronounced the gleeful first line of that cryptic letter, a sudden flurry of "Sh!" sounds filled the air. Here and there someone rushed over with a tape machine and accidentally immortalized Kit's moment of fame. Much the same happened in dorm rooms and a few off-campus apartments.

A moment later Kit Wills read for a third time the enigmatic and perverse epistle, now a bit more hurriedly, while at a dozen cafeterias the silent incredulity and the rush to record were to repeat themselves.

Chapter 5

Crystal Sweet rushed into the booth all aquiver. As Kit finalized his third recitation she nervously informed him that President Hastings had called for his immediate presence at Foley Hall. Kit ignored Crystal's long blonde ponytail, grabbed the Spanish book and, feeling exhilarated and agitated both, ambled out as per instructions. A couple of friends crossed his path and expressed amazement at "that creepy letter." Kit said "Yeah," raised his eyebrows, then ambled on.

At the Richardson-Romanesque stone building, the kind that houses most Northeastern college administration offices, an unflappable President started out by demanding the anonymous note. Hastings then firmly reprimanded Kit for having acted without any prior consultation of others.

"This is not a light matter, Kit. It's only a couple of months before you graduate and head for law school, and that does restrain me. However, I will have to take *some* action as regards the position you hold in the campus information system."

Hastings' voice rose. Kit's spirits sagged. That afternoon Hastings passed on the original document to federal agents. Kit retained the photocopies, proudly displaying them to roommates and friends. The item became known briefly thereafter as "the Kit Wills letter." Some ex-Richies still refer to it by that name.

Meanwhile the entire campus was abuzz over this latest development. The prevailing confusion and rage had been further heightened. The air was filled with morally charged expletives like "Disgusting!" and "Who could write something as sick as *that*?"

In suites and lobbies there were cassette machines of every make, size, and shape, playing back Kit's reading of that mysterious note. And at WRCR, in-house and guest commentators had temporarily edged aside Crystal Sweet's Bach *Passion*.

At the foyer of the radio station, individuals from every political persuasion sought access to the air waves. At one point the lone Marxist professor at Richards strolled quietly past the student throng. In a residual French accent, running both hands through his bushy white hair, he graciously requested a brief spot in order to explain that no true Marxist would speak in such repellent fashion, and that the PMF would never exult in the death of innocent Americans. The managers gave him two minutes.

Directly following him came the lanky, blond, bespectacled and shorthaired president of Campus Conservatives. In an intense and brittle voice he protested the airing of such "treasonous filth" as that letter. Clutching onto the mike, he expressed revulsion at "the lack of compassion for human suffering evinced in that vile note. 'Mercy' does not exist in the Marxist vocabulary." He paused for a moment. "This offensive document puts another nail in the coffin of Karl Marx. It's a timely reminder of the simple fact that only Conservatives value human life."

Late that afternoon Scott Yarmolinsky, a shy, taciturn, hard-working senior and Libertarian Club member, was struck by the writing style of the anonymous note. Sitting in the privacy of his room he put aside the day's computer problems and listened closely to Kit Wills' voice on cassette. The copy four-times removed was dim and required extra attention. He rewound the tape, flicked on his typewriter and began the off-on job of transcribing the message. The fanatical Marxism, the "laugh at yourselves" bit and other such sarcasms, the catch-words like "point of view" and "perspective," and above all the virulent anti-Richards sentiments permeating the prose were ringing a bell in Scott's brain.

He rolled out and stared at the scratch paper, read it three times, phoned Kit Wills, got a busy signal and tried again. On the fifth attempt there was no buzz sound, then Kit's voice. "Kit? This is Scott Yarmolinsky."

"Uh-huh. Yeah?"

"You got that letter still?"

"What letter?"

"C'mon, you know what I mean."

"..." Ten seconds ticked by.

"Look, Kit, I think I've got a lead."

"Whaddoyou mean?"

Scott explained. Kit still held back, then finally mentioned having a xerox copy somewhere or other.

Once more Scott insisted he had this big lead. He asked if they might meet at the Language Center.

"Okay, okay," Kit grumbled.

"Bring the letter, will ya?"

In a matter of minutes they were in the L.C. basement. The lab was open, with only a student monitor present. Scott headed for the coin-operated IBM typewriter and inserted two quarters into the invisible slot. Kit followed phlegmatically and shut the cubicle behind him. From a pad of erasable bond left lying about, Scott tore out a sheet and slipped it into the machine. Though he knew the text almost by heart, he read out loud from the prized xerox that Kit held in his left hand. A two-finger typist, Scott pecked out the note, reproducing the layout of the original. Several exhausting minutes later he yanked out his handiwork and showed Kit the result.

"Yeah, it's just what I thought," he said nervously. The two typefaces were identical.

"Well, I can see you're on to somethin'. So who've you got in mind?"

"Carlos Chadwick, who else?"

Chapter 6

It was inevitable for someone to arrive at that conclusion. Scott's suspect, a class of '75 Richie, had been employed since fall as a Language Center aide, where he'd prepare tapes or type out memos. Following a junior year in France, Carlos had gained notoriety for an irrational hatred of Richards and its lifestyle. His play, *Perspectives Industries, Ltd.*, had been produced—poorly— over WRCR earlier that spring. Some of its viciously satirical lines Scott could almost hear in his mind whenever he'd whisper the sardonic sentences in that anonymous note. Since the day of "the events" Carlos had not been seen on campus. Nor was he among the dead or wounded. By dinnertime many Richies were talking angrily about "the Chadwick letter."

Federal agents were already active on campus. Most probably they'd had Carlos on their lists before getting there, since he'd been rooming with the late Marta Colón plus five other campus radicals. It soon leaked out that the Feds had learned from Quebec authorities that, indeed, at 9:30 on the evening of the explosions, a C. Chadwick was recorded as boarding an Air Canada flight from Montreal to Paris.

Still, the note might have been authored not by Carlos himself but by some clever forger—a rival faction, a personal enemy. And even if Carlos were the actual screed-scribbler, it wasn't clear whether he was trumpeting responsibility or merely expressing glee at Richies' shedding blood. He had once written a letter to the *Richards Booster* saying that many a Peruvian peasant would just *love* to see bombs fall on Richards. Was he now voicing similar feelings? Or had he really been party to those explosions? Meanwhile the FBI had targeted the individual who to this day remains the prime suspect in the Richards affair.

At a small school like Richards one can come close to meeting everybody. Most Richies knew Carlos on a hello-goodbye basis, and his radical rep was known to all. Throughout that confused, mournful, beerless, partyless, gray, drizzly weekend, much of the talk to the reporters who descended on Richards-New Ashford would center around "that Carlos character" (occasionally with profane expletives). And at other Berkshire colleges, from northernmost Williams to remote Sheffield State, there were Carlos Chadwick reports on campus radio or in extra editions of the school newspaper. (Someone detected a note of glee in the Sheffield State accounts.)

Within the privacy of Richards' ivied dorms there was near unanimous fury. Few Richies doubted Carlos's guilt. And his own roommates on Radcliff Road, though still oddly sympathetic to his rabid leftism, expressed to me a quiet anger that Carlos could have compromised them with the Feds. (A pair of brush-cutted agents now seemed permanently stationed in a blue Ford across from the old yellow house.) Understandably these young radicals were also in a state of shock over Marta's death.

Outside the Richards-New Ashford area Carlos was scarcely even a name. In a matter of days, however, the big question bruited over the national media was "WHO IS CARLOS CHADWICK?" (These were the words plastered across the *Daily News* front page next Monday.) When Hal Kipnis, my boss at *Manhattan* magazine, heard via the grapevine that I'd actually spent my freshman fall semester up at Richards (scholarship kid, 1953), he phoned me at home Friday evening to ask if I could get on it immediately and do a piece, "Richards Then and Now."

And that's how I first returned to Richards-New Ashford for a busy three days' chatting with students and faculty, spotting an occasional prof's name, stoking distant memories, and comparing it all to Richards today: 45 percent coed, double in size to 1,600 (before the explosions), the fraternities gone and new modern dorms in their stead (with maid service still provided), the physical scars and shaken self-confidence.

I got a tidy sum for the 6,000-word piece. And yet once the article was out there, photos and all, I wasn't happy with it. My curiosity had been piqued in a big way. Nothing had been solved, no questions cleared, and with the summer I began piecing together some satisfactory reply to that *Daily News* headline.

Just who was this bizarre, disturbing character named Carlos Chadwick?

Chapter 7

Carlos José Chadwick y Labat was a 21-year-old Venezuelan-American at the time of the events. Known as "Charlie" since freshman days, as a senior he started insisting on "Carlos." The networks soon made such facts common knowledge. What no one could figure out, however, was: What forces could have led this scion of a Connecticut Yankee businessman and a gracious upper-class Caracas lady to allegedly take such action against a small, genteel, private school idyllically ensconced in the hills of Western New England?

I spent three years' spare time investigating precisely that enigma, and logged thousands of miles attempting to find an answer. My quest took me to Richards and its environs several times, to Paris, where I reconstructed Carlos's junior year (and indulged hopes of an encounter and a scoop), plus Caracas for two weeks, where every evening I met with Carlos's parents and also saw local relatives, neighbors, old classmates and casual acquaintances from his past. Three continents and many conversations later, here follows a summary of everything from the field that seems newsworthy.

Simply on the surface, Carlos's background seems lifted out of an exotic novel or memoir. Before Richards he'd spent seventeen years growing up in El Bosque, a peaceful and attractive turn-of-the-century neighborhood in East Caracas. There is a romantic aura to his immediate family origins: the never-explained marriage of a sandy-haired, ruddy-skinned, square-faced, blue-eyed, physically hardy WASP expatriate and entrepreneur to a raven-haired, olive-skinned, oval-faced, dark-eyed, bird-like Latina, a middle-level government functionary named Alejandra Labat y

Estévez.

Carlos's parents can boast their genealogies. On her own mother's side Alejandra's ancestry includes a co-founder of the settlement of Barquisimeto in 1563; his name, Enrique Estévez, appears listed on a Spanish royal order from that year. The original document sits elegantly framed at the Estévez cocoa farm located near the town, first planted in the 18th century by African slaves and today in decline. The Labat line (Lah-BAHT) comes directly from Jean-Pierre de Labat, a French adventurer who conducted himself heroically in some key battles in Venezuela's independence wars and was a minor political rival to none less than Simón Bolívar. Alejandra's kin have figured in the annals of the country's history, either in government posts or in the liberal opposition to Juan Vicente Gómez, dictator of Venezuela from 1909 to 1935.

For Everett Phelps Chadwick's less colorful if equally rooted lineage, one can point to the Phelps Streets and Chadwick Courts in several Connecticut towns. Both names were once influential in the economic development of that state. The Phelpses made brass doorknobs in Waterbury and were among America's first makers of cheap wrist watches. The Chadwicks manufactured men's hats and furnished uniforms for the Coast Guard Academy and City Police at their New London textile works.

Hostile to Harvard Unitarianism and also seeing Yale as far too liberal, the Chadwicks had customarily sent their sons to the remote but right-thinking world of Richards. Ev's parents were no exception. Still, a maverick of sorts, young Ev went in not for Pre-Law or Poli Sci but Romance Languages: he was the only graduating Spanish major in '47. There being no peacetime draft that year, Ev had no worries about induction. On July 1 he started work in New York as a management trainee for Omni-Tel Inc., then a medium-sized communications firm with origins in a one-room office in Mayagüez, Puerto Rico, today the worldwide conglomerate known as Omni-Telectrono Chemicals and Containers. For some reason—and much to his relief, Ev confessed to me—he never was called in for army conscription.

Though lacking in charm (he admits to being humorless), Ev's cool composure and appetite for work quickly impressed his Omni-Tel superiors. Add his language background and he seemed a natural for their newly-expanding overseas business and possibly destined for their upper executive suites. By late 1949 Ev had been assigned to Caracas as Assistant Sales Manager for the Spanish Caribbean.

It was his first trip abroad, and he trotted up a good record. He lived for the job, working late into the night to push Omni-Tel goods and services and taking long DC-3 and Cessna flights to San Juan, Havana, Ciudad Trujillo, and many a smaller Latin town. His trips were strictly business—a fast lunch or dinner, a to-the-point conversation with a client, a deal usually, and back to the local airport. Despite a good salary, he drove an old if well-kept '42 Ford, kept a modest apartment on Avenida El Parque in the middle-class foothills of El Bosque, took work home at night, and did little in the way of entertainment—no movies, concerts, gourmet meals or cabarets. On Omni-Tel's account he belonged to the Club Valle Arriba (a central place for Caracas Americans to socialize) but showed up weekends only to swim a few laps. In his spare moments and on flights he might skim *U.S. News and World Report*. Through book clubs he bought the occasional James Jones or Cameron Hawley best-seller. He hadn't bothered reading French or Spanish books since college.

Carrying as he did the individualism of those hat and watch entrepreneurs, Ev soon found the corporate world regimented and confining. His own father, Dawson "Chip" Chadwick, is one of those Yankee Republicans who thought the New Deal a first step toward tyranny, raged against FDR at dinner table as "that man in the White House," defended Nixon to the end, hates labor unions as "monopolies" yet also doesn't like big business.

Ev Chadwick inherited such views in modified form. Moreover they helped him see that an independent businessman with ideas and pluck could do well for himself in Venezuela's free-market economy. The situation—Ev recalled with enthusiasm—compared favorably to the U.S., where big corporations and the Federal Government had everything pretty much sewn up. By the '40s some of Ev's more enterprising relatives had moved to the Carolinas, where low wages, lack of unions, and almost no health regulations made for a favorable business climate. Ev nonetheless ruled out those states, finding them too "hickish" and their Jim Crow laws morally debatable, though he could not accept the idea of Federal "coercion" to abolish them. "As I saw it, it's a matter of individual choice," he said to me.

During his stint at Omni-Tel, Ev had been quietly saving much of his hefty salary and keeping an eye out for investment opportunities. Through his contacts he became aware of healthy growth in textiles. Early in 1951 he tendered his resignation to the firm; his superiors understood his decision and even expressed comradely envy at his courage. Next month he became a partner in Telares Venezuela, a clothing manufacturer with fast-growing sales throughout the country, particularly the public sector. By coincidence, just as a Chadwick firm had once supplied uniforms for the Coast Guard Academy, Telares Venezuela was a regular contractor with the national Air Force.

Ev spent most of '51 and '52 working harder still: twelve to fourteen hours a day, seven days a week, at the textile plant downtown or his flat in El Bosque. The upshot was more good money piling up. Besides the suits and uniforms manufactory he got in some informal middle-manning with imports as diverse as rainhats, saxophones, and Cuban rice shipments. He kept up his lone-wolf ways, with a sizeable network of sales connections and no friends to speak of. He also continued not to bother with anything cultural (morning news excepted) and for food he frequently patronized a couple of American-style soda fountains down on Avenida Miranda. Outside of commerce, his life was a blank. Women, whether for warmth or pleasure, seemed of no interest to him.

The pattern was temporarily abandoned when, on Halloween of '52, he became smitten with love at first sight for Alejandra. I've heard this story from many sources, with only slight variations, and must assume it's true. Ev Chadwick was inching along Avenida Urdaneta in his Ford. It was rush hour on an unusually warm day. For ten minutes all traffic had come to a stop. One heard car metal taking a heavy beating up and down the avenue. (Honking horns is illegal in Caracas; motorists pound their roofs and doors instead.) Meanwhile in the lane to his right Ev had fixed his gaze on the driver of a blue Mercedes: a crisply-profiled young lady with short black hair and smooth coppery skin, dressed in a flowery print. She took slow puffs on her cigarette, exhaling slowly.

Ev stared. Her left hand flicked the burning butt delicately out her window. At this point she became conscious of those Anglo blue eyes looking her way. Her Andean features grimaced as she shook her head. She focused on the road.

A minute went by. She turned abruptly toward the gaping foreigner, raised a dark, angular eyebrow, and snapped in medium-slow Spanish, "What the devil are you staring at, *señor*?"

As she spoke, traffic moved ahead a yard or two, leaving a gap in her path. Ev suddenly pulled up in front of her Mercedes and poised his Ford at a 45-degree angle, blocking both lanes.

He jumped out, bounded over to an amazed Miss Labat, flashed his gold-embossed business card and said, "If you please, *señorita*, I would like to meet with you as soon as possible."

She thought this blond gringo completely mad. In her loftiest Castillian she commanded, "Sir, kindly remove your jalopy right this instant, or I shall call the police, I'm not joking." Not until she agreed to see him, he replied calmly.

"You are out of your mind. Move that stupid machine! *¡Usted está bloqueando tráfico!*'

And indeed for a block behind him there were motorists screaming, tempers boiling, doors being beat. Someone venturesome beeped his horn. The word *yanqui* was in the air. The commuters' wrath seemed fully trained on Ev.

Ignoring the environment, Ev insisted on the two of them getting acquainted over lunch. Fortunately there were no cops in sight—it was the time of the brutal Pérez Jiménez dictatorship. "*Por favor*, just one meeting. My business is in the center."

"*¿Pero quién es usted?* Leave me in peace!" She began rolling up the window. By a quirk of fate the crank snapped off. Ev smiled, pleaded more; a classic *yes!-no!* pattern followed. With a hint of a vulgarism, Señorita Labat fumbled inside her Italian purse, and extracted a rolled-up little card she hurled at Ev.

Around 10 A.M. next morning Ev asked his secretary to "get me the Ministry of Education." Several busy signals later he was told he could pick up the phone; he in turn asked for Development Programs, then for Señorita Alejandra Labat. Despite two intermediaries and a five minute wait, he never doubted that the rumpled card was hers, nor was he surprised at her "*Haló.*"

"*Buenos días.* This is Ev." He reminded her of yesterday.

An only slightly amused Señorita Labat told Ev in all frankness that she found his behavior rather strange.

Still, they conversed a while about their work, her Study Abroad desk, his textiles. He remarked that, with her on Urdaneta and him amidst all those new factories in the old southwestern part of town, only fifteen blocks separated them.

College backgrounds came up. Turned out she'd attended Manhattanville. "Oh, did you know so-and-so?" "Why, yes, she's in Montreal now, married to a . . ." "And did you happen to know that shy fellow from Key West, what's his name?" "Oh, yeah, we were corridor mates freshman year, haven't heard from him since '47."

Alejandra dropped a couple more names; he recognized them from classes and swimming. She'd been up to Richards one weekend, didn't much like their loud beer parties, though.

Well, she just didn't understand Richards ways, he joshed. He'd also been to Manhattanville, for their big mixer. Really? How'd he like the place? Well, nice, but those girls were far too intellectual for my tastes. Ha ha, he chuckled, just kidding. Somehow their conversation had shifted to English.

Out of sheer curiosity she agreed to meet him over lunch; at 1

P.M. they met at a French-style place a block from the Ministry. Despite the years elapsed since his college Balzac, he could read the menu and order in French, a fact they both appreciated. However, he had eaten French food maybe twice before, and a bemused Alejandra had to enlighten him about most dishes. Ev was never to be absent from work as much as he was for the next two weeks. His impetuosity must have touched Alejandra—their betrothal was announced in less than a month's time. Whirlwind courtships were then unheard-of; in Venezuela's high echelons, engagements of several years having been the rule. And so the society columnists got in some wicked if mindless wit.

There were rumors of relatives unhappy with Alejandra marrying a *yanqui* and a Protestant to boot. The Labats and Estévezes had always looked to Europe for their ideas and sometimes for spouses too. But Alejandra was the maverick, as shown by her attending college in the U.S. rather than Venezuela or Europe. Her live-in French Grandmother did, apparently, take some interest in *le yankee d'Alejandra*, but rumor-mongers likened it to the interest felt by a visitor to a zoo for the leopard or the elephant.

Despite all this they were married in mid-January. Ev put aside his Connecticut prejudices and agreed to a Catholic wedding. There being no grand old Spanish cathedrals in Caracas (the city was flattened by an 1812 earthquake), a stone church in Las Mercedes served as site for the moderately lavish ceremony, followed by a typically Latino reception at the Valle Arriba, where a hundred or so couples danced until sunrise to two alternating bands (one brass, the other flute-and-strings) while Ev's ruddy-faced parents and uncles managed to suppress deep yawns and look like fish out of water. Ev made some attempt at adapting to Latin festiveness, doing jitterbug steps to rumbas, and Alejandra obliging with delicate smiles and expert tropical twirls of her own. Still, try as he might, when came the time Ev just couldn't bring himself to fully hug her father and brother, let alone kiss her sisters and grandma and other kin.

Ev tried nothing terribly eccentric thereafter. He'd majored in

Spanish, "parachuted" into Caracas, walked out on corporate pay, then run amok as a man in love. Those youthful follies would fast recede as time came to administer Telares and market its products, for which growth expectations remained high. Ev's work habits far outstripped those of his partners, who preferred taking long junkets to Miami. His own schedule found pause only in Sunday services at the American Church, or in family visits on Saturday afternoons and some weekday evenings, at the mansarde-roofed, marble-floored Quinta Labat at the Country Club's edge. Church as well as mansion were located only a few blocks either way from a stucco highrise, which he and Alejandra rented as they took time watching for a house in the vicinity.

Chapter 8

Carlos Chadwick was born in New London on a chill rainy Columbus Day. Alejandra agreed to confinement up north on the understanding that their child could take up Venezuelan citizenship should it someday choose to. Profiting from a generous Ministry policy on maternity leaves, she and Ev flew off for New England ten weeks before she was due. The future suspected terrorist entered life just a few days prematurely. A small gathering of Chadwicks admired the baby's dark eyes and light-copper skin.

Carlos grew up bilingually, speaking English with Ev and often with Alejandra too. Spanish he picked up spontaneously through his Labat relatives, a succession of live-in maids from Spain, other folks in the building, and local radio and TV.

In Carlos's fifth year the Chadwicks moved a few blocks uphill into a California-modern *quinta* with a red-shingle roof, a banana tree, and "Tropical" as its name. (The Caracas address system uses names rather than numbers. Hence a building will be known as, say, Edificio X or Quinta Y.) The car-free silence of the shady street sounded uncanny after the eternal traffic jams on Avenida Libertador. Carlos's new set of playmates dealt with him pretty much as a native; through college days his life with them would develop in a casual, relaxed Spanish way. Ev and Alejandra still reside there, wondering what went wrong and politely shrugging their shoulders whenever some ex-playmate—now a working professional—makes friendly inquiries about their son.

Carlos Chadwick was "Charlie" to his parents and also the locals, who pronounced it with a Spanish flip of the tongue; Charlie he would remain until 1974. Because of his nickname and nationality, Venezuelans from his early years affectionately call him *el gringo*. Ev further bolstered this identity and assured his growing son that he, Charlie, was an American temporarily abroad who would return to the States for genuine schooling and experience, and then start work at Telares Venezuela. Young Charlie made occasional mention of this American present and future, dwelling obsessively on his U.S. prospects as high school graduation drew near in 1971. Brief trips to New London every other summer further reinforced his Yankee plans and dreams.

Charlie fell smoothly into the pattern by attending Campo Alegre, the local American elementary and middle school. Located atop a slope just five minutes from the church of his parents' nuptials, the school had been built in an earlier era by Creole Petroleum (the Venezuelan branch of Exxon) for the children of its American employees. Campo Alegre still enjoys repute for its fine teachers, high academic standards, and attractive setting. As a pupil Charlie was consistently good, making honor roll regularly and getting 90s even in Conduct. Alejandra recalls Ev once saying offhandedly, "I wish he'd do something *bad* for once."

Ev and New London aside, Charlie's first contact with things American was Campo Alegre, where he would enroll for nine years. Like most beginning schoolchildren he cried the first day of class; Alejandra had to drive and console him all the way to Campo Alegre even for the start of third grade. Because the Chadwicks didn't live in "Gringo Gulch"—the local Americans' humorous term for their enclave in Las Mercedes—Charlie knew no pupils on entering and took some time to make friends.

American students looked down on Venezuelans and avoided them, and Charlie's darker skin and native Spanish must have placed him in that category. Still, with his scholastic, introverted nature he may not have sensed that possibility (he mentioning it to his parents maybe once) and he did have his El Bosque playmates. By seventh grade he had developed some Campo Alegre friend-ships, certain Americans with local ties or who had attended Venezuelan schools, and a few Latins whose parents had lived in the States or wanted their kids to learn English.

On an occasional Saturday morning Ev might take the boy and his neighborhood friends to Telares Venezuela. There they'd watch the looms chugging rhythmically or a cutter patiently shaping a gala uniform. Or, getting restless, they'd run about the aisles until Ev told them to stop. Later, during Charlie's teens, Ev gave him low-paying summer jobs at the office and factory, in order to acquaint his son with the quirks of the business. But in more subliminal ways which I was not competent to grasp, there seem to have been powerful influences from Alejandra and her relatives (as well as from the now-untraceable maids).

Still, Ev's old-Yankee origins and sometime evocations of New England life did carry weight at home and school. *U.S. News and World Report* and the South American editions of *Time* and *Newsweek* all arrived at Ev's downtown mailbox, and after skimming Politics and Business he'd hand the periodicals down to his son, who in turn perused them front to back, including those parts he didn't understand. Only in his twentieth year did "Carlos" actually get around to reading Venezuelan magazines and papers.

One major influence was the *Richards Alumni Monthly*. With miraculous regularity it arrived every third Friday at Quinta Tropical. Beginning at age four, Charlie would turn its handsome pages, pausing to stare at pastoral images of ivied Gothic stone on landscapes suggesting Constable, or candid shots of students in thick sweaters, silently doing math or scanning verse in an old log-heated library, or bright late-summer Kodachromes of happy blond couples, seated under a roof of resplendent gold-hued boughs, books in hand while they recited a classic or discovered a new idea, and in the background a facade of white colonnades. Later, when he could read, Charlie on his return from Campo Alegre would pluck the *Monthly* from the sideboard, sink into Ev's armchair, and savor with hushed delight the written accounts of intellectual, musical, and social life at Richards.

Ev would see Charlie so engrossed right up until dinner, and say to him, "Someday Richards will be your school too. You'll find all sorts of culture there." Charlie would look up and stare silently as Ev went on, "Much more than in this underdeveloped country, where there's not even a decent public library."

Setting down her rum-and-coke, Alejandra would dismiss him with a wave of the hand. "Oh, Ev, come on; you think the U.S. is the only civilized place in the world." Charlie kept reading.

"Well, really, Alé, it is true that Richards has a fine library. So does Manhattanville, no? Any libraries like those down here?"

She'd sigh impatiently as she skimmed *El Universal*. "Ev, dearest, sometimes you sound like the typical American."

Charlie meanwhile displayed musical inclinations. Where they came from is impossible to say, given that both Ev and Alejandra admit to being unmusical. For whatever reason, beginning at age four, Charlie started tuning in to the government radio station and humming to its classical broadcasts. Curiously, however, what first inspired him to request violin lessons wasn't the sound of Bach or Beethoven but a photo of the Richards College Chamber Players gracing an *Alumni Monthly* front cover.

It was a rainy afternoon. Charlie sat gazing at those eighteen string players, their bows poised as one on their separate instruments. He turned to his father. With an earnest, excited urgency he asked, "Daddy, could I learn to play violin?" Ev continued with his *U.S. News*. "Of course, Charlie."

Charlie pointed at the *Monthly*'s cover photo. "Will I be able to play with them?"

"Yes, son, someday you could belong to that group too."

Ev didn't even try to explain that those bright faces would be long gone from Richards by the time Charlie got there. The women players, for one, weren't even Richies (only males could attend then) but were brought in from a nearby women's college and a local secondary school.

Chapter 9

More than once Ev remarked to me that his own feeling for music is, in a word, nil. "Modern, classical, it does nothing for me," he reflected jocularly. Still, Alejandra went poking around for teachers and came up with a cultured, multilingual Czech emigré who happened to live across from Ev's first Avenida El Parque address. The boy started out with a small-sized fiddle, then moved on to the normal kind.

Though no prodigy, he learned fast enough and by age twelve was taking weekly lessons at the National Music School, where he would soon play in student ensembles and recitals. Eventually he worked up decent renditions of the Mendelsohn and Beethoven concertos, doing them at conservatory events and at the American School talent shows. During the two years before college he was recruited by the Orquesta Sinfónica de Venezuela to swell their ranks in command performances of Beethoven's *Ninth* and Handel's *Messiah*. In addition, being formally Catholic was no obstacle to his taking an occasional obbligato job a few blocks down the street at the American Church. Curiously, Ev was to see his son play in public twice at the most, both before the boy's teens.

Charlie had his Music School friends who, like the neighbors, dealt with him as they would with any other Venezuelan studying theory and violin. The music people nevertheless remained separate from his social life as it evolved at American schools or El Bosque. At the same time Charlie's musical involvements led him into an informal role, beginning in ninth grade, as "music programmer" for Gringo Gulch parties.

Summer nights in Las Mercedes were dominated by something

called "Teen Canteens." Hosted by Campo Alegre on the spacious stage of its open-air auditorium, the Canteens featured ping pong, dancing, a U.S.-style snackbar, and general socializing for young Americans and guests—all for about a dollar. In addition, on alternate Saturdays from September to May, the high school sponsored dances at the Centro Venezolano-Americano, a language and cultural facility located at the gates of Las Mercedes and right across Caracas's first shopping mall—the Rockefeller-owned Automercado. Charlie's ex-classmates still have remembrances of him at those social functions, selecting and stacking 45's or LP's, punctuating rock with occasional Latino, taking requests for a slow one or "somethin' fast", or "how 'bout Norwegian Wood" or (less frequently) hard salsa.

Most Campo Alegre "graduates" go on to prep school in the States. At that point, however, Charlie preferred staying in Caracas. Partly it was a matter of recently acquired friends, whom he didn't want to leave behind, plus his ensembles at the Music School. Alejandra understood the attachment and argued for it with the boy's father. Though Ev would have liked him to get some start in the U.S., he acceded, with Richards College still envisioned as Charlie's true goal.

And so 14-year-old Charlie matriculated at the Colegio Americano de Caracas, a 40-minute schoolbus ride from the Automercado's secondary parking lot. At the time the rectangular building stood on a hilltop surrounded by open fields, unpaved roads, and occasional squatter settlements. Since then OPEC greed has brought total urbanizing of the area, and now a row of 45-story apartment towers faces Colegio Americano from neighboring peaks and hollows. Feverish oil developments notwithstanding, the school retains its spectacular northward view of the valley.

Colegio Americano is much smaller than Campo Alegre— Charlie's graduation class would consist of forty-six people. But there was greater diversity, with proportionally more Latins and even a few Europeans, their combined population roughly equalling that of the statesiders. Moreover the U.S. kids were either of less wealthy stock or of diehard southern parents who didn't want their boys and girls being brainwashed at Yankee prep schools. Their fathers, rather than high-paid executives who set norms at Campo Alegre, were small businessmen who might operate a potato chip or pasta factory, an Automercado toy store, or a Dale Carnegie franchise. There were some career military types, both U.S. and Venezuelan (one female classmate had a colonel stepfather who'd been mayor of Caracas). Size and demographics thus allowed for greater mingling between Latinos and Gringos. And so for pretty much the first time Charlie had regular Americans as school friends, going to their homes and parties around Las Mercedes and learning how to dance to rock music.

Charlie continued to be a good pupil, though now making Honor Roll less frequently. Still he pretty much sailed through coursework, doing consistently well in French and History, his maps on How the West Was Won particularly impressing a Mrs. Smith. Teachers at both schools recall Charlie as a sweet and quiet sort, with an uncalculated knack for befriending anyone regardless of nationality. His conduct remained good, though with some lapses in junior and senior year, when he was kicked out of class, once for throwing chalk at a companion across the room, another time for laughing too loud at a neighbor's sex jokes. Young Charlie was finally doing "something bad."

In short, his was the typical life of the Colegio Americano teenager. The long bus ride was lightened by Beatles tunes sung by the blond-American set; he frequently joined in. After school his Venezuelan and U.S. pals would sit around the Automercado soda fountain sipping at cokes, munching on catsup-soaked French fries, chuckling over somebody's *Mad* magazine, day-dreaming about cars, and gossiping about girls (nice buns on that new one, so-and-so's got a real neat personality, etc.). Then, for variety, Charlie sometimes would cross the street and hang around at the Centro Venezolano-Americano library, ostensibly to study but more often to flirt with the young secretaries and business students who took English classes there.

Football is costly, and Charlie would thus see nothing of that classic U.S. experience until Richards freshman year. Casual softball games did take place Saturdays at a playing field across from Sears Roebuck; classmates recall him as an average batter and outfielder. Further stateside cultural contacts included Ed Sullivan, the *I Love Lucy* reruns, and other TV shows that arrived a month or so after their U.S. screenings (sometimes dubbed in Spanish). Weekends there was the usual round of dances with Bacardi rum aplenty, mini-flasks of which Charlie and his American School buddies might carry in their coat pockets (Venezuela having no minimum drinking age, Charlie could purchase liquor in any grocery shop around El Bosque).

Because of these activities, Charlie was spending less time with Labat kin, who not surprisingly viewed with displeasure his defection to the American colony. Whenever Charlie's set of friends zoomed up to Quinta Tropical and honked *pah*-puppuh-*páh páh* impatiently, Alejandra and even the maid reminded him gently about relatives a few blocks up the hill. He'd put on his coat, say "*Sí, mamá, sí,*" and dash down to a station wagon packed with high-spirited horseplaying boys, aged 16 and up. On one of Charlie's increasingly rare visits to Quinta Labat, he sat silently as Grand-Aunt Eliane gave him a Gallic tongue-lashing for spending all his time with "those Yankees." Ev on the other hand seemed quite unconcerned.

And so the station wagon would peel off with a screech and go cruising up and down east Caracas, Charlie and his friends visiting Colegio girls or buddies at their *quintas* around Gringo Gulch or in spiffy Altamira or La Castellana, flirting here, gossiping there while tapping their toes to blaring LPs; or they'd sit by the clear-blue pool at the Theater Club and other American havens in the Las Mercedes hills, playing leisurely card games and ordering tall rum-and-cokes. During his senior year they spent many a night out on the town, starting out at a Centro dance and then making the rounds of night clubs where they'd watch girlie shows and drink more rum-and-cokes, or drop in on a few pleasure houses, and at

3 A.M. head out for the deserted Próceres highway to drag-race against motorcyclists or carefree owners of Porsches and Corvettes, many of them now active in Caracas's expanding retail and real-estate sectors.

Sometimes these adventures took on an ugly twist. One raucous summer night a Charlie well in his cups retired early—luckily, since a 5 A.M. drag race was to end in disaster when a daredevil British cyclist flew off the road, slammed into the edge of an abstract marble monument and spilled out half his brains, thereby involving two of Charlie's friends in bitter legal tangles and family conflicts.

Some of those youngsters had a habit of taunting drivers and passersby, a practice that occasionally backfired. On a bright Easter Sunday a Venezuelan-American named Freddy Arismendi shouted *"Fangulo!"* (Italian for "fuck you") at a short, swarthy man waiting in a blue Fiat at a red light. In a jiffy the guy'd maneuvered to corner Freddy's Lincoln, then sprung out flashing a police badge. He barked, "Driver's license, please." Freddy sheepishly admitted to not having one.

In a cool voice the cop said, "You're under arrest."

A panicked Freddy blurted out, "No, please, no."

It took a $50 bribe, some abject begging on Freddy's part, plus humble pleas from his friends to persuade the offended police officer not to prosecute. He did write down Freddy's plate number, leaving the young senior quite terrified for a few weeks, though nothing came of it.

Another incident had to do with Eddie Phillips, a lanky, dark-haired, brush-cutted mathematical prodigy from Texas, today acne-scarred and an engineer at Arco. Overly fond of Scotch, Eddie became still more intoxicated one evening by the feel of the wheel of his dad's new Chevrolet, and he took to shouting "Eat shit!" in English at random pedestrians, at which the group in the car would roar with laughter. "Eat shit, darkie!" he shouted late that night at a musclebound Black man standing outside a ramshackle café, puffing at a cigar.

The Black turned out to be West Indian. "Wha' you say, mon?" The boys laughed.

Eddie Phillips got more defiant. "I said eat shit, darkie."

Enraged, the islander blitzed over and seized Eddie's left arm, twisting it violently. "I kill you, mon!" he shouted, starting to open the door. "I feel like to bust yo' head."

It was Charlie, sitting right next to Eddie, who saved the situation. He caught the man's gaze and quietly explained that this gringo from Dixie is just some dumb animal who thinks he's hot-shit Texas.

Charlie's jovial taking of the Black man's side—"Aw, leave the guy alone, willya? He's white trash, that's all"—disarmed the avenger-to-be, whose fury subsided just enough for him to shove Eddie clear over to the glove compartment. He then kicked the shiny car door twice before stomping back across the street. The onlooking Venezuelans applauded him.

Soon afterwards, on Avenida Miranda, Eddie Phillips growled resentfully at Charlie for saying those things about him.

"Charlie Shitwick, y' stupid fag. Whyn't you go back to Tchaikowsky?"

From the back seat Freddy Arismendi interjected, "Hey, Eddie, would you rather the darkie'd busted yer ass?"

Eddie turned silent for most of the evening.

Chapter 10

The American colony in Caracas seems a special breed. Before visiting that Latin city I'd always tended to think of the standard stereotypes of Americans abroad—the swaggering, loudmouthed, checker-trousered "gringo" businessman; the awkward and inarticulate yet overly-confident blond youths—to be just that, stereotypes, unkind caricatures launched by reflex anti-Americanism. To my surprise, a fair number of the Americans I met around Caracas came close to fitting the cliché.

I'd also heard of Americans who spend years in a foreign country without learning the language; and I'd dismissed it as knee-jerk exaggeration. But they do exist in Caracas. There I met Colegio Americano students and alums plus their parents and other *norteamericanos*, not a few of whom boasted to me about knowing no more than fifteen Spanish words. Many families hired West Indian maids or gardeners so as to stick with English and cling to their specialness. A couple of Colegio Americano officials—one retired as of this writing, the other now vice-principal at a U.S. school in Japan—knew virtually no Spanish.

More striking were the general attitudes in Gringo Gulch and vicinity. The phrase I kept thinking of for them was "militantly Eisenhowerish." About the good ol' USA the Caracas Americans evinced a faith the likes of which I hadn't encountered in years. One middle-aged laundry owner who hadn't been back to Ohio in a decade said to me after just a few sentences, "It's the greatest country in the world." Even Ev Chadwick, who stands partly outside that expatriate community, used those words more than once.

Perhaps not surprisingly, opinions on U.S. foreign policy were fairly hawkish. One engineer complained harshly about "those long-haired peaceniks who stabbed us in the back" in Vietnam, then fantasized about bombing Libya and "bumping off that Bedouin colonel." I made imprudent mention of the Panama Canal Treaties, and someone suddenly turned red and pronounced with quiet passion, "That Canal is the Eighth Wonder of the World, and we're keeping it," or "*We* built it, and we're not letting any Rooskies get *our* Canal, no sirree."

On the other hand I found that many Venezuelans held rather baffling and frustrating views. At that time the covert bombing in Peru was defended by virtually every adult American I met. (I secretly disagreed with them, it goes without saying.) Ev was a grudging exception, apparently the result of pressure from Alejandra and her in-laws, all of whom uniformly, uncritically saw the action as an instance of "Yankee imperialism." So strange: I'd always thought that tired slogan the exclusive property of Marxist cliché mongers. But when I asked Alejandra about the prospect of Peru becoming a clone of Cuba, she snickered condescendingly, muttered, "Oh, you Americans," and added, "Cuba's just another country. I couldn't live there, but I can't see why you Yankees get so hysterical over Castro."

For the sake of harmony, I held my peace with her too. But I noted that the Venezuelan press also viewed Castro that way, treating him like just another president, hardly seeing him as a world threat and even expressing some occasional admiration for him. Coming as I do from a country that has the best, freest, and most objective critical journalism on earth, I was simply depressed by the lack of balance the Venezuelan media showed toward Third World issues. Its editorialists dogmatically attacked *imperialismo yanqui* while blithely ignoring Cuba's imperial adventures in America and elsewhere. They condemn our bungling in Peru and our tragic mistake in Vietnam, yet acquiesce to Viet Cong and PMF evils with not a hint of even-handedness. Violence in any form is a bad thing, period, and anybody will agree that ideological double standards are self-defeating hypocrisy.

At any rate, Charlie's native Spanish, Venezuelan relatives, and contact with local ways appear to have been an anomaly among Caracas Americans, who mostly insulate themselves from the surrounding society. His language skills also proved useful to Ev during the summers, when the youngster worked as an all-purpose handyman and office boy at Telares, becoming a kind of informal staff assistant by the end of college sophomore year. His growth in that direction, however, was to be cut short ten months later when he returned from France sporting long hair, olive-drab fatigues, and a Marxist chip on his shoulder.

That, however, was to be a unique deviation. For the most part, youth culture in late 1960s Caracas was a tame stepchild of its U.S. forebear. Male hair styles progressed from crew cuts to bold Kennedy coifs—the outermost limit. There were a few hippie shops, and occasional teenagers in beads, but no bandanas, raggedy jeans or cutoffs—Venezuelan mores simply wouldn't permit them, at least not without some jeers. What little pot-smoking did exist was risky, given the stringent local laws.

The preppie students who returned for Christmas and summer were potential bearers of new stateside fashions and poster purchases. But instead they trimmed their hirsuteness just before the long ride from Choate or Emma Willard to JFK Airport. Once in Caracas they'd put aside their counter-cultural ways and avoid antagonizing their super-straight parents, whom they saw three months a year at most. And they'd huddle together at the Valle Arriba or Theater Clubs, radiating an aura of group exclusiveness and largely shunning the Colegio Americano kids who'd once been their Campo Alegre schoolmates. Alejandra recalls Charlie's dejection the day when a tall and talkative blonde, with whom he'd bought Automercado ice cream cones in eighth grade, ignored his approach as she dangled her bare feet in the Theater Club pool.

After a moment's silence, Charlie greeted her with an enthusiastic, "Hi, Sally!"

She shook the long hair out of her eyes, glanced up, then stared down at the water. "Hi there. Sorry, I can't remember your name." Her legs kicked up some clear, white foam.

Of course there were the seemingly endless Vietnam War and the beginnings of the Peruvian mess. But among Caracas Americans no anti-war protests took shape, no SDS, none of the rabid leftism that was tearing campuses apart in the States. Indeed, no one seemed much opposed to the wars, let alone in favor of the Communist guerrillas. The suggestion that the Viet Cong (or the Liberation Front, as leftists liked calling it) had some special right to be in South Vietnam would have been mocked out of existence or ignored. And yet, though they agreed with the wars' aims in some vague, passive way, few actually wished to be called up for active duty. They had their own way out: I heard of a half-dozen cases of Colegio graduates or college returnees who, faced with induction papers from the U.S. Military Mission, solved things by taking out Venezuelan citizenship (back then a painless bureaucratic procedure).

Still, our overseas conflicts couldn't help but bring local repercussions. Even at Colegio Americano there was occasional controversy over Vietnam, particularly after the incursion into Cambodia, with American students variously defending, and the Venezuelans, Latins, and a few Europeans generally opposing, Nixon. At lunchtime or on the return bus two individuals might start arguing heatedly ("We've got our commitments, can't you see?" "Hell, it's just Yankee imperialism." "No, it's not, it's defending American freedoms." "Shit, why defend American freedoms in Asia?") and the dispute would sweep in ten more pupils from either side. And then the afternoon bell rang or the Automercado loomed into view through all the pollution, and everyone would disband, their political debate fast forgotten.

Sometimes the classroom was drawn in. One evening during the invasion of Laos a crowd of Venezuelan leftists broke windows at a U.S. consulate and roughed up an Assistant Secretary of State who was on a speaking tour. Next morning on the Colegio bus there were no Beatles tunes but plenty of bitter exchanges, all of them soon eclipsed by the wrath of Mrs. Smith, who had taken deeply personal offense at the leftists' violence. Both her English classes that day were cowed into silence as she railed eloquently at Latin "ingratitude" and proudly recalled how she and her husband, a successful J. Walter Thompson executive, had adopted Venezuelan baby twins, raised them with love, and were now paying for their tuition up in the States. Charlie's classmates today single this out as by far their tensest moment at Colegio Americano.

Out and around the city, however, the anti-Americanism could get immediate and ominous. One still-remembered street rumble was sparked when, after a grand Christmas dance at the Valle Arriba, six soused preppies confronted a notorious gang of rich Venezuelans from that Beverly Hills-style area. The American kids were singing, sometimes dancing as they sauntered down the road. From the now-silent clubhouse the equally drunk Venezuelans barreled down in their black Continental. The Americans heard the unusual sound of a honking horn, followed by screeching brakes. Startled, they jumped aside; one of them nearly stumbled down the 20-foot drop. In the moonlight they saw two handsome Latin faces leaning out the left window.

"Death to the Gringo imperialists," they shouted in unison Spanish. "Yankee assassins," shouted another. The tires made a peeling noise and rolled on.

"Come back and say that ya goddam spik!" shouted a ramrod-cool Mike McDermott. He was the only one from Colegio Americano.

Again the car screeched, then blitzed all the way up in reverse. Again the Americans had to jump, getting their bearings as six sleek, fashionably dressed Venezuelans emerged from both sides of the car. Someone carried a stick, another a chain; one preppie grabbed hold of a rock. The rest was a matter of a minute or two: bloody noses, black eyes, a shattered wrist watch, Mike McDermott twisting a Venezuelan's arm clear out of its socket, and the Continental blasting off, its rear window cracked.

No one really "won," and anger against the rich hoodlums was to persist into the summer months. But there's a long and secret history of Gringo-Latino street brawls around East Caracas, and in '69 something so ordinary could take on ideological overtones.

In retrospect it's surprising, but Charlie Chadwick was even more apolitical than other Colegio Americano pupils. During the angry debates he remained mostly mute, at best interjecting a set phrase on the order of, "What about the threat of Communism?" From his pre-Richards days the only instance I heard of anything like political discussion took place one afternoon with the Busta-mante brothers, who lived across from Quinta Tropical. Charlie had once played many rounds of tag or stickball with them.

"Hey, Charlie, come play us a tune," shouted Victor, an Engineering student, bearded and bespectacled, the eldest.

Charlie walked over and joined them. He did a whiplash with his left hand. "My fingers feel like jelly." He gestured as if he were bowing. "But otherwise . . ."

The Bustamantes liked classical music, so they chatted about violin concertos. Then Victor asked, "Hey, Charlie, tell me, what'll you do if Nixon drafts you?" It was the day after the Cambodia speech.

Charlie shrugged his shoulders. "Can't say. Don't like Communism, so I suppose I'd fight if I had to."

"But are you for the war?"

"Who can be for any war? All wars are bad." He paused. "What do we do about Communism, though?"

"What's so horrible about Communism?" Pepito asked. He was the youngest and cockiest.

"People aren't free under Communism," Charlie replied.

The middle brother pointed at the slums covering the north mountain slope. "How much freedom do those people have?"

"They're free to vote and can say whatever they want," said Charlie. "Just last week I learned in World History that Russians live four to a room. You can't even own a *quinta*."

The three brothers laughed as Charlie turned red. Pointing again, Alfredo said, "And those families have luxury housing?"

Charlie turned defensive. "We also learned how Russia's economy is a complete failure."

"*That*'s strange," said Pepito. "My *liceo* geography book says Communist Russia has made great industrial advances."

Víctor now was sitting on the lounge-chair up on the porch. "How d'you account for Russia's being the world's second industrial power?"

Charlie was apparently taken aback. "Russia's the second industrial power in the world?"

Alfredo patted Charlie condescendingly on the back. "*Sí*, Charlie, *sí*. What did you think? That they're some under-developed country like us?"

In the light of his subsequent ideological manias and uncritical Russophilia, Charlie's teen-age indifference to politics seems astounding, really. But the one probably leads to the other. After all, some Symbionese Liberationist crazies were once cheerleaders.

Chapter 11

War or no war, politics right, left or nil, Charlie was approaching senior year. And there never was any question as to which college he should attend. Four generations of Chadwicks had gone to Richards. Why should a fifth do differently? Charlie had spent a warm June weekend at Richards in 1962, when he and Alejandra rented a car at Idlewild Airport and later met up with Ev on campus, where his fifteenth class reunion was coming to an end. Richards made a lasting impression on the nine-year-old kid, who found himself entranced by the tranquil beauty and the stone, brick, and vegetable reality of a place he'd so far known only via the *Alumni Monthly*.

In their Hertz car Charlie asked Alejandra countless questions about Richards. Her honest answer was mostly, *"No sé."* At Richards he besieged Ev with endless inquiries about this or that building, and are concerts mostly in Putney Auditorium? Could I see the music rooms? oh, is this the lawn where people sit around with their books? Cooper Hall is where you used to eat, Dad, right? The library was virtually empty, but as his parents talked in the foyer he stood silently in the reference room, staring at book spines for a long minute or two.

Living as he did under Ev's influence, Charlie had no idea that other places might be worth consideration. It is Ev Chadwick's belief that nothing anywhere can equal the elite small colleges of New England, and that within this high breed Richards is the best, finest school in the hemisphere and on the globe. Universities like Harvard and Yale he thought contemptible—too big, and corrupted by urban leftism and bohemia. State universities were simply out of the question—educationally beyond the pale and morally wrong, an indefensible intrusion of government into so private a matter as individual schooling.

Richards thus represented Ev's ideal of a small, self-contained community untouched by big government, big industry, and big labor. (The school is known for busting all union attempts; some years ago two young electricians who'd been threatening to go before the NLRB suddenly and mysteriously disappeared.) As is natural, Ev passed on his views to his son.

The last few months of Charlie's senior year were dominated by Richards. Admitted already in January, he was the only member of his class who had applied to a New England institution. Owing to their southern ties and technological career plans, most Colegio Americano students put their sights on, say, Georgia Tech or U. of Oklahoma, noted for their engineering programs. Charlie's uncommon path was viewed with curiosity by his friends and awe by his teachers, and he'd often volunteer information about life in the "Little Ivies," all of it taken from Ev's remembrances, *Alumni Monthlies*, that single visit, and especially the 1970-71 Richards catalog, which he carried about for weeks, just as other students might tote *Mad* magazine between classes. The clover-green book soon turned grimy, its course offerings section a thicket of underlinings and check marks. Ev later saved this catalog as a memento; some of the pages he showed me were all but buried underneath Charlie's array of scribblings.

On the other hand Charlie felt unsettled and surprised whenever he'd mention Richards to Venezuelan friends and nothing seemed to register. The day after receiving his letter of acceptance, well-wishers at the Colegio had deluged him with congratulations. Later that afternoon he saw the older Bustamante polishing the family station wagon. Charlie chugged uphill and announced excitedly that he'd be at Richards next fall.

Bearded Víctor stopped briefly, then asked, "What's that?"

Charlie explained the liberal arts school setup to him.

"But isn't that a high school?" Víctor wondered.

Slightly piqued, Charlie elaborated on its being like a university, only smaller.

Víctor queried in all innocence, "Oh, that's where they play football, right? But I didn't think you were a *futbolista.*"

The catalog happened to be among Charlie's schoolbooks. He produced it and showed Víctor the latest picture of Richards Chamber Players.

"*Ahá,*" Víctor remarked. He stroked his beard, tapped at the photo, and commented, "Nice girls." (Women had been in attendance since 1969). He smiled. "You're going to enjoy yourself."

At home, Ev recalls, Charlie was like a little boy counting the days until Christmas, saying once too often at dinner, "I can't wait until I'm at Richards." Throughout the summer he day-dreamed out loud about this course or that ensemble. Over the last year he'd strayed a bit from music, skipping lessons and getting rusty; now to his parents annoyance he practiced non-stop evenings or Sunday afternoons, getting ready for Chamber Players audition.

He worried about being good enough for Richards. And he wondered if being on U.S. soil might make him draftable.

Ev was uncomfortably aware of the young Americans who'd been draft-dodging in Canada or Venezuela. The night before Charlie's departure Ev decided on a face-to-face chat with his son. Alejandra had gone up to Quinta Labat, where all three of them were soon due for a celebration in Charlie's honor.

Father and child were seated in the living room, on the very sofa where little Charlie had once savored the *Alumni Monthly* page by page. There were suitcases and a trunk lined up in the foyer.

"Charlie, I know there are young people who won't fight for their country. Seems they'll do anything to wiggle out of it."

"Yes," was the breathy answer, "one guy at the Theater Club's been talking about taking Venezuelan nationality."

Ev cleared his throat. "Don't forget, Charlie, giving up your U.S. citizenship would be a terrible mistake. You know, there've been many attacks on America recently. They come from people who envy us or don't understand us. But you must remember this: America is the greatest country in the world."

"Yes, Dad, I've always known that."

Ev's final words in that intense meeting were, "And Richards is the greatest college."

"I know, I can't believe I'll be there tomorrow."

At the Labat house they toasted Charlie with champagne.

Chapter 12

Dear Mother & Dad,

You can't imagine how exciting it was, after all that ocean blue and the heat at JFK, when our Commuter Airlines dwarf plane rolled to a halt at Albany Airport. There was a Richards couple sitting up front in the airport limousine. They both had long red hair; from their kidding around I could tell they were seniors. It would've been nice to talk with them about Richards. But it's really begun now—four glorious years, packed with good times and good people and culture amid the creme de la creme. I know they'll be the happiest years of my life, and nothing will equal them—nothing. It was so beautiful when we entered the deep-green valley with its touches of gold, and I saw the College ski paths carved out on Brodie hill, and the tall white wooden church steeple, just like the ones in Grandma Chadwick's Xmas cards. Then I saw the Perkins Hall cupula with its old clock and huge bell, and I wanted to decipher the 180 degree shaped Latin on the granite archway. As the limo swung into College station I saw the rows of white trees filing down toward the campus glen. And when I saw the groups of Richies milling around on their doorsteps I said to myself, 'This is it. This is what I've waited for, and I'm finally here!' After getting my room key from Buildings and Grounds I trudged up to Berkshire Hall feeling high, and I kept saying, 'I'm at Richards!...'

These excerpts from Charlie's first letter home give some idea of his state of mind that September. Friends and acquaintances still remember the rapturous high that made them slightly uncomfortable. Though Richards does inspire strong bonds of loyalty, Charlie's peers tended to find such quasi-religious ecstasy rather cloying and, in retrospect, even pathological, given his later flip-flop and alleged bloody deeds. Phil Ormsby, his freshman roommate, recalls this foreign-looking type stepping into their wood-paneled suite saying "Greetings!" in a vaguely foreign accent, stretching out a vigorous hand, and declaring, "I'm Charlie Chadwick from Venezuela, and I'm here to spend four incredible years at this greatest of schools!" They exchanged introductions and small talk. Charlie went out for his bags.

Another Charlie letter goes into wild lyric transports such as "If there's anything like paradise on earth, this is it!"

Sometimes Charlie would speculate about getting his Ph.D. and then coming back to Richards forever.

Ev didn't take these fantasies very seriously. He saw it as little more than a 17-year-old boy's enthusiasm for small college life and its cozy beauties. Add to that Charlie's intoxication with living in New England for the first time, and hence the spell cast over him by this rare new world. Ev had no doubt that Charlie would soon settle down and come to his senses. "Being an intellectual's a nice hobby," Ev said to me, "but let's face it, the payoff is minimal, and Charlie knew that."

In a perverse way Ev was proved right—Charlie didn't stay at Richards, though Richards stayed too much with Charlie.

The letters of Charlie Chadwick from that year are replete with place names dropped, classmates cited, professors judged. (One of them had taught young Ev, and then been my Freshman advisor.) Charlie's prose gushes over every little detail—the college hills, the library, evening meals with his corridor mates at Cooper, concerts in Putney. Falling leaves and first snows elicit a string of superlatives from his Smith-Corona. Sometimes he recounts and summarizes certain abstruse arguments from Philosophy 101, where Plato's doctrine of ideas gets him all fired up. He sees his first French and Italian movies, and writes back delighted at being able to follow much of the dialogue, but also slightly puzzled that none of his corridor mates want to go to those films. "Phil Ormsby can't stand subtitles in movies. Incredible! I've been reading subtitles all my life!"

His overstatements aside, Charlie led a more or less typical Richards existence. He suffered through academic requirements (choosing Astronomy; Congress) and complained. He kept fit via Phys Ed (following the rule: two years, eight courses) and did indifferently. Unlike most Richies he wasn't much drawn to athletics, but he outdid most everybody in his indifference to politics. For extra-curricular activities he made it both into Symphony and Chamber Players. Weekends he practiced violin, and also partied. Christmas he spent in Caracas, shorter breaks with Connecticut relatives, though they appear not to have been at ease with one another. In fact, Charlie Chadwick was a subject that his New London kinsfolk refused to discuss with me under any circumstances.

About the rest of the United States, Charlie exhibited minimal curiosity. He did visit friends' homes in New York or Boston but, save for a tourist's glances at buildings, his interest wasn't much sparked—his letters or postcards say little about those places. For the time being Charlie's world was Richards College, the town of Richards-New Ashford, and the Berkshire Hills. Eventually it would be Caracas and textiles—such was the understanding as he now lived his "dream come true."

So much to do here! Vladimir Ashkenazy played to a full house last Thursday. I've still got goose-pimples from his Beethoven.

Phil's going to major in American Studies, a cross-disciplinary thing combining history, lit, etc. For me, it's probably French. Then I'll really be able to understand foreign flics.

The work here is incredible. How do people ever graduate? There's at least a paper a week, plus gobs of reading. I remember the dean telling us way back at Freshman Picnic that "hard work will be your best antidote to mischief, and will keep you from becoming Marxists" and I can see how he's right. The skinny little

guy who teaches philosophy even says we're getting plenty of prac-
tice for law school or Wall Street, then he laughs and so do we.

It's weird, lots of people here don't even know where Venezuela
is. I have to keep explaining that we're above the equator and
speak Spanish not Portuguese. Some chick I met the other day
thought Caracas was Buenos Aires, and McNab down the hall
asked if Venezuela's part of Mexico!

Last week the trees were all orange or yellow, and gorgeous it
was. Remember, folks, you've seen it before, but I haven't. Some
of the trees look like huge walking sticks. I'm looking forward to
seeing a real winter, snow and all. Love, Carlitos

Needless to say, nature, art, and intellectualism weren't
Charlie's sole interests that first year. True, pot hadn't caught on
at Richards, but beer and its rituals still endured as the age-old way
of filling up weekend evenings. Charlie is only slightly discreet in
his allusions to aluminum kegs multiplying in the Berkshire
common room Friday afternoons. By 10 P.M. the parquet floors
are coated with spilled beer, the stucco walls atremble with the
plunk-a-plunk of amplified guitars, and the air thick with student
voices frenetically trading campus gossip or sports facts, or softly
taking note of someone from the opposite sex now dancing loosely
and floppily, or just standing alone, tightening her sash and puffing
at her cigarette.

Charlie fell right in with the pattern—by his second Saturday he
had gotten reelingly drunk. Some of his shared antics that year
inevitably recall Caracas. One of them, "the billiard-ball mis-
adventure," involved his entire Berkshire Hall corridor. As Phil
Ormsby and I sipped coffee at Cooper snack bar, he guffawed
throughout his recollection of the episode. Phil remembers how
they'd all consumed twelve pitchers of Pabst at the Saloon down at
Signet House. This reconverted old mansion, conveniently located
right across from the College gray stone gym, actually serves as
setting for semi-formal gatherings Monday through Thursday. On
weekends, however, its sawdust-covered basement floors become

the arena for competitive heavy-duty boozing.

It was 1:30 A.M. The Saloon was shutting down, but not without a thick-armed bartender politely explaining to Phil and Charlie and the whole crew that it's time to split, guys.

The unseasonable warm weather came as a slight shock. Charlie and two of his mates ambled arm-in-arm onto campus, croaking an off-key *Summertime.*

Suddenly something fell from the sky.

"Why it's a billiard ball! A red one," Phil noted, examining it closely.

Charlie peeked, exclaiming, "A billiard ball!"

They all turned 'round and saw their neighbor, Tom McNab, solemnly taking aim and discharging spherical projectiles toward a great bulbous moon.

"What're you up to, McNab?" said a voice somewhere.

"Can'tcha tell? I'm tryin' t' hit the moon!"

Some tittered. Another nodded, puckering his lips. Up went a fourth ball, a fifth and sixth. The spent missiles came thumping right back down onto the yellowing lawn. McNab was toting a bagfull, presumably liberated from Signet House pool room.

"McNab," said Bruce Kelly, another neighbor, now facing the guy and grasping his shoulders, "I'm gonna tell you the truth."

"The truth? Tell it."

"You can't hit the thing."

"Why?"

"'Cause it's too far away."

McNab took a long sniff. "Too far away, eh?"

They all faced him now, nodding.

"Tom," said Charlie, "it's 'way too far. You can't possibly reach it, Tom. Never! Sorry, that's just how it goes."

McNab staggered around a bit. "Well, that'sh jusht your point of view, you dopey South American." (He smacks his lips, then wags his left index finger.) "Shuppozhe I *did* hit the moon?" (Phil Ormsby provides me some expert mimickry of all the voices, particularly McNab's.) "Ya gotta have the ol' can-do shpirit, y' see. There'sh no limit to the ol' can-do shpirit."

So now McNab winds up like a Red Sox professional and hurls *two* simultaneous pool balls at that moon. One of them unfortunately veers off the wrong way and comes crashing down and shatters the rear window of a BMW parked nearby.

"Oh, Jesus," says Charlie.

"Well, whaddoyoo want? Shit! Damn thing was in my way!" At which point McNab stops, spins around once, and then plops right down onto the dewy grass, thoroughly bezonkered.

It was all Phil could do to hold back his belly laughs as he wound up his reminiscences. I laughed too.

For Charlie it was a very good year. A happier frosh Richards College has never seen.

The spell remained with him all summer long, as he talked about the school at any opportunity back in Caracas. A couple of his old Colegio Americano chums at times resented it.

Freddy Arismendi got particularly impatient with him. "OK, Charlie, OK, we know it, Richards is the greatest, OK."

They'd still go out on their madcap drives and meet at the Automercado or the Valle Arriba, though less often than before. And Eddie Phillips, in a baiting mood, might say—leaning up and slapping on the back of his head—"Hey, it's God's green acre up there, right, Charlie ol' boy?"

Some erstwhile Preppies from the States who used to ignore Charlie at Theater Club now started greeting him. For the first time in years a gold-tanned Sally said, "Well, hello, Charlie," and sat down with her rum-and-coke by his pool side bench to talk about Mt. Holyoke and her sort-of-boyfriend up at Richards, a senior in American Studies, pre-Law actually. Charlie recognized his name without knowing who the guy was.

Ev and son now had lots more to discuss and remember. Driving to Telares and later enduring the evening's slow-traffic creep, the elder and the younger Chadwick would invoke their school, comparing past with present. Alejandra, if she rode along, either sat smoking quietly in front or noted parallels with

Manhattanville. Now and again Ev might tease her by expressing mock-envy at the female Richies Charlie had in class—so unlike his own day!—and she'd respond with an ironic little slap.

Richards College had become a shared family fact.

Charlie worked hard with order forms and inventory through June and July; the American Church choirmistress welcomed him back for a couple of violin obbligato numbers; at the marble foyer of the summer-silenced Music School he ran into his former violin teacher, all excited about a forthcoming pilgrimage to Bayreuth; and weekend afternoons were dutifully reserved for visits to Quinta Labat, where few understood what Richards was about. For Charlie, however, Richards was now a second home.

Chapter 13

Charlie's initial bliss and contentment is largely attributable to the policies of Richards itself. From day one a Richie can count on top-quality treatment. First struck by the rural setting and its lush greens, the incoming freshman soon catches sight of the ivied buildings and the diverse architectural specimens of Gothic, Renaissance, Neo-classical, British brick, Berkshire frame, and contemporary geometric, each and all a stone's throw away from each other.

Next he/she is welcomed by an array of junior Richies who serve as advisors and guides, and is further attended by faculty volunteers whose job it is to make the Richie feel welcome. The suites in the student houses (never referred to as "dorms") come equipped with private baths, built-in maplewood desks and bookcases, and black-leather chairs, and there is weekly maid service in the rooms. The older official structures will further move him with their pink marble floors and vaulted ceilings, illuminated by crystal-teardrop chandeliers. And though at dinner time some Richies might poke fun at today's "mystery meat" and "plastic gravy," the dining-hall fare, prepared by former chefs from old-Yankee inns, easily rivals the better offerings at many a respectable New England restaurant.

Once settled in, the Richie and his work are supplemented by intense socializing, not only during mealtime but at enormous special gatherings—guest dinners, cocktail parties everywhere, wine-and-cheese receptions at academic departments, informal get-togethers at professors' homes, and weekend bashes. The 3-to-6 o'clock slot is for group sports exclusively, and many Richies belong to two or more athletic teams—for example Phil Ormsby did varsity squash and swimming plus intramural lacrosse whenever he could.

Hence from the very start the Richie is integrated into the larger Richards "family." This feeling is particularly enhanced during the four-week January Intersession ("J.I." as it's known), when all Richies are virtually free to study whatever they want—their own family trees, or boat building, or simulate the stock exchange, or draw maps of the Battle of the Bulge, plus sleep late, go skiing, and be with their house and college friends. At the end of the final year comes "Senior Recess," ten glorious and unstructured days of outings, barbecues, and beer busts, complemented by golf, sailing, and other warm-weather sports. A Richie departs Richards with fond summer images and happy memories inscribed on his/her young mind.

The feeling of "family" is much stronger today than during my brief stint as a Richie back in 1953. At that time the fraternity system virtually monopolized and set the tone on campus. Meanwhile the scholarship students—twenty percent of the student body, as it is today—found themselves excluded from the Greek houses and consigned to special dorms (humorously known to the frat crowd as "turkey farms"). Ironically the "turkey farmers" got the highest grades. This wasn't as tough as it seems since good grades were considered bad form by the frats, who held annual contests rewarding the house with the *lowest* collective grade-point average (prize: a twenty-gallon keg of beer). Because of the strange mixed atmosphere of prestigious college and "finishing school for rich boys," not a few "turkeys" felt confused and occasionally dropped out (as did yours truly, who instead joined the National Guard and later started all over again as a Spanish major at Indiana U.).

A tragic incident was to shake up this state of affairs. In 1959 a bewhiskered young Ethics professor launched a personal crusade against the fraternities' special privileges and ways. He ridiculed them in class with heavily loaded instances ("Now, suppose a frat guy rapes and murders a drunken Smithie"). At the austere "turkey farm" lounges or in half-empty lecture halls he gave informal chats with titles like, "Any good reasons for fraternities?" One night he debated two house presidents and an alumnus, outshining the whole sick crew according to the "turkeys," looking like a contemptible fool to the Greeks. And he blitzed the editors of the *Booster* with his highly technical letters with their syllogisms arguing for abolition of all frats.

By pure chance, in the fall of 1960 at Kappa Delta Nu house, a Nebraska farm boy was made to swallow half a roll of fresh toilet paper. The boy was soon choking; an ambulance arrived swiftly. The brothers, however, told the white-coated pair that the kid had "a spasm in his throat," a falsehood that was to mislead the staff at the college infirmary where, alas, the young Nebraskan promptly perished. The *Booster* and WRCR kept silent on the misfortune, but word leaked out and ran as a sidebar in the distant *Boston Globe*. The Philosophy prof read it over breakfast; now really driven, he ignored his wife's pleas and that morning speechified in class against the Greek houses, referring to them as "private gangs" made up of "murderous hoodlums." With redoubled force he called for their "total termination."

In response a trio of Sigma Alpha seniors took matters into their own hands. In a brown DeSoto they whizzed down to a Lanesboro sports shop, purchasing a shotgun. Back in Richards-New Ashford they checked addresses and planned their move. After a fine dinner with their fifty-seven S.A. brethren, the threesome went cruising by the professor's small house, going round the block a few times until human forms appeared at a shaded bay window. The man in the driver's seat took calculated aim, then two shots. His S.A. brother in the back seat grabbed the gun and pumped four fast ones at the chosen target.

This time the news travelled with all due speed. Within a half hour's time the WRCR announcer interrupted Johnny Mathis's smooth voice and reported that unidentified snipers had taken potshots at Professor Fulano's home and that a bullet had grazed the man's young son in the shoulder, another the prof's left ear.

Commotion followed. Local non-Richards media kept mum, but the snipers were the sole subject of conversation in frats and dorms that night. Many a Greek man publicly praised the vigilantes' "initiative" and expressed a wish that they'd been successful. On the other hand the "turkeys" held what was for Richards a major rally, with seventy-five scholarship students assembling in front of Cooper and listening to condemnations of all such "vicious and immoral acts." Meanwhile quick police work retraced the spent bullets to that sports shop and thereafter to the S.A. trio.

The aftermath was anti-climactic. The instructor chose not to press charges, and the snipers were expelled that week. Today the professor teaches at a small college in South Florida. Two of the three S.A.-ites remained within the national fraternity fold and are prominent business leaders in the Maryland area; another is with the Foreign Service in South America. Curiously, save for a few faculty old-timers, almost nobody I talked to at Richards knew of the incident. The *Alumni Monthly* appears never to have run a report, and Ev was incredulous to hear of such a thing transpiring at his alma mater.

Later developments did vindicate the professor. Giles Hastings, a then-new president who wished to show his strength, convened a College-wide committee to consider abolition of fraternities at Richards. There was bitter rhetoric on all sides, but by 1966 the Greek houses had effectively disbanded and the nationals donated their imposing facilities for conversion to dorms or classrooms.

One notable exception (which shall remain anonymous) chose instead to demolish their secluded stone manse and leave the lot unoccupied: so it is to this day, rubble and all. A notorious rich, conservative alumnus from Belmont, Massachusetts, also broke ties with the school on grounds that "abolishing fraternities will open Richards to infiltration by Communists."

And yet, these are aberrations. If anything, Richards alumni are fiercely loyal, their per-capita contributions to the school far outstripping those of "Big Ivies" graduates. And in Homecoming Parade every October, when thousands march under iridescent golden trees lining the College byways, pride of place is reserved for those alumni who have shown exceptional generosity. With the abolition of the frats, moreover, grades are now taken very seriously indeed and worked hard for. And whereas in olden times (such as during my brief stint) Richies went right from graduation into pa's and grandpa's business, today they might take a graduate degree before striving to be leaders in management, medicine, and law.

Admissions standards and workload aside, however, Richards College's most singular distinction is a quietly-kept secret: namely, its students' parents' income, which on average is the nation's highest. The fact does show in the array of new cars parked by the "houses" and the abundant furniture issuing out of U-hauls come September. A few of these Richies will one day feel at home in Richards-New Ashford township, with its two tax-paying billionaires and forty-nine resident millionaires, several of them retired Alumni Richies themselves.

On the town streets, of course, one sees many recent Cadillacs and Porsches, but also little auto pollution, no neon, and not a single red light. The one "STOP" sign at a highly dangerous 5-way intersection was put up in order to mollify those citizens who'd been pushing for a full-fledged stop signal, left-turn arrows and all. The town worthies considered this a potential eyesore and argued that what takes place at a Richards-New Ashford intersection should be the business of the individual, not government.

From its beginnings the College has been associated with conservative wealth. The place was almost single-handedly founded in 1829 by Jeremiah Wright Richards, a white-haired Virginia patriarch whose twin sons Isaac and Isaiah had enrolled up north at venerable old Williams College. The two youths felt "grievously unhappy" there, owing in part to the large number of economically humble students at that school but mostly because of the outspoken Abolitionist views of certain professors who in 1823 had founded the first Anti-Slavery Society in Massachusetts. Mr. Richards expressed his profound displeasure at "unthinking fanatics" being given quarter at "an educational College." In thunderous epistles he called for their removal, though no one at Williams took him seriously, least of all President Chester Dewey. A wrathful Mr. Richards then bought up huge tracts of farmland down in New Ashford and succeeded in persuading the town notables to add his own name. The stage was set: in the summer before his sons' junior year, a dozen anti-Abolitionist students, two like-minded professors, and J. W. Richards, with members of his clan, all solemnly gathered together at a big house in Richards-New Ashford. It was July 4th. There they signed the Richards College charter, in which it is proclaimed that "all Individuals' Opinions must be tolerated, inasmuch as Tolerance is the very Bedrock of this God-given Republic."

Jeremiah Wright Richards's strong "Opinions" eventually proved an embarrassment following Fort Sumter. College officials aimed thereafter at quiet neutrality and minimized the school's origins. War and defeat notwithstanding, the Richardses were to give bounteously to their College throughout the 1860s; descendants continue to do so, if on a lesser scale. The result is that Richards has something of a "Southern" flavor, with a relatively higher proportion of students from that region. In my time there existed a Southern frat house, notorious for the anti-Black songs its brothers sang at meals and football games. During my most recent visit I noted Confederate flags in student rooms. But values change, and Abolitionism no longer elicits controversy in New England.

Inevitably the anti-Abolitionist orientation had to be supplanted, and for a century the guiding doctrine at Richards has been that of "building individual character." An inscription on the Roman archway that leads to a quiet little courtyard says: WE CELEBRATE THE SINGULARITY OF EACH MAN WHO TREADS THESE NOBLE PATHS. And the entrance to Putney bears in gold the legend: KINGS AND QUEENS HAVE HAD THEIR ANCIENT SAY, BUT WHAT IS MORE ENDURING THAN THE INDIVIDUAL?

In spite of the respected academic standing of the school, its course catalog and other publications regularly state that "fullness of character" and "all-around individuality" matter far more than the achievements of pure intellect.

These doctrines were first formulated by Marathon Fitzwill Cooper, the remarkable President of Richards from 1861 to 1901, immortalized by Cooper Hall. A Philosophy man, Cooper none-theless remained convinced that inordinate booklearning "can do irreparable harm to our unique, individual essence;" his own reading later in life would be restricted to the daily press. Moreover he took pride in scarcely having glanced at any thinker outside the Anglo-Saxon "guild of masters"—Locke, Hume, and Herbert Spencer. Occasionally, with exaggerated gestures, he would recite randomly out of Hegel to his freshmen, thereby mocking the Teutonic windbag and showing them how not to do Philosophy. Geology he dismissed as "nonsense in a new way," Evolution as "one man's idiotic theory." A passionate Calvinist, what he most believed in was wealth and piety as the prime guarantors of salvation, and was always strict about compulsory chapel attendance (daily back then, only monthly when it was dropped in 1960).

The Cooper "creed" and style have left their unmistakable stamp on Richards. Whenever some undecided senior would come for advice on apprenticing to a scientist in Germany or—worse yet!—becoming a writer in France, a crusty old Mr. Cooper would urge the young dreamer to put such misguided fancies out of mind and seek a well-paid clerking job in textiles, or in the new iron and steel works, bright and dynamic in their future. Richards has since had some prominent scientists and poets in its employ, and in the 'Sixties did graduate a playwright, a photographer, and of course Livie Kingsley in 1975. Most Richards B.A.'s, however, still make their names in upper executive suites and certain high government posts. Not for nothing has the College earned a reputation as "the West Point of Wall Street."

The admission of women beginning in 1969 has not significantly altered the Richards "way." From the start, female Richies have been much like the males—robust, athletic, moderate to conservative in politics, basically well-adjusted, and headed for business careers or the professions. (Two of the smartest new women in the C.I.A., for example, are Richie alumnae.) And of course their numbers boast a high proportion of third and fourth generation Richies, only they're female now. Certain explosive tensions did at first flare up with the presence of women at a once all-male bastion. But actually the implacable demands of work, sport, and group socializing all serve as an efficient curb on desire. Few Richies I talked to were terribly surprised at that much-cited Princeton survey of campus sex life, with its recurrent news that the northeastern school with consistently the least erotic activity—whether casual flings, torrid romances, or just holding hands—is Richards. Accordingly, one sees few sexy young dressers walking about Richards-New Ashford.

It may seem strange to say so but, April 1975 and its horrors notwithstanding, there are few places as happy and harmonious as is Richards. Its dissenting element is minimal; even in the 'Sixties tranquility was the Richards norm. Anything resembling, say, Berkeley, was entirely gentlemanly. At one point in Spring 1969 a group of Black students staged a one-day sit-in inside Foley Hall and politely enumerated demands for more Afro-American faculty. The Economics Department soon hired a young Black Ph.D. from UCLA—a conservative opposed to all government social programs. Because many Black Richies are conservative, the choice didn't create much of a stir.

Then came Cambodia in May 1970. Richards did cancel classes for a day, so that students and faculty could assemble in Putney and discuss the pros and cons of Nixon's bold move. Following the Kent State shootings, a second one-day forum was declared. President Hastings set the agenda by urging all Richies to shun emotionalism and remain open to every possible viewpoint. And so they did; some in fact opted to shun the forum altogether and play racketball on the greening lawn. Meanwhile back inside Putney spokespersons from all sides had their say. Some deplored the senseless deaths; someone called Nixon psychotic, raising eyebrows thereby; yet another insisted that the National Guard has a right to defend itself against aggressive violence; and a popular Philosophy professor called for a healthy skepticism and resistance toward all dogmas of Right and Left, the speech eliciting enthusiastic applause. Except for some heckling from a few SDS people, things went smoothly.

Back then, radicals at Richards were scarcely more than a few dozen campus marginals. A tiny SDS chapter had fourteen malcontents among its ranks. Today the entire left is about that size. And it's not as if Richards leftists suffer from much red-baiting. If anything, the left's problem is one of feeling pointless, of getting worked up over issues that, at Richards, are considered not subversive but out of place or just plain boring. Anybody weird enough to wave slogans like "imperialism" at dinner table will simply be told, "Hey, look, don't spoil my meal," or elicit blank indifference. Campus life is a force that far outweighs leftist ideology, and even Richie radicals like to guzzle from the kegs. During my ill-starred Richards semester there were in my dorm a couple of gangly Brooklyners, one of them actually Marx by name and both needless to say "turkeys." Inseparable, they worked serving tables at Kappa Nu, where a wittier brother might greet them, "Well, here they are, the Red busboys" or jokingly address them as "Amos and Marxy." Even we "turkeys" generally ignored the pair and giggled whenever they'd trot out old slogans about "exploitation" and "the ruling class," ideas which to us seemed as hot as planet Pluto.

Today's leftist issues are equally remote—literally so. Just before my last visit to Richards the bombing of Peru had been stepped up to round-the-clock status. The *Booster*, which since 1975 has declined in quality, carried nothing about the re-escalation, and few Richies would even have thought of discussing Peru except in Poli Sci 220 ("U.S.-Latin American Relations"). One young sophomore I talked to, a Quaker, mentioned how at breakfast time he sat with two guys wearing prep school T-shirts; he casually mentioned having heard over National Public Radio that entire Peruvian villages were being blotted out by B-52s.

Preppie Number 1 started giggling uncontrollably.

Preppie Number 2 chuckled and said, "Well, well, Peruvians being blotted out, how'bout that now?" and lumbered off for O.J.

Preppie Number 1, still giggling, looked over at two brunettes sitting alone at the next table. "So whattaya think of that, Allison and Pat?"

Allison giggled too, nearly choking on her Cheerios. "Hey, I can see it now. Great one-liner! 'Peruvian Villages Gone Blotto!' Boy did I need a laugh today." Pat also laughed.

At this point in our conversation the Quaker kid slapped the edge of the table with both hands and exclaimed, "Jesus, I can see why Carlos might do what he did." Thus spoke the pacifist.

And yet the young Quaker deeply loves Richards, a well-nigh unanimous attitude. To a graduate of a state college—where grousing about the school is a daily sport—such institutional pride and loyalty strikes me as exotic and enviable. This loving attitude is shared by the faculty, most of whom feel pleased to be shepherding America's high society.

"Some students in your classes might be multimillionaires," said a short, elegantly dressed History professor to me, puffing on his pipe. "From looking at them you'd never know it, though. They don't flaunt it in any way."

"And they don't have to, really," said a tall, stout colleague of his, "not when so many of their friends on the playing fields might be equally well-to-do."

A professor of Political Theory, after expressing his scorn for Carlos and his play, went on to inform me with genuine satisfaction, "A lot of my seniors have gone right from our seminar room to the State Department, and I don't feel any arrogance when I say I've helped groom them for those positions."

Faculty identification with Richards is additionally reinforced by such customs as house "guest meals," or the occasional game of softball with the Richies, followed by snacks at a faculty home. Fifteen percent of the professors, incidentally, are Richards B.A.s.

Of course there are occasional young malcontents who gripe about Richards anti-intellectualism and make wisecracks such as "Richards is a country club, and I'm like a golf instructor." And there's the story about a neatly-dressed high school senior whose mother throughout his admissions interview kept referring to professors as "the help." The boy was supposedly turned down.

Such a story may well be apocryphal, and it was cited to me by a couple of new leftist teachers whose judgment may not be exactly objective. At any rate it's a jaundiced view held by a tiny minority. If anything Richards College and its environs seem like the model for Dr. Johnson's Happy Valley. The majority of its professors and virtually all Richies are damn proud to be there, and the place maintains its tone in great degree because some enterprising individuals have chosen to make it that way—founding it, attending it, raising their boys (and now girls also) with it in mind, contributing cash, making sentimental visits, and sometimes retiring nearby. Richards shapes one's future; there the Richie makes business contacts and meets possible lifemates, for the school now boasts a high rate of intramural marriages-upon-graduation. Summer issues of the *Alumni Monthly* are filled with photos depicting garden-party receptions, in which smiling Richards seniors combine commencement festivities with wedding joys. In sum, most everybody at Richards loves Richards and will do so until their dying days.

Perhaps the sole doubt that burdens them is being in the shadow of their more esteemed forefather to the north. In most everything that counts, Williams College has its edge over Richards—higher admissions standards, greater national reputation, more solid traditions (it's the second-oldest college in Massachusetts), and a long list of alumni prominent in education and the arts (names such as Sterling Brown, Elia Kazan, Jessie Winchester, John Sayles, and Stephen Sondheim). Richards's campus is more varied and beautiful, and its sprawling library a source of pride, but, in the larger world, its contributions other than commercial have been slight. These invidious comparisons are routinely shrugged off by Richies, who look upon Williams kids as studying machines whose real life experience is nil. Williams nonetheless remains the premier college in the Berkshires. It was Charlie Chadwick who brought to its neglected southern offshoot an undesired attention.

Chapter 14

Charlie's sophomore year was less idyllic.

Things may have started to crack on his arrival at Babcock House. He was the very first person there that gold-hued day; his single room was bright and airy. He lay down his bags, feeling blissful. Then he saw inscribed on the closet door, roughly carved capital letters, about 2" high: "LEON EATS IT."

Charlie at first was amused, but not for long. "Can you believe someone actually wrote *that* in my own room?" was his peeved comment in a short note sent off that day.

Leon Kramer had previously held the suite and changed rooms last minute. The inscription was obviously meant for him.

Then there was the matter of Chamber Players. Lugging his fiddle up to the music building, Charlie thought he'd warm up for rehearsals.

"Hi, Charlie." Marsha, the spunky redheaded secretary,

headed for the Xerox. "How was summer? Actually winter, right?"

He stopped to chat. "Oh, hi. No, it's summer, we're on the Caribbean. Working was great, but I didn't practice much. Hope I'm still eligible for Chamber Players."

Marsha bit her pink lower lip. "Well, you need not worry."

Charlie perked up. "What do you mean?"

"Haven't you heard? Chamber Players is being discontinued."

"What?"

She was earnest now. "Yeah. Budgetary reasons. Actually they're consolidating Players with Symphony. Same thing, tho'."

At which point Charlie simply rushed off without a word. Marsha was surprised at his abrupt reaction. Of course she had no idea how much Richards Chamber Players meant to him.

Disappointments aside, Charlie was now a member in good standing of the Class of '75. Richards was his school, and Babcock his house. A few of his old corridor mates also ended up at Babcock. In addition there would be women students housed on the second and fourth floors, the result of what *Life* magazine, in a glowing 1970 photo-essay on the new co-ed dorms, called "The Good Revolution." Charlie was pleased as punch with the arrangement, mentioning it in his letters and making sly comments like "So how's this red-blooded American boy going to get any studying done?" His humorous remarks were eventually to prove just a shade prophetic, though not in the way he'd intended.

And his routines were pretty much the same as before. He studied hard as ever, and his grades rose higher. He practiced some and attended weekly orchestra rehearsals. Occasionally he'd go out for coffee with someone from French Lit or Symphony. On the other hand he went to no football games and was indifferent to them. If he spent Saturday afternoons at Richards he might play violin or go to some movie or just sleep.

That indifference to football seems to have piqued a couple of his corridor-mates—unexplainably, since they'd already known of Charlie's lack of interest. It was a bright nippy morning after the big annual Williams game. Dining hall was quiet. Bruce Kelly and Tom McNab were sitting at a spacious round table, leaning back after having cleaned up their five-high waffles and link sausages.

As Charlie joined them they kept up their flow of talk about that amazing last play. "It was truly beautiful," said Bruce.

Adding three sugars to his coffee, Charlie asked, "Who won?"

Tom and Bruce froze. After an astonished silence Bruce finally snapped, "You mean you don't even know who won?"

"No. Should I?"

The sound of stacking plates could be heard. "It was the Williams game," Bruce elaborated.

"I guess I must've been playing Bach."

Tom said with an ironic grin, "So Charlie fiddled while his fellow Richies fought."

Charlie was puzzled. "Yeah, right. Listen, suppose football doesn't interest me?"

A half-minutes dead silence, and a more serious Tom remarked quietly, "Who won doesn't seem to interest you either."

Another brief silence, and Bruce interjected, "For your information, Chadwick, we won the big game, 28-22. C'mon, McNab."

The two grabbed their trays and left, saying no more.

According to a letter home from Charlie, McNab and Kelly both ignored him for a while after that incident. Tom and Bruce deny that this was so.

"Paranoid, that's all," Bruce said to me in his E.F. Hutton cubicle in Boston. "That Charlie—*Carlos*, ex*cuse* me!—he was just being *paranoid*, the s.o.b."

When Ev Chadwick read the letter recounting the episode, his initial response was to deplore Colegio Americano's lack of football facilities. Today he sees himself as in part responsible. "I should've taught my boy about American traditions."

Chapter 15

The episode that did more than its share to shake up Charlie's confidence was a brief but intense relationship with fellow sophomore Olivia B. Kingsley.

Livie, as she is known, contributed Part 2 of this book.

Readers may also remember her as the college junior who, in Spring 1971, published a memoir entitled *Living the Good Life: Report from a Small College in New England* (Doubleday). With its loving evocations of the Richards landscape and activities, its slightly blasé dismissal of the dogmas of 1960s love-and-leftism, and its serene and lofty balance, the 150-page volume attracted some attention when it first came out, garnering good reviews in high places. First-year sales were modest, and the remainder houses were expecting shipments of *Living the Good Life*. As fate would have it, the bombings sparked interest in the school, and 10,000 new copies of Livie's book were promptly issued and sold.

Livie was the very first Richie to have published a book while still a student. This was one of the many items in "Livie's legend."

There was Livie the top student, who consistently made Dean's List and received early Phi Beta Kappa nomination.

There was Livie the star musician, the impressive flautist whose virtuosity brought solo appearances around the Berkshires as well as with the Hartford Symphony and Boston Pops, prompting speculations about her being another James Galway.

And there was the journalist Livie, who as a sophomore was placing articles in the national press, and who in her junior year became Editor-in-Chief of the *Booster*, a for-seniors-only position. In that capacity she was to succeed in reforming a sophomoric sheet hitherto printed on shiny paper but with a journalistic level "somewhere between sixth and seventh grade." Such were Livie's words in describing it to me, and I know that during my own brief Richards spell the *Booster* was an unreadably smirky and self-congratulatory grab-bag of campus gossip, crude cartoons, hair-splitting debates, in-crowd references and fraternity humor, and no reviews of concerts or books, no news stories or comments, *nothing at all* about what might be happening beyond Richards-New Ashford. I find it a minor miracle that Richie graduates with only the *Booster* and *Time* as their outside reading could land plum jobs in Washington D.C. back then.

Luckily for me Indiana U. had a real newspaper where I got my start as reporter. Livie's strategy in her freshman year was to turn the *Booster* around. She did well: by the time she'd become Editor it was appearing twice a week and running news summaries plus lively opinion pieces on the presidential crisis, on Vietnam and Peru, or on the economy, many of them by faculty members and some even by student leftists—a first in Richards history. Also, for the first time anyone could remember, there were books being reviewed once a week and regular coverage of concerts and lectures. In all, the journalistic level at Richards had risen by 1,000 percent, and for the first time there was an incentive at Jeremiah Wright Richards's secluded old school for good writing on non-Richards subjects.

"Livie's Legend" at Richards began as early as Freshman Week 1971. Like most private schools, Richards starts things out by distributing a "facebook" with photos of all new Richies. Many a freshman's spare moments will be spent leafing through its pages, noting where so-and-so's from, wondering what he/she's like. As it turned out, during that first weekend many an all-male gathering ended up on page 82, at the luminous 1.5" rectangle where, right between Valerie Kemp and Andrew Bliss Kingston III, you could find and gaze at the portrait of Olivia B. Kingsley from Ohio, Queen of the Class of '75 facebook.

It was a striking photo, what with the provocative tilt of her head, the model-like poise, the hint of a grin on her pouty lips, the clear though not quite innocent eyes, the smooth skin and smooth neck, all framed by the perfectly molded blunt-cut of her hair, vaguely resembling Louise Brooks's Lulu yet also classically American in its good looks. One didn't flip past that picture, which some young blood reportedly tore out and slipped inside his wallet.

Idle rumor, perhaps, but what matters most is the fact that people were saying it. By the second freshman night, after the swimming tests and placement exams and ice cream bashes, a group of 17-year-olds might be sitting around till 3 P.M., swapping backgrounds and asking, "Oh, do you know X?" And of course sex would come up and all talk lead to enigmatic Olivia, the object of collective lust at countless men's suites across campus. She was literally something to write home about, as Charlie did. Every male body wanted to bump into her at Science Center or watch her strolling down the quad, or they'd stand around the P.O. at Cooper, hoping as much to end up having her at their side as to get pink envelopes from old flames elsewhere. Naturally she never showed up, and their young hearts ached.

Nothing like her had been seen during three years of women at Richards, and there's been nothing since. At the first freshman mixer she wore white dress, high heels, and a red sash that brought out her swaying waist; and a cigarette highlighting the dark-polished fingernails further enhanced her leonine femininity, making the callow youths burn all the more with desire for just one dance with her. Save for dark blues in winter, plus a gray beret, that clothing ensemble is the one she has largely stuck with to this day. Shunning as she did the casual jeans-and-clogs image of the Preps, Livie's look was part of her aloofness from rah-rah pressures and college socializing. Ironically, what she would defend the most about small schools in her book was, precisely, the socializing.

Being one of those creatures who effortlessly elicit male infatuation and can count on a hundred eyes glancing at her wherever she may be, Livie remained on men's minds the next four years. Her talents, her patrician family background, and her having been high school valedictorian all added to her aura. In a place where things cultural aren't looked upon that seriously, Livie Kingsley had the odd knack for getting men to try wooing her with their intellect. A mustachioed Swiss professor recalls the effect

Livie had when she showed up for second half of Intermediate French. Throughout first semester the Conversation class, 95-percent male, had been shamelessly indifferent as they slouched in their seats, coming solely for the requirements. With Livie now there beginning in February, those blasé boys perked up and sat straight, leaping into the fray and marshalling their French as often as possible, anything to look good in Livie's eyes as she sat still and statuesque in the second row. By March the group's quality had shot up and all grades had risen.

Livie already had a record of disturbed and broken Ohio hearts to her credit. Soon there were Richies on that list, including an aspiring concert pianist, an art professor, and an Amherst man. One Richie after another yielded his mask and found his self and soul shaken by La Kingsley, and as the string of "Livie's Loves" grew so did her reputation as a dangerous charmer. In what I inferred was the common set phrase, Phil Ormsby snidely alluded to her as "the body snatcher Livie Kingsley." From his tone of voice I gathered that the term might in fact express resentment at *not* having had one's body "snatched," though the exact opposite reason may at times have been the case too. And there were the verbally less adept who bitterly dismissed her as "Livie the bitch," for like motives, no doubt.

Charlie at first resisted the Kingsley lure but, during sophomore year, he at last succumbed and joined "Livie's Loves." Dazzled with the events and his own fire, he wrote home in December about some vague if passionate plans to "marry that girl someday," his ecstasy over engagement probably sharpened by a subliminal realization that there really was no engagement. "What incredible nights & weekends! We spend whole evenings together, eating and studying and all the rest, and I love her!" Further details of their brief amour are to be found in Part 2.

Charlie went back to Caracas in high bliss, and wrote her twice a day, Special Delivery. Then, over Christmas she abruptly left him for a Young-ADA activist from Cleveland, and so informed him in a Dear John note mailed to Richards. Charlie all but collapsed following his return. January Intersession doesn't require much study, and with the minimal pressures he was reading almost nothing at all. He spent entire mornings lying in bed, staring at the walls and letting the phone just ring, skipping early meals, later maybe wolfing down some soup and losing nine pounds in the process. After dinner, before stretching out once more, he'd stack up the same old Brahms and Ravel LP's, much to the annoyance of his quiet, studious neighbor Dick Betsky.

The whole experience threw the adolescent into a long-term lethargy, a numbed indifference that had him in its grip for the remainder of the year. His letters home dwell obsessively on that contradictory lovelorn sensation of both heaviness and void, of feeling overstuffed as well as drained. At one point he even wished (casually, no doubt) that he were dead.

It was with lofty indifference that Ev read and dismissed those epistles. "College girls matter very little, you'll understand that once you're in the real world. So forget these trifles and settle down to work." He now regrets not having comforted his son a wee bit, just as he wishes he'd given him a more patriotic upbringing, but that's another story.

Chapter 16

Charlie's progress was further disrupted by a bizarre college prank. It all began on a warm evening in April, when at about 10 P.M. some twenty drunken males showed up at the library reading room. Among the fifty-five users present were a shy and very pretty student librarian (my informant) and Charlie himself.

The roisterers now furnished a concert of less-than-delicate songs. One glorified rape; a milder one went, *"Here's to the girls of Richards, Richards, / And the streets they roam, / 'Cause one of those urchins on Main Street, Main Street, / Could be our very own."* The performance lasted some fifteen minutes. Meanwhile a reveler inflated a feminoid mannequin which, for their closing number, they sprinkled with red wine and plopped onto an astounded librarian's desk. They exited raucously.

Throughout the spectacle almost everybody sat in incredulous, if sometimes pleased, silence. A street-tough actress from New York's Little Italy did snarl at them once. Most of the men, however, clapped and cheered after each tune.

A diminutive blonde freshwoman strutted over to a claque member and politely asked him not to encourage the serenaders.

He waved her off. "Aw, c'mon, Sue, they're from my corridor," and went on clapping.

With the singers gone a debate began in earnest. Some of the men were laughing uncontrollably.

"What's so damn funny?" shouted the actress, but the laughing continued even louder.

Half a dozen women and two men got up, spewing rage. They huddled out in the hall and drafted a sharply-worded condemnatory letter. Back inside they read it out loud and called for signatures.

"Oh, jeez, what's the matter with you girls?" shouted a guy. "You're all gettin' too emotional," shouted another. Some men did sign, among them Charlie Chadwick. Two days later the signed protest showed up in the columns of the *Booster*. There also appeared the first of many bitter individual statements and a high and mighty editorial pronouncement by Livie Kingsley, who suggested that, "In the interests of balance, our frustrated choir boys might have sung at least one song about their moments of impotence, their recent days as virgins, and other of their sexual lacks."

The "library incident" sparked controversy at Richards the likes of which were not seen during Vietnam or Watergate or Peru. For the remainder of Spring classes the atmosphere was charged with dispute, and few could talk about anything else at mealtime. As a side effect, broader political discussion flourished briefly. The esplanade area in front of Putney became a "Little Berkeley" where half a dozen political groups from Richards as well as the Berkshires set up card tables with their pamphlets and other literature. Only a few score Richies, including Charlie, ever took with any regularity to the idea, but those few were often seen milling about at the tables, and the College feminists did hold a rare rally there, drawing good speakers (Livie among them) and a couple hundred chanters.

Meanwhile the *Booster's* Letters to the Editor pages brimmed with opinions ranging from bumptious amusement to righteous anger. Critics talked of "sexism," "violence toward women," and "male sexual fascism." Defenders dismissed the plaintiffs as "hysterical," applauded the "fun joke" of "regular guys who like drinking beer and looking at beautiful dames," and mocked "those puritanical females" and their "prude attitude" (*sic*). The most frequent refrain from the anti-feminists was, "Hey, girls, grow up and learn to laugh at yourselves." A byword of both sides was "intolerance." Feminists complained of "intolerance" toward women. The prankster faction decried "feminist intolerance of our views" and even "intolerance of intolerance."

Over the next two weeks the verbal volleys became thicker, the sentiments sourer. In one incident, two of the serenaders strutted up to Charlie as he sat with his half-melted ice cream in Babcock dining hall.

I look up and see the bulkier of the two waving a huge index finger at me. "Listen, Chadwick, you shouldn't've signed that dumb letter."

I stare back and blurt out, "And why not?"

And now the short, skinny kid bares his upper teeth and mocks me, "Why not? Why not?"

"Yeah, yeah, why not? Isn't this a free country? Can't I say what I want?" Mr. Brawn now raps his knuckles on the tabletop. "Yeah, right, Chadwick, and so can we. And we're tellin' ya not t'go signin' dumb letters from asshole feminists."

"You watch out, Chadwick, or we're putting you on a banana boat to Rio or whatever jungle it is you come from."

I've got to admit I felt scared, but, trembling and all, I

managed to say, "Well, I mean, if those chicks're such assholes,
how come they c'n get you so riled up?"

So Shorty slams his cup on my table and snorts, "Aw, Jesus,
c'mon, Hines, this guy's a moron, let's go."

The two of them stormed out through a side door. The April
twilight showed it was well past closing. Three self-absorbed crew
types in a remote corner seemed oblivious to the spat.

The little exchange darkened Charlie's evening and briefly
brought back his January inertia. Again he lay silently in his unlit
room, not once cracking his Camus, and with Brahms and Ravel
again spinning a way. Yet when the day dawned, the sheer force
of the ongoing debate and the threats from the Laurel-Hardy pair
seem to have swept an apathetic Charlie into the war of words.
Like other Richies at the time he wrote a letter to the *Booster*—
nothing angry, just some reasonable, pleas to the jesters to be
open-minded and see the feminist "perspective."

To the Library Serenaders and their Spokespeople:

Look, guys, laugh at yourselves all you want, but don't do
other people's laughing for them. How would you like it if twenty-
five women paraded into the library and sang songs about the time
you couldn't get it up, or the other time when you made a pass and
got turned down? How would you like it if they paraded this plastic
statue that looked like you and then kicked it around the College
green? I wouldn't like it, you certainly wouldn't like it, so why do
it to others? Try to understand other ways of looking at things,
other perspectives. That's why we're at Richards—to learn about
differing perspectives and points of view.

The letter brought him more than he'd bargained for. While a
few individuals, mostly women, expressed their gratitude the day
it appeared in the *Booster*, others were to confront him or simply
stop greeting him on the street. A mild-mannered fellow in French
Lit asked him why was he so hysterical and closed-minded about

the pranksters? In a democracy, don't they, too, have a right to their perspective?

More ominously, Leon Kramer informed him while showering, "Chadwick, you're a traitor. You've betrayed Babcock unity." Charlie said nothing, and the conversation ended there—forever. By pure chance Babcock was the most jockish and anti-intellectual of all Richards houses. Four of the serenaders were Babcock men, and twenty-seven residents had signed a letter to the *Booster* flamboyantly ridiculing the feminists' complaints. Most of Babcock gave Charlie the silent treatment uninterruptedly through May.

April had been cruel enough. Charlie now simply wanted to have done with his courses, get back to Caracas and then head for Paris, where he'd been accepted by the Montrose College in France program. "I need a nice long break from this place" was the refrain in his otherwise confused, sometimes desperate letters. One moment he hates himself, another moment he despises his corridor-mates. A brief angry note expresses "absolute loathing and disgust" toward Babcock residents, and in a longer letter he wonders about Richards itself. While the target varies from day to day, the constant lament is one of isolation.

"It's weird, I'll be slushing through the mud on my way to Cooper, and I'll see five guys I'd chugged beer with since I first got here, and they'll walk by without saying a word."

All this plus his jilted-lover feelings weighed heavily on Charlie's mind. So totally caught up was he in his problems as lonely male and Babcock marginal that he took no note of an event later to loom large in his life—the arrival of eighty-seven U.S. advisers and the first major U.S. air raids over PMF-controlled areas in Peru. Richards was far too much with Charlie at the time.

Family feuds upon return to Caracas further blocked out the war from his consciousness. In Ev's troubled recollection, when Charlie finally made it past the slow customs queue at La Guaira International Airport and rushed through the glass doors, he hugged his parents, effused about being back home, and at hectic speed began retelling the entire story of the library, the protests, his signature, the aftermath, his own letter . . .

As they got onto the La Guaira-Caracas highway, Ev gently interrupted Charlie and said he might have best stayed out.

"The whole shabby affair was really none of your business. Besides, what's wrong with an occasional college prank?"

Charlie remained silent as he took in the mist-topped mountains, the four lanes of steady traffic, the deep gorges at his right. "You think I shouldn't have written that letter?"

Ev was silent in return.

From the back seat, Alejandra intervened. "Tell me, Ev, do you really believe it was just a harmless prank?"

He snapped back. "Of course it was harmless. Literally so. Who got hurt?"

"Some people's feelings got hurt," Charlie interjected.

"Well, those people should have risen above their petty personal feelings and not been so darned weak. Intolerant too."

"But, Dad, it was those twenty guys who were being intolerant. Can't you see that?"

"You and those coeds shouldn't be so hysterical. Pranksters have feelings too. Ever consider that possibility?"

Alejandra now said with conviction, "Listen, Ev, if I had witnessed that incident I would certainly have written a letter. Maybe I would have flung my books at those guys too." In fact she threw her cigarette stub out the back window.

Now the western Caracas shantytowns intruded with their cesspool odors; some of the newer skyscrapers loomed into view; but the bitter spat continued all the way up to El Bosque. As the car pulled into Quinta Tropical, the three of them agreed not to discuss the matter any further.

Charlie spent the summer in a daze, going through the motions as a gofer at Telares. People remarked on his increased personal polish and slightly rustied Spanish.

He still visited the Theater Club and Valle Arriba once a week and swapped college stories with old chums, but the cruisings of yesteryear were no more. Instead he spent his evenings and many a Sunday at the table in his room, reading French novels and building up French vocabulary, getting ready for the Fall. Ev wondered about this dedication, while Alejandra was pleased.

Three thousand miles South, Phantom jets were on their first strafing missions over enemy villages in the Andes. Burdened with his own conflicts, Charlie could hardly notice let alone make out what was going on in those distant heights. At the clubside pools his friends never talked about the war and it didn't concern them since the draft was gone. The Bustamante brothers across the street might rave about "Gringo Imperialists," to which Charlie, shrugging his shoulders, would say, "I don't know. I suppose it's a bad thing."

Meanwhile September drew to a close, and all Charlie wanted was to get to Paris.

Chapter 17

It seems strange but, save for Charlie's grandfather, who'd served briefly as an interpreter for our World War I doughboys, not a single Chadwick had been "over there" for at least a century.

Britain was another matter. Charlie's Gilded-Age forebears occasionally did pack their trunks and board the steamer for London, but the Continent was off-bounds. The Chadwick view took its extreme form in a letter by Charlie's great-granduncle Adam to the *Hartford Courant* in 1905, wherein he crustily dismissed all Continentals as a crew of "half-crazed poets & subversives."

Curiously, some Chadwicks—including Adam himself—had done well in languages at Richards or Mount Holyoke, but in spite of their linguistic skills they never evinced much interest in French or Spanish places. They seemed to pick up languages much like an earnest collector builds up a library of 18th century leatherbound Americana or early- Victorian antiques.

By contrast the Labats liked vaunting their European links. They were descendants of Jean-Pierre de Labat, the freedom-fighting swashbuckler who'd stayed on in the new Venezuela and become active in food exports with a couple of his brothers, all of them marrying locally. Throughout the century the Labats of Venezuela summered in Europe with their dwindling French family brethren. By 1911, however, the Labat clan had all but died out in Paris, and the visits from Venezuela became fewer and shorter.

A more recent flesh-and-blood France existed through Héla Montesquiou de Estévez, an upper bourgeoise from St. Cloud who chanced to meet Alejandra's uncle Federico on his grand tour in 1913, married the 38-year-old gentleman and debarked with him to a then-sleepy Caracas. Childless, Héla survived Federico's 1921 death by almost four decades. Eventually she would stay at Quinta Labat and sing French songs to infant Charlie right until the morning of his fifth birthday, on the afternoon of which she heard a radio soap opera come to its lachrymose end, then muttered a Gallic obscenity and breathed her quiet deep last.

In addition to Héla's trusty rocking chair, the Labats' furnishings and home were of French design. From his Venezuelan kin Charlie heard frequent intimations that, somewhere across the Atlantic (they'd point toward Europe, saying "*allá*"), there existed an Old World far more refined and civilized than these youthful Americas, still so rough and primitive. Alejandra herself had done her Master's in psychology at the Sorbonne, a time she recalled with nostalgia. Such differences caused no dissension in the Chadwick household. Ev hadn't inherited Uncle Adam's narrow Europhobia, but was equally indifferent to his inlaws' dreamy Europhilia. The demands of the textile market were too great for him to be concerned with rating remote cultures.

Charlie Chadwick boarded the Air France jumbo jet with expectations surpassing those he'd once held for Richards College. Meeting up with the Montrose group at JFK Airport and arriving with them at Orly helped further fuel his excitement. For the initial few days, however, he felt oddly disappointed. To begin with, the cab driver who drove him and a fellow student into Paris, upon noting that they were Americans, couldn't resist taunting them on Vietnam and Peru.

Cab-sharer Nick merely grinned and rolled his eyes in silence, while Charlie replied, "I know nothing about that affair, monsieur." The two passengers peered out the window, catching glimpses of the Eiffel Tower and not believing their eyes.

The cab pulled up at a tiny street near Odéon. Charlie was the first off. "*Amusez-vous bien, monsieur,*" barked the driver. Charlie's attractive host family of three, Bidot by name, lived in a sixth-floor flat near the Latin Quarter. The elegant graying parents were Mitterrand socialists who made no secret of their views though did not insist on them. By contrast their svelte and feisty 17-year-old daughter Francoise was friendly with young leftist extremists, and on Charlie's second morning there she took to baiting him with some ugly news about *l'Amérique*, further challenging him with, "How can you live in a country like that?"

Feeling defensive, Charlie replied, "Because it's the greatest and free-est country in the world, and it is our task to defend freedom."

Little Francoise chuckled loudly and said, "Oh well, certainly it is the richest and most powerful country."

Madame Bidot scolded her from the kitchen. "Francoise, stop that. Monsieur Chadwick is our guest." The lady might have added that, through Montrose College, they were getting good if devalued U.S. dollars.

That afternoon Francoise gave him a copy of *Le Monde*, supposedly so he could practice his French. The issue carried a front-page feature reporting alleged U.S. "atrocities" in the Andes. Charlie was annoyed and bewildered, and said so in his first letter home that night.

In all it wasn't an auspicious beginning. Back in Caracas the Labats or Bustamantes might pan "the States" in a friendly way, but for the first time Charlie was in an environment where many of the people seemed down on America. The notorious nastiness of French functionaries seemed to make things worse for him those first few days.

In a couple of weeks, though, he starts warming to Paris. With some American friends he improvises a walking tour of the city, and takes notes. Aiming especially at Alejandra's memories, he zeroes in with enthusiasm on those Parisian details. Crisp breads, creamy sauces, and the refinement of the waiters and shop girls (*"when they're not snapping at you"*). The elegant Rue de Rivoli arcades. Cafés and more cafés, one after another! The pungent roast aromas on the Blvd. St. Michel, and students sitting around talking about ideas etc., Shakespeare & Co., of James Joyce fame. Two-hundred movie theaters with films from all over the world! The polyglot atmosphere, the myriad cultural activities, the prestige of the arts. (*"Can you believe there's actually a Ministry of Culture here?"*) He is astounded to see everyone consuming croissants, something he'd thought only the Labats had occasionally at breakfast.

Charlie was in the process of discovering "Europe" and all that that has meant for expatriated Americans, only now there was a crucial difference. As a freshman he seldom drew invidious comparisons between Richards-New Ashford and Caracas. In France, his songs of praise are at America's expense. As he reports it in his letters, everything, I mean absolutely everything is better in Europe—from the food to the subways, from the way women dress to media reporting of the news. Even Europe's destructive wars are looked upon as instances of rich human experience and high virtue.

And it was in Paris that a susceptible Charlie became enamored of leftist politics. The transition came fast. Throughout most of November Charlie scarcely sent even a picture postcard. Then, around Thanksgiving, he scribbled a note and mentioned that Francoise had introduced him to a couple of Venezuelan students who were friendly with local Trotskyist groups, and since it's next to impossible for a foreigner in Paris to meet "natives," he was availing himself of the opportunity to attend a few of their informal meetings. From what I've dimly gathered, the left-wingers soon had him ideologically hooked.

Not that Charlie's leftist friends were all that activist. Aside from marching in rallies against Pinochet or Peru, mostly they huddled in their garrets or cafés discussing fine points of Marxist ideology, or holding study groups to wade chapter-by-chapter through the famed obscurities of *Das Kapital*. In addition, at the prompting of some Venezuelans (their exact identities have eluded me) Charlie took to sitting in on lectures at the Latin American Studies Institute near St. Germain. The bias in those courses was to portray the United States as an aggressive bully in the hemi-sphere—there was no attempt at a balanced view of U.S. foreign policy. As the year progressed Charlie hung around increasingly with Institute students, and through his Venezuelan cronies he even got to know one of the profs, a suave, bearded leftist by the name of monsieur Guy.

What was it about the French scene that could draw a young American toward Marxist arcania? In my search for an answer, I asked Monsieur Guy to enlighten me on the subject, and he politely if coolly agreed. His English was surprisingly good. Occasionally he shifted to Spanish.

At the café next door he ordered two expressos and insisted on paying. He lit a Gauloise and inhaled deeply. "You must understand that, in France, Marxism is accepted by many people."

"And how many is 'many'?" I asked.

"Oh, per'aps one-half of the population."

I was astounded. "Is that so? Have there been polls?"

Monsieur Guy smiled. "In every election the parties of the left receive approximately half of the votes. I think that in your country they receive maybe one-half percent, no?"

I was surprised they'd get even that much.

"Also, in France, many of the intellectuals are affiliated with the Parti Communiste."

I thought of asking him if he's a Communist, but held back. Still, feeling mystified, I asked, "How can so many intelligent people adopt an ideology as closed and rigid as Communism?"

"Mr. Jennings, what you call Communism is part of our history. The French proletariat (he actually used the word) has always been on the left. And during the Occupation, Communists played the leading role in the Résistance."

"What about De Gaulle?"

"He hardly fought. The majority of the Résistance were Communists."

Given his bias, I knew Monsieur Guy was exaggerating. And yet I couldn't let him wiggle out of the basic issue. "Really, isn't all this Marxism here due to Russian influence?"

Monsieur Guy snickered, almost smugly. "Oh, you the Americans, you always arrive at that question there. But no, there is no Sovietic influence. There are no Russian companies here, only the example of their successes. They defeated the Germans. They reconstructed their nation without American aid. No, Marxism in our country is product of the class struggle, not Moscow."

So Russia defeated the Germans! Not our G.I.'s! If this inability to get away from Marxist manias is typical, one can see how Charlie—disillusioned with Richards and hungry for a new faith—could be seduced by it all. And that Soviet-style vocabulary seemed to be present even in the mainstream media. The issues of *Le Monde* I made my way through actually spoke of "the capitalist class," "the industrial élite," and "the bourgeoisie." And its writers liked alluding to that fabled "American imperialism" while appearing indifferent to the Russian brand thereof.

There are gaps in Charlie's Paris phase, though Ms. Kingsley has additional details. It's clear, however, that Charlie's radical contacts had cast a spell over him. One hears of him burning midnight oil, studying Marx, Engels and their apostles and also numerous left-wing books of history and politics. (Somehow he manages to make B plusses in his Montrose courses.) He diligently follows the news from Peru on radio and TV, and devours every pamphlet about the war. In a few months he's become quite well-informed about the ever-shifting situation there, if one-sided in the extreme, blithely dismissing the *International Herald Tribune* as "Yankee propaganda," but eagerly gobbling up *Le Monde*'s thick articles on the U.S. bombing and the "Peruvian powderkeg."

Charlie sent some of those bombing stories to Ev and accompanied them with letters expressing his moral horror at the so-called "criminal deeds" of his country.

"How can we do things like THIS?" Charlie writes. The emphases are in the letter, and *Le Monde*'s references to free-fire zones and obliterated villages are underlined in yellow.

Ev at first replies with muted resentment, refusing to take Charlie's "anti-American propaganda" and "Communist influences" seriously. The father's staunch position appears further to encourage the son to fan the flames of debate. Charlie starts openly vilifying U.S. foreign policy, then Ev informs Charlie that his vehement criticisms of the United States are only the "youthful nonsense" of a passing phase. Then the language gets hotter and the rift widens. Charlie brags in letters about having demonstrated before the U.S. Embassy, claims to feel sheer joy about that B-52 crashing in the Pacific, and gives vent to a lurid fantasy about seeing Amarillo, Texas "go up in one great big beautiful nuclear cloud!"

On the edge of tears Ev uttered ruefully, "It shocked me, seeing my only son becoming so fanatical. He just seemed enamored of the idea of violence." Lips puckered, the hardy Yankee kept his self-control.

Charlie had lugged his fiddle to France, but in an April note to Livie he boasts about not having so much as tuned it in months. "No time for toys!" he writes.

Chapter 18

During his first two months Charlie mixed quite a bit with the students at Reid Hall. Located on Rue Les Chevreuses in the arty old Bohemian area of Montparnasse, the elegant old mansion houses several American study-in-Paris programs and serves as a hangout for U.S. college kids. Charlie became acquainted there with Amherst junior Jason Willis, whose French family lived a few blocks away from the Bidots.

So Jason, Charlie, and a coed or two would amble over to a renowned café like La Coupole and sip capuccino and talk about their profs or discuss last Saturday's excursion to Chartres. Or they'd take the Métro to St. Germain des Prés, slip into an inconspicuous table at the Café Flore and catch a glimpse of James Baldwin or other literary expatriates. Young Francoise happened to stroll by on one occasion; Charlie signalled his "sister;" she joined the group briefly, warming the boy's heart as his friends practiced their French with her.

And of course, being red-blooded American boys, they'd have a good time whenever possible. Charlie once got royally drunk with Jason and two Dartmouth guys.

"It was incredible," a brush-cutted redhaired Jason said to me in an Amherst diner. 'We'd just come back from the Flea Market one Sunday afternoon, and I said, 'Hey, when in Paree, do as the Parisians do!' So we stopped and bought four bottles *of rouge ordinaire*, and each of us started imbibing the old grape juice right on the Métro! Got wine spots all over my T-shirt. And when we exited at St. Michel I felt this urge to run alongside the train as it pulled out. Believe it or not, I managed to stay neck and neck with the French girls who'd been sitting across us in the back seat of the last car. I ran all the way to the front end and waved and smiled at the threesome, but they didn't seem to want to reciprocate. It was incredible."

Jason was almost splitting his sides with laughter; I smiled sympathetically and asked, "What was Charlie like?"

"Real nice and quiet back then. Didn't say much, even when he was drunk that Sunday."

"Any sign that he might've turned into a dogmatic Marxist?"

"None. I couldn't believe the change that came over him."

Starting November, Jason and other junior-year-abroad types

started seeing Charlie huddled in cafés with Latin leftists. Oftentimes he'd bring to class a Marxist tome or a pamphlet about Vietnam or Peru, and he'd try striking up conversation about these things with his fellow students.

At first Charlie was rational, even reasonable. Hanging around Reid Hall or La Coupole he'd attempt friendly persuasion. He'd quote statistics purporting to demonstrate that the U.S. "ruling class" is "imperialist," that it needs ever more investment markets, that our tragedy in Vietnam and Peru was somehow caused by that economic drive, and that all our wars were nothing more than a succession of "land grabs" and "real-estate deals."

Show 'em "the facts" as he put it, and they'll see how it all fits together. Charlie expressed it thus to one of his scant sympathizers, a bearded radical from Columbia University. The latter (who requests anonymity) grimaced and said to me half-bitterly as he shook his frizzy part-balding head, "That Charlie and his naive faith. Did he really think arguments could convince *anybody*?"

Indeed, few of the American students took to Charlie's arguments. Most of them didn't care about Vietnam or Peru, and they'd plead ignorance and switch subjects. A surprising number of them defended the U.S. role and laughed in his face.

I managed to pick some of those kids' memory lobes during my field work in New England. One, a Colgate student named Bob Seelye, commented with nervous disdain, "I mean, Charlie'd come on to me with these stories about U.S. planes leveling every village in some part of Peru. How the hell could he be so sure? That was only his point of view. The facts aren't in yet, nobody really understands those wars, and I'd inform him he was being simplistic, but he'd get miffed."

Charlie would repeatedly come back with comparisons to Nazi Germany. "Well, you know, Bob," he'd state emphatically, "a lot of Germans still say 'we didn't know what Hitler was doing.' In America they don't *want* to know . . ."

"Aw, come on, Charlie," he'd snap back, "that's just ridiculous. How many protests were there under Hitler? Back in

America you can say anything you want and nobody'll put you in jail."

Among the juniors at Montrose that year was Sally, the blonde from Charlie's seventh- and eighth-grade classes.

"What're *you* doing here?" the two said virtually simultaneously, trading a Latin-style hug-and-kiss in Reid Hall lobby.

Social distance had divided them elsewhere, but here they shared a bond as the only Venezuelan-Americans studying in Paris. So over a late-morning coffee they'd reminisce about Caracas and Campo Alegre.

Then came Charlie's radicalization, and it seriously strained their friendship.

I saw Sally at Mount Holyoke a couple of weeks after the Richards events. It was a bright, porcelain-blue day and she was wearing a white dress she'd just bought for use in graduation.

"Charlie started showing me these biased reports taken from French papers. 'American Bombings Destroy Civilian Areas.' And he'd never question them. Never seemed to realize he was uncritically accepting their point of view. No balance whatsoever."

What with Charlie's increasing hard line, the two were soon barely on speaking terms: "Hi" in Reid Hall was about it.

As a result of these clashes Charlie became increasingly isolated from his fellow Americans, save for a tiny handful who more or less shared his views on Vietnam and Peru. That radical from Columbia (whose parents had been subjected to McCarthyite attack in the 1950s) mused to me at the 116th and Broadway Chock Full 0' Nuts, "Charlie took the war issue as more than a political problem. Oh, sure, those wars are criminal and fascist, I agree with him all the way there, but to him they were a personal issue. I got the feeling the wars had shattered his lifelong image of America. Let's face it, Richards College isn't the United States. Or maybe it is, who knows?"

The radical student munched on his cheese danish, then added, "Charlie couldn't get enough of those Peruvian bombing stories. He'd collect them like kids collect baseball cards." Charlie's life in Paris underwent yet another shift in April, when Monsieur Bidot's firm suddenly assigned him to an emergency job in Bucharest. All three family members would go at company expense, and Francoise, feeling thrilled with the idea of seeing Rumania, talked about it excitedly. Charlie felt most sad about her leaving. He'd gotten to know her as well as any visiting American can know a French person, and it was through her that he'd met the Venezuelan leftists. Along the way he'd developed a crush on her, doing his best not to show it.

It being so late in the year, Montrose College had some difficulty locating a suitable family with which Charlie could be placed. So they approached the Fondations des Etats-Unis, convinced its director to make a brief exception for Charlie's being under 21, and got him a room for the duration. In a way it was like being back at Richards. A somewhat decayed yellow-brick, slate-roofed dorm for U.S. students mostly, the massive edifice stands at the gate of the Cité Universitaire, that lush campus south of Paris, with its dozens of handsome dorms, one per country— Norway House, India House, a sumptuous Iran House and the like. The U.S. house is among the oldest, hence its faded look, chipping paint, and austere furnishings. The rooms are monastic if clean, the corridors long and dark, and the aging showers operated not by knobs but little push-buttons that summon ten seconds of deliciously hot water, the bather then pushing enough times for a satisfactory scrub and rinse. On the other hand the cafeteria in the Fondation basement is the only one in the vicinity that, for a mere seventy-five cents, serves American-style breakfasts. Students from neighboring houses habitually converge there for bacon-and-eggs plus the chance to meet American girls.

Charlie used to come down every morning around 8 A.M. and get the whole works, including corn flakes. He tended not to mix with the Junior Year types, while the couple-dozen medical students who set much of the tone at the Fondation were dismissed by him in a letter to Livie as "frat guys in their late twenties." And there were the Nadia Boulanger pupils and other musicians who occasionally gave performances around the Cité but whom Charlie, having renounced music, pretty much avoided. About his only relationship with most of the American set occurred when he might overhear someone in the lobby casually mention Vietnam or Peru or OPEC, and he'd horn in with, "That's utter bull shit," proceed to "correct" the poor startled ignoramus on his/her "facts," and then storm off his own merry way.

Charlie now hung around with the Latin students who, from Casa Argentina or neighboring Maison de Mexique, would regularly penetrate into that U.S. enclave and its underground café. Over long breakfasts they'd engage in fervid discussions about the war, with Charlie as a frequent participant. He was increasingly resembling some of them—with his longer hair he looked Indian, an aspect further accentuated by his slightly morose stare.

The Latino students were mostly dogmatically leftist, but there was the occasional conservative who'd serve as friendly gadfly. One serio-comic instance involved Adolfo Robaczek, then 26, a proud scion of Chile's old oligarchy, who looked more like an Italian dandy than the descendant of German immigrants he was. A Wharton graduate and owner of half-a-dozen parking lots in Santiago, Robaczek was doing a year's stint at the prestigious Ecole Nationale d'Administration, part of his game plan of learning a wide range of management styles and using his know-how with multi-national firms. Coincidentally he now works as a junior executive in the South American section of Ev Chadwick's first employers, Omni-Tel.

By contrast with Charlie's growingly fanatical leftism, Robaczek was and is staunchly committed to the ideal of unfettered individual enterprise. He gives General Pinochet's junta top grades for their free-market policies and welcomes the rumors of their plans to send support troops for U.S. operations in southern Peru.

I visited Mr. Robaczek at his white-walled red-carpeted office in Omni-Tel's sleek new skyscraper. From his picture window you could see one World Trade tower and part of the other. After the amenities he said in his slightly German-accented English, "You know, Mr. Jennings, back in Chile my family and I have a tradition of eating three broiled steaks per week. Good French bread every day, and we like an occasional endive salad too. Those are not unwarranted needs, you will agree."

"Well, I will tell you, during the Allende tyranny, our steaks were down to one a week. *One!*" He gestured with his thumb. "And we Chileans were forced to eat *black* bread. And *that*, Mr. Jennings, is socialism. Can any decent people live that way? Look, I'm no reactionary, I had my radical phase years ago, but then I visited Russia and saw totalitarianism's ugly face, but no charbroiled steaks. And no endives. What I did see lots of was *ridiculously* slow restaurant service."

Robaczek snickered. "But today, Mr. Jennings, today Chile is free from Soviet oppression. I enter any restaurant in Santiago, and someone rushes over to serve me immediately, just like that." He raised his hand, snapped his fingers, and proceeded with noble indignation, "You try finding a good waiter anywhere in Communist Russia."

He shook his head earnestly. "You know, I cannot believe the ignorance of those Russians. I met an Intourist guide there, a student of Economics, and that bloke knew nothing about stockholding corporations, he could not even grasp the concept. An Economics student! All he could talk was Marxism. And the onesided Russian press is so depressing. You see, I am addicted to *Time* magazine—the best magazine in the world, let me say. I read it cover to cover. It is a work of genius, even great literature." (As a *Manhattan* staffer I could only disagree—but I kept quiet.) "And nowhere in bloody Russia could I find *Time*. Nowhere. Very frus*tra*ting." (He pronounced it "frus*tra*ting.")

Having once served in Henry Luce's sweatshop, I wasn't eager to join in Señor Robaczek's praises, so I switched and asked about reports concerning malnutrition in Chile.

"Sentimental rot. And even if it is true—whatever that means, 'true'—those so-called hungry Chileans have something not a single Russian has: freedom. Talk to any Russian and you will find a classical instance of what the great Marxist philosopher Marcuse called 'One-Dimensional Man'."

I inquired about the principle behind Chilean troops possibly being sent to Peru.

"Principles do not exist," Robaczek replied with a wave of the hand. "Who can point to a principle? Balance sheets are reality. Mr. Jennings, there are only single problems. Today's top problem is the Marxist threat in the Americas. Since seeing Russia's horrors, I dedicate my free time to fighting Marxism. And if that means defending Pinochet, then I will do so."

Robaczek's Fondation room was directly above Charlie's, and oftentimes the Chilean's cot could be heard squeaking and banging whenever someone from his bevy stayed over with him. After the Richards College ambiance of sexlessness, Charlie appears to have been fascinated by Adolfo's cosmopolitan charms and success with the ladies. Sometimes an American girl would sit with the Latino bunch, and Robaczek soon captivate her with his honeyed voice, dreamy eyes, and recurrent invitations to join him on his next trip to the Riviera. At least two of those young creatures seem to have taken him up on it.

And then there were the lively political discussions over croissants and coffee. Charlie and Company would stubbornly defend the Castro regime; Robaczek would counter eloquently by saying he'd seen Russia and didn't want *his* Chile to turn out like *that*.

Things turned sour one May morning when Robaczek and a sultry Cubana from New Jersey—his current amour—sat with a lonesome Charlie and started taunting him about Marxism.

"Hey, Charlie, listen, how can you, a Marxist, eat those Yankee-imperialist corn flakes?" was Adolfo's opening gambit.

Juan José Suazo, a quiet bronze-skinned fellow from Mexico House, joined them just as he heard Charlie's brusque reply, "I happen to like cornflakes, so screw Marxism."

Robaczek put down his cup and applauded lightly. "Bravo, Charlie! Naturally I agree. 'Screw Marxism,' right. So why the devil do you believe in that outdated nonsense?"

"Makes more sense than any other theory."

The Cubana now interjected, "So move to Russia if you believe it. *Practice what you preach*, as the Gringos say."

Charlie answered smilingly, "I couldn't take the winters. Besides I don't know Russian."

Juan José saw Robaczek make a grotesque face, mimic Charlie's answer, and snap, "What a *stupid* argument."

Juan José interjected, "On the contrary, Robaczek, there's no better argument."

Dismissing this, Robaczek now baited Charlie with a pun invoking Mao, Fidel, and oral sex, too convoluted to translate.

The Cubana giggled and Juan José grimaced, but Charlie took the pun seriously, getting the point only moments later. He sat silently as the Chilean and Cuban kept up their barbs.

"Come on, Robaczek, let's not push things," Juan José said. Suddenly Charlie got up, picked up his cereal bowl and plopped the soggy corn flakes right on top of the coiffed head of Adolfo Robaczek, who sat stunned as Charlie strutted toward the door. The whole incident took a second or two.

Juan José was the first to laugh, after which everyone in the vicinity, including the slinky Cuban, was guffawing loudly.

That morning in the Fondation lobby a freshly-scrubbed Adolfo warned Charlie, "Listen, Chadwick, you imbecile s.o.b. You do that again and I'll bust your face." Charlie walked off with an audible chuckle. "You hear me Chadwick?"

After that they never spoke, and would sit at separate tables at the cafeteria. But *l'affaire* of the corn flakes wasn't the end of it. Readers of Charlie's play *"Perspectives Industries, Ltd."* will note that key character, a mock-sinister German scientist by the name of Doktor Adolph Robaczek.

From the real-life Robaczek there came another, unexpected influence. The rich Chilean's taunts had spurred Charlie to go check out Marxism for himself, and so that June, Charlie and two Venezuelan leftist friends rented a VW camper in West Berlin and embarked on a full tour of Iron Curtain country.

Feeling that such a trip would temper the boy's extremism, Ev Chadwick supported his East European journey.

"I thought it'd be good for him to see Communism first hand. Once he realizes what a hopeless failure the Communist system is, he'd be cured of his Marxist dogmas. That's how I saw it."

The strategy failed. Soon the twenty-year-old pilgrim was sending back flamboyant praise for everything around him—the chic "elegance" of Warsaw women, the beauty and "efficiency" of the Moscow subway, the "high cuisine" in Hungarian restaurants, the alleged "civil liberties" in Yugoslavia ("They sell *Time* magazine here!"), plus "free medicine" everywhere.

Both by mail and in conversation he'd state his refrain: "Nobody's starving in Russia, there's no shantytowns, everybody's got the basics," repeating such utopian notions like a litany. Somehow East Germany's being the world's number 11 economy impressed him, though its notorious grayness elicited from him not the slightest attempt at balance. That the Soviets can't feed their people simply eluded him, and nowhere does he cite the restrictions on free expression, while on the other hand he makes wild claims, e.g. saying Communist Yugoslavia has open borders.

He wrote his parents, "A lot of Venezuelans would like to have what these East Europeans have."

"None of the Venezuelans *I* know," was the retort to Charlie. "You know," Ev told me in a fit of passion one Saturday afternoon, "those commissars seem to think filling people's bellies is something special. Really, Fred, animals can do that! But people always accuse us Americans of being materialistic. As *I* see it, though, Man is fundamentally spirit, not matter. We're spiritual beings. There's more to Man than teeth and a stomach."

Nevertheless Charlie kept baiting Ev with his Marxist ideology (Alejandra apparently stayed out of the debate), and heaping more praise on what he chose to see as Communist achievements.

"The Russians lost 20 million people and a third of its industry to the Germans. And then they rebuilt from scratch," was an idea he kept harping on.

And Ev would counter, "Listen, my boy, America also lost millions to Hitler."

"Sorry, Dad, it ain't so. Fifty thousand Americans died fighting Hitler—less than in Vietnam."

Such brash statements convinced Ev that his son had been brainwashed. Everybody knows that Intourist guides do little more than deliver Marxist pep-talks about Soviet glories. I didn't ask Ev if he regretted having funded Charlie's East-bloc junket, though I wish I had.

Chapter 19

The long line at Venezuelan customs creeped, and Charlie's clothes and coif must have aroused suspicion, since two quiet men in gray suits appeared and invited him to step aside, please. One of them helped wheel Charlie's luggage cart to a small austere office, the other asked him to open up his bags and empty out his pockets. They were consistently polite as they looked through his suitcases and pocket effects.

"Good thing I mailed my books directly to Richards," he would say later.

They thanked him; as he wheeled out the cart he was saluted by a guard, then waved on by a policeman at the exit door. He saw Ev and Alejandra at a remove from the anxious crowds, their backs to a picture window. Lugging his bags he made a slow approach, then poised himself directly within their line of vision.

He said nothing. Nor, thinking he was some hippie, did they. "Well, how are you?" he finally asked in Spanish.

After a split second they burst out with "Charlie!" and "Son!" and "Good heavens." They hugged, beamed; she wept some. During the awkwardly joyous reencounter they had trouble seeing their Charlie through his sullen aspect, khaki shirt, and long straight hair.

It was about their only moment of shared gaiety that year.

There now followed four weeks of unmitigated tensions. Evening meals were marked by angry disputes or slow, painful silence. Though never arrived at, a breaking point seemed imminent. Actually Ev and Alejandra saw little of their son. He'd sleep late and avoid them for breakfast, while after dinner he'd scoot out with no hint as to where. And unlike previous summers he never once showed up at the textile plant, which had just undergone renovations plus a change of name to Telares Chadwick, Ev having bought out his partners. Charlie, however, evinced not the slightest concern with the factory's progress or working there.

In addition Charlie ceased visiting the Valle Arriba and Theater Clubs, and steered clear of the old Colegio Americano crowd. There were phone calls from Eddie Phillips and Freddie Arismendi, but the maid was told to say he's out. Whenever he'd catch a glimpse of one-time friends strolling about Las Mercedes, he'd duck into some shop or byway, and if there occurred a face-to-face encounter and somebody addressed him, he'd reply, "Fine, thanks," and rush off without further ado.

At one point Sally spotted him (his hair longer, khakis scruffier) sipping coke at the Automercado. She slid into the empty stool at his right.

"Hi, Charlie." Sally made an effort to be demonstrative, tolerantly ignoring his looks, which she'd grown used to in France. "*Ça va?*"

At first he didn't respond, keeping the straw to his lips. "Oh, hello," he finally said and kept on sipping. His subsequent replies were all curt monosyllables or slow head motions.

"It was *sad*, Mr. Jennings, real sad to see my old friend Charlie so closed and *snobbish*, even *rude*. Didn't pronounce my name *once* or even have the decency to treat me like a human being." She pursed her lovely lips.

Owing to this inaccessibility there floated around Gringo Gulch vague rumors to the effect that Charlie was headed for Cuba or getting himself ready for the Andes. As Eddie Phillips said to me, "You just couldn't get to him anymore, and I guess he really looked the part of the terrorist, so the scuttlebutt at least made sense."

On the other hand Charlie's Venezuelan kin had the privilege of seeing the boy on Sundays and could therefore assert that those Gringo Gulch rumors were false. They didn't much like his angry Marxism, but in their quiet way they were almost as critical of the war in Peru as was Charlie himself, and they'd interchange views whenever he might be around and the war news would come up on TV.

Such obligatory visits aside, Charlie spent that August in isolation, sleeping till nine and then going right to the card table that served as his desk, scribbling furiously and only venturing out for the bathroom. After a perfunctory lunch he'd place his note-books into a shopping bag from Librairie FNAC and promptly disappear. I gather that the writing had become an obsession with him (something any professional word merchant can spot), since he'd reportedly been seen taking notes in the front seat of Caracas taxi buses, and was also sneaking the stuff (against his mother's wishes) up to Quinta Labat, where he might tear out a page or two while everyone else was engaged in conversation. Scraps from his writing marathon still crop up. In a hidden cranny underneath Charlie's bed, Ev and I found a minutely crumpled-up paper containing on one side a rough first sketch for Dr. Robaczek's allegory of the elephant, and on the other the first two Laws of Perspective.

Former classmates claim to have seen him strolling by the Las Mercedes river shortly after lunchtime. It's possible; Charlie was spending afternoons at the Centro Venezolano-Americano Library, and surely must have stepped out for breaks and fresh air. Once at the Centro he'd start out by perusing local dailies and maybe leaf through *Time* and *Newsweek*, smiling sardonically and emitting a belly laugh here and there. Eventually he'd settle into the same table in a corner, where he'd plunge into work and fill up sheets of block-lined paper. He talked only to the librarians and refrained from flirting with the language students and secretaries (these much more chic now than when he'd first ventured in some years earlier).

What does add up to a mystery is Charlie's evening activities that August. It's a given that he was out there with his new-found left-wing life and friends, but so far I've picked up no substantial lead on the matter. Access proved to be a problem—you don't just look up *"Marxistas"* or *"Trotskyistas"* in the Yellow Pages. What leftists I did manage to track down were hopelessly vague and uncooperative, with no identifying data permitted as to age, gender, or occupation.

And then there was the sole exception. Out of a number of younger Universidad Central academics who (rumors claim) had been with the guerrillas during the 'Sixties, the one who agreed to speak to me in less than airtight conditions was a medium-height, stunningly attractive woman with enormous dark eyes and the darkest hair imaginable. In a manner both tough and cordial she furnished me some minor recollections from Charlie's Paris days (where she'd met him), but was unforthcoming about August 1974 or his current whereabouts. She also fired quite a few questions at me there in her office, as if it was *she* who were doing the interviewing; I had the odd feeling of being personally sized up.

A Trotskyite twosome did allow me a half hour, but the interviewees (again, no details permitted) actually claimed to know nothing about Carlos Chadwick other than what the media had said. So many fruitless attempts gave me a taste of Marxist paranoia. At first I'd been quite concerned and hoped to reach out to these people, but now I can only ask: How is the American public to know anything about the Latino left if the leftists themselves remain so closed and adamant? How is their ideology to be understood if they hold at bay a professional journalist from a reputable weekly who is interested only in gathering objective information for a book-in-progress?

Of course I heard rumors aplenty: Carlos had been seen in a picket line; had been attending rifle practice at a shooting range in the eastern suburbs; had been linked with a splinter group that planted a time bomb in a Caracas Omni-Tel washroom; and the like. If even half of these accounts were true, they'd take up approximately a decade of Charlie's short life. For all I know some fraction of the gossip may be accurate, but at this point the best thing to do is to take these rumors with a grain of salt and treat them all as equally undependable.

One thing is certain: Charlie wasn't too keen on returning to Richards. He packed his bags without the high spirits of yesteryear, and his last dinner home was also the tensest, three Chadwicks supping in silence. After Alejandra had called for dessert, Ev turned jovial.

"Well, by this time tomorrow you should be back in quiet old Richards."

Remaining mute for a moment, Charlie then said, "Richards is a fraud."

Ev's pride and pocketbook felt injured. "Now look here: Richards is the best damned school in the United States. And it costs money . . ."

Charlie shrugged his shoulders. "It's a fraud. So it's expensive. Big deal."

Ev took the approach of the injured parent and played on loyalties. "That's *my* school you're talking about. Yours too."

"It's about as much a school as the Caracas Country Club."

Other than exhorting him not to talk that way, Alejandra held to a noncommittal silence throughout, even as father's and son's tempers kept rising. The ice cream did nothing to cool things down.

"Some education that doesn't even recognize Marxism."

"Marxism, Marxism. You and your outdated ideology. What did Marx know? Does *anybody* believe that man anymore?"

"Millions."

"Yes indeed, millions of dupes and fanatics."

"Dad, tell me something. How much Marx have you read?"

"Oh, Charlie, why bother reading trash? Marx didn't know a blessed thing about economics. Or human nature. Surely you are aware that none of his predictions have come true."

Snickering, Charlie shrugged his shoulders once again. "Well, I guess you've answered my question."

"What's that?"

"I mean, you've obviously never read Marx."

"If you want to see what a mess the Marxists can make of things, look at Peru."

"Mess, hell. It's our military that's messing things up."

Ev laughed disdainfully. "Well, Marxist Mother Russia has her Gulag Archipelago." He pointed in a vague northerly direction.

Charlie answered in a calm voice. "Yeah, right, and we've got our Cotton Archipelago."

Ev recoiled slightly. "What *are* you talking about?"

"Oh, you know, those slave camps in the South."

"That, my dear boy, was a good many years ago."

"Yeah, and so was the Gulag."

After a silence during which the maid set up the coffeepot, Ev scoffed, "Well, when the Russians land at Richards you might feel differently."

"Aha, I see, yes. And how're they getting there?"

"They have the Red Army stationed all over Eastern Europe. What will keep them from invading us next?"

"The Atlantic. The Pacific. And our 30,000 nuclear weapons, just for starters."

"They could use Mexico as a launching pad."

Charlie sighed. "And tell me, Dad, how're they getting to Mexico?"

"Charles, *you're* being ridiculous with your questions."

"No, Dad, you're being ridiculous. You've got it all backwards. It's *us* who's invaded them in the past, never vice versa."

"Nonsense, my boy. We've never invaded them at all. We're a peace-loving nation that just wants to be left alone."

Charlie now started laughing and laughing, first a suppressed giggle, then an ever-louder series of guffaws. Cupping his hands around his face, he stared down at the table and simply kept laughing—forced, prolonged laughter that was faintly audible all the way from the Bustamantes' front porch.

Alejandra snapped. "That's enough, Charlie. Stop it."

Charlie held back, but soon was sputtering more giggles and guffawing once again. He now wiped his lips, folded the napkin, stretched up and scurried off to his bedroom, laughing as he gently shut the door.

Ev and Alejandra disregarded the whole performance, finishing off their *café con leche* and discussing their respective work days.

The ride to the airport next morning was virtually speechless. From the back seat Alejandra smoked a Salem and gave motherly advice about diet, dress, and health care. Otherwise their fifty-five minute drive and a spell at the airport went by with minimal exchange.

Departure time was approaching as they stood about the Pan Am area.

Ev remarked with great earnestness, "Charlie, it's important for you to dialogue with your parents. It's a way to hear other perspectives."

"That is true," said Alejandra.

"You don't often get a chance to hear perspectives other than your own."

Charlie nodded almost exaggeratedly. "Oh, yes, Dad. You're right. Other perspectives, that's what a guy needs."

"Exactly, son, I knew you'd understand. So keep it in mind when you read my letters and answer them."

"Oh, I will."

When the call finally came for his flight to JFK, Charlie looked up at them and answered a brief "Yeah" to their "Study hard" and "Have a good semester."

He ventured a smile, gave them a perfunctory hug and kiss, and picked up his trusty beat-up FNAC bag. As he filed through the exit he waved at his parents. So far it's the last time they saw him.

An American businessman who claims having sat next to

Charlie says the boy scribbled throughout the entire flight.

"I've never seen anybody more obsessed with writing something down," he said to me.

Chapter 20

At first Charlie took up quarters in his original suite at Babcock. Also housed there were some neighbors from '73, but Charlie seemed set on outdoing them in their silent treatment of that year.

On his arrival two male Richies, dressed in tennis shorts, were sprawled out on the lawn by the front steps.

"Hey, Charlie, how's it goin'?"

Charlie marched straight on without a reply. Seldom was he to talk again to his erstwhile friends, and he never addressed any of the newer Babcock assignees.

"The guy was just unyielding. He kept clinging to that grudge of his and taking it out on all of Babcock," said Phil Ormsby in our Cooper Hall chat.

Several of those individuals perished in the bombing.

Presumably to steer clear of housemates Charlie took his meals at other dining halls or ate in his room, using Brahms LPs to seal himself off from Babcock sounds. Ev and Alejandra got letters that contain gripes about Richards or sentiments so indecorous as to be unprintable.

Charlie Chadwick was clearly another person. Gone were his starry-eyed openness and enthusiasm about most aspects of Richards College life; now he'd attend few activities other than political talks plus the weekly meetings of a tiny leftist student group. But mostly he holed up in his Babcock suite with his books and scratch paper. When socializing at all, he mixed with campus radicals or the small set of campus Hispanics, and with these "marginals" he showed his once-sweet self.

It was around this time that he began styling himself "Carlos" Chadwick, so signing his checks, mail, homework, tests, and forms, and asking to be so addressed as well.

In the third week of September Carlos (as I'll henceforth refer to him) went to the Dean's office and requested permission to move to an apartment.

Richies are traditionally discouraged from living off campus, inasmuch as it conflicts with the residential nature of the school and the goal of a total Richards experience. Nevertheless a few dozen juniors and seniors who show special maturity or maladjustment are allowed to reside elsewhere. At a small school everyone knows most everyone's business, and the Dean who handled Charlie's "case" was fully informed as to the returnee's alienation from the campus life. Seeing no need to complicate things and hoping to reduce such tensions, he and Carlos met privately and cordially for less than fifteen minutes, at the end of which the Dean signed an official memo authorizing him to move out of Babcock into an address in Richards-New Ashford.

Dean O'Rourke tightened his glasses and stood up. He cleared his throat and mentioned the 1971 Freshman Picnic. "Remember when Dean Forbes said that hard work is your best antidote to Marxism? I hope you're following his advice."

Carlos looked at him and smiled. "Oh, yeah, that's right. I'd forgotten about that."

"You've kept your good grades, so you must be doing the right thing."

Carlos bit his lower lip and said, "Well, yes, I've been working pretty hard."

There was an awkward silence. "Okay, good luck to you, Ch...Carlos." He patted the boy on the back and shook his hand.

"Thank you, sir," Carlos replied, glancing toward the exit.

That afternoon Carlos boxed his Panasonic stereo, packed his clothes and library, and dialed Town Taxi. No one saw him leave. Dick Betsky later noted the open door and abandoned suite.

By dinnertime Charlie was fully moved in with the five Richie leftists who shared the elaborate 19th-century frame house on Radcliff Road, a brownish-yellow three-story structure with assorted gables and turrets, a rambling three-sided porch, and eight spacious rooms. The ground floor frankly awed me with its thirty-foot ceilings, ornate central stairway, and bannister posts crafted at every inch—a skill I doubt is much practiced anymore. The elderly Yankee couple who owns the place had long ago retired to Florida, and the house is just too big to sell off at a decent price. So their fifty-year-old son—an alumnus who stayed on in Richards-New Ashford—makes the best of it by leasing to tourists in summer and Richies in winter.

Situated at the terminal incline of a winding cul-de-sac, and then humorously known as "Subversives' Den," the aging manse shares scenery with bright birches and a dozen picture-postcard Yankee homes. The residents were a proverbial mixed bag. There was Marta from San Juan, who died horribly and is buried in the College cemetery. And there were the others: Paul, a gentle, bearded, blue-eyed San Franciscan; "Joe," a taciturn Nigerian raised partly around Washington D.C.'s embassy row; Jake from Bay Ridge, a lanky Jewish fellow with a drooping moustache; and Laurie of the granny glasses and bright long yellow hair, the daughter of a Yale history professor. There were activist pasts: Jake's parents had once swelled Norman Thomas's socialist vote; Paul's mother was involved in Henry Wallace's disastrous 1948 presidential campaign; and Laurie's father, while too sane to be leftist, had at one time defended the right of a Marxist to teach at Yale. Marta herself, a brilliant scholarship student, had flirted since age fifteen with far-left Puerto Rican nationalists.

From the moment I entered the big house I couldn't help but note the singular atmosphere. Almost in defiance of the FBI pair stationed down the road, their living room walls flaunted Bolshevik placards, colorful posters of Che Guevara and Uncle Ho, plus photographs of long-forgotten labor agitators, mere names to me—really, who out there remembers Big Bill Haywood or Mother Jones? (Laurie and Jake duly identified them and furnished me biographical sketches of each.) Marxist volumes, including plenty of heavy fare by founding saint Uncle Karl himself, spilled out from chipped bookshelves onto coke-stained end-tables and a frayed sofa. From a record player there came earnest folksongs vocalized by some South American leftist singer named Jara or Mara. I was struck with how many more books there were in their crash pad than in regular Richie suites.

During my visit they were under suspicion for complicity with the Events, but have since been cleared. I'll admit that they seemed the folks least likely to plant so much as a firecracker. While I can't see anything to recommend in their leftist dogma, they did seem gentle, hard-working kids, scholarly types, frustrated professors in a way, the farthest things possible from terrorists. They were all terribly shaken, for one, over the death of housemate Marta, and simply horrified about all of the rest.

"Whoever'd do something like that is just plain sick!" said Laurie to me.

They ventured no speculations as to the culprit. The Montreal note to Kit Wills, they granted, resembles Carlos's prose style, but they really don't think he had anything to do with the actual bombings. The guy didn't know the first thing about explosives, and to imagine him toying with all that hardware struck them as laughable—he spent too much time at his desk. And once they'd shelved aside their pique at Carlos for having brought them into trouble with the authorities, they remembered him sympathetically. Any anger they felt was reserved for a Pittsfield editorialist's suggestion that Carlos and the entire group might have deliberately murdered Marta as a means of throwing off the police.

The Radcliff Road group functioned communally, and Carlos seems to have been happy among them. They shared cooking and cleaning, often ate together, and, despite the heavy Richards workload, devoured plenty of left-wing literature and then discussed it, also together. From their descriptions I was reminded of Bible study, except that, rather than immerse themselves in one sacred Book, they devoured lots of books from the same creed.

And they'd draft leaflets, mimeo them, and then show up together at campus lectures dealing with Vietnam or Peru. After handing out the leaflets they'd file into Putney or whichever hall it was and join up with other radicals. When the talk was done they'd pile on the questions—civil and concerned ones if the speaker was left-wing, hostile and scornful if he was moderate and balanced. They once viciously heckled a State Department official who was sincerely defending the U.S. role in Vietnam and Peru, and the poor guy could hardly get through his speech. It was with glee that they reminisced about the episode, and expressed to me no regrets about it. I reminded them that, like Hitler, they'd infringed upon an individual's right to free speech. Paul stretched out on the sofa as he laughed. "You serious, Fred? *He* was like Hitler, with his fascist war."

"That's not at issue," I replied. "In a democracy, everyone has the right to speak. You folks were abrogating that right."

Jake turned unusually petulant, made a dismissive wave of the hand. "Hey, come on, man, it's not like we've got the power to abrogate *anything*. That was the fuckin' U.S. government throwin' its weight around up there."

"No, Jake, I'm sorry, it wasn't, it was an individual with a point of view, that's all. *You* were the ones 'throwin' your weight around.' And there's nothing more important than individual free speech."

Laurie snapped. "That guy's bosses murder Asians and South Americans. I think the freedom to live is more important."

"Well, that fellow's boss is the State Department. And it's not they but the Defense Department that makes war. So be careful about making accusations." I paused a moment, and then added, "Can anyone live without freedom of thought?" I realized, however, that making a dent in their ideology was impossible. Such was the dogma that at times degenerated into shouting matches or worse. There was the fabled fist fight that broke out one time between a brush-cutted Libertarian and Paul.

It happened at a lecture entitled "The Soviet Threat to Latin America," by a very famous Harvard professor.

Throughout the first ten minutes of the talk Paul kept mumbling out loud, "Utter nonsense."

Finally that young Libertarian lost all patience, turned around and scolded him, "Would you please shut up? The man's got a right to speak."

"He's got no right to spout bullshit and lies," Carlos interjected.

"If you don't like it you can leave."

"I don't like fascists telling lies," Paul lashed back.

"Who's a fascist?"

"That dude's a fascist. Maybe you're one too."

Before anyone knew it the Libertarian had leaped two rows and grabbed Paul by the collar. They bruised each other's faces; Paul ripped the Libertarian's shirt. Joe from Nigeria quietly cut between them and sent them back to their seats.

The Libertarian more or less won since things settled down thereafter. The Radcliff Road crowd left their provocations for the question-and-answer period.

Of course the South American war had recently gone into a major escalation, so tempers on both extremes were running high. On December 1 the President announced round-the-clock aerial bombing of the city of Puno as well as routine strafings of PMF sanctuaries in Bolivia. Richie Libertarians in their TV rooms applauded the Pentagon's ill-advised bellicosity, while leftists reacted by turning destructive in their rhetoric and deeds. The morning after that absurdly emotional and overstated December 1 speech—in which our mellifluous President delivered his sermonette about sacred missions against evil atheists—some hapless shopkeepers on the town Main Street arrived to find their storefronts sprayed with simplistic slogans like "U.S. OUT OF SOUTH AMERICA," "STOP THE FASCIST BOMBING," and other sorry substitutes for thought, plus shattered plateglass here or there.

It was a familiar dynamic: government high-handedness and sabre-rattling leads to extremist violence from leftists, who cast all moderation to the winds.

The same extremism was part of their language. About the time of Puno a well-meaning Richie raised his hand in Introductory Economics class, and asked how our agricultural sector might be channelled into alleviating the growing problem of world poverty.

"Well, poverty *is* a problem," said the intense young woman professor. "I don't have a simple answer. Any suggestions?"

"Yeah," said Marta Colón in the front row. She'd been doing excellent work in the course. "Kill all the Gringos."

There were a few nervous titters but mostly a brief silence. It was surely the first time these kids had ever given any thought to "Gringos," let alone imagine themselves as targets of such a notion. The professor politely disregarded Marta's remark and went back to her discussion of comparative advantage in the global trading system.

Carlos's private journals, apparently dating from about that period through his sudden departure, show the same shrill rhetoric. He'd saved and pasted in a notebook a *Time* clipping about the surprise typhoon that hit and sank a U.S. aircraft carrier in the Pacific, killing a dozen pilots and crewmen. In the margin of the page was the scribbled reflection, "Some typhoons do good"

Facing that page was a well-known UPI wire photo showing a PMF woman pointing her automatic at a felled U.S. pilot's back, his hands straight up, his face gazing down. In a crudely-drawn comic-strip balloon, positioned so as to represent the pure girl's thoughts, were the block letters, "SERVES YOU RIGHT, BUDDY!"

The most drastic and really creepiest of these inscriptions was "EXTERMINATE THE BRUTES!" scrawled in red ink across a grainy *Time* photo of a squadron of B-52s. Just who is meant by "brutes" and who is to do the exterminating aren't exactly clear within context. These private jottings, however, do reveal something about the dark underside of our supposedly idealistic young leftists.

Chapter 21

Carlos most probably began filling notebooks about the time he moved into the Fondation des Etats-Unis. The elderly, vivacious cleaning lady, Mme. Durand, recalls the sheets of French grid paper accumulating on his desk, plus the crumpled wads in the wastebasket every morning. So caught up was he in his world of scribbling that at times he'd reply with scarcely a grunt to her *"Bonjour, monsieur!"*

The obsession presumably followed him to Eastern Europe, and we know that, back in Caracas, he kept at it some six or seven hours a day. Of all the people who noted this compulsion, only Mme. Durand seems to have registered his total absorption in it.

"So much paper!" she exclaimed to me. "Was it a book?"

I grinned. Through my interpreter, a Smith College junior, I explained to her that the "book" was fairly short but, to Carlos, all-important.

"I saw that boy referred to last week in *l'Humanité* (the French Communist daily) and I read in there that he wrote a theatre piece. Was it the same one?"

She brings this up because she'd once commented to Charlie about his diligence. "Monsieur writes all the time. A thesis?"

This time she'd penetrated the wall. He looked up and smiled. "Oh, just a little comedy to make people laugh."

At Richards he burned midnight oil working on *Perspectives Industries, Ltd.*, typing far beyond everybody's bedtime, to the occasional annoyance of Dick Betsky and then his Radcliff Road housemates. On a brisk morning early that November he limped down slowly for breakfast, sweater and gray corduroys rumpled. Through his crooked eyeglasses sizeable rings could be seen.

Marta and Joe were at the kitchen table sipping coffee.

Carlos plucked a donut from the fridge, poured himself some instant, and informed them he'd just pulled an all-nighter. "I've thrown together this play about the Gringo mind. C'n you guys give it a look-see?"

Perfunctorily they answered "Okay" in an identical tone of voice, making all three of them laugh.

Yawning, Carlos swilled his coffee, clunked back upstairs and trotted down once again, handing Marta the typescript and Joe the carbon. They both nodded and kept up their conversation as Carlos ran off to morning shift at Language lab. Barely on time, he then scarcely stayed awake at the central monitor, though he did perk up during Sartre seminar. In the dusk he yawned repeatedly as he sauntered toward "Subversives Den."

The entire crew save for Paul were seated around the kitchen, coffee cups in hand. They were exchanging light gossip about that lone faculty Marxist and the right-wing dolts (so they saw them) who were always trying, unsuccessfully, to demolish his arguments in class. Jake nodded at Carlos's silent entry as he told of that day's dumb questions from the Libertarian clique. Laurie followed up Jake's anecdotes with a story about some rightist congressman who, going after the Red Menace, had investigated the New Deal's Federal Theatre project back in the '40s.

"So this Committee member, Martin Dies or Joe Starnes, I forget which, notes that among the plays produced by the FTP was something by Christopher Marlowe." She paused. "And the congressman asks, 'This Christopher Marlowe, was he a Communist?'"

Naturally the group roared at this alleged illiteracy. Carlos also guffawed and joined them with a glass of cider.

After a brief silence, Marta said to Carlos, "Well, you really threw in all the official American clichés."

Carlos blushed, sipped at his cider. "I hope so."

"Invented some new ones, too!" Jake interjected.

"I believe I have heard everybody at Richards say those things," was Joe's single comment.

"And I mean everybody," Marta emphasized.

Laurie laughed. "And everybody at Yale. I could actually hear my father's friends spouting lines from *Perspectives Ltd.*"

Carlos chuckled back.

By the evening *Perspectives Ltd.* had been handed on to Paul and two New York friends of his, leftists naturally. By next day the phrase "It all depends on your point of view!" was the going joke around "Subversives Den."

A radical-symp with access to a Xerox machine succeeded in running off twenty copies of Carlos's closet farce, circulating them among Richie leftists plus fellow travelers and the idly curious. By Thanksgiving more than leftists had read *Perspectives Industries*. Reception among radicals needless to say was favorable, but opinions outside that narrow circle ranged widely.

Carlos gave a copy to Livie Kingsley following one of their political disputes. She read it several months later, when the play gained notoriety. At our first editorial conference she owned up to feeling a bit embarrassed by *Perspectives Ltd.*

"It was weird, all the arguments I'd been giving him were right in that play," she said to me, flipping through her copy-edited manuscript. "How'd he anticipate what I'd say? I still wonder."

Others were more negative. A couple of days after completing his satire, Carlos gave it to a white-haired Yankee gentleman who teaches Drama Lit and directs an occasional play, in the hopes that it might be staged at Richards. The pipe dream was soon shattered. In the quiet of the faculty lounge, the Lit professor expounded to me vehemently, his thumbs in his vest, "I am a centrist, and I would *never* say the things Carlos attributes to us. Oh, sure, a left-wing terrorist is entitled to his odd ideas about centrists, fine, but a play that does not provide a balanced view simply fails as art. It is not a good play."

Sitting on the same sofa an hour later, a balding, bespectacled professor of Political Theory remarked, "Chadwick thinks conservatives are fascists. That's typical of leftists. Well, I'm a proud conservative, one who welcomes diversity in the marketplace of ideas. But I'm Jewish, and I draw a sharp line at seeing any good whatsoever in Nazism. So what if Hitler was anti-Communist? I'm *not* of the view that Hitler's anti-Communism cancels out his anti-

Semitism." The good professor pauses, and sighs. "Look, I'll admit that the Soviets suffered more than any nation in World War II. So does that crazy Carlos think conservatives actually *applaud* Hitler for having killed twenty million Russians?"

Phil Ormsby, preferring to reminisce about good times, had little to say about his old roommate's opus, other than characterize it twice as "incredibly biased and one-sided."

Non-leftist readers thought of Carlos's "Militants" as too idealized and romanticized. Leftists on the other hand felt the Militants come across too negative and simplistic. I suggested to Carlos's housemates that *Perspectives Industries* might have been improved had he balanced his Karlist Militants with anti-Karlist activists from the Right.

"Are you kidding?" Paul exclaimed. "The Company anti-Karlists are right up on that stage, talkin' to Phil Wilson."

Somewhat piqued, Jake added, "Why the hell should things be even more stacked against the Militants?"

Laurie knitted silently. Joe leafed through a *Booster*.

I pursed my lips, then tried to explain. "I think Carlos could have shown *more* 'perspectives.' There's a basic contradiction in his play. The company men up there say they're open to all ideas, and yet in the course of play they turn out to be too anti-Karlist. It's inconsistent and illogical."

Even as I uttered my last sentence I could hear the sound of four leftists laughing. "That, Fred, is precisely the point," said Laurie, putting down her knitting. "Those guys *are* anti-Karlist."

"So why have them say they're open to all ideas? Are they just hypocrites?"

There was raucous laughter; it's difficult to argue with ideologues who see only their own "perspective." By contrast, I remember some open-minded Richies who, though well aware that Carlos had put into his play some of the very things they'd once said to him, were still generous enough to find *Perspectives* "real funny" and "very clever."

Despite initial rejections, *Perspectives Industries* eventually was started on the path to its odd repute. An energetic junior in Music named Rick Lehman took on *Perspectives*, producing it as a radio play with whatever actors he could instantly round up, including a mellifluous senior from Williams to do Phil Wilson plus extras bussed in from Bennington to do audience's voices and some Militants. The hastily conceived production was taped and then broadcast over WRCR in mid-December and again in January. A few Richards people listened to it and talked about it some. At this point the satire's underground reputation seems to have begun spreading beyond the Central Berkshires. Next month some Harvard students did *Perspectives* at the university's science center—appropriately, given the striking similarities between that variegated edifice and Carlos's Multifacetia.

Back in November Carlos had mailed out the play to a dozen New York publishers, in the naive belief that a young unknown, with zero theatrical status, can achieve publication just by submitting xeroxes of his "closet farce" blind to, say, McGraw-Hill. Needless to say everyone of the publishers mailed it promptly back. In early February, however, a tiny left-wing South Boston outfit prepared a cheap photo-offset version with a stapled yellow cover, the crude volume cropping up in select northeast bookstores. By April its initial printing had sold out. The morbid curiosity since aroused by Carlos's alleged lurid acts has, alas, much enhanced the saleability of his acrid lampoon, so much so as to make possible a first hardcover edition of *Perspectives Industries, Ltd.*, this literary oddity concocted some while ago by a 21-year-old Venezuelan-American student at a prestigious New England college, now an expatriate on the lam somewhere.

Carlos apparently had hopes that *Perspectives* might help end the war or at least persuade people to his left-wing biases. Nothing of the sort, needless to say, could take place. Americans simply aren't drawn that much to ideologies, whether right or left. And the war was considerably stepped up around then, with three more aircraft carriers dispatched to Peruvian coastal waters and serious discussions of a combat role for U.S. troops in that beautiful, tragic, war-torn country. There was also the surprise landing by U.S. Marines to protect Americans from nationalist violence in Mayagüez, a move which, though brief and successful, only reinforced Carlos's and his cronies' dogmatic prejudices about "U.S. imperialism." Public opinion in the meantime steadily backed our military policy, with 61 percent favoring South American escalation and 39 percent opposed—and for his Mayagüez rescue mission the President got a whopping 76 percent support. Among Richies the ratio was lower, about 52 to 47 percent, but still a majority favoring air war against PMF guerrillas.

Part 3 of this volume provides readers with Carlos Chadwick's rather subjective view of "American centrists, conservatives, libertarians" and such. Leftists will undoubtedly lap up his bile and dogma, while more sensible folk will see *Perspectives Industries* for the lopsided caricature it is.

When I said this to Laurie in the Radcliff Road living room, she shrugged her shoulders and scornfully blew out a little puff of air.

"Sure it's a caricature. It's a spoof on vulgar liberalism, which is itself already a caricature."

I was taken aback. "What, pray tell, is 'vulgar liberalism'?"

She remained cool. "Russia's got vulgar Marxism. China's got the Little Red Book. And America gets its slogans from John Locke and Adam Smith."

I shook my head. "That's highly dubious. Most Americans haven't even heard of Adam Locke or whatever. And we tend not to believe in slogans. What we most value is the individual who thinks independently and avoids all slogans of left and right . . ."

Laurie now turned slightly vehement. "Fred, you're spouting dogma of the center!"

"What *are* you talking about? There's no such thing, Laurie. It's just that truth always lies somewhere in the middle."

Paul shouted from the kitchen. "*That* is a centrist slogan."

I could not conceal my irritation. "You kids are completely closed to other points of view."

"Which others?" Laurie blurted out defiantly.

"*All others, it seems.*" Paul now stood at the kitchen door as I tried reasoning with them both. "*You won't grant that there are as many viewpoints as there are individuals, and that a free system accepts them all.*"

Laurie and Paul again turned to their tactic of laughter, abruptly cutting the discussion short. It was a grim reminder of the intolerance that can flare up in a free society.

It's amazing when you think of it. What with murderous Gulag slavery and insane Swedish taxes, Marxism is a hopelessly discredited system. And yet any U.S. citizen can walk into a library and browse in Marxist books if he so wishes. Some states actually require a semester's course on Communism in high school. I doubt that any of the Marxist empires require analogous study of democracy other than to propagandize against it through outdated pamphleteers like Karl Marx and his ideological slant. Soviet Aeroflot stocks exclusively Communist publications on its Transatlantic flights; airlines in the United States, by contrast, offer a broad spectrum ranging from *Newsweek* through *U.S. News and World Report*; and if they carry no Communist literature, it's because nobody wants to read the stuff. The simple fact that *Perspectives* is being printed here—despite Carlos's obsession with a "slavery" long gone since 1865, his sinister suggestions of American businessmen favoring Hitler, and his paranoid delusion that sees "anti-Karlists" everywhere—is the strongest possible proof of American openness and freedom. And while our dissidents are on Martha's Vineyard, the Kremlin exiles or incarcerates theirs instead. Is that perhaps not sufficient reason for a strong nuclear defense and a stand against fanaticism in Vietnam, Peru, and elsewhere?

I'm honest enough to admit that I haven't the slightest idea what Marxism is, though the little I've read strikes me as arrant nonsense. But I know this: while Marxist countries lash out at capitalist evils and mouth their utopian rhetoric about a "classless society," the one true success story in our world is this capitalist America, a country where you can be anything you want, where everybody feels middle class, where descendants of slaves drive Cadillacs and tote fancy radios, and where thousands of yearly rags-to-riches stories show *ours* to be the classless society and prove hard work and individual effort to be the best answer to poverty.

That is mere economics, though. For what matters most is our unique freedom. We are at war with a group that frankly calls itself the Peruvian Marxist Front and that espouses doctrines posing a threat to our way of life. And yet recent documentary movies like *The Trembling Andes* go so far as to portray the PMF as noble, valiant freedom fighters besieged by evil, cold-hearted U.S. bomber pilots—the tired old good-guys/bad-guys formula. Well, I can only hope that those filmmakers are somehow grateful to a society that allows them and their viewers the right to choose between pro-war and anti-war ideas—in contrast to the PMF, who're hardly known for allowing those smiling, colorfully-clad Indians any comparable free choice between pro- and anti-U.S. viewpoints. Indeed, the PMF's projected "New Information Order," with its proposed limits on American journalists working down there, is in flagrant violation of the U.S. Constitution. It may well be argued that our openness is ample justification for combatting an adamant PMF, though I personally don't subscribe to so simplistic a view, since I realize that things are terribly complicated and that there is no easy answer to the manifold dilemmas posed by the responsibilities of power and the commitment we have made to global freedom.

Granted, there's the argument that insurrections are always harsh. As the Radcliff Road leftists remind me to the point of exhaustion, during our Revolutionary War the Loyalists were tarred, feathered, and sometimes executed; following the Patriot victory their properties were seized; and they themselves were hounded into Canadian exile ("boat people" is what Joe had the temerity to call them). No doubt that was a deplorable episode, but it's ancient history. Today, anyone can express pro-Crown ideas without fear of reprisal. In fact, just recently a man published a book arguing that independence from England was a stupid and wasteful mistake. He received highly favorable reviews, and today leads a tranquil, comfortable existence in Western Connecticut. The day that the Peruvian guerrillas allow analogous sort of books to be printed and reviewed in their territory is the day I'll see something positive in them.

Carlos's whereabouts remain unknown. Ev and Alejandra have not heard from their son since April 1975, and Livie Kingsley, now Arts Editor at a respected neo-conservative monthly, has no new info to offer about her former boy friend. Her current beau—who is Managing Editor for the magazine—feels it's just as well.

With passing time Carlos becomes a remote memory at the college. Among today's Richies he scarcely receives mention, and nobody in this year's freshman class seems more than dimly aware of old associations between those deeds and his Anglo-Latin name. At Freshman Picnic Dean Forbes still tells them that hard work and discipline is the best antidote to Marxism, and the exhortation continues to ring true. A few individuals might know vaguely about a play called *Perspectives Industries, Ltd.*, but Richies don't do much reading outside of class, and the campus bookstore doesn't stock crudely-made small press volumes. In the interim the FBI has been assigned the case and there are rumors of arrests being imminent. The culprit may well be announced by the time this book goes to market.

In the wake of the bombings, a massive fund drive brought record sums from Richards alums, including a check in the high-five figures from Ev. Babcock and Chapman Halls have been rebuilt to look exactly as they once did. The sole reminder of The Events is a modest pair of marble slabs, dark gray in color, 3-inches high by 1-inch wide, each of them located in a discreet, tree-shaded corner in the front yard of the respective dorms. They bear the simple heading "IN MEMORIAM" followed by a list of the victims' names. In spite of the bloodshed and suffering endured by the Richies, and notwithstanding our stupid, senseless, disastrous and costly South American war, there are now six young Marxists on the Richards faculty.

□

As readers read on they will find in Livie's memoir an intimate look at Carlos's traits, notably his emotionalism and his ideological manias. And then there's *Perspectives Industries, Ltd.* The play is too long, maybe by half. Readers should feel under no obligation to swallow it whole and in all good conscience can just dip into its lines here and there so as to get an x-ray of its author's less-than-balanced mind.

Perhaps more revealing are the eight sets of epigrams, reproduced verbatim from the Richards College notebook found sitting in Carlos's desk drawer. His bizarre thoughts will trouble many readers who hitherto may have believed they'd seen enough forced comparisons between a free America and a totalitarian Germany and Russia. (It's tiresome, this analogy between Indians and Jews.) However simplistic and naive they are, the documents help furnish some "perspective" into the strange and as-yet-unsolved mystery of Carlos Chadwick.

□ □ □

PART 2

Carlos Chadwick: A Personal Memoir

by Livie Kingsley

(Arts Editor, The *New Dial* Magazine)

Chapter 1

I first met Charlie—his name then—in October of our freshman year. The Richards College Orchestra had just played its first full concert and dazzled them all with splashy pieces like Debussy's *Nocturnes* and Ravel's *Daphnis*. The audience loved it, they clapped and clapped. The mixed chorus, the percussion people, the wind soloists, our conductor Mr. Adams, and I with my flute, we all got to bow more than once. All of Berkshire County seemed to be cheering us in Putney Auditorium.

Richards may be small but that night I'd never talked with Charlie Chadwick. We were all backstage now, packing our horns and fiddles and meanwhile catching our breath. Some women had slipped into more comfortable shoes. I was brushing my hair when I saw this medium-height, vaguely Hispanic-looking fellow in horn-rimmed glasses, walking up to me, violin case in hand. Like all the others, he congratulated me on my *Daphnis* solo.

"Nice job on the Ravel, Livie," was his comment.

115

"Thank you," I replied with a nod, flashing my best smile.

"Only somehow I thought it sounded better in rehearsal."

My Logic professor now stood next to me, his hand extended. Out of the corner of my eye I could see a less-than-civil Charlie Chadwick heading for the side door. I simply didn't know what to make of his parting remark. It troubled my evening, since I thought my performance had gone real well.

Something similar happened next week, the day my glowing account of Vladimir Ashkenazy's recital came out in the *Booster*. Just as we're all stepping out of RCO rehearsal at Putney I see Charlie at my left. And he sings the praises of my reviewing style, and we share our excitement about Ashkenazy's playing, so as we're walking by Cooper Hall I invite him to join me in the snack bar. We grab an empty table and I ask him where he's from. I thought he might be from somewhere out West.

"From Caracas."

"Oh, Argentina."

He grinned, fixed his gaze on his coffee, stirred it, and said, "No, dear, Venezuela."

Frankly I felt a bit stupid, but not for long. I was soon quite taken with Charlie's enthusiasm for the RCO. He loved talking about it, and we had fun quoting melodies from the pieces we'd worked on, comparing one Beethoven movement to the other ("I like the scherzo best," "Oh, I prefer the finale"), raving about this or that passage, and speculating about Spring concert.

He was happy at Richards in a way that is rare even among Richie loyalists, something new to me. My father and grandparents are all State University graduates, and they seldom speak of their student days (other than fraternity parties) with the affection Richies feel for their school. Charlie was the first fourth-generation Richie I ever met. All his life he'd had his sights set on Richards, and his love of the college outdid most everyone else's. Probably his only complaint was the lack of interest in classical music on campus ("WRCR plays exactly an hour of it a day!"), which sort of bothered me too. Charlie's disappointment in that fact was intense, though the plusses still outnumbered the minuses in his mind.

After that chance meeting we often took walks or had coffee. I was fascinated with him and his strong feeling for Richards. He would walk by one of the old neo-Romanesque buildings and exclaim, "Beautiful, eh?" He had an almost religious belief in the college life and culture. His courses excited him, and he'd go into ecstasy over a Faulkner novel or wax lyrical about the cars we saw in the Museum of Antique Automobiles; He thought nothing of inviting me to his room to listen to *The Magic Flute*. And I mean listen. We sat there on the two designer chairs that furnish every Richards suite, talking to each other only when commenting on the music, like when he'd say "Great passage!" during the Overture, or I'd remark "Listen to those high notes!" at the second Aria of the wicked Queen of the Night.

I was the tender age of seventeen, but already I was engaged to a boy from back home, a junior in pre-med at Princeton. We planned to have our nuptials the summer before his starting med school. He loved me and treated me pretty well, but for some reason I always felt deeply dissatisfied. And I must confess I found myself drawn to Charlie and his boyish way of putting me down. By December I realized I wanted him and was a bit in love with him. I'd hint about it to Charlie, and yet he'd never make anything like a pass. The later it got, the more I'd expect something that just failed to materialize.

Occasionally we'd have these odd disputes. I remember a time in early November—Charlie, Bruce Kelly and I were watching *Bonnie and Clyde* in the TV lounge of my dorm. Charlie and Bruce were sprawled out on the floor. I was on the sofa, my legs snuggled underneath me. The incident was sparked by that scene when Bonnie and Clyde rob their first bank and make a getaway, and an admiring lustful Bonnie tries to take his bod right there in the car. But Clyde won't give in, he pushes her off and just won't.

Feeling struck by Clyde's reaction, I blurted out, "Wow, if some guy did that to me I'd really get turned on."

Bruce looked back, staring at me with a sardonic smirk. "Well, well," he said, laughing as he switched back to the tube.

" 'Well, well' *what*?" I asked coldly.

"Well, well, so you really get turned on when a guy pushes you off, ey?"

Charlie cackled, clapped his knees, and gave Bruce a fellow-macho pat on the back. "That's good, Bruce, that's real good!"

I felt stung by Bruce's comment, but more so by Charlie's siding with him. It seemed so cruel. No one had ever accused me of anything like that. My Princeton boy friend had always told me I was the sanest, most wonderful person on earth, and while that's overdoing it one way, these two were just being nasty.

"That's mean," I said to them. "You're ganging up on me."

"Aw, come on, Livie," Charlie said.

"And I'm surprised at you, Charlie. I think this is a betrayal of our friendship. You're getting pleasure out of hurting me. It's unkind, and I'm most unpleasantly surprised."

"Hey, Livie, can the lecture, will ya?" Bruce interjected. "You ain't my Mom."

"Listen here, Bruce, you've just about told me I'm sick, and that's really low."

"Well, Liv," Charlie mumbled, "you just about admitted it."

Refusing even to dignify such an accusation with a reply, I sat in silence, my gaze fixed on the TV.

Charlie made a dismissive gesture and got up. "C'mon, Bruce, let's go." Bruce grabbed his windbreaker, stumbled up, and the two left me to watch car chases and gunfights by myself.

For about a week thereafter Charlie seemed distant and didn't go out of his way to chat with me. And yet when I took the initiative and sat with him in Cooper dining hall, he was his usual cheerful self. Back then, there was in him a certain innocence that came forth despite his wariness with me. The innocence manifested itself as we once again shared our enthusiasm for Beethoven's *First*. Others at the table kept silent, and a couple of them were smirking ever so slightly as they munched on their salad and

Charlie and I quoted from the first movement's main theme.

Tom McNab joined us and sat down at Charlie's left. The two were classmates in Philo 101. Charlie had apparently picked up some notoriety for raising fine points about Plato both in class and out. Opening his napkin, with poker-faced seriousness Tom asked softly, "Uh, Charlie, listen, got a question for ya. Listen, d'you think ideas exist in the world or in the mind only?"

Looking up, Charlie began expounding the pros and cons of each view. I touched him on the arm but he just went on. People around the table now tittered, me included, I couldn't help it.

A minute maybe had gone by when Tom shook his head, chuckled in falsetto, patted him on the shoulder and interrupted, "Hey, c'mon, guy, I was only kidding."

Charlie stopped in mid-sentence, shrugged his shoulders, and went back to his clam chowder. As I look back, I now realize there was a streak of anti-intellectualism in the whole episode, but I wasn't able to see it at the time, so awed was I at being at a small, prestigious Eastern liberal arts school.

The last night in November a gentle but extended snowfall whitened everything in the Berkshires. Next morning Charlie and I ran into one another in freshman quad. He was wearing a hat and scarf, his first time ever, he told me.

He gestured toward the bright snow-blanketed surfaces. I walked alongside him.

"Wow, I can't believe it, Livie, it's just like in the alumni mags, or the movies. This is the real thing, though."

Being from Ohio I'm well accustomed to those long cold snowy months and the indoor warmth. But to Charlie's tropical eyes this was something new and strange. Plus there's a legendary quality to New England snowfalls—on campuses especially. What would Edith Wharton, Hallmark cards, Hollywood love stories or *The New Yorker*'s artistic staff ever do without those chill wintry scenes?

"Everything's so white! Looks like fresh linen!" He stopped in his tracks, took off his hat and glove, and, for a short moment, held out a bared left hand. "Melts to the touch," he said, closing his fist.

I had the impression he got pleasure as much from living the legend as from feeling the physical flakes themselves.

Chapter 2

In January I got involved with a Richards senior, a concert pianist with movie-star eyes who just last May had gained local fame for his rip-roaring rendition of the Rachmaninoff *Second*. For the RCO veterans he was a hero who'd brought them that memorable standing ovation and cries of "Bravo!" plus bouquets of flowers flooding the stage.

By month's end my beau from Princeton had broken up with me, and in a most ungracious fashion. He phoned, at 3 A.M. no less, and *demanded* to know where I'd been the last two nights, and I was completely honest with him, told him everything and asked him to share me with the pianist, but instead he got hostile, then hysterical, then started crying and then just barked at me, "No, Livie, I never wanna see you in my life."

He took it very hard, swearing never to write me again and even charging me with being "two-faced" and "manipulative." Childish though our relationship had been, I felt stung by this show of unkindness and have never gotten over the sheer spite I could hear in his voice. To this day I look back with sadness at the hurt his parting accusations caused me.

That aside, I was feeling extremely happy. The pianist and I couldn't see each other as much as we would've liked, since he followed a strict practicing and studying schedule and was free late evenings only, and besides he had a busy calendar, with recitals somewhere around New England almost every week.

Still I was happy and didn't mind being alone now and then. One frosty February night—the first day of the semester—I was sitting around, getting started with studying at the Library's snack bar, with its futuristic white tables and its red mushroom-style lamps depending from the ceiling. Out of nowhere who should plop into my booth but Scott Yarmolinsky along with a skinny guy from freshman crew plus some nerdy friend of theirs.

"Hi, Livie," said Scott.

"Hi." I kept my eyes fixed on Samuelson, Chapter One.

They tried their best to make conversation, but I just wasn't interested and really wanted to get away. Then I caught a glimpse of Charlie at the coffee dispenser. I would've much preferred to talk to him instead, and I signalled him to come by. He turned as if he hadn't seen me gesture.

"Excuse me a second," I said, and Scott got up to let me by. I ran up and asked Charlie to join me. He stood in silence a split second.

"Oh, y'know, I've got some reading to do."

"Oh, I see, you're trying to get rid of me."

He said nothing.

"Charlie, we haven't chatted since before Christmas. Besides I want to know what you think of the guy I'm going with."

"Mr. Pre-Med? But I've never even met him."

I laughed. "I found someone else."

"Who?"

I told him the pianist's name.

"Oh, that stud," he wisecracked.

I thought this unfair and told him so.

He attempted to elaborate on his snide remark. "The guy's got girls coming in and out of his life like flies in a kitchen."

"So?"

"So nothing." There was sarcasm in his voice, then a pause as he took his first sip. "So where'll it all go?"

"Oh, I don't know, maybe he'll leave me, we'll see."

"Well. He must've turned you down a few times, 'ey?"

"What?"

"Didn't you say if a guy pushes you away you get turned on?"

I saw the beginnings of a nasty grin.

"He is a real artist. Right now he's playing at Smith."

"Yeah, but he's a stud. Betcha he's got groupies tonite."

I suppressed my fears, but also suspected Charlie was jealous. Still, he did finally agree (after much persuading) to join me in a nearby booth, and we talked up a storm about our Christmas vacations. Oh, he'd had a great time in Caracas seeing family and friends and old haunts, but he was so glad to be back at good old Richards, where you've got the RCO and Chamber Players, and exciting classes where all kinds of ideas are discussed, and where the faculty makes constant efforts to communicate with, and the school truly *cares* about, you.

I've never seen Caracas, but Charlie's descriptions reminded me of Dallas or Houston and their oil wealth and flashy new skyscrapers but few cultural attractions. He also expressed the complaint that a lot of his Venezuelan friends were obsessed with U.S. foreign policy and always wanted to talk about it, but he just wasn't interested in politics, what interested him was Richards and the many beautiful things he'd discovered there . . .

I understood what he meant, though in a different way. Like most Midwesterners I still felt overwhelmed at being at an Eastern college of Richards's standing. I particularly admired the school's tradition of preserving, in Matthew Arnold's words, "the best that has been thought and said." To be at Richards was to be in an oasis of peace and reason that—in a world racked by irrationality and hate—helps promote open, civilized discussion. I believed that then and still do so today. But unlike Charlie, I'd always had politics in my blood, and so I especially appreciated Richards's acquainting me with every political idea imaginable, even Marxist ones. I remember the time in Freshman Week when I went to buy my textbooks for Intro to Political Theory and noticed *The Communist Manifesto* among the titles. Back in the dorm I informed my roommate Kathy how shocked I was that we'd be reading Karl Marx. Kathy had been to Phillips-Exeter, however, and was more aware of how things are done; she said, "Well, you've gotta be open-minded and see all sides."

It wasn't long before I saw the wisdom of Kathy's comment. Early that Fall my PoliSci professor explained to us that "the best way to deal with our enemies is to know their minds." And yes, it's crucial to know and understand the ideology that motivates the Soviets as well as the many guerrillas, terrorists, and parliamentary Communists the world over, that's basically what he said. I soon realized that it's not enough simply to say that Karl Marx was mistaken, or that Marxists are dogmatic and fanatical. We must study the man's doctrines in order to refute him and his followers. And so I became aware of the importance of every individual deciding for himself or herself which ideas are valid and which ones aren't. That is what Richards taught me.

So these were the aspects of Richards life that appealed to Charlie and me. It was as if we'd gone beyond our backgrounds and moved on to a higher world of "culture." And while Charlie's devotion to the school was exaggerated, almost fierce, it's true that many of us felt pretty much the same way.

Granted, those of us who'd come to Richards for its educational strengths weren't the only group on campus. Lots of guys seemed to be there for football, beer, and ski slopes, and similarly not a few girls had as their chief aim and function to keep those guys company and cheer them on.

That was not my style. In four years at Richards I went to exactly one beer-bust, for maybe twenty minutes, but the beer-busters persisted in knocking on my door and inviting me, week after week, hundreds of them, I can't remember their faces.

There were also the guys christened with three last names and a Roman numeral, who attended Richards only because it was in the family, and who'd take off for Switzerland for a weekend. (Charlie was exceptional in this respect. True, he was fourth-generation, but I suppose his being South American played some role in his being different.)

And then there were the truly repulsive cases, like the handsome hockey player who rode into Econ class on a skate-board, to the admiring laughter of a female foursome; I was glad when the prof booted him out of class. At any rate, those of us who had come for an education could mostly ignore the obnoxious elements and stick with Richards' many positive features. So now as I sat there talking with Charlie, I could see and hear these things running through my mind. It'd been fun sharing these impressions with him, but the time had come for me to toss off a movie review for the *Booster*.

As I got up I said, "Charlie, do call so we can talk some more."

He looked up from his half-emptied coffee cup. "Oh, for sure."

I ran to pick up my coat and Econ book. Scott and Company were still lounging about.

"Hey, Liv, what's this? Aren't you gonna join us again?" Scott pleaded, looking desolate.

"Sorry, fellas, got work to do." I rushed out of the snack bar, drafting much of the review in my head en route to the news room. I felt pleased about encountering Charlie, and as the months went by we remained good friends, chatting after rehearsals or over tea at dinner. Whenever he'd see me with my tall, wavy-haired pianist friend he'd avoid me, while a couple of other times he managed to sneak into our conversations some nasty comment that harked back to *Bonnie and Clyde* and my supposed "problem." But he seemed not to mind my company. Little did I suspect the ups and downs that were in store for us, though that is another chapter.

Chapter 3

Back in Ohio that summer I faced the usual difficulties of a college freshman returning home. From Charlie I got occasional letters mentioning wistfully how much he missed Richards, a sentiment I warmly shared in my replies to him. And from my pianist friend I got mail almost daily and a phone call once a week. He'd just graduated, but stayed on in Richards-New Ashford when our relationship turned serious in May.

Around downtown Columbus I more than once encountered my ex-fiancé (the pre-med student) and felt terribly hurt at his ducking into a store whenever he'd see me approaching. It did make me feel glad that Princeton had turned me down.

Aside from that I practiced my flute and did the initial drafts for *Living the Good Life*, which I'd already gotten the inspiration for in April.

Meanwhile my father got me work with the local Democratic Party Committee, and early on I met an Amherst guy, a senior pre-law major and impressive public speaker whose grasp of national issues was awesome. Tall and blond, he was a Columbus native, and we had lots to share. And it was hard, so hard, my pianist was so constant, such a dear with his steady correspondence, yet I felt dissatisfied and soon realized I wanted the Amherst boy. At first I didn't want any love "relationship" because Richards-New Ashford could be sticky and explosive. But things quickly ran their course, and by mid-July we were deeply involved, and in my party work around Columbus he'd become terribly important to me.

And so the time had come to put my cards on the table, time to send Mr. Pianist a note of concern explaining that I no longer was his lover. But now he insisted on inundating me with ever more passionate letters, so many I lost count. Any reply was impossible, and the one thing that had me worried was that he might go committing suicide and leave a note pointing the finger at me. That aside, it was a simply marvelous summer—not bad for Columbus! The first draft of my book was about done, and late that August the Amherst boy and I agreed (between hugs and kisses) to see each other weekends back East. Our last few days in Ohio were unfettered delight, their glow surpassing any Silhouettes or Candlelights or other such romances!

In Richards-New Ashford I had an eerie sense of history repeating itself when Mr. Pianist and I crossed paths at the town Post Office. He thoughtlessly averted his gaze, blithely ignoring my presence at the neighboring stamp window. Later that same day I ran into Charlie, and he gave me a warm Latin hug, and despite a chill breeze we stood there between two willows in the campus glade, reminiscing about our three months' glories. We quickly gave each other the rundown on summer activities, family and friends, movies seen. We traded happy feelings about now being Richards *sophomores*, summarized our respective course loads, and commented on the early cold and bright blue sky, all this for at least a quarter of an hour.

"And how's the pianist?"

I felt a touch of pain as I was reminded of the cruel snub at the P.O. "Oh, I'm not seeing him anymore."

"What?"

"Charlie, that was last year!" I told him about Amherst.

"I see." He smirked as he glanced over at one of the willows, its spindles shaking in the wind. He guffawed. I wondered, what's with him? Now he turned mock-serious. "Gee, Livie, a lot of guys seem to turn you down," was his shallow wisecrack.

Coming as it did just after the P.O. encounter, I felt badly stung by this sarcasm and insensitivity, and in my most glacial voice I replied, "My *dear* boy, you haven't the *faintest* notion of what you're *talking* about." Spinning around and departing at a fast clip, I left him to laugh by himself, regretting ever having trusted childish Charlie with my casual reaction to a dumb gangster film.

In the dorms, at Cooper snack bar, outside faculty offices, and all over campus a new year was alive with the friendly spirit of greetings and fresh gossip. We now knew that Richards was *our* school to love and cherish, and so it would remain forever. And I was pleased as punch about my Assistant Editorship at the *Booster*.

I was really excited about turning the weekly around. But it'd be an uphill battle and I knew it. The paper had long been in the hands of old-school types whose exclusive "beat" was athletics or socials and who blissfully ignored cultural happenings and printed scarcely a line of "hard" news. My little story on the Ashkenazy recital was their first such piece in five years! That Fall I skimmed three decades of *Booster*s and in issue after issue I found politics and book reviews drawing an absolute blank, oh yeah, but there were abundant junior-high jokes about "goils" and "broads," stiff cartoons about some shy-but-handsome jock waxing horny at Smith College tea parties, longish "surveys" comparing the different houses' beer busts or weekend meat markets, and a prose style aimed at the mentally deficient. I remember how when Nixon mined Haiphong harbor and expanded the Vietnam bombing there wasn't a peep about it in the *Booster*; I thought it unprofessional and a scandal, and said so at a staff meeting. The editors (all males) simply laughed. The one good thing I can say about the weekly before my arrival was that it came on shiny, expensive high-grade paper.

Somehow it took me most of my freshman year to arrive at so unsettling a realization. My young mind couldn't see all this squaring with Richards College and its high-power academics and renown. But I'm not exaggerating when I say that the old *Booster* was one of the worst newspapers you could conceive of, and I was set on doing something about it. I'm proud to say that I did.

What with tough courses, flute practice, *Booster* deadlines, and my writing, I was deluged with work. After RCO rehearsals I'd dash off to the newsroom. Weekends I saw my friend at either college, but I did lots of work then too. Charlie I'd run into only occasionally, and the few times he ventured up to Park-Davies dining hall he'd either sit elsewhere or join me in a group, where I was spared his barbed comments.

Meanwhile the Amherst guy was making demands, writing daily, phoning just about every night, "declaring himself" at every turn, and once again I felt dissatisfied. Early that October I began an intense relationship with a visiting prof, a writer from New York who'd just gotten divorced and was at Richards teaching journalism courses, one on feature-writing which I audited. (He recently died tragically in a scuba-diving accident down in Florida.) Following an RCO rehearsal I broke with Amherst over the phone, and good God did he sulk and pout and accuse me of this and that, and he was so uncivil as to hang up on me and leave me standing there with nothing but the cold sound of a dial tone.

But I certainly wasn't going to call back and try pulling teeth.

So I didn't need Charlie mocking my dilemmas and finding fault with my decisions. Somehow, though, I managed to run into him whenever I didn't particularly want to. One weekend the writing prof and I were in New York visiting some friends of his, a charming literary couple who had a gorgeous, sunlit townhouse on Washington Square. She was an arts freelancer, he an editor at Doubleday, and they took an interest in my book and asked me for a sample, which I sent him promptly on my return to Richards. Meanwhile they honored us with a light but tasty French lunch, and later my friend and I took the uptown train to the Modern Museum. Just as we approached Picasso's *Guernica*, there, at the picture's far side, staring my way, was Charlie Chadwick.

"Well, hel-lo, Livie Kingsley." He said it as one word.

"Oh, hi." I introduced them.

"Oh, yes," Charlie remarked. "You're at Richards, aren't you?"

"Yes, yes, that's right," my friend replied, feeling flattered. He shook hands enthusiastically, keeping his left thumb in his blue jeans' waist.

There was something cocky and insinuating in Charlie's voice, but my professor-friend couldn't hear a tone I knew too well. The cockiness increased when he corrected my Spanish.

"I've never seen *Guernica*," I said, "so I thought this was the perfect chance."

Charlie giggled, then remarked, "Oh, you mean Gare-NEE-cah." He winked, waved mechanically, and moved on to the opposite wall. His conduct wasn't exactly appreciated.

There was a kind of reprise in Cambridge next week, where the writer took me to a *Boston Phoenix* cocktail party and gave me an inside tour of his venerable alma mater. Just as we're emerging out of Harvard station I hear this brisk voice uttering the words, "Well, well, it's Livie Kingsley!"

I look around and amid the crowd I see Charlie scurrying by with a gleeful grin on his face, scarf blowing in the wind.

Still, Charlie's popping up unexpectedly is what gave me the opportunity to know him better. It was Thanksgiving break; I was alone. My writer friend had gone away to interview Cape Cod restaurant owners, while I needed to finish off research for a piece I was drafting on the last remaining textile mill in West Adams. The factory would soon move to Mexico, the old shell then to be transformed into fast-food joints and specialty shops. My entire Friday morning was spent hearing both workers and managers tell me about how the change would affect their lives.

Famished at day's end and worn out from hearing their sob stories, I was about to dine at a nearby pizza parlor with one of the factory foremen. Suddenly I spotted a Richards face, ashy young math prof who, pizza box in hand, was heading over to his VW bug. I rushed over and asked him for a ride to campus. He stammered out, "Oh, all . . . all rightie."

I looked back and saw the poor foreman still standing there where I'd left him.

"I'm going back to Richards. Sorry!"

He raised his hands, affected a hurt look. "Suit yerself, lady."

The math professor tried to make small talk; I duly answered all of his questions. A leafless Route 116A was already quite dark, the traffic thin, and it took less than ten minutes for a sparsely lit Richards College to come into view. My one-shot chauffeur invited me to share his pizza; I declined the offer as graciously as possible and asked if he might drive me up the hill to Babcock, the only dining hall then open. I clambered out, gave him my best smile, quickly thanked him ("oh, you're very w-w-welcome," I could hear his voice replying), and scurried up the front ramp. Inside it was toasty; as I reached the stairs I saw a familiar shape trailing the food line. I tiptoed up to him, trying my best to minimize the squeaking in my new boots, and said softly, "Well, hello, there's Charlie Chadwick."

He turned around and beamed through his blushing.

"So what're you doing here?" I asked.

He'd been to New London briefly to see relatives but had just come back to work on his Gabriel Marquez paper. *A Hundred Years of Solitude* is simply out of this world, he felt.

"It's weird," he said, "nobody in Caracas ever mentioned the book in class or anywhere."

He was completely taken with Marquez and thought the two last chapters of the book were the most beautiful thing he'd ever read. Now he was devouring the man's other books too. I'd never read any Marquez, but as Charlie fetched me a glass and poured me a Tab I agreed that the guy (I cautiously avoided pronouncing his name) seems to be a pretty good writer.

Charlie was being nice, and a lovely surprise it was. He followed me to a square table, and once settled in he made no cruel wisecracks about men or Clyde's Bonnie or me. We lingered over our ice creams, trading flavors. Slowly we sipped at our coffee, and eventually were the last ones there, and only the darkened lights hinted at the hour. We bussed our trays, filed out lazily, and after a short idle stroll (he singled out Orion, I Venus), we shuffled into the warmth of Park-Davies. We tried the TV, found nothing worth seeing, and so I decided on us going upstairs, the stairs that resounded in the empty house, and we sprawled out onto the floor, talking some, talking more into the frosty night, and we did things like get high on my remaining half-bottle of Cold Duck, listen to Act I of *La Boheme*, some Brahms, some Ravel, and quietly recite poems from a collection I always keep at ready on my night table. He made some explanatory gesture; my right hand caught his wandering left. He'd planned to start drafting his paper that night. He didn't.

We took all meals together the next two days, and on Sunday we read through my entire *New York Times*, and sad (or glad?) to say we got far less work done than we'd expected. But oh! did we feast and play together and more. Oftentimes I would say "Charlie! Charlie!" in long melodious murmurs *pianissimo*, while applying my skills and methodically seeking out his softest and most sensitive spots, and his husky moans to me were sheer pleasure. Sometimes while he'd rest we'd read aloud a dirty episode from the last chapter of *A Hundred Years of Solitude* and he'd giggle and then spin happy fantasies about us doing the same. And oh, it seems bizarre, I know, me harboring romantic memories of a suspected mass terrorist, but I can't negate that brief spell when Charlie Chadwick was the source of delight to me, because his surface innocence hid a passionate, fiery sort easily satisfied, far more than I could be. Sure, in my life there's always been someone around and available, but Charlie in particular showed a charming willingness to please my every whim. He was so easy to love, so constant, and how this squares with the angry, bitter Charlie I was to discover in scarcely more than a month is something that defies comprehension.

The situation was a bit awkward on Monday after lunch, when Charlie and I were about to enter the library, and out of the door comes exiting the journalism professor.

"Well, hello," he says.

I excuse myself from Charlie and ask him to wait for me in the lobby while I take the poor man aside and explain in my most caring voice. He took it very well, in fact with a smile and casual comments like, "Oh, yeah, right," which had me wondering how much I'd meant to him.

So he extends his hand with a "Well, 'bye-bye, Liv," our handshake is kind of ordinary, and off he goes saying, "See you around," in a disturbingly flip tone of voice. But we were to remain on speaking terms, and my book did eventually get published through his friends in New York. One time the following week he, Charlie, and I even gabbed over coffee together at the snack bar, an episode I couldn't help but find comical.

November and December with Charlie were just perfect. He was so good, so sweet, the most affectionate of all my boy friends so far. I need hugs like some people need morning toast, and whenever I'd demand a hug, he'd provide. Or I'd say how much I'd like to see Venezuela with him, and he'd glow, and I'd say "Hug!" and hug he did. Many was the time I asked him to do some xeroxing for me, or fetch me a book, or type up a review I felt too tired to type myself, and my asking was his doing.

Still, despite this pliability, he held back his emotions. Here's a typical instance: We're in his room, sitting on his bed after dinner, my *Boheme* on his stereo, and I grab hold of his hand and say, "Charlie, you're so important to me."

He answered nothing.

"I've become so dependent on you."

More silence, and a frown.

"You don't believe me, do you."

Utter impassivity, and it was the pattern day after day, and oh! it was frustrating. No matter how much I'd pour out my soul to him, no matter how much love I gave him those Fall nights, he'd remain sphinx-like before my deepest feelings.

The tension dragged on until the day before exams, when things broke out into the open. We'd just had a quick lunch at Cooper and were checking the P.O. *Newsweek* was all that Charlie had got, but I turned white when I opened my mail box and saw a letter postmarked from Amherst. I shivered in the wind as we headed toward Park-Davies. He took my arm; I jerked away.

"What's the matter, Liv?"

I simply could not speak as I tore open the square, light-green envelope. And, oh, yes, it was just as I'd feared, the Amherst boy had sent me a long love letter filled with passionate declarations. I felt visibly upset.

We'd climbed the stairs to my floor when Charlie again asked, "Livie, what *is* the matter?"

My voice trembled. "Oh, God. Why don't some people forget?" As I reached into my pants pocket for my keychain I could see Charlie freeze.

"Who . . . what do you mean?"

"Just, you know, *forget*. I certainly forget. Why don't they forget me. Why sign a letter 'I love you' ten times?"

Charlie shut the door behind him and stood there giving me a pale stare. From the bed I could hear his heart pounding.

"You know, Livie, it scares me to hear you talking like that."

He slumped down beside me on the bed, breathing hard.

"Why? Because it strikes you as cold and callous, or because you think someday I might be saying that about you?"

"A little bit of both." He breathed through his mouth now. "Am I gonna be the next one?"

Two women ambled by in the hall, their nervous talk of exams interrupting our discussion. Their wooden clogs echoed in the stairwell. Charlie was breathing harder than ever.

I tried to reassure him. "Charlie, those guys just weren't for me. All they wanted was to use me." I took his hand in both of mine. "You're different, Charlie. You're special." I put my head on his shoulder. "You're so important to me. Nobody's ever treated me like you have." As I held him tight I could hear my wrist watch ticking fast. "Charlie, you're perfect for me."

After more of this tortuous conversation he calmed down, though still saying very little. He seemed to believe me. We spent the afternoon in my room, he was as serviceable as ever, and a very nice time it was indeed!

I didn't feel fully satisfied, but everything appeared pretty much smoothed over, and we studied till 2 A.M. at the House library. He stayed on in my room and furnished me more hugs and kisses and such. We had breakfast downstairs in the morning; he looked real pleased to be with me amid the Parke-Davies crowd. I gave him a goodbye squeeze as I ran off to Econ final, and breezed through it painlessly. Outside in the hall some wimp asked me to join him in lunch, but I said I wasn't hungry which was true, and I trod home in the falling wet snow, wishing I'd stayed with the wimp and his umbrella. I skipped lunch and went right up for a well-deserved nap.

As fate would have it, the relief proved short-lived. Sometime in mid-afternoon, still groggy, I peeked into my mailbox and instantly spotted the minuscule neat hand of my pianist friend (he had moved to New York in late October). The regulation P.O. envelope was thick, with a long letter ten times more frustrating than yesterday's from Amherst. His defenses were down; his every line was stuffed with words like "adore" and "worship" and the rest. He claimed to be crying about me, night after night, claimed his piano playing was doing badly just because I wasn't there at his side. Passionately, abjectly, he begged me to come down and move into his Soho loft. ("We'd make beautiful duets. Each day of the week we could play a different Bach sonata!")

I skimmed the six pages in an absolute dither, walking fast, lips tight and shaking my head in frustration.

"Livie!" Coming from the library, books in hand. Charlie.

I stopped, looked up at him, hesitated, said nothing. I started to fold the letter.

"So what is it now?" he said with a flutter of sarcasm.

"From New York. It's real upsetting."

"Oh, I see, just another jerk who won't forget you." His voice trembled. "You know, maybe there should be a first time."

I asked him quietly, "A first time for what?"

He stared down at the fresh snow, furrowing it with the tip of his loafers, and said, "A first time some guy just ups and forgets *you*."

He started treading briskly toward Babcock, then stopped in his tracks and whirled around. His mouth was distorted, his voice bitter. "I've heard you laugh at the old boy friends you've ditched." He turned again toward Babcock as he screamed, "Well, you're not doin' it to *me*!"

I hurried after him, grabbed him by the sleeve of his down jacket, and explained to him animatedly, "Charlie, listen, you just don't understand. If I don't like hearing from those guys it's for a reason." Waving the letter, I took a deep breath. "Can't you *understand*? Can't you see it's 'cause its you I care for?" He gave me this blank look. "You see, I . . ." (he kept staring at me) "I *love* you."

He was absolutely still and silent for, who knows, half a minute, and asked softly, "How can I be sure you mean that?"

My voice implored, "Oh, Charlie, how can you *accuse* me that way? Please, trust me, I do love you." And I truly meant it.

He looked down, again said nothing. Then he took his right hand out of his pocket, squeezed me on the shoulder and said, "We'd better go inside and study. You've got geology tomorrow."

So in his actions he was receptive, if refusing in kind. Next morning I repeated it to him over scrambled eggs in our quiet little breakfast nook. Oh, I must've told him I loved him a hundred times, right into the last morning of finals week, when we each had exams scheduled, and still he'd fail to reciprocate, though we were constantly together. Our last two nights we spent cuddling nicely since I was too tired to do much else. Charlie, however, was feeling desirous, oh, was aching from lust, really, and I just couldn't, wouldn't do more, and with all my heart I'd plead with him, saying, "But Charlie, you're the love of my life!" And he'd insist, even beg, and I would ask, "Is that all you care about, Charlie? Is sex just the frosting or is it the cake?" And he'd turn sad, making me sad too.

By the afternoon of the last day there was scarcely a soul on campus, and we spent it all in his room, hugging to the strains of *La Boheme* Acts 3 and 4, and Charlie indulging me with a two-hour-long back-and-shoulders massage. After a quick dinner at Cooper we shared a cab to Albany airport.

"Give me your paw," I said as we settled in, and he held my hand the entire ride. The thick charcoal-gray cloud cover and recent snows gave the New York mountain villages an even more desolate look. He lay his head on my shoulder, we kissed and cuddled, and at the airport he almost forgot his small bag on the car seat. After check-in we had a couple of hours to spare, owing to delays, and as we sat watching the planes lift off one by one I put my hand on his neck and whispered into his ear. "Charlie, Charlie, I love you so much." The usual silence. "Sometimes I'd like to have your child, that's how much I care."

Now he pressed his face against mine, kind of choked and, almost embarrassingly loud, confessed, "Oh, Livie, I love you too." He sobbed. "I'm going to miss you these three weeks."

It was the first time I'd heard him say the words, and I felt pleased. I squeezed him tighter as I purred, "Say it again, Charlie, say it again."

And say it he did, "I love you," "I adore you," and variants thereof, maybe fifty-two times, maybe more.

Calmly, quietly, my fingers dried his face as I whispered, "That's a good boy!" We embraced, and kissed, it was *glorious*, and passionately we promised to write each other during holidays.

It was bitter cold on the way to the DC-8.

Charlie's declarations opened up the floodgates, it seemed. We'd parted on a Saturday. On Monday I received a beautiful, adoring note postmarked at Albany and another from NYC. Soon after that there was mail from him every day, sometimes two or three letters, all of them Special Delivery, and before that there were telegrams. It was utterly strange, getting so much concentrated emotion by mail. I'll admit I'm not the sentimental type who wraps old love letters in pink ribbons, but I do regret having discarded his materials so soon after our relationship. They might have revealed some crucial facets of his personality. Certain traits Charlie exhibited could well have accounted for his political conversion and possible terrorism two years hence, I think.

Chapter 4

The last note Charlie sent me that Christmas vacation showed a cruel streak. True, I hadn't written him in a while, but his final note to me was inexcusably bitter. Earlier on I'd caught only glimpses of this side of him, and now I felt less hurt than deeply saddened and surprised. That frenzied reaction of his was sparked by my mention of (really!) *Madame Butterfly*, which was being staged near Columbus around then. So anyway I'd mailed him this postcard saying I hoped to get tickets just to see Pinkerton being such a *bastard* to that sweet woman who's so loving and devoted to him. "MEN!" was my zestful parting comment.

Well, the casual musical reference somehow aroused his

righteous wrath. On my next-to-last day at home I receive this incredibly nasty letter, Special Delivery of course, in which I see Charlie getting mileage out of some big words from Psych class. I've forgotten his exact text, but I remember his saying my *Butterfly* remarks were pure "projection," that Pinkerton merely treats a "girl" the way I treat "guys," that "after Pre-Med, Pianist, and Writing Prof, Charlie's next," and that I, Livie, was playing Pinkerton to his Butterfly! Such was the gist of his harangue.

It was a vicious, spiteful letter, I must say. Such unkind thoughts and insults were being hurled at me, plus the cheap parallels—Livie equals opera villain! Charlie equals Mr. pre-Med! He showed no sympathy for my situation and, in a long letter I composed that day and sent straight on to Richards, I spoke my mind. Calmly I reminded him of the bond of trust between us, and in my concern I assured him that, though a diatribe like his could be quite damaging, I felt that our trust had not suffered, despite impending changes in our relationship. Notwithstanding his cruelty and our no longer being lovers, *we still had mutual trust* and should strive to preserve it.

Moreover I told Charlie the whole truth. I may not entertain too high an opinion of myself, but I've always taken great pride in my honesty and sincerity. And I thus informed Charlie that in my first days in Ohio I'd met someone, a former alternative-press journalist currently studying Law at Yale, where he was head of Young Democrats. A handsome fellow in his late twenties, with an earthy look to his salt-and-pepper beard, I'd interviewed him at a regional A.D.A. convention in Cleveland, his home town, but because of a death in the family he'd actually been spending Christmas with relatives in Columbus. Doug was his name, and I'd seen him daily and many a night, furnishing him solace and support, and oh! did I feel joyously happy.

And so I advised Charlie of this fact and explained how his defensiveness and distance toward my affection had been terribly hard on me at Richards, causing me sadness and dissatisfaction through December. I told Charlie I cared very much for his feelings and that he would forever remain a dear loved one but that, alas, the nastiness of his attack now precluded any renewal of our romance, however splendid it once was . . . And yet for all his wariness with me I still trusted him and did not want to hurt him, and so I clearly expressed it in a P.S.

That January we met exactly twice. On a still, sunlit day the first week of J.I. he calls up at the *Booster*.

"I've got to see you immediately."

I pronounce myself at his disposal to talk about whatever he wants for as long as he'd like.

"How 'bout right now?"

"Charlie, I'm busy at the moment, but you could come, oh, let's see, maybe two hours from now."

"Livie . . ."

"Charlie, you'll have to wait, I'm sorry."

"Okay, okay, I'll see you at 3:30."

Contrary to what we'd agreed he shows up at 3:20, but I let him help me with my coat, I fumble for my keys in my bag and lock up, and we tread silently to Park-Davies.

No sooner have we stepped in than, giving me no time to catch my breath, he starts haranguing me with those cruel parallels between himself and other men and also throws in his cheap shot about—yes!—Pinkerton!

"It's a pattern with you, Livie, and now it's my turn. The only thing I regret is not having ditched you first, when the ditchin' was still good."

I heard hatred in that voice, it was disturbing. After a while I raised my still-gloved hand and cut his lecture short. "Charlie. Listen. I didn't let you into my private space so you could stand there and . . . vilify me. I think some mutual trust is in order. I have no desire to hurt you. So why hurt *me*?"

At that point Charlie collapsed on the bed, bursting his reservoir of tears.

"Livie, please," he sobbed, "tell me, what am I to you?"

I must confess I was upset by his whole song-and-dance. I've never been able to stand emotional scenes, they unnerve me.

"Charlie, come on, you're putting me on the spot."

"Please, please, what've I meant to you?"

"Look, Charlie, I'm tired from work, you can't expect me to reason like a rabbi. You're being really manipulative, and I will not let you play on my guilt."

"Livie, I'm so sorry about the mean things I said to you."

"It's all right, don't worry."

"And I never was good enough to you, was I?"

"You've been very good, Charlie."

I felt pleased that he had the decency to apologize, and he seemed genuinely repentant about his aloofness last semester.

But on the whole I found the episode distasteful.

Charlie's explosions were something the like of which I hadn't as yet experienced, and when he kept telling me, "Livie, you're an ideal woman," and "Livie, you're the most wonderful person on earth," I could only wince and insist that he stop saying those things since they weren't true and most probably all he wanted was to bribe me anyway.

I suppose it sounds unnice but after a couple of hours I welcomed with relief his getting up for departure, and besides I hadn't had any lunch.

"Livie, " he asked, "do you have a kleenex handy?"

"Sure," I answered, as I reached for a blue packet in my desk drawer. I pulled out a tissue and handed it to him.

"Thanks, " he said.

He dried his tears, placed the kleenex on my desk, then kissed me on the cheek without any noticeable bitterness, said "Thank you for everything, Liv," and, rather briskly and breezily, walked out, leaving the door open. I dropped the used kleenex into the wastebasket.

My next meeting with him took place two weeks later in his room, during the thaws. The slush was considerable on my way to Babcock, and in the lobby some guys in T-shirts were lolling about, playing Monopoly. From among them voices said, "Hi,

Livie," and "Hey, Liv, how's it goin'?" Upstairs I knocked on Charlie's door. As he peeked out his face brightened. He expressed utter surprise, saying, "Livie . . . Hi."

"May I come in?"

"Yes, please do."

"Charlie, are you all right?"

He shrugged his shoulders. "I'm okay." We sat down, he on the bed, I by his desk.

"You haven't called or anything, so I was feeling concerned."

There was a moment's silence, followed by some small talk, or rather I talked and he'd answer monosyllabically.

After about a half hour it got frustrating so I asked, "Incidentally, Charlie, isn't my *La Boheme* still here? I know what you're thinking, but I'll appreciate your not saying it."

He looked at me stiffly, then said, "It's in my music locker. I'll bring it to you sometime soon."

"Oh, no hurry." I stood up, smiled, and asked, "Well, how 'bout a friendly hug?" He put an arm around me casually, almost perfunctorily. "Now, really, is that all I get?" And both his arms clasped me, and his hold became strong, almost clinging. As I broke off I told him, "Call me, please do."

Next morning I find the record album sitting on my office desk all by itself, with no note or communication of any kind.

I bring up these intimate, somewhat embarrassing details of our personal relationship because I believe they shed light on the "Carlos" Chadwick who later became so notorious. Charlie was the sort of person who gets mad when reality doesn't live up to certain expectations he's created for himself. Recalling his spiteful letter to me I can see in embryo the same bitterness he eventually felt toward the school and this country. He would form these excessive attachments to people and places and cleave to those attachments with all the fire and conviction of a true believer, but, once disillusion set in, he'd transform them into hatred. And then, rather than examine his own conscience, he'd take to blaming those people and places. As a freshman Charlie arrived at Richards with unrealistic notions about its cultural and human climate. When the school turned out to be something else than what his mind imagined, his abhorrence for the place turned fanatical, and the same could be said about his drastic shifts in attitude towards me. But I'm letting myself get ahead of events.

Chapter 5

I didn't run into Charlie until February at our first rehearsal. As I entered Putney backstage I saw him standing there, fiddle propped under his stubbly chin.

"Hi, Charlie, how are you?" I smiled at him warmly.

His nod was infinitesimal; he averted his gaze and went on to tune his E-string; thereafter he stopped greeting me, period. For two months he'd drift right by me in the music basement, the library, at rehearsals or Cooper Hall, and refuse so much as to acknowledge my presence. I'd say "Hi Charlie" and he'd move on without the slightest gesture. And oftentimes I did feel the impulse to walk up and grab him by the hand and ask him, "Charlie, what is the matter with you? Are you okay?" But I can only take so much rejection.

At any rate I thought his conduct less than proper or considerate. I've always felt it's best to be civil and polite. Plain old human decency—that's what it's about. And it was tough on me personally when, to compound my woes, yesteryear's pianist showed up on Thursdays to rehearse Tchaikowsky's *First* with us and then played it at our big spring concert. More than once, as I settled into my chair onstage, unpacking my flute and piccolo, I would reflect on the sheer pain of being in the midst of a crowd where there are males who make no secret of loathing you. The experience of sensing such cold and heartless hate from all sides is something I would not wish on my worst enemies. Men are such pigs, so thoughtless and cruel!

Meanwhile winter shifted slowly into springtime. Tall snow

banks shrank, turned shapeless gray and trickled off into murky puddles, and in overheated rooms the tensions of overwork gradually loosened up. Trees blossom late in the Berkshires, but April warming trends would help ease those biweekly visits with Doug in New Haven, where warm weather was in full bloom.

What seemed a peaceful New England's midwinter spring was soon shaken up by the Library incident, so powerfully recounted in Fred Jennings's account. I didn't actually see those creeps doing their routine, but it was enough just to hear the news, first via the librarian who phoned me at Park-Davies and could hardly tell the story in between sobs, then from three angry and hyped-up "sister" Richies who, just as I lay down the receiver, pounded on my door, shouting, "Liv, it's urgent."

They stormed in and proceeded to report the episode in all its ugly details. I stood there listening in outrage.

After they'd each relayed the facts and reiterated them in their fury, I thanked the threesome, put on my coat and boots, and with a fiery Francesca (a spunky actress from Little Italy) I rushed off toward the newsroom and started rehearsing my angered thoughts with her (she was the perfect sounding board).

I switched on the IBM Selectric, almost tipping it over in my rage, and there I sat banging out the phrases at full speed and reading them aloud to Fran (who laughed throughout, and applauded and cried "Bravissimo!" at my final sentence).

Two days later it ran in the *Booster* as a signed editorial, and I felt proud of it. We also printed the protest letter Charlie had signed. Starting that week there was a constant round of debate in the *Booster*, making its pages livelier and more stimulating than they'd been in fifty years. There were also feverish discussions all over campus, a feminist rally condemning the repeated harassment of women at the school, and a team that went around washing off the "COED GO HOME" graffiti that had cropped up recently on building walls.

For every *Booster* that spring and the local press I produced stories and editorials concerning the affair. I also had pieces in the

Berkshire Eagle and the Boston papers. I doubt if I will ever write with as much conviction as I did during those weeks.

Charlie's signing of that protest letter made me glad. I felt even more pleased next week when, tacked right in the middle of the mail board, I saw the typescript of his own letter. A few days after it was printed I ran into him in the library stacks. The afternoon was warm and sunny, but the shades were down in his cubicle, where he sat buried amid French books. He still wasn't talking to me, so I approached him myself.

"Charlie."

He looked up slowly and silently from his marked-up copy of Sartre's *Nausea*.

"Charlie, I really liked your letter. Thanks so much."

He gave me a long, quiet stare as he fiddled with the button on his ballpoint pen. "Thanks for the appreciation." He paused a moment, doodled on his yellow scratch pad, looked up again and said, "And boy do I need it. The guys in my corridor've stopped talking to me." Another pause. "I'm getting the silent treatment from their girl friends too."

"I'm real sorry to hear about it." In fact it made me mad when he reminded me just how many women Richies were defending the Library incident and joining in the clamor against feminists. At the rally, I remember, one short girl with long blond hair went so far as to stand up before the crowd and say, "In my three years at Richards I've never seen any sexist abuse. So where's all the sexism?" There were hisses and applause.

A frecklefaced redhead from the women's swimming team contributed to the *Booster* debates with her own brief letter saying, "Any woman who gets mistreated probably deserves it anyway."

Unfortunately I was in no position to comment too specifically on all this, since I could jeopardize my reportorial objectivity.

So anyhow here was Charlie, bearing some of the brunt of sexist intolerance, and all because he'd written a letter making a simple plea for open-mindedness. Now, he tells me, others are accusing *him* of closed-mindedness.

"I've gotten phone calls at midnight." He tilts his head sideways into his hand. "Some voice drawls, 'We're gonna get you yet, you damned traitor,' then hangs up."

"That's slimy."

"Yeah. Another time the same voice mumbled something about a banana boat." Charlie closes his fist, holds it up to his ear, and mimics a hoarse, raspy bass. "'Whynt'cha go back to Tijuana or wherever it is ya come from?' Click." He taps on the edge of the desk with his Parker, muttering "Bastards!" under his breath.

I wasn't completely ignorant of these attitudes. At the *Booster* we'd received an unsigned note which I and another woman reporter summarily discarded, and which had as its entire text, "There's guys at this school who're nothing more than hysterical females." But I had no idea the intolerance had gone this far.

Charlie was still holding me at a distance, but we managed to become friends once again. And I was glad for this because he looked terrible and felt unsure about staying at Richards. I felt concerned that someone should talk with him and help him survive the semester. The prevailing topic that week was not Nixon or Watergate but the Library episode and related matters, so every time Charlie and I would go for coffee after orchestra we'd chuckle over the stupid sexist arguments floating around campus or in the *Booster*. (That pianist on the other hand still adamantly refused to have anything to do with me.)

Around this time Charlie began hanging around with the assorted little political groups that had set up tables and started congregating in front of Cooper just after the Library incident.

The tables were something completely new on campus, as was the commitment of the people running them. Richards students traditionally have been either apolitical or Republican, and even the Democratic minority during my days was either indifferent or conservative. But now for the first time there were six to a dozen card tables manned by groups representing a much-expanded spectrum of opinion. There was a non-partisan coalition advocating impeachment of Nixon, while a few yards down there was another group defending Nixon. At one long table you could always find, ever faithfully, a tall, tough, wooly-haired senior from Brooklyn and her two bearded comrades, calling for a complete end to all U.S. involvement in Southeast Asia. Their publications could keep you busy for a week.

The fellow who occasionally ran the table for Young ADA had heard of my New Haven friend and spoke highly of him. A Nicaraguan guy gave away anti-Somoza leaflets and sold pamphlets favoring the Allende regime and the PMF. A Trotskyite table came and went, and sometimes there were a few guys from the Black Student Alliance. Once in a while I saw the Ayn Rand Club or Young Americans for Freedom sitting about, looking terribly respectable in their crew cuts and horn-rimmed glasses. Besides the anti-war threesome, the one group on hand every afternoon was the Richards Left Coalition, who gave the impression of having parachuted in from Chicago '68, and would later figure heavily in Charlie's life. But things were liveliest whenever the Richards Feminists set up their books, leaflets, and bumper stickers, and several dozen bystanders would gather around to argue or just chitchat. For the most part, however, the number of people who stood about and talked to the "politicals" seldom rose above the thirty mark.

Charlie was frequently to be seen among the bystanders, probably the first time he'd gotten involved in something other than academics or the endless rites that keep us Richies ever so busy. On more than one bright spring afternoon I'd walk by the tables and find him milling about and observing the exchanges taking place between a table activist and her opponents or questioners.

One time I saw him listening intently on the sidelines; I asked what he thought about all the political talk coming at him. "It's sort of interesting," he answered, "but I don't know what to make of it. You see so many arguments from every side."

Fred Jennings touches on this in recounting Charlie's progress, but I'll emphasize it myself. Before the advent of the tables,

Charlie's interest in politics hovered at zero. Except for the Sunday *Times*, which I'd introduced him to, his only window on the outside world was *Newsweek*. And despite his being South American, I knew fifty times more about the situation down in Chile, Peru, and Nicaragua than he did at that time. Through my New Haven friend I often attended ADA meetings where student members read position papers on Chile and Peru. More than once I got informally involved in the discussions and then wrote about it for the *Booster*. On the other hand Charlie's info level on Allende and Somoza and the PMF was either cliché or confusion. "We have no business in Asia or Latin America," I'd argue.

He'd then say either, "But, I mean, what about the Soviets?" or "I just don't know what to think. Does *anybody* know what's going on?"

What fascinated Charlie about the tables was the sheer drama of ideas being tossed back and forth. I suspect it resembled the image he'd once entertained of student life at Richards. I gather also that the daily excitement and high-pitched talk were a relief from the silent treatment he was getting around Babcock. The tables were a kind of halfway house or temporary home, something like the *Booster* was for me. And for all I know the people around those tables may have planted in his mind the initial seed for *Perspectives Industries*.

Suddenly our little forums disappeared. Exam week arrived and swept them away, steering us back to our textbooks. One sunny Friday in May the *Booster* came out with a centerfold containing Letters to the Editor exclusively—angry, wise, or witty or just plain puerile letters on every imaginable subject—and then we shut down for the summer. The six-week activists packed up their literature, carted off their tables, and hid away in their suites and cubicles, leaving Cooper Quad to a dedicated core of frisbee addicts. The RCO concluded its big spring bash with the *Eroica*—and our audience jumped to its feet with applause the minute we thundered out that last E-flat chord. I took apart my flute with a slight feeling of sadness.

A nervous silence now descended as everybody from militant feminists to professional beer-swillers put aside their various obsessions and buried themselves in academics. The bitter disputes from earlier in the semester now vanished into oblivion. Charlie was exceptional in that he had forgotten nothing. Or rather his housemates and their friends wouldn't forget his "betrayal" and were still disregarding his presence around the college. (I couldn't help but see the poetic justice in this, inasmuch as he'd been giving me the silent treatment since April.) One evening after a particularly long rehearsal we'd gone to Cooper, where over a tall Coke he talked excitedly about his upcoming junior year in Paris. It was the first time in months that I'd heard him feeling positive about anything at all, and I agreed with him that he needed a nice long break.

"We've got to get you out of here, Charlie." I told him to send us stories for the *Booster*. He liked the idea, though I really didn't expect much to come of it.

I ran into Charlie one more time those next few weeks. My New Haven friend had already flown to Ohio, and by a quirk of fate Charlie, me, and Crystal Sweet from WRCR ended up sharing the same Albany Airport limousine, he and I both aware of our ride on that same mountain stretch last December, but saying nothing about it now. The three of us settled in and joshed with relief at the year being over. Crystal and I reminisced angrily over the Library incident and hoped for a change of heart among male Richies next fall. A quieter Charlie smiled most of the way, clearly glad to be departing Richards-New Ashford. During the 50-minute trip I caught glimpses of Charlie the cheerful freshman I'd met a couple of years back. Little did I know it was the last I would see of that person, for a Charlie Chadwick different even in name was to return to Richards in just over fifteen months.

Chapter 6

The changes in Charlie started manifesting themselves in a letter from Europe that September, with its glorification of everything French. If I recall correctly, it was in that same note that he first expressed serious dissatisfaction not just with Richards but with America as well. Then, in October, he made in passing what may well be his first set of political references ever. He was, he said, "horrified" at the American devastation in Indochina and the repression in Chile. He alluded to the upcoming French elections with some vague hope that the left would win. And he engaged in paranoid speculations about a CIA-engineered coup if Communists came to power in France, or about a United States "nuking" Peru if the PMF made gains in any of the big cities.

These were wild political fantasies the likes of which Charlie had never talked about at Richards. Clearly he was picking up leftish attitudes from the Latino students he'd been buddying with in the City of Light. Of course, influences of this sort are more to be expected in Paris than around Richards. And though I believe strongly in America's system of pragmatic, nonideological problem-solving, in all fairness I will say that Charlie appeared to be gaining from exposure to those ideological passions for which the hot-blooded French and Latino peoples are so renowned the world over.

So discovering politics, even if left-wing, at first seemed good for Charlie. I seriously considered excerpting his reports and running them as short articles. The accounts Charlie sent me of anti-Pinochet demonstrations right in the Latin Quarter and of pro-PMF rallies near the Sorbonne were particularly vivid. But in the end we decided he should have shown less bias toward the left and provided a more balanced view. Besides, the anti-Americanism in his letters was turning shrill. He'd send me *Le Monde* stories in which one Jacques DeCornoy actually claimed that every single village in northern Laos had been levelled by round-the-clock B-52 raids, a charge I thought dubious and exaggerated, but which Charlie accepted on faith. Another set of articles by some Norwegian "reported" how the PMF's noble and lofty programs were being systematically sabotaged by CIA agents and U.S. warplanes—and again Charlie relayed those allegations as truth itself.

And it wasn't as if the views and "facts" Charlie dwelt on were new to me. My uncle back in Ohio had always insisted that the Vietnam War was a stupid mistake, and that any more such foolish episodes "would cause needless suffering to Americans," as he said in a much-reported speech. Through Doug, my New Haven friend, I'd helped draft documents aimed at lobbying against U.S. aid to South American generals. I'd also written *Booster* editorials questioning Nixon's sabre-rattling in Peru and his instant recognition of Pinochet. So while Charlie's ideological raps from Paris did understandably raise his father's hackles, he was really obsessed with things I'd been dealing with all along. But then he had just found out that United States foreign policy is far from perfect, a realization that didn't fit the rosy images of America he'd picked up in Venezuela and nourished at Richards. That our high-minded idealism could lead us into such tragic misadventures abroad was something completely novel and therefore shocking to him.

Though my own environment wasn't halfway as exotic, there were things in Richards-New Ashford keeping me busy all day. For one, my life had taken a darker turn when Doug, in a rare letter, told me he could never love and much less marry me. He expressed it in a few curt sentences and no uncertain terms, and once again I was rudely reminded of the cruel streak lurking within the best of men's hearts, and after all I'd given him, all those nights spent together . . . I remember dialing area code 203 countless times those terrible November weeks. And I remember the pain of my suffering bringing me to the verge of tears for the very first time since ninth grade. In my desperation I got briefly involved with a couple of men around Richards, but each of these guys somehow got it into their heads to make demands and expect a commitment, wanting to be with me tomorrow night, and then maybe every meal including breakfast, why not? By Thanksgiving I'd gotten sick and tired and decided to stick by Doug and the admiration I felt for him.

Still, there was the agony, and to stave it off I plunged into work. Talk of municipal bankruptcy coming out of West Adams kept me borrowing cars or hitching furiously back and forth to meet with city councilmen and the new mayor. A couple of *Booster* cubs transcribed and edited the tapes, and I ran the lot as a feature article and even placed a short note in *The New Republic* on the town's troubled future. At nights I sweated over academics, doing intense research for my Econ paper, focusing on the constructive role that U.S. firms play in leading Third World nations to growth and "take-off."

Afternoons I worked like a fiend on the Mozart flute concerto, which I was scheduled to perform next May with the RCO and the Hartford Symphony. An ever-thoughtful Music Theory prof came down to the practice rooms and faithfully accompanied me on the piano at least once a week until the concerts were done. (A smashing success they were! They could've been perfect if Doug had bothered to attend . . .)

I think it was in January that Charlie reported being absorbed in Marx and Engels. And he was clearly impressed with their teachings. Charlie came to Marxist ideology with the same conviction I'd once seen him exhibit for Richards, now citing long stretches of *The German Ideology* and *Das Kapital* in order to "prove" how such and such a quote applies to capitalism *today*, or simply remarking in block letters, "WHAT A GREAT PARA-GRAPH!" I got the distinct impression Charlie was now trying to bring me 'round to all that Marxism he'd gotten so involved with. But, as I wrote him in reply, though Karl Marx had provided some interesting perspectives and beautiful ideals, I simply didn't believe in becoming attached to any particular point of view at the expense of all others. There is something to be gained from *every* theory which no single theory can provide—that's how I felt.

Well, he didn't much appreciate my skepticism about his left wing "progress." Every time I'd express my doubts he'd answer right back with a long letter in which he'd aggressively defend his hard-line perspective. I remember once, when I wrote him and politely suggested he was getting a little bit, you know, dogmatic, within two weeks I get a lengthy reply with the perfectly nasty opening line, "Dear Livie, Really, you liberals don't know shit from corn shucks." And so forth. And he goes on to insist that American liberalism is "an ideology that has very little to do with anything anywhere else on this globe," that his two years of Richards education had been "an utter farce," and that life in the United States is "spiritually sterile and joyless." Strange, and sad, it was. Across the ocean, 3,000 miles away, I could see the gentle Charlie I'd once known, a lover of Mozart and Marquez, now falling under the spell of his radical friends and readings, becoming fanatically obsessed with U.S. foreign policy, and with the seed of an ugly hate inside of him.

And I was by no means unsympathetic to Charlie's views. In fact, before Spring break I announced that the *Booster* would throw open its editorial pages to free discussion of U.S. policy in Latin America. The move was a success. During the next two weeks our clerk sorted out mail from over seventy students, professors, and townspeople and staff. The letters ran the full range, and in our second April issue we printed samples from every position—left, right, and center. On the far right a notorious reactionary freshman from Elizabeth, N.J. advocated that the U.S. "nuke all of Peru, where life is cheap anyway." A similar letter from nine campus libertarians made the argument that Chile's Allende ("he's dead now—and we're *glad!*") and the Peruvian guerrillas were part of a Kremlin "shopping list"; it heaped praise on the Chilean generals for "restoring individual liberty" and called for like measures elsewhere.

From the center there came agonizing reappraisals of our policies, expressions of the wrenching dilemma of not wishing to "abandon our Latin friends to Communism" while having to "depend on corrupt generals in order to combat that very tyranny." And from the far left a brief statement sent in by Charlie blithely assured us that the PMF is right and the U.S. is wrong and that Pinochet is nothing less than "our hired killer, he's Nixon's Pétain, and therefore deserves the same fate."

We printed a few letters like Charlie's, and some elements around campus openly criticized me for "being biased" toward Marxists. But I refused to succumb; I knew we had to accept every shade of opinion if we were to arouse concern for the terrible problems confronting U.S. policymakers. And so Allende, Somoza, the PMF, and other South-of-the-Border phenomena briefly became hot topics for the *Booster*. I also got a well-known Boston University prof to contribute a piece criticizing our Peruvian intervention, which I balanced on that same page with an essay from a Fletcher School analyst, who convincingly demonstrated "a grave leftist threat in South America" and called for "quick and effective action" against that threat.

Charlie's Marxified letters to me, then, were really a case of preaching to the converted, inasmuch as I welcomed *all* views, including his own.

Toward the end of April we received from Charlie a brief if grandiose analysis of human history through the notorious prophecies of Karl Marx. While its overstated conclusions struck us as beyond belief, his broad argument was so novel I decided we'd use it. And so, on a lazy, breezy, May afternoon, the year's final *Booster* served its affluent Richies this abstract theoretical essay demonstrating how (of all things) Marx's predictions were on-target even when they hadn't come true! For those of you who wish yet another instance of Carlos Chadwick's delirious writings I reproduce his article herewith. For those who find such sweeping reflections a crashing bore, there should be no compunction about skipping Charlie's heady generalities and moving on to Chapter 7.

HOW MARX WAS RIGHT
by Charlie Chadwick

"None of Marx's predictions have come true." This cliché has been tirelessly intoned by a regular army of barstool thinkers, instant-idea columnists, silver-haired TV sages, and every imaginable anti-Marxist jester, choirmaster, and scribe. Behind the familiar phrase there lie millions of atrophied brains and an ignorance of Marx, history, and geography which, in its scale, cannot but inspire awe.

The obvious points first: The way simplistic anti-Marxists like to put it, Marx saw the capitalists getting richer and the working poor sinking deeper into the bog of misery, but of course it hasn't happened that way since (as EVERYONE knows!) workers today are much better off than they were in Marx's time. Neither this facile dramatization nor the supposedly "real" counter-outcome have anything to do with what was actually foreseen by old Marx, who focussed on the proletarianization of ever more bourgeois citizens, a dynamic whereby more and more shopkeepers, farmers, artisans, and other small businessmen would inevitably be stampeded out of capitalist status by their big competitors, subsequently be driven into the ranks of the propertyless (i.e. without productive property) and would thereby be, technically speaking, proletarianized.

Well, that's what's happened. In 1830, around 80 percent of the U.S. population was self-employed. Today that figure stands at under 20 percent! For every few hundred millionaires emerging each year, there are hordes of graduates eager to work on salary for capitalists, and the same is true of engineers, lawyers, hospital doctors, lab scientists, and computer technicians. Oh, sure, they may think of themselves as "free professionals," but at bottom what they are is fortunate functionaries, high-paid employees.

Workers in key industries (e.g. autos, steel) earn decent money and work eight hours instead of the obligatory fourteen of a hundred years ago. Such gains workers owe, however, not to any fabled capitalist benevolence but to the hard collective struggle waged by their unions to secure acceptable working conditions and pay. And if some big anti-union firms like DuPont provide high wages, they do this precisely because of the standards established by the labor movement, which they try with all their might to keep out! Still, the living standard of the dishwashing, floorsweeping, and grape-picking sectors has remained, down to this day, solidly Dickensian, and each decade the number of unemployed slowly but steadily rises . . .

Hand-in-hand with this proletarianization there goes a dynamic which Marx (and back then only Marx) predicted: the increasing concentration of capital. That is pretty much how it's turned out. A "big firm" in Marx's time had 700 employees. Today General Motors has a global payroll of 700 thousand (all of them, I suppose, free and independent individuals). In the 1920s there were dozens of auto manufacturers in the U.S. As of this writing there are three and a quarter. (In case you've forgotten, Pontiac, Mercury, and Dodge were once separate companies.) Only nineteen nations have more money than Exxon! The big corporations are richer than most of the nation-states where they do business. Of course, some diehards out there find concentration more "efficient" (i.e. it provides ever-shoddier goods at a faster rate, with fewer hands, at lower cost) and therefore a Good Thing. It's funny to see those big-business apologists praise the very thing Marx said would happen . . .

So much for the obvious (which, not surprisingly, the anti-Marxists can't perceive).

The "failed prediction" which anti-Marxists never tire of bringing up is that socialist revolution hasn't come about in the "advanced" societies of Europe, where Marx implied it would. Instead it's happened only in backward nations like Russia, China, Vietnam, Cuba . . . Well, there's lots swept under the rug here (see next paragraph), but for now I'll just say this: that these revolutions took place at all, against such odds, is no small matter, though their self-evident existence leads us to forget they happened. And their making was just as Marx outlined it. China, a pretty good example of an "advanced" civilization (even if non-white), had become totally "proletarianized" by Western capitalism and later by the Japanese militarists. (The same applies to Vietnam.) Cuba, among the more "advanced" countries in the Caribbean, had been "proletarianized" by U.S. business. If capitalism can ignore national boundaries and spread overseas, then so can the twin dynamics of class struggle and revolution. (Regarding 1917: the Romanov Empire, where there had been massive European investment, then found itself up for grabs by whatever group commanded the most effective tactics and mass support.) To predict a species of event and then have it come to life someplace is already to be partly right. To fail to predict the exact time and location of the event is a lesser fault. After all, meteorologists, seismologists, market-researchers, and high-paid generals do it all the time.

And indeed, what about the revolution which hasn't come about in Europe? And what about Fascism, which (I've often heard said) Marx "didn't predict."

Actually, the first dirty little secret is that the Revolutionary left has scored several victories across Europe during the last century: the Paris Commune in 1871; Bela Kun in Hungary, and Rosa Luxemburg and the German Spartacists in 1919; the Left's sweeping electoral victory in most of Spain in 1936; Tito's partisan's throwing off Nazism in 1944; and the Greek guerrillas in 1946. Tito's excepted, these revolutions were ruthlessly crushed either by local reactionaries or by invaders from Antonescu's Rumania, Hitler's Germany, or Churchill's Britain, which repression was applauded by Western center-right forces! In brief: the wise men who claim Marx was wrong are the same ones who've done everything possible to overthrow and bump off mass activists who prove too well that Marx was right!

Dirty little secret no. 2 (which is the flipside of no. 1): Fascism has always emerged in reaction to threats to capitalism from the left. Growing worker agitation in Italy drove Mussolini to seize power and smash the militant unions. Germany in 1932 was more or less divided between left and right parties; Hitler's first major repressive measure in 1933 was to destroy the German Communist Party and send its members to Dachau. Many anti-Marxists thought this a Good Thing. TIME-LIFE tycoon Henry Luce, for example, visited Germany in 1934 and praised Hitler for ending class war. At the Nuremberg Trials, twelve years after Luce's junket, Hitler's finance minister Hjalmar Schacht was to justify his own complicity on the grounds that, were it not for Nazism, Germany would have fallen "to the left, to Communism." I suspect a lot of people out there breathe an approving sigh of relief with Herr Doktor Schacht . . .

Dirty little secret no.3 is that Hitler's and Mussolini's empire-building responded to the same insatiable drives that stood behind EuroAmerican empire-building: the search for more land, more raw materials, more markets, more and cheaper labor (slave labor in the case of Confederacy and Reich). In the late 1930s, Germany was the West's richest nation. And in 1939-41, German business experienced phenomenal growth. (Guess why!) Which brings us to Western "prosperity": among the unexamined bases for the affluence of American workers is the control that U.S. power exerts over the globe's primary products. Fully half of the materials that go into the making of a Cadillac comes from abroad—and comes cheap. As Marx said, capitalism cannot survive without growth; and the most logical setting for it to grow is . . . elsewhere, especially if that elsewhere consists of weak, defenseless nations. So you invent an external enemy and whip things up for war! It's the oldest trick in the street hustler's book: steer attention away from what's at hand. "Hey, man, look over there . . ." Zap!

What clearly emerges, then, is that Marx was so on-target about future events that the capitalist system has since done all it can to forestall, conceal, or openly combat those predictions. And though Marx admittedly didn't foresee that fascism would be welcomed by businessmen (i.e. failed to recognize businessmen's tolerance for absolute evil), their last-ditch solution is an expected, "predictable" response. Most anyone who sees a possible threat gestating somewhere will inevitably take measures against that threat. To take an analogy: suppose a chicken farmer finds out that the nearby woods hold foxes. He thereby "predicts" that the foxes will go after his poultry. To counteract Fox Power, he builds a chicken-wire fence. He sets up fox-traps about the chicken coop, as many as he can afford. He posts a few Dobermans (his security forces), the more vicious and bloodthirsty the better. One night he hears foxes breaking into the coop. He leaps out of bed, grabs his shotgun, rushes over to the window and takes aim—bang!— shooing off a fox, blasting another to bits, and accidentally wounding a couple of hens in the process . . .

The doltish need not take my fable too literally: workers most emphatically are not chickens, nor do Marxists belong to the vulpine mammals genus. The chief difference, however, is that the Chickenologist does not hire learned experts in Fox Science to write thick books demonstrating that "Vulpinist predictions of a coming triumph of Foxism over Chickens have not materialized, and are thus proven false." By contrast, most of Western and 99 percent of American "intellectual" life is one long footnote to Marxism, in the sense that tens of thousands of "thinkers" are engaged in a vast, century-old attempt to overshadow, discredit, "refute," or otherwise show that we can explain our lives without Marx. The chicken farmer need not convince anyone of his rightness. He knows that, so long as he has his shotguns, fences, and dogs, he will prevail and the foxes won't win . . . (END)

Leave it to Charlie, as they say. Only someone who'd accepted Marxist ideology to the hilt would go so far as to defend its crystal ball even where history had proved it wrong! And the idea of a vast intellectual conspiracy to "refute" Marx simply staggers the imagination. But then Charlie had closed himself to all other views, to the point where he couldn't see anything else, least of all what was before him.

This came through most clearly during his "junket" through Iron Curtain totalitarianism. Unlike most normal folks who perceive all too clearly the scarcities and horrors of life under Communism, Charlie sent me rave reports with no attempt at evenhanded balance between good and bad, and claimed to see no Latin-type poverty or starvation there. When I asked him why Polish workers rose up in revolt in 1970, he replied that it was because they wanted more than they already had! What was eerie, though, was the way Charlie would compare Poland or Hungary not to the United States, as everyone does, but to Venezuela! Really, it seems to me there should be some set of universal values we can go by, instead of everybody just taking up any old yardstick of his arbitrary choosing.

Chapter 7

The pattern was too uncanny for comfort. The one Richie I met up with when going for my bags at Albany Airport was Charlie Chadwick. His new-grown shoulder-length hair gave him an almost Indian aspect. And instead of jeans or corduroys he was wearing olive-drab fatigues of the kind associated with the PMF.

It was this person I now saw exit from the little burger-and-franks joint and nod at me in silence. Strolling at my side, he said softly, "Hi."

I gazed straight ahead as I marched toward the baggage area.

"Well, Livie Kingsley," he said, "not saying hello anymore?"

Feeling puzzled and a bit annoyed, I frowned and glanced sideways. It took me a few seconds to recognize him.

"Charlie!" I gasped, stopping in my tracks. We'd reached the luggage carousel. His new "look" reminded me of some migrant Mexicans I'd seen around Ohio.

He grinned ever so slightly at my delayed response. "By the way," he interjected, watching the first suitcases come down the ramp, "it's Carlos."

"How's that now?"

He reflected. "The name isn't Charlie. It's Carlos."

"Oh, I see." Pause. "Well, so why the name change?"

"No change." Deadpan expression. "It's my real name."

It had been a while, but I now remembered. The College Directory always listed him as "Chadwick, Carlos José." I'd asked about it soon after we'd first met, and he explained, "Oh, that's just the name I got at baptism."

I'd never given it any thought since then. At Richards your full given name was something seen and not heard. I knew enough Richies whose foreign or biblical names had long ago been scrapped for monosyllables like Cal or Mal or Skip or Chip. My neighbor from freshman year was listed as Marie-Augusta Belfiore, though you'd never guess, inasmuch as its melody was reduced by all to "Mab" or "Mabbie." I don't think I heard anyone at Richards call me "Olivia" until graduation ceremonies, when we were marching one by one onstage, solemn in our green robes, and the Dean said my full name and announced my summa as he handed me my sheepskin.

And here a Richie was reverting to his "real" first name.

Carlos (as I'll refer to him now) read my predictable thoughts and added with a chuckle, "I could go by 'Carlos José,' but no Richie could pronounce it."

I asked him if he was glad to be back.

He answered simply, "No."

We headed for the limousine, handed the chauffeur our bags, and climbed into the middle seat. We were the sole passengers.

"And how was Paris?"

"Quite a place," was his answer, followed by silence.

The limousine had left Albany's outskirts and was nearing the Berkshire foothills. I asked him about his month home.

"Real bad and real good." Only now did he start opening up and mention the family feuds, the disputes with his dad over Vietnam and Peru and Marxism, and the vicious quarrels over which is better, Europe or the United States. Whenever he praised

France his mom seems to have cautiously taken Carlos's side, but if he chanced to defend the PMF, she'd withdraw, letting father and son fight it out. On the other hand Carlos reported having made some new friends in Caracas, leftists apparently, though on that score he was pretty vague.

Carlos's speech made me uneasy. While in his letters I'd indirectly witnessed the metamorphosis he'd undergone during the last year, the experience of now actually seeing and hearing him surpassed any notions I'd entertained about just how much the old "Charlie" differed from the new "Carlos." Where the one had never talked or thought politics, the other seemed to have little else on his mind. Add to that the physical change and you'll get some idea of my feeling throughout the 50-minute ride. Oh, certainly, up at Richards some guy might complain about family tensions, but none had come so close to breaking with Pop just over politics, let alone geography. After all, few of us spend much of our college careers outside Richards. We figure, if Richards is just about the best school in the world, why bother taking courses someplace else? So any differences we might have with our parents come out in other areas—say Democrat versus Republican, Eastern versus Midwestern. There's not much question of radically opposed ways of life.

And now here was Carlos talking about a possible total rift, with his father particularly.

The limo turned the sharp curve where you get your first glimpses of the bright white spire of one of the Richards-New Ashford churches. The late afternoon silences out there seemed total. A few minutes went by; some college buildings now loomed over the hill. Two male Richies in gym shorts jogged past us at our right, waving at me enthusiastically. I believe I recognized them.

Carlos exhaled noisily, then mumbled, "It's God-awful."

I knew but inquired all the same, "What is?"

He pointed with his hand. "This place is. It's God-awful."

And I just couldn't get over it. Charlie, who had seen himself as attending Pa's and Grandpa's school and feeling like one of the

Richards "boys" in ways that I obviously never could have, was now Carlos, going to extremes in despising the whole thing.

By now we'd arrived at the limousine stop across from the western edge of campus. The car came to a sudden halt; the driver barked vigorously, "Richards-New Ashford."

What was left of our conversation also reached an abrupt halt as we shuffled out into the street. The bearded chauffeur unloaded Carlos's bags, then handed me mine with a smile. I got a good grip on my garment bag and leather suitcase and turned around. Carlos was standing ten yards off, hands in pockets and legs apart, staring at me with that defiant new stare of his.

"Going for your keys?"

I grinned. "Yes, I am."

We walked the few blocks up to Buildings and Grounds, stopping on occasions to lay down our bags and rest our hands. Save for a stray reference to balmy weather and crickets, there seemed to be nothing to say en route. We got our keys from a jolly lady with a French name who gave us a warm "Welcome back!"

I thanked her and smiled; Carlos moved on morosely. He and I then exited together through the plate glass double doors. Without so much as looking my way, he turned left and blurted out, "Well, see you later." I assumed he was heading toward Babcock.

"Oh, yes, well, goodbye, Cha..., I mean, Carlos." As I trod uphill toward Park-Davies I felt quite disturbed by the drastic change, everything from the name to the negativism.

I saw little of Carlos that September. Through the gossip mill I heard he'd been eating at odd hours. Much to my surprise he had also quit the RCO, so I wasn't running into him on Thursdays. At our first rehearsal that year, however, as I stood poised to read the flute solo for the Bach *Second Suite*, I looked up from my music stand and caught sight of Carlos Chadwick, sitting in a dark and distant back row of Putney. Faithfully he stayed through my, or rather our, initial read-through of the *Suite*, his legs propped on the pew in front of him, and when I reached the end of the finale I think he may have flashed me the thumbs-up sign, though I wasn't sure.

At Babcock, I heard, he'd been returning his housemates' silent treatment with a ruthless consistency, and from afar I saw him occasionally, conversing with some campus radical or trekking to the library with the now-late Marta Colón. As for yours truly, I was busy applying to journalism schools and spending weekends in New Haven, marking time to see which way things were to go with Doug.

Toward Thanksgiving I saw Carlos in a corner booth at the library snack bar, sitting alone. He had both legs up on the bench and appeared to have gone further in his "metamorphosis." A few Richies like sporting well-groomed beards or mustaches, but Carlos's unshaven face had a look that was simply scruffy. His PMF fatigues had also gotten messier.

He stared up from his book and said nothing as I approached. With my most cheerful air I greeted him, "Hi, Carlos."

It was almost a new voice that replied "Hello." Of course he was reading something called *For Marx*, by some German.

I now noted that he had a slender brown cigarillo between his second and middle fingers. He took a puff.

"May I join you for a few minutes?" I asked.

"Yeah, go ahead."

I detected a slight note of sardonicism, and so, touching his right arm lightly, I asked, "Are you all right, Carlos?"

"I'm perfectly fine," he answered, withdrawing his arm and flicking some ashes. He kept his feet up on the bench and stared off in space, giving me a stubbly profile to look at.

Time was ticking by, and I didn't have all day, and I remarked to him, "Haven't seen you around in quite a while."

He took another puff, blew out a mini-cumulus cloud. "Yeah, I've been staying away from this place all I can."

"Do you attend classes?"

He shrugged a shoulder. "That's the one thing I do here."

I didn't inquire about campus social life since everyone knew he'd turned his back on *that* entire business.

He laid down his cigarillo. "And what've *you* been up to? Feeling the pinch of senioritis?"

I smiled, then mentioned journalism schools, maybe a newspaper job, it all depends, etc. "How about you?" He had asked me the question we seniors hear every day, and I reciprocated with a "What're you doing after you graduate?"

Both his shoulders shrugged now. "Don't really know. Maybe go to France, study Marxism." More ashes for the ashtray.

"You're really involved with Marxist ideology, aren't you?"

Another puff, and a nod. "If that's what you like calling it, yes, I am."

"Why France, though?"

"People teach it and read it there."

"So? People teach it and read it here too."

He smiled, a bit smugly. "At Richards? No way."

I believe he'd misunderstood my remark, but I continued, "Well, look, there's Mr. Schiffmann in Philosophy."

"One." He gestured with his right thumb.

"Well, Carlos, just what is it you want, then?"

"Seems like there could be more than one Marxist prof." He flicked some ashes into his empty coffee cup. "Why not have five? Or ten?"

His cocky attitude was beginning to unnerve me. "Please tell me why." I paused a few seconds, got no answer. "Since when does any view whatsoever enjoy a monopoly on truth? There's no such thing as a privileged outlook."

He made a grotesque face, then responded emphatically. "We're enrolled in what is supposed to be a high-quality school, in a so-called 'advanced' country." He raised his cigarillo hand and pronounced in a nya-nya-nya sort of voice, "'Fifth-highest admissions standards in the United States,' as they like reminding us here. Well, big deal. So why does a major way of thinking have exactly one, and just *one*, representative at this great American college of ours?"

His speech was thick with sarcasm. I was determined to avoid stooping to his level.

"It's *not* 'major,' Carlos." I kept my cool. "It's just one point of view like any other."

"What do you mean, 'like any other'?"

"It's just a perspective. There's many possible perspectives and they're all equally right."

Fixing his glance on the cigarillo poised on the ashtray, he let out an odd guffaw. "You don't think some ideas might be better than others?"

"Every idea has something to offer."

"What about Hitler's ideas, f'r instance? What do *his* ideas have to offer?"

I paused and mulled over his question for a moment. "That's different."

"And how? Is it maybe because Hitler's ideas were worthless and wrong?"

"Carlos, you're absolute. Nobody's really 'wrong' as you say. Someone might present a well-reasoned pro-Hitler argument. Then it would have something to offer."

"O.K., What about the argument that women are mentally inferior to men?"

"Now wait a second..."

"Aha, see...?"

"Carlos, that's a prejudice, not an idea..." I tried to elaborate my point but he kept bulldozing ahead.

"Yeah, see? There *are* some ideas you won't accept..."

"I will not accept an idea that is prejudicial to me and..."

"Hey, wait, I thought you said there's something to offer in any idea? Well, then, why doesn't our dear Richards College have more Marxist teachers?"

It seemed futile, but I tried to reason with the guy. "Richards offers a bit of everything. It's like a supermarket. You know, John Stuart Mill and the marketplace of ideas."

There exists an arrogant, dismissive laugh which, both around

Richards and elsewhere, I've found to be typical of male radicals I've met. Carlos now laughed that laugh. ("Marketplace! That's a good one! Ha!") I stared at him silently. His laughter died down as I kept staring.

He finally turned civilized and asked what I'd been doing.

I mentioned my involvement with Young ADA politics, my working to try to get more Democrats into office.

"D'you really think it would make much difference?" Now for the first time Carlos started talking earnestly.

"More Democrats in Congress would get us out of Peru and avoid future mistakes."

Carlos blew on his lips, like horses do. "The war is no mistake."

"And what do you mean by that?"

"The U.S. wanted war. The mistake was inability to win."

"Really, now, Carlos, why should United States *want* war?"

"Why else?" He took a deep breath and began rattling off his alleged "explanations," gesturing with his fingers for each one. "There's the military industries. There's access to raw materials. And there's the need to protect U.S. investments."

I couldn't help raising my voice. "Markets? Investments? Carlos, that's absurd! You're not going to sit there and tell me we've expended all that blood and treasure just to save a few investments in little old Peru."

"Peru *is* 'old,' Livie, though 'little' it's not. Anyway the guys who control the American empire" (that was his exact word) "know that if they lose Peru to U.S. investment, then other countries might drift away too. So you've got the Pentagon and the CIA serving as a global police force." He stopped.

"Are you done?"

"Yes."

"Carlos, there *is* no American 'empire,' as you call it, except maybe in your mind. I've heard those leftist theories before, and I just don't buy them. Everything gets reduced to an economic conspiracy. You know, people also fight wars because they have ideals. And I believe we got sucked into the Peruvian war so we could defend our ideals of open-mindedness and free expression. We've tragically misapplied those ideals, but I don't think you can deny the Soviet threat."

Carlos's closed-mindedness now came forth with a vengeance. "BULL SHIT," he growled. The two couples at a neighboring table looked over and, amused, grinned. Carlos ignored them. "Livie, there are no Russian combat troops in all of South America." He snorted contemptuously. "The Soviet threat. The magic formula of all the right-wingers. It's false and that's that."

"Well, you're as wrong as all those right-wingers. They see Communist conspiracies everywhere, you see capitalist ones. You're both extremists and both equally wrong."

"Oh, come on, Livie, American business is *everywhere*. Russian soldiers aren't."

"There are Russian troops in Cuba."

"And there's hundreds of billions of U.S. dollars invested all over the fuckin' globe. Those investments add up to the world's fourth largest economy, after the U.S., Russia, and Japan. If a single *nation* were the world's fourth economy, d'you think they'd tolerate a Marxist revolt in any of its provinces?"

I couldn't take his economic obsessions. "Well, Carlos, you've got to consider other reasons for the war."

"Like what?" he asked defiantly.

"Technology, for example. Once you have all that technology at your disposal, it takes on a life of its own."

"That's like the bully who says, 'Hey, I didn't hit him, my baseball bat did!'"

I just about shook my head in frustration. "Carlos, you've got these quickie comebacks. You keep twisting and distorting everything I say. And I don't like it." But I held back my irritation in order to marshal further points. "Anyway, the Peruvian war has psychological roots too."

"And what is it this time?" he smirked.

"Well, it's been said that the President feels insecure. So the war's a way for him to prove he's tough and *macho.*"

Carlos snapped right back. "Would you apply that to every single president who's sent troops down there since 1840?"

"No, but why not to *this* president?"

"The U.S. has invaded Latin America some seventy-five times, usually to protect U.S. business interests. Why should it be any different this time 'round?"

"Things *are* different now, Carlos. We live in post-industrial society."

"And what does that fancy phrase mean?"

"Our economy is rapidly shifting from manufacturing to services. So there's much less need for overseas investment."

"Ha! That's a laugh! Do you know why there's a shift from manufacturing? 'Cause U.S. industries are fleeing lock, stock and barrel to Haiti, Singapore, and Taiwan, where the labor is fuckin' cheap." He paused, his eyes lit up, and he added, "To cite small, tropical islands only."

"There you go again. All you think about is money. Well, my friend Doug is chief researcher for Young ADA, and his statistics demonstrate that Latin America and the Third World are un-necessary for United States investment. Look, we've got at least ten times more money invested in Europe than in South America. So why aren't we at war over *there*?"

"You've forgotten, Liv, the U.S. has half a million troops over *there*. But you tell me now, if Peru isn't all that important, as you say, then why the hell is Washington sending bomber pilots down *there*?" He pointed south.

"Because the President has some ignorant advisers who aren't aware of the latest data on Latin America."

"And pray tell, why, if American companies don't need Peru, why oh why do they support that dirty little war?"

"What you're saying simply isn't true, Carlos. Look at International Computers. Its chairman recently criticized the war and said we should negotiate a withdrawal."

Carlos now got heated as his absolutist view faced challenges.

He raised his index finger and snarled, "ONE company."

"Well, you just said American business favors the war in Peru. That's clearly inaccurate."

With an impatient gesture he replied, pedantically, "O.K., so 99.9 percent of American business supports the war. Why?"

"Again, they lack the proper information. That's why Doug and other ADA people have been approaching executives to persuade them about disinvesting from Latin America."

"Per*suade* you say?" Carlos almost shouted. "You think those guys are persuadable?"

"There's no better way." I smiled. "What do *you* suggest? Picket lines? Anyway, Doug is very good at persuasion."

He put his hand on his forehead, shook his head, whispered, "Oh, boy," and tittered with his lips still tight. "So Doug can persuade people, eh? How is Doug, by the way?"

"He's fine."

Fidgeting, Carlos again stretched his legs out on the bench, leaning against the wall. "I'm surprised it's lasted this long."

"And why do you say that?"

"I'm just surprised. You mean you haven't found some other guy lately?"

"Now, now, Carlos, let's not start sounding like a bitter little boy."

His shoulders twitched as he looked down at the table, putting out his cigarillo. "Well, so how's things with Doug?"

"Fine. I'm very happy." There was a brief silence.

"Getting married?" he asked softly.

"It's none of your business, but no, I'm not."

His voice suddenly showed great concern. "Oh, that's too bad. And why not?"

"Doug doesn't want to."

Now he looked up and, with a smirk that was plainly gleeful, stared me in the eyes. "Hmm. I see. Very interesting."

"And what, pray tell, is 'very interesting'?"

"Well, you've just explained why things lasted with Doug.

Rejection. *Bonnie and Clyde*, remember?"

I felt as if I'd been tricked, and my blood neared a slow boil, but I spoke softly. "Look here, Carlos Chadwick, or whatever it is you're calling yourself these days. I sat down here for a friendly chat. The last thing I expected was for you to insult me and say I'm sick."

"Hey, wait a second, you're putting words in my mouth. I *never* said 'sick' or . . ."

I resisted gritting my teeth as I raised my voice just sufficiently. "You seem to think your leftist ideology gives you *carte blanche* to be obnoxious."

He waved his hand aside, saying, "Oh, Livie, you're so full of it." Shrugging his shoulders maybe for a tenth time, he added, "You American liberals are all so full of it."

"You've become terribly fond of labels." Getting up, I tossed my cup and spoon into the nearby trash bin.

A redheaded guy at the next table remarked supportively, "Hey, Liv, fanatics are fanatics, you're wasting your time." His woman friend interjected, "Yeah, it's hopeless, why bother?"

"Fanatic *is* the word," I replied. I saw no point in bidding Carlos goodbye as I headed upstairs and on to the newsroom.

After settling in I reflected with disbelief on how totally Carlos had changed, just how far along he'd gone in becoming an arrogant ideologue. Feeling high on the wine of Marxism and its alleged ability to "explain" everything, he'd taken to making claims so vast and exaggerated as to appear laughable, and unless someone agreed with his rigid ideology, he'd cut the discussion short with rude phrases like "You're simply wrong," or his standby, the vulgarism, "You're so full of it." But any time a more open-minded Richie would question these dogmas and reason with him for a more balanced view, he'd inevitably turn insistent, vocal, his vehemence and anger covering up for his lack of flexibility.

Again, though, when you come down to it, I think Carlos's anger grew largely out of his disappointment with Richards. For one, he had come back terribly enamored of Marxist lingo, and not being able to hear more of it around his alma mater is what frustrated him. Richards of course offers no special privileges to ideology but, had our school been more indulgent with the true believers and dogged followers of Karl Marx, "Charlie" Chadwick might very well have stayed on as a dedicated Richie and blissful graduating senior, and then duly gone back to Papa Chadwick's business in Venezuela.

Chapter 8

The last extended encounter I had with Carlos took place in mid-February. It was a follow-up to my J.I. project, a Richards opinion survey I had completed on the week-long bombardment of military targets near Cuzco, Arequipa, and Ayacucho. To gauge views around campus I had a team of *Booster* volunteers poll some 400 Richies. The results were 52 percent in favor, 42 percent against, and 6 percent undecided. Those opposed cited exclusively moral reasons; only a few leftists believed the PMF was right and should win the war.

So we printed the results, and next day we got this brief Letter to the Editor saying, *"I note that close to 60 percent of Richards students (a typical exaggeration) favor the fascist bombing of Peru. Well, folks, I feel compelled to inform you that more than 60 percent of South Americans favor the reciprocal bombing of fascist Richies. "* (Signed) *Carlos Chadwick.*

Carlos's bombing fantasies appear all too prophetic now. But at the time I saw nothing wrong in principle with printing his letter, though *Booster* staff did divide evenly and bitterly on running it. Eventually we did, and in an accompanying note I took sole responsibility as Editor-in-Chief. Criticism came promptly and furiously from all quarters, but the negative reactions and emotion-alism scarcely worried me since I felt right in airing Carlos's views, hate-filled and repellent though they may be. Those ideas are out there—shouldn't they be recognized? Still, inasmuch as the

Peruvian war was giving rise to increasingly irrational attitudes on campus, I thought I might get a good feature article out of interviews with people from both extremes—the rightists who enthusiastically favored "atomizing Peru" (in one letter-writer's quaint phrase) and the leftists openly sympathetic to the PMF.

The day of my appointment with the Radcliff Road people was a frozen, still, cobalt-blue afternoon. There was no breeze as I trudged up to the big yellow house. The wooden stairs were slick with uneven ice cover. Tacked onto the door was a note saying, *"LIV—COME RIGHT IN. BACK SHORTLY."*

The door scraped and squeaked. My footsteps echoed as I ambled through the spacious and disorderly living room. I sought out the kitchen. Last night's dishes were piled high in the sink. A sad brown mutt was snoozing idly in the corner. From nowhere a yellow cat appeared, meowed once, rubbed against my leg (I felt almost nothing through my suede boot and thick levis) and then scurried off quietly. I plucked a plastic glass out of the drainer, filled it with tap water, took a sip, and saw something unsettling. Taped visibly on the refrigerator door there was the famous wire-photo of a PMF woman pointing her machine gun at a downed United States pilot, a crew-cutted giant twice as big as she, with his back to her, his arms up and head down. Somebody—I have two guesses as to who—had scribbled something in Spanish across the picture. On the opposite wall I noticed a homemade dart board, its playing surface crudely composed of drawings of United States government officials, business leaders, an army general, and photographs of two downed pilots. There were darts sticking into most every picture.

Yes, it all faintly disturbed me. On a shelf a few feet up from the mutt I detected a small radio. I flicked it on and got Amherst NPR. They were playing some Sibelius; it was soothing. The mutt glanced up slowly, stretched and dozed off again. The cat seemed to have disappeared. Laurie later informed me that the dartboard was Carlos's idea. Only Marta actually favored this decor; the others found it unattractive and even, in Jake's words, "just a bit sick," though they all would admit to playing with the darts occasionally.

As I walked back toward the living room I heard footsteps on the porch stairs. Carlos came in puffing and took off his shoes. I'd left my boots on, it was just too cold. He caught sight of me sitting on the arm of the sofa. "Well, well," were his words.

I asked about the pictures and the wirephoto.

He chuckled. "Oh, yeah. Feels good to see those bullies getting it. 'Specially after all the killing they've done."

I felt it important to be reasonable. "You're glorying in someone else's suffering."

"What the hell, they glory in their bombing."

"How so?"

"I mean, like they *enjoy* dropping bombs."

"Are you so sure about that? What's your source?"

He sighed impatiently. "My source." He reached into his down jacket and dug out a *Newsweek* clipping. "Here, Livie, is my source, as you say." He unfolded it and handed it to me brusquely. "Get the headline," he snapped.

"BOMBER PILOTS—PLEASED WITH THEIR JOBS," it stated.

"Go on, read it."

I settled onto the sofa, crossed my legs, and skimmed through the piece. It wasn't pleasant reading. Yes, indeed, here was a *Newsweek* correspondent talking to United States pilots then active over Peru. One pilot was quoted as saying, "I love to bomb!" Another allegedly rhapsodized, "There's nothing more beautiful than bombs going off. The patterns, the color, they're gorgeous! Just like a Fourth of July fireworks display." A young ace admitted to feeling both gung-ho and cowardly: "Everybody here likes getting a piece of the action over the Andes. None of us wants to get shot at, though." Still another showed a vengeful streak: "Whenever I see anti-aircraft rockets coming my way, I feel I could make beef stew out of those sneaky little spics, or whatever it is they are."

I frowned, nearly shuddered as I folded the clipping. "What I cannot figure out," I mused as I handed it back to Carlos, "is how anybody can feel such hate."

"Bah, most of those guys don't feel *anything*. To them it's just fun and games, like a panty raid. What d'you expect from fascists?"

A few seconds of silence rushed by.

"Now you're showing the same hatred they do."

"No, Livie, I am not a hired killer. They are."

I wondered out loud, less to Carlos than to myself, "Why is there so much hate in the world? It doesn't make sense. I don't want to hurt anybody. Why hate another human being?"

He made a hissing sound and said, "What about hating fascists? Does that make sense?"

"The fascists were immoral, but that was years ago. Really, why hate? I can't see much of a point to it."

"Oh, Jesus, this is like Lieutenant Pinkerton again."

"Pinkerton?" I had to think hard to guess what he was driving at. I thought maybe he meant the detective agency.

"You know," he said, "it's easy to feel self-righteous about other people's hatred when no one's ever done you wrong."

"Carlos, I beg your pardon, I came here to interview the residents of this house, not to get a lecture from you."

"No, really, you rich WASPs can be so lofty and high-toned" (he put his nose up in the air) "about the anger of the oppressed when nobody's fire-bombing your homes . . ."

"Just a second . . ."

". . . or poisoning your crops . . ."

"Will you stop?"

He pointed at me. "When nobody's ever even *ditched* you."

He finally stopped.

"Listen to me." I put on my coolest, edgiest, and most business-like voice. "Don't you give me this left-wing Billy Sunday stuff. We're not here to thrash out my personal life or your old feelings. That's ancient history and I've forgotten all about it.

It's high time you forgot about it too."

We sat there in complete silence for who knows how long. Finally I took out pad and pencil, tested my brand-new recorder, and said, "I'm trying to get far Left and far Right opinion on the United States escalation of the bombing in Peru. I'd like to ask about your view of the President's action."

I could see his lips curling into a little smirk. "Mm-hmm. Interesting. Why ask *me*, though?"

"I've told you. I'm polling far Left opinion on the expanded United States bombing of Peru."

He smiled wider and smirkier. "I'm not on the far Left."

I tapped pencil on pad, took a deep breath, looked up at the ceiling. "Oh, God, really. Come *on*, Carlos."

"Hey, wait, I'm serious, it's true. I'm on the Left, but that's not the same thing. Left isn't far left."

"Okay, okay, so the *Booster* would like to know what *you*, as a student on the *left*, think about the bombing of enemy positions around Cuzco, Arequipa, and Ayacucho."

"The bombing of *what*?"

I repeated my statement.

"Oh," he said smugly, "I didn't realize they were enemy positions."

If he was expecting a reaction from me, he didn't get it.

Finally he said, "Well, you know what I think."

"Say it then."

"Come up to my room." He got up in a jump. I followed him to the top of the wide stairway. His room in Babcock House had been fairly neat; this one had books, pamphlets, and leftist magazines all over the floor. "Have a seat," he signalled.

I set up the recorder and sat down in a faded round wicker chair, writing pad and pencil on my lap. He was poised on the edge of the mattress.

"What do I think of the bombing? I think it's one of the vilest spectacles imaginable, those overfed blond boys razing peasant villages. And I hope the Peruvians shoot them all down and execute them in public."

The tape spun on, and I wrote silently. There was pure hate in his voice.

I heard the sounds of people entering the foyer, someone's boots dropping onto the floor, plunk plunk, and Laurie's voice shouting, "Jesus, it's cold."

Carlos stopped for a moment. I noticed that tacked onto his bulletin board there was a news photo of the crew of a recently downed United States Air Force jet. Underneath the picture of the three POW's he'd scribbled, "Feel so tough now, flyboy?"

He raved on. "I only wish the PMF had planes so they could bomb a few gringo Air Force bases and maybe a U.S. village or two and give these imperialists a taste of their own medicine."

"Have you ever attempted a more balanced view?"

He looked at me, smirked again, and gestured toward the bulletin board.

I added, "As you know, there are always two sides. And one side argues that we're fighting down there so you'll have the right to say whatever you want."

"What is your question?"

"The question is, suppose the war is being fought to further freedom of expression."

"And why isn't the Pentagon fighting for freedom of expression in fascist Chile or Guatemala?"

"It's terribly complicated, I know, but we've got to start somewhere."

"Well, suppose *I* say those Peruvians are fighting not for freedom of expression but for land and food and life?"

"Don't you find that terribly materialistic? There's more to life than just stuffing your belly."

He sat there smug and self-assured, refusing to answer.

Having gotten all I needed from him I said, "Thank you, Charl— Carlos. Much appreciated."

He still said nothing as I slipped pencil inside the ring of the pad, turned off my cassette, and slowly marched out from his room. It was the next-to-last time I saw him.

Downstairs I found his roommates sitting around the living room, taking in the toasty fire. Already they were on the subject of the expanded bombing, and since it dovetailed nicely with my idea for a group interview, I got permission from them to run the tape recorder. From time to time I'd ask my set questions, and I'll admit that in those forty minutes (I had to flip the cassette once) I heard very little hate in their voices, none whatever in the case of Jake or Paul. But, like Carlos, they didn't feel unhappy about United States aircraft being shot down by the PMF, and Marta positively rejoiced at the idea of Phantom jet pilots being taken prisoner. (I won't dwell on the matters of poetic justice and Marta's tragic fate.) And all were convinced that the guerrillas were right and United States wrong—black and white, with no grays, no gradations in between. Such was the thinking in the house on Radcliff Road.

The experience of overhearing these ideas (or emotions rather, since I found little rational content to them) had an unsettling effect on me. Never before had I heard Richies actually rejoice in the destruction of American property, much less applaude United States military casualties. Really, I'd always thought of such sentiments as the stuff exclusively of Third World terrorists and fanatics. Oh, sure, in some metaphysical way I could understand the frustration of these fellow Richies, in spite of their being far Left, but somehow they'd coldly and callously lost sight of a simple, undeniable fact: namely, that our Air Force pilot is a human being every bit as much as a Peruvian peasant is, and that he too possesses such basic rights as life, liberty, and the pursuit of happiness in a career of his choosing, in short that he too is a victim of war. I nonetheless remained cool and kept my personal feelings to myself.

I must say, though, that I do take friendly issue with Fred Jennings's romanticized portrait of the Radcliff Road radicals. Presumably his aim is to indulge them with the benefit of the doubt when he characterizes them as "scholarly types," "frustrated professors" who liked collecting labor posters, holding Marxist study groups, and leading ye olde communal lifestyle. It's an idyllic view, and all that sort of thing might be fine and dandy. But as their peer, what *I* saw during my visit was a hardened clique of selfish, inflexible, coldhearted ideologues who feel no loyalty to America's uniqueness, and who are ultimately interested neither in ideas nor intellect—but in *power*. I'm not attributing the college bombings to them, but I would venture to say that, if given any responsibility for other individuals, they'd prove purely exploitative and do loads of harm. Of course this is meant not as a personal criticism of Mr. Jennings and his superb journalistic skills but as a corrective counterview to balance out his picture a wee bit. I can't exactly put my finger on it, but there was something profoundly ruthless about Carlos's cronies, a disturbing lack of compassion. And I feel called upon to single out their ruthlessness.

Having obtained more than enough material from the far left, I spent several days interviewing far right Richies who favored expanded bombing. They tended to live in separate individual suites around campus, and it took me longer to sample their opinions. A couple of guys worked so hard and constantly that they agreed to a quickie interview only at lunchtime or while walking from point A to point B.

Once I got them to talk, they showed little emotionalism or hysteria, and the contrast to Carlos's white-hot hate was refreshing. Calmly they dwelt on the threat of Marxism, the dangers of Kremlin penetration of the Americas, the fact that PMF chieftain Hugo Soto had studied in Budapest, and the way that the PMF was exploiting peasants for its own selfish ends, brainwashing them with fanatical slogans about "Yankee imperialism." Occasionally the rightwingers made a stray reference to "commies" but their attitude was impersonal rather than angry. I caught just one rejoicing note: a short, wiry, dark-haired fellow I buttonholed en route to the gym, who answered my first question with "Bombs away! Hooray!" and promptly rushed off. More typical, however, was the President of Richards Libertarians, who gave me a cool and logically reasoned deduction to the effect that aerial bombardment of Peru was *protecting* American freedoms, for otherwise draftee troops would have to be sent to the Andes, and he was completely against reviving the draft. Hence the bombing of Peru was saving lives and liberties, not taking them.

It was an unusual but interesting way of thinking, concerned yet rational.

Chapter 9

I never again chatted with Carlos, except for perfunctory greetings and one distasteful group incident. A couple of days after the Marine landing in Mayagüez, I see Carlos and Marta come running into the newsroom, out of breath. They rush up to my desk and without further ado ask me to run an in-depth story they'd co-authored on the Puerto Rican affair. More than once they referred to alleged "brutalization" of the locals by the American troops.

"Well," I answer after hearing them out, "a guy on our staff is already putting together an analytical piece."

After an awkward silence Marta interjects, "Hey, yeah, but, look, I'm Puerto Rican, from Ponce, and I can give you an insider's perspective." She elaborates on this for a minute.

I can't be sure whether her presumed insider's view would be sufficiently balanced, and I inform her so.

"Balanced?" Carlos now breaks in. "Livie, how do you show balance about a God-damned invasion?"

"It is our aim to present the news free of bias. The *Booster* is not a party newspaper. Will your story show both sides?"

Now I get this cold stare, then vociferous oratory, from Marta. "Look here, I have *no* reason to show both sides. The U.S. media show the Yankee side *every day*. I want to explain my side." She waves her arms frenetically, emphasizing her words.

"I'm sorry, that is propaganda. I cannot accept it."

"Livie, listen, this is your chance to get a Puerto Rican look at the events."

"I'd be getting a one-sided look, and a hard-line one at that. It'd give the impression that it's the only valid viewpoint, the 'real' truth, as if there's any such thing." I paused a moment. "I'm sorry, the answer is no." I reflected and added, "You're always free to start your own paper."

Carlos started fuming with something like "How can you . . ." when Marta grabbed him by the arm and jabbered away in angry Spanish. Carlos nodded, said something unintelligible in return, and the two did an about-face and stormed out, shouting excitedly. I caught the word for "idiot" somewhere. "Hot blood" was the phrase that inevitably popped into my mind.

I had little use for ideological manias, and so that was the last I saw of Carlos Chadwick. But then I was hardly seeing anybody around Richards. What with winter, the mounting work, disappointing sales figures for *Living the Good Life*, and professional uncertainties (I had yet to land a decent job) I'd hit a new low in depressed feelings. I desperately needed the upcoming Spring break and Doug's manly company. Alas, things being what they are, my stay was to start out not with Wedded Bliss but with Amorous Agonies and Tribulations in New Haven.

"Doug Friday" I used to call him teasingly, since our "marital visits" began usually that day, when we'd have dinner at a Chinese place called Blessings. A favorite of the Yale Law School crowd, it boasts a huge menu, top Mandarin cuisine, and an elegant atmosphere. But the evening had few blessings in store for us. From the cocktails and the won ton soup to the crisp fortune cookies ("you have a soaring and romantic soul," mine said) we traded bitter blows in a lovers' quarrel. I was feeling simply furious at Doug for not having so much as lifted a finger in support of my job search.

"I can't believe how selfish you are, Doug. All those journalistic contacts and you do absolutely nothing to help me. I feel like a first-class jerk."

"Well, I like *that* just great. So you thought you could get some fancy job connections through me. *Uh*, uh, honey. I ain't *your* stepping stone."

"That's so horrible. How can you attack me that way? I give you everything, and now you accuse me of using you."

"Baby, that's exactly what you're doin'."

Then it happened, I couldn't resist, I shed hot tears at the injustice of it all—my plight and his inconsiderate and brutal treatment. "You're cruel, Doug. You're ready to sell me down the river." There were quick sad-eyed glances from the party of Divinity School students finishing up across the aisle.

"Aw, come on, Liv, can the crocodile tears."

Laying down my chopsticks with a thud I wept profusely, using up three kleenexes. "That's low, Doug." One of the Divinity people, a motherly type with short graying hair, pursed her lips and averted her gaze.

"Aw, Livie, look, I'm sorry, I didn't mean to hurt you."

Between moans I managed to cough up, "Hurt me? Oh, no, you haven't hurt me." I sobbed. "You've simply said I'm a hypocrite and," I sobbed again, "wrecked my fragile ego. That's all."

There were recriminations; I stood my ground; he eventually turned contrite. He took my hand and apologized, "Yeah, Liv, I guess I haven't done enough, I'm really sorry." The Divinity students, their backs to us now, were stretching for departure.

And he went on in his newly apologetic vein, his first time ever. I wept silently, preferring not to play on his guilt.

Doug insisted on paying for the meal, tip and all. We giggled about our fortune cookies as we headed for his Crown Street highrise, our arms wrapped about each others' waists. I wasn't feeling too physical the next few days, but as we kissed and cuddled, the entirety of my being throbbed with my love for him, and my pleas that he "Give me a more virile hug than that now!" would spark surges of desire that I'd defuse, holding him off with a delicate balance of wholesome expectation. But he was as important and challenging as ever, the love and glory of my life!

And the Chinese restaurant trauma had a happy ending. As I sweated over my seminar paper on lobbyists, Doug spent most of the weekend drafting notes about me to his media contacts and even telephoned a couple of New York guys, including Lance, his buddy from the good old days at Columbia, rumored to be launching a new monthly. Doug also wrote a glowing "To Whom It May Concern" letter on my behalf, and that went a long way toward making the first week of Spring break a nice one.

And yet there still gnawed in me a vestigial depression, a lingering dissatisfaction having to do with my sense that we seemed headed nowhere. For two years I'd gotten not the slightest commitment from him, and what climaxed my frustration was the following Saturday, when Doug and I went to his sister Josie's wedding up at Harvard Memorial Chapel. The dawn came a crisp rosy red into our hotel suite on Harvard Square, and the ceremony itself proved a spectacle to behold. Doug escorted her up the aisle, and as I gazed at them, gliding with such dignity side by side, I found myself wanting to look as gloriously radiant as Josie now looked. In a blinding flash I realized that the beauty of matrimony is not its promise of lifelong happiness, but rather its miracle of devotion and trust, a bond sealed to the end of time by the golden rings traded by bride and bridegroom. There I saw Doug and Josie, arm-in-arm in their quiet, resplendent glow, and I wanted Doug to be mine!

The reception was short, and soon thereafter Doug and I settled into our rickety old train for New Haven. We sat silently until Providence, but I figured the moment had arrived, and, holding his hand I asked, "Doug, do you really love me?"

"How come you ask me that now?"

"I often wonder. Like last weekend, the nasty things you said to me . . . I mean, I actually had to goad you to help me in my career. If a man truly loves a woman, does she need to coax him that way?" I paused and reflected, "Can it be that you're just using me?"

"Look, honey, I've been with you for two whole years now."

I stared into his deep-blue eyes. "D'you want more?"

"Yes, hon, but what is it you want me to do?"

The train was stopped on the bridge near Old Saybrook. Night had fallen, but over the horizon a bright full moon was casting its aura upon the shimmering ocean waters. And finally I heard Doug say, "Livie, I love you with all my being. You're the girl of my dreams; I want us to live as the happiest of professional married couples, and I want you to be a mom to the two little geniuses we'll have. I love you madly, now and forever."

My heart skipped a beat, then accelerated to a *piu allegro*. "Oh, Doug, my darling." I raised my blissful eyes. "What you say is music to my ears, and if I knew a good aria I'd sing for joy. You simply cannot know how much my soul has *ached* to hear those words on your lips." I cleared my throat. "Except one thing's missing. It's old-fashioned but very important to me."

Doug groaned. "Oh, no, hold it. If you expect me to carry you across the threshold, no, sorry, I won't."

Playfully I made a fist. "Do you want a punch in the nose? Silly oaf, no!" I took a deep breath. "I want you to propose on your knees, just like they do in those Harlequin books."

He stared in disbelief. "Here, in this creaky old Amtrak smoking car? Livie, you're being Victorian, or worse!"

"It's what I want," I said firmly.

And what I wanted is what he gave. He slid down, squeezed in front of his seat and, kneeling at an angle, clutched my two hands, kissed them both, and said, "Miss Kingsley, I, your humble servant, must urgently inquire, will you do me the highest honor of marrying me, your loyal, loving Douglas?"

There were nimbus clouds streaking across our moon. The sparsely populated coach was quiet, and its passengers mostly lost in sleep. I would have been oblivious, however, to any sound but that of Doug's sweet voice, and I exclaimed, "Yes, my precious, a million times yes, I will, yes." Pulling him toward me, I clung to him with my arms, opened my eyes and saw our enormous moon shining bright, and after many loving kisses we decided on the last week in July as a possible date. Back in New Haven we spent the rest of my Spring break in domestic bliss and ate at

Blessings as a happy couple, and I looked forward to the satisfaction I hoped to achieve when, sometime next summer, we would drive into the Ohio sunset, bound for a wedding of our own.

My return to Richards on Sunday the fourth felt unreal. As I gave Doug a passionate embrace and got into my Toyota (bought last summer with the advance on my book) I pondered the strangeness of my heading back to Richards and attending classes with everybody else. But more good news was in store for me when I checked Cooper Hall P.O.: an envelope with my Columbia Journalism School acceptance! In addition there was a beautiful letter from Doug, plus a professional overture from his friend Lance, who told me he'd just gotten a generous commitment from Omni-Tel/America Foundation to launch his magazine, where they'd be needing cultural staff, and would I phone him collect? Phone I did, the moment I reached Park-Davies, and Lance said he was coming up to the Berkshires to do recruiting that week and he hoped for a preliminary chat with me, so we set the date for Thursday at Richards Placement Office. I was elated yet so exhausted from it all that I passed out overnight on my bed, without having called Doug or parents or anyone whatever.

The week's weather irregularities came as an eerie backdrop to events. Sunday's sky was dark and low; next A.M. we're being hit by a major winter storm, with whirlwind gusts and whiplashes. Everyone in class looks not so much Florida-pink and freshened as stoned breathless by the wintry April morn. Then, Wednesday around lunch, a warm front starts making itself felt. By the small hours it's a heat wave, and at 5:00 a handful of campus jock types are out greeting dawn with a noisy game of Frisbee. Thursday all day becomes one long carnival, with guys lolling on doorsteps, scantily clad women sunbathing in chaises longues, clowns in cutoffs wading through the slush, and most everybody on a high, feeling carefree and giddy.

I first met Lance in Spring break of the year before, at a New Haven singles bar. His BMW having fizzled out en route from some big bash at Newport, he'd phoned Doug and invited us for drinks while the guys across the street installed his new alternator and tape deck speaker. Scruffy and predatory, the singles' joint had its charms, though the hard rock emanating from the juke box was too basic for my tastes.

Lance was dirty-blond and handsome; I could easily imagine him on a white horse, that or playing Jimmy Stewart in a 1930s romantic melodrama. Back in the mid-60s he and Doug had organized pioneer protests against Johnson's bombing of Vietnam.

"I've since grown up a bit," he boasted, serenely, over beer. "I haven't the slightest desire to waste my precious time on anybody's lost causes."

Doug smiled, sneered almost. "You haven't grown up, old man. Corrupt is what you've become."

"Silly boy. You still believe in ideals, principles, that sort of thing. Well, super; go ahead. You'll never make the big time, though." He swilled down his last few drops of Beck's.

There was tension between the old friends, I could sense it. Strange, though. Lance's cynicism was off-putting and worse, yet I found it refreshingly frank. As I slipped into my bunny-shoes later that evening I caught myself imagining Lance, could not get him off my mind, and I feared that, given the right circumstances, I might want something with him. By next morning I'd forgotten about it, but I was to feel the same ineffable sensations when we paid him a short visit at his elegant little West Village studio next October.

And here I was, decked out in my best white silks and red sash, strolling in semi-high heels with open toes toward the Placement Office, ready to talk business with Lance himself.

Feeling calm, I approached, with cat-like leisure, the spacious old fraternity mansion where RPO is housed. Parked in front was a shiny new wine-colored BMW. Sitting in the driver's seat, combing his hair, was my future boss.

"Hi, Lance," I greeted him melodically. "Been waiting for a while?"

He was pocketing his comb. A smile flashed onto his face.

"Oh, he*llo*, Livie. No problem, really. I thought I'd get here early, it's *such* a beautiful day."

Just as he unlocked his door I gestured "Wait" with my left hand, leaned on his right fender, stilled a softly swaying antenna, then pointed my scarlet-tipped index finger toward the house. "Lance, it can get *so* hot and stuffy in there. Why don't we drive over to Cooper Hall snack bar instead?"

"Sounds good, tell me about it."

"Well, they've set up an open-air terrace with white metal tables, real nice and breezy, you'll see."

"Yes, I do like the sound of it, so let's do it, yes."

The interview went smashingly, and we hit it off in a big way, talking about all kinds of stuff. The checkered light gave the impression of us being inside a Monet canvas, and Lance ventured the comparison. By the first hour of our conversation he'd told me I was exactly what he was looking for, that from the moment he'd read my book he knew he wanted me, and that Omni-Tel/America Foundation would probably be calling me soon for a New York interview, and of course I felt pleased, and then we went on to chat for a couple more hours about everything under the sun, from Mostly Mozart to imported cars, and had it not been past the allowable deadline I would gladly have invited him to Park-Davies for that evening's guest meal.

"It would've been so nice for you to come, Lance. And Park-Davies is real pretty."

"Well, Livie, I know we'll be in touch; there'll be lots of time to do it again."

Before moving on he hoped to get a peek at the Museum of Antique Automobiles, and once there I heard him moan breathlessly at the vintage Cadillac, the Bentley, the Hispano-Suiza, and the 1920 Rolls-Royce. As we sauntered back toward Cooper parking lot we took great pleasure in a pair of bluejays fluttering about a nest; our final handshake was excited, vigorous; I waved, almost sadly, as I watched the BMW turn north on Route 7.

Probably no guest meal was looked forward to as much as that warm Berkshire evening's. I felt sheer joy at the prospect of sitting down to a candlelit dinner at Park-Davies, that New England row house where I'd spent three marvelous and exciting years, always with a room of my own on the upper floor. And in the crowded lobby I found myself reflecting on how the ice-cold cocktails, the cool-jazz combo, the residents and guests in spring attire (flowery dresses, white ties), and the generally festive atmosphere were inspiring in me a special emotion about Richards, something I hadn't felt in years. A black trumpeter and a towhead trombonist were blaring out a bouncy first chorus to *"The Lady Is a Tramp"*; two short, tipsy preps, barely recognizable to me in their plaids, attempted to sing along; and as I observed the scene I felt glad to be a Richards student, and sad to think that it was just a matter of two more months...

I stood there talking to a bearded young English prof who had once praised my journalism, and now expressed admiration for my book. We're discussing the relative merits of small colleges vs. big schools when I hear the first blast—Babcock House, I will later find out. As Fred Jennings remarks, we explain it as thunder, but it does send chills up some spines, including the professor's. He floats a quizzical comment, and the two of us gulp down the last few drops of our Bloody Marys. The horn men repeat the final phrase of "Lady/Tramp;" their drummer prolongs the grand close with a brief, spirited solo.

The professor and I are filing in for dinner when we hear the second explosion—Chapman this time, though it will be minutes before we know anything. We sit down, season our salads, and hear sirens on Route 7. Then I see an acquaintance rush in through the double doors, a blond senior in a cream-colored blazer whom I danced with once at a mixer, and whose name included a Roman numeral III. His light, wavy hair is a bit of a mess and his rectangular face whiter than a freshly-bleached sheet. He approaches the housemaster, a balding chemistry professor who now gets up to confer with the messenger. From my perspective two tables away I can see the man making a little jump, then turning equally pale.

He straightens his tortoiseshell spectacles, returns briskly to his place at head table, and taps nervously on his wineglass with a spoon.

"Attention, please."

Some sophomores at the table next to mine are laughing loudly while flicking wads of bread at each other.

The housemaster looks their way and addresses them firmly, "Excuse me, please be so kind as to desist for a moment."

They play dumb and sit up straight, with a mock-innocent look on their faces.

Suddenly, from outside somewhere, a female voice shrieks, "Oh my God, they're dead!" Her cries recede in the distance.

Some giggles. Some murmurs of concern. Silence.

The housemaster announces, "According to a report we just received, explosions have occurred at Babcock and Chapman houses."

Most everyone draws a deep breath. I frown. "The damage is extensive. For the sake of caution, I suggest to all present that we exit and wait calmly outside, pending further instructions." We rise as one. He adds, "There are doors in front and back. Please do not rush."

Everyone shuffles out, nervously but keeping cool enough. Once outside they stand around in the crisp twilight, awaiting further announcements. I wave silently to the English teacher and hear him say, "So long, Livie." Despite high heels I tread quickly over to a deserted *Booster* office, grab a pad and cassette recorder, and go galloping down to Babcock for a story. As I approach I see hordes of stone-frozen people plus a few cops, girding the site and blocking my view. The first items on my tape will be sound effects such as water spewing from thick hoses and firemen barking their lines in the night. Press Pass in hand I efficiently elbow my way to the front of the crowd so as to get my first close look at the ghastly spectacle.

"Ghastly" is the word; it was a scene out of a Hollywood World War II movie. The most modern building on campus had been reduced to its rear wall; the rest was powder, jagged rocks, and chunks of concrete. Two firemen were laying bodies on stretchers side by side. I almost felt sick. I'd never seen a corpse before, and my first emotion was immense relief and even an "I'm sure glad it's not me." From the crowd I heard sobs; I taped them as I took notes and jotted down my thoughts.

Soon I'd elbowed my way out, hurried over to a nearby booth, and coaxed a sad-eyed music major into wrapping up his phone call. The only *Booster* staff I could reach was our pretty-boy photographer, who lived off-campus in an austere and secluded studio and, blissfully dozing in his big soft queen-size bed, had not yet gotten wind of the events. Some *Booster*ites were already out getting stories. I ran into one of them at the Putney meeting, a junior named Stacy seated in the front row. We exchanged greetings and statements of disbelief. I settled in to transcribe the President's and other speeches, and after about fifteen minutes I handed her my recorder and an extra tape, suggesting she stay on and record everything.

I was still wearing my high heels, and today I'm amazed at my having traipsed around barely conscious of them. I hastened over to Cooper, quickly banged out a story from my notes, and dashed down to the printers' shop on Main Street, arriving just in time to have them expunge a bland filler and insert my piece into next day's *Booster*, plus advising them to be prepared for Extras soon thereafter. The two grumbled, I smiled my best and expressed my concern, and they acquiesced as I knew they would. Walking barefoot now on my return to Cooper, I converged with Dick, our business manager. He briefed me on the remainder of the meeting and provided a tentative casualty report. As we hurried toward the newsroom I wondered to myself, "*How* can someone (whoever the culprit may have been) perpetrate such cruel and inhuman deeds? *Why* do people not care for one another, *love* one another? *Why* is there evil?" Again and again I heard my unsettled mind say: bombing rejects civilized values; violence shows callous disregard for the sanctity of life.

There's little to add, inasmuch as Fred's summary does full justice to that ugly episode. I really can't say how much Carlos had to do with the Events, and of course in this country a suspect remains innocent until proven guilty. Still, I can't help noting the parallels between Carlos's futuristic ending to *Perspectives Industries* and that traumatic Thursday evening a half decade ago. It's almost as if, after he'd given vent to his extremist rage against "American centrists, conservatives, libertarians" and the like, his "Militants" somehow sprung to real life and made his grisly finale come true.

As far as *Perspectives* is concerned, I can only say that Carlos doesn't understand America. He spent a mere three years in these United States, though in an environment that is admittedly the best. At first he came with an open mind, but, seduced by overseas dogmas in his junior year, he eventually broke with our willingness to consider all perspectives (his Marxist ones included), and then conceived his "play" from a narrowly Third World radical vantage point. Like all dogmatists he scorns our balance and objectivity, our skeptical individualism, our rejection of true-believerdom, and our uneasiness with closed views like socialism. (And where did he pick up the notion that American business leaders could favor the collectivist Hitler? *That* is a "revisionism" that stretches the imagination! Everyone knows that Nazis were anti-business and pro-Soviet. Hasn't Carlos heard of the Nazi-Soviet Pact?)

He really seems to believe there's some vast conspiracy brainwashing Americans to go out and buy this or that idea. He invents simplistic economic reasons for our openness, and in the end refuses to see the beauty of our being free to choose among the widest range of options, unfettered by totalitarian control, free to select whatever product (material or spiritual) best suits our individual tastes. Oh, certainly, I'll grant that he took things I've said and then put them—grotesquely exaggerated—into his play. It's Radical Chic triumphant; cold, hardhearted, unbending Marxism made fashionable, sexy. *Perspectives Industries* is a leftist's, a foreigner's, and therefore an unreliable, unbalanced, and

I'd say unAmerican, portrait of America. Read it with the proverbial grain of salt as you laugh at its forced jokes.

Monday after the tragedy I rose at daybreak, dressed my best, and boarded the early car to Albany Airport. I was New York bound. Omni-Tel/America had invited me to meet with *The New Dial*'s editorial board. I was also scheduled to appear on a couple of afternoon talk shows and say something about Richards plus belatedly promote my book, which I of course appreciated, though on the matter of Carlos I would not speak.

A groggy media crew was sprawled out on the front seats of the limousine, headed home. The youngest guy peeked back at me; the woman of the group was sound asleep. Suddenly it dawned on me how distant and remote Doug seemed, how far he had receded from my thoughts. I didn't marry him; I'd cared for him and his feelings, and we still had our bonds of trust, but our love had been shaken by the events. That day was a day that changed my world, forever and always, and once again dissatisfaction reared its ugly head. As I watched the still-barren trees rush by I whispered softly to myself, "I've lived enough for a lifetime this last week." And again, I heard my mind say, "I've done my stint as a revolutionary." And I looked back on my radical days with wise disenchantment and no regrets.

I yawned, knowing that a major chill had descended over my commitments to the liberal cause, and I bade a starry-eyed utopianism adieu. I was embarked on a business trip that would blossom into five long glory days with Lance, who was to show me the beauties of New York, the strengths and wonders of the American dream, and the genuine attractions of achieving fame and fortune by one's own efforts. When I boarded the Allegheny mini-jet the following Friday, and waved from the ramp as he waved too, I was recalling our first kiss, our impassioned embrace, and I fully intended to pursue and bring to utmost fruition my human right to live happily ever after.

□ □ □

PART 3

PERSPECTIVES INDUSTRIES, LTD.

by Carlos J. Chadwick

an Ideological-Epistemological Closet Farce
dedicated to all the American centrists, conservatives,
libertarians, solipsists, and the many distinguished
thinkers, dreamers, and crackpots
who've provided me so much material

The Time: The Twentieth Century
The Place: An auditorium in a large U.S. city
The Characters:
Phil Wilson, the host
Huntley Hunt
Ted Stanford
Dr. Adolf S. Robaczek
Male Militants 1, 2, 3, and 4
Female Militants 1, 2, 3, 4, and 5
Group of Militants
General Audience
Albert
Three workmen
Two policemen

*(Darkness. Three electronic bleeps. Five measures of fast big-band
jazz are heard coming from backstage. Lights. A podium at right,
three arm chairs at left, a giant screen in back. Phil Wilson enters,*

191

wearing white suit, gray tie. Applause. He waves, smiles, sits down at podium.)

WILSON: Good evening, ladies and gentlemen. I'm your host, Phil, and I'm here to welcome all of you to another presentation of *(drum roll)* Meet the Companies! *(Jazzed up version of Handel's "A Trumpet Shall Sound." On the giant screen a swirling montage of images: abstract shapes, portraits of famous thinkers, chic boutiques, women in furs, skyscrapers old and new, single-story electronics firms, tourist sights including Stonehenge, the Parthenon, the Eiffel Tower, and more.)* Ladies and gentlemen, tonite we're pleased to have as our guests three executive officers from Perspectives Industries, Ltd., the idea-manufacturing and marketing firm that is outstripping all growth records! It's another success story we can tout in our great Kingdom. But before meeting our guests, a message from Perspectives Industries, our sponsor this evening!

(Moderate-paced piano-trio jazz is heard. Images now appear on screen in slow sequence, showing colorful books, magazines, cassettes, computers, colleges, data-retrieval centers, radios, and toys. Out of nowhere there appears Huntley Hunt, tall and lanky, with short, neatly-coiffed blond hair, long face, tortoise-shell glasses, and a light-blue three-piece suit. Music fades. The images continue as he speaks in his urbane Northeastern accent.)

HUNT: Hello, I'm Huntley Hunt, speaking for Perspectives Industries. We're in the business of processing and selling ideas. If you're looking for an idea to fit your needs, come and see us—we've got it!

(Next to him there appears Ted Stanford, average height and stocky, slightly round-faced, with light-brown hair and moustache, bright green pants, and a plaid sports coat. Midwestern accent.)

STANFORD: Our firm sells ideas to any person who chooses to buy from us. It doesn't matter whether that person's a slaveholder or a slave, rich or poor. If he wants our wares, we'll sell.

HUNT: *(More earnestly and aggressively)* Our clientele includes

people of every rank and hue, whether royalists or constitu-
tionalists, abolitionists or Karlists. The Royal Family's
staffers buy their ideas from us. So do anti-royalists and so
does the King. *(A plateglass multi-story building appears in
background.)* This is our chief customer, the Ministry of
Philosophies and Thoughts. Their idea orders keep us busy all
year 'round. We're always designing, manufacturing, and
packaging ideas for the Ministry of Philophies and Thoughts.
We're proud to serve His Majesty's Government.

STANFORD: But above all Perspectives Industries is proud to
serve you. *(A multitude of faces appears on the screen.)*
Because we've got ideas of every shape, size, age, and color.
And we want you to have that variety and come to our Idea
Boutiques. *(Soft violin music. Two or three futuristic shopping
malls appear successively on screen.)* There's one in every
shopping center, usually next door to our stationery outlets.
*(Closeups of shiny storefronts; clerks and customers moving
about; neon signs saying "Idea Shoppe," "Variety Views,"
"Perspectives Boutique")* They stock our latest goods, and
our staff will help you pick out the idea of *your* choice. Check
us out today! You're sure to want an idea or two.

*(Fadeout. Big-band jazz briefly returns, stops. Lights now on Phil
Wilson)*

WILSON: Welcome back. And now, ladies and gentlemen, allow
me to introduce our guests. First, Huntley J. Hunt, Chairman
of the Board at *Perspectives Industries. (Enter Hunt from
backstage. Nods. Applause from audience. He bows, sits
down.)* Next, Ted Stanford, Vice-President for Sales. *(Same)*
Last but not least, Dr. Adolf S. Robaczek, Head of Research
and Development. *(Ditto. About 5 feet 10 inches, with dark,
wavy hair, dreamy dark eyes, and the civilized air and metal
eyeglasses of a cultured European)* Mr. Hunt, could you start
things off by telling us what it is about Perspectives Industries
that you're proudest of?

HUNT: You know, Phil, a lot of answers come to mind, but just
off the bat I might mention our extraordinary productivity.

And our global outreach too. Because together with our ink and eraser factories, our paper and pencil farms all over the world, well, we're one happy family. Each of these groups pursues its private interests, but at the same time we all work together and help each other out, thanks to our guiding hand. We handle the ideas, though, that's our line. We've produced every kind of idea, millions of them. The more variety the better, it comes down to that.

WILSON: How about you, Ted Stanford? Could you describe your vision of the Company? How d'you explain its success?

STANFORD: *(Slowly, a bit folksy)* Well, Huntley just mentioned variety. That's the key word, Phil. It's my conviction that people should have at their disposal the widest range of ideas. What it boils down to is whether we're going to have a one-perspective or an all-perspectives society. And there's nothing drabber than a one-idea society. Look at Muscovy or West Nepal. So the only alternative is a pluralistic all-ideas society like ours. Every idea is fine for our marketplace. We've marketed pacifist as well as militarist ideas. Copernicus was a big seller ten years ago. This year Ptolemy's made a comeback, we sell him too. I personally abhor German anti-Semitism, but we've always sold about equal numbers of pro-Semitic and anti-Semitic perspectives. And we've marketed neo-abolitionist views, even though Lincoln's abolitionist doctrines were fully discredited a century ago. So you see we offer choices. It's not for us to decide what's true or false or right or wrong. If someone down in Florida wants to believe the Earth is the center of the universe, that's his business. If a guy in Boston thinks abolishing slavery is going to solve anything, that's his belief. Same if they think the opposite. 'Cause beliefs are nothing more than fictions. And our job is to manufacture *all* beliefs and fictions. We do the processing and marketing, and our customers do the choosing.

DR. ROBACZEK: *(With a slight Middle European accent)* The ideal society offers the consumer a maximum number of choices.

HUNT: Exactly. We produce in quantity, but what the consumer buys is his business, not ours. We're strictly neutral on the issues, and that's why we've done such a fine job of supplying the market with every possible point of view.

WILSON: Or, as you call them at Company Headquarters, every possible Perspective, right?

(The three men nod, saying "Oh, yes!")

DR. ROBACZEK: Right, Mr. Wilson. And we call all views Perspectives because we know that there is no truth. There are only Perspectives. The quest for truth was first unmasked some 2,000 years ago when a Roman consul named Pontius Pilate, faced with a mob of true believers, asked of them scornfully, "What is Truth?" And he would not stay for an answer, because he knew there was no such thing. The real hero of that dark drama was not Jesus, it was Pontius Pilate. And Pilate's words ring deep for us today. He lacked our scientific methodology, but he already perceived that every question has many sides, any of which is as valid as any other. *(More emphatically)* One *must* see all sides. It is unhealthy not to. For example, while I consider myself a moderate, I believe one must be open to perspectives from the Right, and even to the occasional idea from the Left. All positions have their views, all of them equally plausible. Clashes and disputes go on; those doing the clashing and disputing have their own sides, which in turn have secondary sides, and so on into infinity...

STANFORD: *(Interrupting)* Truth is a tired myth. People bought it many years ago. But it's a notion that's had its day, and it's got no place in our modern society, with its idea-processing plants and shopping malls. What we've got plenty of is Perspectives, and *(pointing his open hand to the audience)* we invite everyone to come and shop with us.

DR. ROBACZEK: *(Weightily)* The history of mankind is a history of Perspectives.

□ □ □

(Three electronic bleeps. Two measures of fast, big-band jazz music ending in a long-held eleventh chord)

WILSON: Ladies and gentlemen, you're now going to see some footage of the world-famous skyscraper that houses Perspectives Industries. Mr. Hunt, could I ask you for some running commentary?

HUNT: Oh, sure, glad to, Phil. *(Electronic bleep. Hunt gets up with authority, stands before screen with a flashlight. The eclectic building now appears. Ooo's and ah's from audience. As Hunt's comments go, so goes the building.)* Well, ladies and gentlemen, this is our Company headquarters, known as the Multifacetia Complex. And, as fits our scientific view of history, it contains every architectural style known to Man. You see *(with conviction)*, we have discovered the non-progressive, non-developmental nature of human history. Nothing improves, nothing changes. Because *(wistfully)* for all his differences, Man is always essentially Man. His inner essence can never—*will* never—change. *(Brief pause) (Out of his trance, more matter-of-factly)* Anyway, our skyscraper contains an infinite number of shapes and colors. And so, depending on the weather, the season, the time of day, and the angle of vision of the individual viewer, the appearance of Multifacetia will alter dramatically in a split second. Now watch. The cameraman is moving some ten paces to the left and—presto!—the building shifts to High Gothic. *(Electronic bleep. A Gothic facade appears on screen. Ooo's and ah's)* But now the sun is going behind a cloud and—what do we see—a swirl of images and—some Art Nouveau. *(Same set of actions)* Astounding, I must say. You'll find everything there from Pharaoh's pyramid *(Bleep. The Great Pyramid appears, Hunt points.)* to the most avant-garde specimens of Geometric Crystallism *(Same. With cool enthusiasm)* It's really quite something, isn't it? Just looking at Multifacetia gives me a feeling of pride.

WILSON: So much stimulus can only enrich our lives. How 'bout a round of applause for Multifacetia? *(Applause. One hiss)*

□ □ □

(Two bleeps)

WILSON: Dr. Robaczek, you're the Company philosophist and a brilliant scholar who's designed many ideas—

DR. ROBACZEK: Really, you are too kind—

WILSON: —so maybe you could tell us the philosophy that guides Perspectives Industries?

DR. ROBACZEK: *(Clears his throat. Speaks with extreme deliberation.)* By all means. We have a poetic image for our philosophy, Mr. Wilson. *(Brief pause)* It is most significant that for our official coat-of-arms we have the famous Persian fable about the five blind men and the elephant. *(On the large screen, a group silhouette of an elephant and five ragged men, each one respectively touching the animal's trunk, back, left leg, left side, and tail.)* You see, Mr. Wilson, Man's existenz on Earth is a *(pause)* a tragic one. *(faster)* Supremely tragic, there is no other word for it. *(Again deliberately)* Hurled onto this dark planet, he is Man the Seeker, and he feels his way through Life, grasping at whatever objects may fall within his reach.

WILSON: Hmm, that's kind of abstract. How 'bout some details?

DR. ROBACZEK: Well, what this means is that, as private individuals, we do nothing more than stake out our strictly private claims as to what "reality" is like. And we are all equally right, just as each of those blind men is right. Because after all, Mr. Wilson, an elephant *is* like a garden hose or a hairbrush or a tree-twig. What right have we to dispute those men's experiences? Each one knows his elephant, and, by Gott, that is good enough for him.

WILSON: *(Brief pause)* I never thought of it that way.

STANFORD: Makes sense, though, Phil.

WILSON: Well, it sure puts a new *perspective* on the old story!

DR. ROBACZEK: That precisely is our task, Mr. Wilson, finding new meanings in old myths! Putting them in *perspective*!

WILSON: *(Coolly but politely)* Yes, you have a question?

FEMALE MILITANT 1: *(5'2", long brown hair, levi's, Mexican blouse, educated accent, soft-spoken, delicate)* Dr. Robaczek, I find your interpretation of that ancient Sufi tale extremely clever.

DR. ROBACZEK: I thank you, Miss.

FEMALE MILITANT 1: However, I believe your theory does ignore something rather basic.

DR. ROBACZEK: And *what*, may I ask, is that basic something?

FEMALE MILITANT 1: What's basic is that those men hold such differing ideas about the elephant because they are all blind.

(Murmur in audience)

STANFORD: *(Slightly scornfully)* Well, obviously...

DR. ROBACZEK: *(Loftily)* Miss, isn't that rather brash and, oh, snobbish? Are you implying that blind men have no right to their own ideas about elephants?

FEMALE MILITANT 1: *(Her voice rising and trembling slightly)* I'm *not* saying that. The point is, an elephant isn't like a hairbrush or a garden hose. Only parts of it are.

DR. ROBACZEK: *(Brief silence)* So?

FEMALE MILITANT 1: Each of those blind men makes contact with one part only.

DR. ROBACZEK: Miss, I do not get your point. *What*, in your privileged view, is an elephant like?

FEMALE MILITANT 1: *(Somewhat impatiently)* An elephant isn't like any of those things. An elephant is like other elephants, it's a large mammal with a hose-like trunk and twig-like tail—

HUNT: Can't you come up with anything more original than that?

FEMALE MILITANT 1: *(Taken aback)* What?

DR. ROBACZEK: *(Without pause)* Miss, I am afraid I cannot take your circular reasoning seriously. *(Scornfully)* "An elephant is like other elephants." Really, that is quite banal.

STANFORD: You know, Phil, I'd trust those five blind men before these young militants anytime.

(Female Militant 1 sits down, shaking her head.)

HUNT: It's a problem nowadays, Phil, these ideologues, so dogmatic and closed-minded.

(Scattered hisses from audience.)

WILSON: I think I see what you mean.

DR. ROBACZEK: Really, Mr. Wilson, why should those blind men's ideas of the elephant be criticized by anybody? Their perspective on elephants is a profound symbol of the human condition.

STANFORD: Some people just have no use for mercy.

□ □ □

(Two bleeps. Silhouette of elephant and five men vanishes)

WILSON: One hears a lot these days about Robaczek's Roulette.

(All three nod enthusiastically, "Oh, yes. ")

HUNT: Phil, I daresay Robaczek's Roulette is fast becoming a household word. And it's the brainchild of our Dr. Robaczek.

STANFORD: Huntley? Could I interrupt just one minute? I'd like to remind our audience that it was Dr. Robaczek who formulated a concept that at one time shocked people, but today is a key notion. I'm referring to the idea that quote—Principles Do Not Exist—unquote.

(Words appear one by one on screen.)

HUNT: That's right. For that matter, some people still can't accept the Robaczek Corollary on Methodologies *(Words appear on screen)*, which goes roughly, "Let it be granted that there are no Principles. It therefore follows that each separate fraction can be approached only through new Methodologies." Ergo, "Methodologies Are Knowledge."

(Words flash on screen.)

WILSON: Sounds consistent enough.

HUNT: But you're probably wondering, why the Roulette? After all, we've got books, brains. Do we really need a machine?

WILSON: Well, do we?

HUNT: As things turned out, we did, yes. Dr. Robaczek devised his apparatus to keep up with the unstinting demands made on us by His Majesty's Government.

WILSON: Which branches?

HUNT: Ministry of Peace, but most of all the Ministry of Philosophies and Thoughts.

STANFORD: You've gotta understand Phil, we're always on call to produce new ideas at moment's notice, boom, like that *(snaps his fingers)*. The whole process grinds us down even today.

HUNT: So imagine what it used to be like for our idea teams. All those sleepless nights spent reassembling old materials into bright new concepts, and vice versa, melting down last week's conceptual package and recycling its components, with new parts added here and there.

STANFORD: During lull periods we did experiment with pre-fab ideas. But it was a stop-gap that solved nothing.

DR. ROBACZEK: Ah, yes. How the Ministry had us running about! Most difficult of all was their tangled style of thinking. I remember, when the war in Nepal was just starting, we received an order for multiple-circuit concepts to sustain the following proposition *(words flash on screen)*: "The Nepalese terrorists are a pitifully weak minority that has no support, and are being pacified by our Royal Air Cavalry with minimum bloodshed and maximum efficiency." Well, a month later the Ministry totally shifted its conceptual system. The perspective now upheld was *(words flash on screen)*: "The Nepalese terrorists are international aggressors who intend to overrun all of Nepal and then seize Burma and Australia." Alas, we were forced to discard the initial package and start from scratch. And the pattern was relentless. One week we are told to demonstrate that, with

9,000 Nepalese terrorists dead, a cruel and tiny minority has been neutralized. Three months later, with 47,000 terrorists killed and the war still widening, we receive an order to show that the fanatical minority was pitilessly shooting down our air convoys, thereby provoking the Royal Air Cavalry to a war of self-defense. The Nepalese war is now in its sixth year. So you can imagine the difficulties we would have faced had the Company not had its Robaczek's Roulette.

STANFORD: And the complications still multiply. Years ago, the Ministry put in an order for some sophisticated modular syllogisms illustrating how Karlist Muscovy and Planet Mars are the true power behind Nepalese terrorism.

HUNT: Just try to imagine, Phil. Production quotas, work schedule, the constant shifts—we were pretty close to the breaking point. Some of our best conceptual engineers went berserk.

WILSON: *(Shaking his head)* Good heavens, what a nightmare. Well, Dr. Robaczek, we're all very anxious to hear how your machine works.

DR. ROBACZEK: *(As he speaks, the original Robaczek's Roulette is wheeled onstage by three swarthy workmen.)* Mr. Wilson, my colleagues have dramatized things. Yes, I did design my Roulette in response to Ministry demands, but out of a sense of duty. *(Points)* This is my original test model. The outer shell seems crude, as indeed it should. It was built from scrap metal taken from an automobile graveyard of mine.

WILSON: Aha.

HUNT: Oh, yes, I might inform our audience that Dr. Robaczek is a well-rounded individual who still runs a prosperous line of automobile graveyards and parking lots.

STANFORD: If anyone's a Renaissance man, it's our Dr. Robaczek.

DR. ROBACZEK: *(Smiles)* Gentlemen, please, I do not deserve such praise! *(With steely determination, and faster)* Now then, the shell being cast, I topped it with this large funnel which I had cast from an innovative amalgam of highest-grade plastic ores, synthetic silvers and iron pyrites. And into the funnel I slowly poured, over a period of weeks, a molten alloy composed of millions of Basic Idea Cells *(words flash on screen)*, or as we now call them, BICs *(flashes on screen)*. The BICs comprise the widest conceivable variety of Man's thoughts. These include, first of all, the complete writings of John Locke and Adam Smith, as they appear in the famed editions prepared by top idea technicians at Company labs. And there are also selected materials from David Ricardo and Dale Carnegie, as well as poems by Wallace Stevens, for example, the one that says, "Twenty men crossing a bridge/ Into a village/ Are twenty men crossing twenty bridges/ Into twenty villages." That was the beginning. To it I added, and today still add, every weekly issue of *Wealth Magazine*, *Forbes*, *Kingdom's Business*, and *Human Trade*. There are also selected issues of *National Enquirer*, *National Review*, *Daily News*, *New York Times*, *Field and Stream*, *Foreign Affairs*, *Aviation Weekly*, *Anti-Abolitionist News and Planetary Report*, and the Wall Street News. For reasons of balance I include random issues of the *Daily Muscovite*, some Nepalese terrorist propaganda, and a few well-known works by the now-discredited abolitionist, Marcus Karl, in the classic edition prepared twenty years ago by Dr. Oscar S. Hak, now Deputy Minister and Head Philosophist at the Ministry of Philosophies and Thoughts. The BICs were held together by common tap water which hardened into ice as soon as the rest of the alloy froze solid. All of this serves as the PTIB *(flashes on screen)*, the Permanent Traditional Idea Base *(on screen)* for the machine. *(He gets up, walks over to the machine)* To operate the machine is most simple. Here *(points)* is the Input Slot, where we must insert the problem set from the Ministry. Albert, please? *(From backstage there appears a swarthy assistant, about twenty-five, wearing gray slacks, white short-sleeve shirt and black tie, and carrying a thick bundle of paper which he drops into slot.)* Thank you, Albert. We have inserted for consideration the following question: "What to do about West Nepal?" *(Bleep. Question flashes on screen)* The measurable seriousness of the problem is now being computed here on the Specific Severity Scale, or Triple S. *(Points to series of dials. Some whirring, popping, and clicking. Stops. Fast bleeping)* A number has registered, indicated that we must spin the Idea Roulette *(Assistant turns a round 15-inch crank on front of machine)* exactly 14 times. *(More and louder whirring, popping, and clicking)* The Ministry problem is now being melted and processed with the PTIB. By the way, the inserted material from now on becomes part of the PTIB. *(Machine slows down)* The machine builds up ideas through a process of eternal accumulation. Now it is slowing down. What you will soon see being ejected into the output basket here are the ideas procured by the Ministry. *(Several reams of paper spew out one by one; Albert picks them up and hands them over to Dr. Robaczek, who leafs through material as Albert exits.)* Thank you, Albert. And here is the response, with title provided *(slower)* —"Some Suggested Parameters for Problem-Solving in Designated Trouble-Spot, West Nepal." There are chapter headings too, as for example, "To Expand our Expeditionary Aerial, Naval, and Alpine Forces in Nepal." Or, "Nepalese Karlist Threats to the Security of our Shores." Or, "Considerations toward a Plan for Invading India." Or, "How to Contain Muscovite Aggression in Nepal." Or, "To Roll Back Martian Expansionism in Nepal." Well, you have seen the Roulette at work. From here our conceptual aqueducts will pipe these ideas in liquid form down to the Ministry of Philosophies. Within hours the report flows on to thousands of editors, scholars, and teachers, and next day it appears in solid form in our kingdom's print products and broadcast boxes.

(Dramatic silence. Sudden applause, with a few more boos and hisses)

WILSON: *(Excitedly)* This is utterly fascinating, Dr. Robaczek. You've left us all here, I mean, simply speechless. I'm reeling with awe. I mean, our kingdom's machinery is the envy of everyone on our planet and on Mars too. But Robaczek's Roulette qualifies as the Eighth Wonder of the World.

DR. ROBACZEK: Thank you, Mr. Wilson, I am very appreciative.

WILSON: *(More cautiously)* I've got only one quibble.

DR. ROBACZEK: Oh? With what, specifically?

WILSON: Specifically with the supposed involvement of India, Muscovy, and Mars with Nepalese terrorism.

DR. ROBACZEK: *(Somewhat discomfitted. Takes a deep breath.)* I do not understand. Would you kindly explain?

HUNT: *(Clears his throat.)* Phil, you're aware that His Majesty's Government assures us that India, Muscovy, and Mars are the prime instigators of Karlist terrorism in Nepal.

WILSON: Oh, yes, I'm well aware of the triple threat posed by India, Muscovy, and Mars to individual liberties on this planet. But still, I thought there weren't any soldiers from India, Muscovy, or Mars in Nepal at this time.

DR. ROBACZEK: They are there by proxy. Nepalese terrorists are Martian and Muscovite agents.

STANFORD: The terrorist bosses get their slogans from Martian books. And Marcus Karl's mother was Martian. That's a clear sign of Martian meddling.

DR. ROBACZEK: I might also point out the disturbing fact that, since 1941, India has openly praised Muscovy's war on Germany.

WILSON: Yes, but, still, there're no Muscovite or Martian or even Indian troops in Nepal. I mean, what proof is there that they're expanding into Nepal?

DR. ROBACZEK: Mr. Wilson, don't forget, this is not just a war to defend Nepal. One must see the grander planetary strategy. Our real aim in this war is to block Indian, Muscovite, and Martian designs on Australia and Brazil.

WILSON: But I don't see any evidence for Indian, Muscovite, or

Martian intervention in Nepal *today*.

HUNT: Phil, the clearest proof I know for Muscovite meddling into Nepal is the fact that there's no free thought in Muscovy. Someone disagrees with the government, and off he goes to an Arctic labor camp.

STANFORD: Just last week they arrested their most renowned agronomist. His crime? Criticizing Muscovite wheat policy. If that doesn't show Muscovy's threat to Katmandu, nothing does.

DR. ROBACZEK: Exactly. Karlist Muscovy is fanatical. It is no surprise that she wishes to conquer Nepal.

STANFORD: It's sad, though. I read the other day in *Planetary News* that the Muscovites are real cynical. They believe nothin' their government tells 'em. And *nobody* over there believes in Karlism anymore.

WILSON: Oh, sure, I know that Muscovy exhibits a callous disregard for the individual perspective. But how will invading India solve the problem of Nepalese terrorism?

DR. ROBACZEK: It is simple, Mr. Wilson. The Nepalese terrorists are puppets of India, India is a puppet of Muscovy, and Muscovy in turn is a puppet of Mars. If we invade India, we shatter the weakest link in the Karlist chain.

WILSON: Yes, question?

MALE MILITANT 1: *(Stands up. Short, frizzy-haired, mustachioed. Blue work shirt, corduroys. Hands on hips, tough urban manner, speaks politely.)* Yeah. Dr. Robaczek, I *must* take exception to your analysis.

DR. ROBACZEK: Oh, no, no, please, it is not my analysis. This is the work of the Roulette.

MALE MILITANT 1: Fine, all *right*. I must take exception to the analysis produced by your *machine*. Really, if India, Muscovy, and Mars, as you yourself admit, do *not* have combat troops in Nepal, then *how* do they pose a threat to Nepal or *Australia*?

STANFORD: Well, that shows you how sly and cagey Karlist Muscovy and Mars can be. Today they're taking over Nepal, tomorrow Australia and Brazil, and all without a single Muscovite or Martian soldier.

DR. ROBACZEK: A point well taken, Ted, I would say the same.

MALE MILITANT 1: *(With a hint of passion)* It strikes me as somewhat nonsensical. *(Rustling in audience. Mixed reactions, agreement as well as anger)* So far I've heard no mention of the peasant uprising in Nepal. *(Growing noise in audience)* How come? Besides—

WILSON: Just one minute! One minute, please. *(Noise recedes.)* Silence! *(Silence.)* Young man, ours is a great kingdom precisely because someone like you can stand up and disagree—

STANFORD: You should be thankful. I'd like to see you disagree like this in Muscovy—

MALE MILITANT 1: *(Still polite, but with suppressed anger)* I *do* believe you gentlemen are evading the issue, which is that Royal Air Bombers have killed lots of Nepalese, and now I hear talk of our *moving* into *India*—

WILSON: Young man, listen, you've every right to talk back, that is the beauty of our system, but let's not get emotional simply because you don't agree.

HUNT: Besides, you've deprived my colleague here of his right to speak. *(Momentary silence)*

MALE MILITANT 1: *(Calm again)* I *understand*. I simply would like to *ask* Mr. Hunt and his associates why so far they haven't alluded to the *peasant* revolt in Nepal.

HUNT: What revolt?

STANFORD: Yes, what revolt?

MALE MILITANT 1: The revolt by mountain peasants organized under the Nepalese Liberation Front.

HUNT: Young man, you're too gullible. That high-sounding NLF is the most outdated Karlism, and a mere cover for

Muscovite terror.

DR. ROBACZEK: Young fellow, what proof have you for the existence of this so-called peasants' revolt in Nepal?

MALE MILITANT 1: *Dozens* of books and articles by French and Norwegian reporters.

STANFORD: Well, that's just their point of view. Who's got a monopoly on truth?

HUNT: You seem unaware, young man—what is your name?

MALE MILITANT 1: *(With some hesitation)* Jake.

HUNT: Jake, in my candid opinion, you are confusing fact and theory. What those French reporters are doing is expounding their theory of what's going on in Nepal. And it's important to mistrust all theories.

DR. ROBACZEK: My dear fellow, I know those so-called reports by French journalists. They are uniformly left wing. And what stock can we put in any ideas from the left? One such journalist was active in a French terrorist group some years ago. Between 1941 and 1944 that group coldbloodedly murdered sixteen German officers and industrialists stationed in Paris. And your Norwegian "journalist," well, he was convicted in 1943 for conspiracy to assassinate Premier Quisling. These are hardly men of balanced perspective. Given their terroristic pasts, what kind of objectivity can we expect from them?

WILSON: No answer, Jake?

MALE MILITANT 1: No, except I'm amazed. Nepalese are fighting our Royal bombing every day, and I hear *those* actions referred to as a *theory. (Sits down.)*

STANFORD: *(Breathes out heavily.)* Phil, isn't this an eye-opener? Shows how badly folks need Robaczek's Roulette.

(Some hisses from audience)

WILSON: It's upsetting, this emotionalism.

HUNT: Irrationality is a real threat that's got to be combatted. So we're developing home model Roulettes to give Ma and Pa lots of help with grocery lists, raising kids, and choosing views on foreign policy.

STANFORD: Don't forget, Phil, life in this kingdom consists mostly of buying and selling. Families now spend entire weekends in the Multiplex Malls, eating and sleeping there and leading lives far richer than they would've in an old-fashioned park or museum. They shop in our Idea Boutiques, and that's where they're gonna buy their Home Roulette, which in turn'll help them plan for their buying and selling.

HUNT: But our truly big product is our forthcoming mini-model, the Toddler Roulette. Believe me, Phil, kids are the next big market.

STANFORD: There's cash in your kids, and we're gonna teach 'em to reason from an early age. You'll see how outbursts like Jake's are held in check before a kid can even talk.

(Hisses)

HUNT: I get excited at the prospects. Everybody's children —yours, mine, *everybody*'s—will be tasting variety-in-ideas from the moment they're born. Polyvalent interpretation and balanced perspective will come as second nature to our kids. By age five they'll know that everything is just a matter of perspective. *Our* Roulette will start *your* toddler off in this richest and most complex society in history.

STANFORD: They'll learn the Robaczek Principle from our toys!

DR. ROBACZEK: They will learn that Principles Do Not Exist.

WILSON: *(Awed)* Boy, with all the dogma I see nowadays, your Toddler Roulette just might start opening up people's minds.

STANFORD: Toddler Roulette and nursery school will soon be mentioned in the same breath. It will be indispensable day care equipment.

DR. ROBACZEK: "Indispensable" is an understatement. For we are at a most unusual juncture. *(Emphatically)* Everything now exists or has existed. Except for improving his machines and increasing productivity, Man can never go beyond what now exists. Abolitionism was attempted by Lincoln. Karlism was attempted by Muscovy. Alas, the waste and suffering caused by the carpetbaggers, the Freedmen's Bureau, the Generals and Commissars only prove that these ideologies do not work. It is only since the Restoration proclamation of 1884 that this Kingdom has attained the utmost in human development. And all other lands must either become like us or succumb to Karlist terror. But—and this is crucial— precisely because every possibility does exist and has existed, no one can grasp the entire picture.

STANFORD: Nobody can. I certainly can't.

DR. ROBACZEK: No one can say what is "there," because there is no "there" anymore. And thus Robaczek's Roulette.

HUNT: Of course you'll always find malcontents with simplistic answers. Some people think abolishing slavery, confiscating lands, and pulling out of Nepal will bring Utopia.

(Brief hissing. A female voice shouts, "We never said Utopia.")

WILSON: It's a heavy burden.

HUNT: Oh, it's incredible.

STANFORD: It's our responsibility, though. We owe it to all our customers, whether they're in corporate offices or cotton-fields, here or overseas. 'Cause our processing plants are busy manufacturing and marketing ideas all over the planet. And we want to help people use their minds and chuck all their superstitions about "truth." That's why we're designing every conceivable idea toy or idea gadget or idea anything. We'll produce plurality and we'll sell it to everybody.

HUNT: People everywhere will learn that "truth" is something that belongs in quotation marks.

STANFORD: And we're gonna make big sales too.

(Hisses from audience. Voices shout, "Aha!" and "That's why!")

HUNT: You said intolerance, Phil?

(The three workmen reappear and begin rolling Robaczek's

Roulette away.)

WILSON: Oh, well, there's always misfits. How 'bout another round of applause for balanced perspective and Robaczek's Roulette?

(Applause. A few bars of moderate mezzo-forte big-band jazz from backstage)

□ □ □

(Three bleeps)

WILSON: I keep hearing about the Six Laws of Perspective. Supposedly they guide all Company policy, right?

STANFORD: They're like a Bible to us.

HUNT: They're posted all over Multifacetia. And we hand them out in brochure form to visitors' groups and teach the Laws in our courses.

WILSON: How do those laws work?

STANFORD: We were waiting for you to ask that.

HUNT: You see, Phil, our aims are vast, and our philosophies abstruse. So we've put our grand system into a few formulas. That way ordinary folks might sort their way through the complexities of our operation, much as researchers hack their way through the tangles of science and thought. So here goes. *(Laws flash onto screen one by one as he utters them. Bleep precedes each one.)*

One: THERE IS NO TRUTH, ONLY PERSPECTIVES. Two: NOTHING IS ABSOLUTE, EVERYTHING MUST BE BALANCED.

Three: NOTHING IS CERTAIN, EVERYTHING MUST BE VERIFIED.

Four: ANY EXCEPTION IS AS IMPORTANT AS THE RULE IT REFUTES.

Five: ALL IDEAS ARE EQUAL, and

Six: 'GOOD' AND 'EVIL' ARE IRRELEVANT TO SCIENTIFIC PERSPECTIVISM. Now let's examine Law

Number One. *(Words flash: THERE IS NO TRUTH, ONLY PERSPECTIVES.)* Yes, you see, every individual has his perspective, just as he has his factory or plantation, his wife or slaves or sports cars. His point of view is his unique and sacred property.

WILSON: For example?

HUNT: Well, take some of the perspectives we apply in dealing with ethnic problems in Europe. A senior biodemographist at our Company, Dr. James Q. Edwards, has gathered evidence showing that Jewish people have what he calls a "financial gene," and that Gypsy people have a "larceny gene." In Dr. Edwards' view, these genes push Jews into finance and Gypsies into theft. Dr. Edwards has devised a renowned Financial Quotient Test *(words flash)*, the F.Q., and he notes that Jews tend to score high in their Financial Quotients, whereas Gypsies score high in Larceny Quotients. Now, on the opposing side we've got staff researchers who argue doggedly that there's no proof for the existence of a financial gene. There's a prominent Karlist who asserts without a hint of a doubt that the role of Jews in finance can be explained by medieval history! You see, Phil, in Karlist theology, history serves as a kind of substitute God. One Jewish staff member has expressed dissatisfaction with biodemography, and of course that's his right. So you see we've got differing perspectives on Jews and Gypsies. And we're selling them all in our Idea Boutiques. None of them is "true," but they're equally valid.

STANFORD: It's like the elephant again, Phil.

WILSON: *(Very slightly confused)* This is fascinating, gentlemen, but, I mean, what about the moral factor? *(Embarrassed silence)*

HUNT: Could you elaborate, Phil?

WILSON: Isn't this biodemographist, Dr.—

HUNT: Edwards.

WILSON: Isn't there a moral problem in Dr. Edwards's views?

STANFORD: Phil, we get into that in the Law of Good and Evil, Number Six.

WILSON: But you don't see anything wrong with Dr. Edwards's view?

STANFORD: Phil, our job is to market ideas, not judge 'em.

WILSON: *(Slightly more troubled)* But, well, what about Hitler's ideas. Would you have marketed them?

HUNT: If they were scientifically researched and well written, yes, we would have. We'd even hire Hitler for our research staff, if he were a good researcher.

WILSON: Dr. Robaczek, being from Germany, you must have some thoughts on the matter.

DR. ROBACZEK: Oh, yes, Mr. Wilson, Hitler made some appalling mistakes, no doubt. His ethnic policy was worse than immoral, it was stupid and ill-conceived. A German tragedy it was. Moreover I believe Hitler did something even wronger than his treatment of ethnics. I am referring to his indefensible policy of not allowing idea processors to disagree with the government. One thing we all agree on is that there is nothing more precious than the freedom to dissent, to talk back and express one's opposition.

WILSON: Yes, of course, this forum is living proof.

DR. ROBACZEK: And it is precisely because we abhor the evils of suppressing individual views that Perspectives Industries encourages the fullest spectrum of ideas on Jews and Gypsies.

WILSON: But—

HUNT: Actually, Phil, our company has several products roundly condemning the worst features of the Hitler years.

WILSON: Oh, such as?

HUNT: The absence of free elections, for example. People should have the right to vote, and Hitler took it away. Why, here in this Kingdom we've been voting for almost two hundred years. And then there's the study by three young researchers who harshly criticize Hitler's reviving the draft. They believe military service should be strictly voluntary.

STANFORD: Our top-selling idea this year rips into Hitler for the crippling paperwork he imposed on businessmen. They really suffered under Hitler—

MALE MILITANT 1: *(Stands up quickly)* How many business-men were sent to concentration camps? *(Sits down)*

WILSON: Please, let's—

DR. ROBACZEK: Young fellow, let me inform you that in my time I wrote numerous articles in which I attacked the Hitler administration on that score. In those articles I deplored the lack of free thought in the concentration camps. I felt then that Hitler violated our most sacred rights in not allowing multiple perspectives in those camps. And I also defended the right of researchers to study the camps and publish their findings freely. In short, I protested the lack of individual freedom in Germany in the '30s and '40s, and am proud to say so. *(Some applause from audience)*

HUNT: Besides, you're too young to remember, Jake, but Hitler's successors soon restored those liberties we cherish. The very rights Dr. Robaczek called for were implemented in 1945, with our advice, by the Bormann administration. Jews, Gypsies, and even Karlists were given complete freedom to protest against the camps. A lot of those dissidents started bookstores and newspapers. Some of the books now being marketed in those places came from the German branch of this Firm.

STANFORD: Not only that, those tyrannical regulations Hitler imposed on business and industry were also lifted by Mr. Bormann. Actually, Phil, a lot of Bormann's 1945 reforms owe their existence to conceptual packages sold to his government by us.

WILSON: I didn't realize that.

HUNT: What's more, Phil, we've shed light on problems right here at home. The slavery issue, for instance. We've got a biodemographist who's spent years researching the cell structure of slaves, and he's concluded that cell structure is the chief reason for their being slaves. So the slave comes programmed by Mother Nature. That's how our biodemographist sees it. Then there's Dr. Moses Franklin, our house neo-Karlist, who's made it his crusade to seek out the causes of slavery somewhere in the social structure and of course *(with polite scorn)*, that godhead of Karlism, economic history. Like all Karlists he thinks he's got a privileged view on the subject. It's an interesting view, though.

STANFORD: Yeah, he really overdoes his economic forces thing, but as an idea it's as good as any other, so we'll sell it. What I don't like is the way some extremists have made Dr. Franklin's views into a battle cry. *(A few hisses from audience)* Some self-styled leaders are even reviving abolitionist ideology and trying to impose it on the slaves.

WILSON: *(Circumspectly)* Well, the slaves do lack some rights.

STANFORD: *(Conciliatory)* Phil, don't get me wrong, I'm not a sadist or oppressor. I truly sympathize with the slave's tragic plight. 'Cause after all, I'm a slave to my company position.

HUNT: It's the human condition. We're all slaves to something.

STANFORD: Besides, we've had reforms. Slaves are now entitled to a three-fifths vote. And their leaders' views are packaged and sold by top idea companies. Some former slaves have started idea companies of their own, right in their living rooms. 'Cause don't forget, Phil, thanks to recent legislation, a slave who works hard enough and saves his cash can buy his freedom in ten to twenty years. After that he'll be free to invest in a plantation and become a slaveholder in his own right.

HUNT: Any slave can now emulate that great man, William Ellison, who way back in 1830 purchased his freedom and later became the richest slaveholder in his county.

STANFORD: So you see, if someone's a slave after twenty years, it's either 'cause he hasn't worked hard or isn't too bright.

HUNT: Phil, did you know that many of these reforms came from our drawing boards?

WILSON: So you work to widen slaves' rights and freedoms.

HUNT: We work to widen *everybody's* rights and freedoms. We just don't like extremism of any kind, whether by slave-holders or slaves. That's why I get put off by neo-abolitionist dogma.

DR. ROBACZEK: It is most coercive, these rallies where they make angry speeches and chant "Freedom! Freedom!" I am uncomfortably reminded of Nazi rallies at Nürenberg.

STANFORD: Right, right. They're incredibly intolerant of slave-holders and anti-abolitionists. Only they're right, that's their mentality. It's pure fanaticism.

DR. ROBACZEK: I do detect Karlist influence among them.

HUNT: What most upsets me, Phil, is their failure to tolerate diversity among slaves. It doesn't occur to them that many slaves are perfectly content with their lot. What about the slave who chooses to remain at the plantation? Are we going to take away his individual right to choose? The dictator Lincoln tried to impose his abolitionist ideology on our nation. *That* utopian scheme led to a half-million dead and lots of cities burned to the ground. *(Heaving a sigh)* Thank God our British friends moved in and put an end to carpet-bagger tyranny. *(Applause from one portion of audience, followed by some hisses)* Thank you. Really, how can anyone defend a cause that engendered terrorists like Nat Turner or General Sherman or John Brown? Anyway, the royal troops are a bulwark against any neo-abolitionist monopoly over the marketplace. *(Scattered applause)*

STANFORD: It kinda gets me. Those neo-abolitionists claim there's no freedom under slavery. Then they go and disprove it by getting their ideas packaged and distributed by Perspectives Industries! *(Laughs. Some laughter in audience)* Could they do that in Muscovy? Big deal, hotshot abolitionists raking in fifty thousand a year in royalties. Makes me wonder about the alleged purity of their beliefs. *(Laughs bitterly.)* But do they show the anti-abolitionist side? I've listened to their broadcasts. They never have *anybody* presenting the case for slavery.

HUNT: They do go too far. Take one of our company slaves, an upright, dignified and highly trustworthy fellow. He's Chief Doorman at Multifacetia, has a dignified look and a deep, rich voice. And he put it beautifully once, he said, "Why should I shake off the Company if it lets me believe what I want? I'd only be trading this slaveholder for one who'll make me believe what Muscovy and Mars want." Well, *there's* a slave who's pro-slavery. Will the neo-abolitionists respect his beliefs?

WILSON: Gentlemen, time's ticking by, so why don't we move on to the next Law?

STANFORD: Sure, Phil, but I just wanna say that individuals should be allowed to think for themselves. All propaganda is bad, right or left. There's always a balance in the middle.

WILSON: Oh, I agree, but how about Law Number Two?

HUNT: *(Two bleeps)* Yes, Phil, it's *(words flash on screen)*: NOTHING IS ABSOLUTE, EVERYTHING MUST BE BALANCED. In other words, there's all kinds of factors operating on our planet. To single out any factor for special attention is unbalanced and unscientific. So the only alternative is to treat each and every element as equally important in those complicated phenomena, Man and Nature.

STANFORD: Everything is terribly complicated, Phil.

WILSON: For example?

HUNT: Well, take the war in Nepal. There's a Karlist ideologue at our lab who insists that the Royal Air Cavalry is fighting in Nepal simply because our idea-processing firms own ink deposits, graphite mines, pencil trees, and extremely fertile paper plantations over there. He also has this neat little theory that our industries merely want access to Nepalese slave labor.

WILSON: Gee, that's an interesting idea! I'd never heard or

thought of it before. It makes some sense, doesn't it?

STANFORD: *(Sighs.)* Yeah, but it's just one view, Phil, don't forget. There's a less simplistic theory currently being worked out by Dr. Robaczek. He argues that the reason for the war in Nepal is that our King was badly traumatized by his cruel and incompetent wet-nurse up until age four.

WILSON: Good heavens, all these theories, it's so confusing! It's almost impossible to know what's really going on!

DR. ROBACZEK: *(Smiles.)* Mr. Wilson, no one knows what is "really going on," as you put it. Of course, I have formulated my own private theory, but there are others. For example some outstanding physicists at Perspectives Industries have noticed a major increase in sunspot activity during our decade. From this they have reached the disturbing conclusion that the war in Nepal may well be caused by sunspots.

WILSON: It's amazing.

HUNT: So there you are, Phil—pencil trees, wet nurses, sunspots. That's three out of countless possibilities, and plenty of proof for each. And yet there's nothing, *(slower)* absolutely nothing, that's going to have a monopoly and explain —quote—what's really going on—unquote—in Nepal.

DR. ROBACZEK: What is far more important is that we have processed and sold some extremely stimulating ideas.

WILSON: *(Clearing his throat)* Could I ask you gentlemen a delicate question? *(They gesture assent.)* Is Perspectives Industries for or against this Kingdom's war in Nepal?

(Momentary silence. Some mumbling in audience)

HUNT: Phil, as Chairman of the Board, let me say that we're neither for nor against. We believe in keeping business and politics separate.

WILSON: How about as individuals?

STANFORD: As independent individuals, we most all of us believe His Majesty's war in Nepal is a necessary and optimal measure.

WILSON: *(Cautiously)* Mm, well, isn't that pretty much the same thing as the Company itself being in favor*? (They gesture in disagreement, "Oh, no!")* And wouldn't Company ownership of paper plantations be a reason for favoring Royal actions in Nepal?

HUNT: No, no, Phil. You're latching onto a conspiracy theory. We're driven by ideals, not greed.

DR. ROBACZEK: If anything, Mr. Wilson, it is Muscovy who is greedy. It is Muscovy who trains terrorists to seize *our* mines and trees and other resources vital to our security.

STANFORD: Look, Phil, this Company paid *twenty-four hundred* plastic beads for those paper lands. If a Nepalese farmer wants to sell us his fields, well, that's his personal business. *(A bit passionately)* Really, who's anybody to say what can or can't be sold? Come on! It's a free market out there!

HUNT: Phil, what do you say we drop it for now?

WILSON: Agreed. Besides, I'm wondering, could Perspectives take a balanced view toward, say, Hitler?

STANFORD: We take a balanced view toward everything.

HUNT: There are lots of factors here, Phil. We believe Hitler's bombing of London was a terrible crime.

WILSON: Obviously. So how could this terrible deed be balanced?

STANFORD: Well, don't forget, Phil, Hitler rounded up the Karlists and threw 'em in jail. Before 1933, the Karlists were too powerful in the polls. So Hitler came and neutralized 'em. They've never recovered. *(Smiles.)*

WILSON: *(Confused)* But—is that a good thing?

DR. ROBACZEK: Well, Mr. Wilson, if Karlism poses the greatest threat to freedom, then jailing Karlists is a *very* good thing.

WILSON: Gee, but—

STANFORD: Look, Phil, the last thing anybody with half a brain could want would be a Karlist victory in Germany. Hitler at least respected the property rights of businessmen. During his reign the factories made a lotta money. Our own branches over there did, 'specially our telephone and aircraft branches. But I mean, Karlism? Those businesses would've been confiscated! *(Shouts of "Aha!" from militants' side)* No way! 'Course, some people think makin' money's bad.

WILSON: *(Frowning)* But why go jailing all those people?

HUNT: Phil, it's not just "jailing people." Hitler confronted Karlism all over Europe. He fought them in Spain and saved that great kingdom from Karlist rule. And after that he spent years fighting against Karlist terror in France. What's wrong with that?

DR. ROBACZEK: And do not forget, Mr. Wilson, Hitler did confront Muscovy and kill 20 million Muscovites.

STANFORD: Right. I mean, anybody who killed 20 million Muscovites can't be all that bad. *(Momentary silence)*

WILSON: *(Still confused)* Hmm, I can see it's a complicated thing, this balance. On the other hand, can you take an equally balanced view toward, say, Muscovy?

HUNT: Very balanced. We produce millions of idea books showing that Muscovy is the worst tyranny known to man.

WILSON: For example?

HUNT: The absence of free elections and private business.

STANFORD: Still, though, none of these things are as shocking as Muscovy's forced labor camps. Decades of labor camps prove once and for all the bankruptcy of Karlist ideology.

WILSON: *(Smiles.)* Well, we've got labor camps here, too.

STANFORD: *(Sighs impatiently.)* That's different, Phil. Our camps grew out of the free market. And the free market's the only road to freedom. Besides, nobody ever froze to death in a cottonfield.

DR. ROBACZEK: Not only that, Mr. Wilson. Consider Muscovy's war on Germany in 1944, and the millions of Germans who died in that imperialist attack. And consider the cruel Muscovite occupation of a third of my native land. To this very day it goes on. To this day. *(Tears well up in his eyes.)*

STANFORD: Can you imagine, Phil? Those Muscovites blitzed into Germany just like that. You know, if Royal troops hadn't come in from the West, you can be sure the Muscovites would've gobbled up all of German territory. We saved the rest of Germany from Karlism, and glory be for that!

HUNT: So you see, Phil, there's a multitude of sides.

WILSON: *(Smiles, a bit confusedly)* Well, it's true that "Multiplicity" is one of your mottoes.

DR. ROBACZEK: Precisely. And that is why our coat of arms says *Multiplicitas* on one side and *Pluralitas* on the other. But *Veritas*, well—that fanciful word carries no weight with us.

HUNT: And our French branch has for its slogan the words *Liberté / Pluralité / Multiplicité*.

WILSON: I'm not one for languages, but I get the idea, I think. *(Looks at screen.)* Law Number Three looks interesting. How is it that nothing's certain? *(Three electronic bleeps)*

HUNT: Yes, well, the entire Law reads *(words flash)*: NOTHING IS CERTAIN, EVERYTHING MUST BE VERIFIED.

WILSON: Now what does that mean?

HUNT: Phil, nobody can be absolutely sure of anything. Prejudices and suspicion just aren't enough. So our Company sponsors a lot of studies that end up either confirming or invalidating all sorts of common sense notions. *(Emphatically)* Our firm shows no mercy toward received ideas.

WILSON: Well, how'bout a for instance?

HUNT: Take the popular belief that low income leads to undernourishment. About ten years ago a dynamic young social researcher named Burton Kratt wanted to find out what connection there is, if any, between scarce financial home revenues and low intake of calories and protein. It was a heroic labor of scholarship. Dr. Kratt interviewed each and every member of all the low-income families living in two rural counties, one in the Far North, the other in the Far South. He burned gallons of midnight oil organizing his facts and figures, then fed the data into Robaczek's Roulette. The result of his four-year efforts was a monumental 2,000-page *Report on the Possible Causes of Undernourishment in Two Counties.* And in Chapter 1 he launched "Kratt's Law." *(Words flash on screen.)* This law states that, in those counties and at the time of his researches, there exists an apparent correlation between monetary disadvantage and dietetic deficiency. *(A few nervous titters from audience)*

WILSON: Aha. Interesting.

STANFORD: Right. The key phrase is "in those two counties." Dr. Kratt isn't a man given to irresponsible theorizing. He's got a tough skeptical streak, and that's why he steadfastly refused to say whether Kratt's Law is applicable to other places. *(More titters)*

WILSON: Good heavens, you really accept nothing on faith.

DR. ROBACZEK: Nothing, Mr. Wilson. Besides, let us not forget, Dr. Kratt's project was completed five years ago, and there is the possibility that his conclusions are now dated.

(Titters and one guffaw from audience)

WILSON: I'm beginning to wonder what all I can believe in.

HUNT: Phil, it's hard to accept anything on faith anymore. So we entertain a healthy skepticism toward *all* beliefs.

STANFORD: Yeah, Phil, here's another instance. We had this young Karlist researcher recently. And look, I disagree with Karlism, but I'm open to any idea, so long as it's scientifically proved. Fine. Trouble was, though, he didn't follow the Law of Verification.

WILSON: What was his project?

STANFORD: He put together a 700-page thing titled *On the Grass-roots Popularity of the Nepalese Liberation Front*, as he chose to call the terrorists. *(Words do not flash on screen.)*

And he claimed that the reason the Royal Air Cavalry have had their problems winning the war in Nepal is that the terrorists enjoy the support of fifty-five percent of the Nepalese population. And we paid the young Karlist a nice sum for his findings, he can't complain. Once he'd handed it in, though, we decided not to process the study. We also discontinued his contract.

WILSON: That's sad. Why the negative decision?

STANFORD: His research wasn't scientific enough. I mean, look, Dr. Kratt went and interviewed literally every individual in two counties, and then was real careful about his conclusions. Well, that young Karlist should've combed every nook and cranny in Nepal and asked everyone how they felt about the terrorists.

WILSON: He didn't go to Nepal?

STANFORD: Oh, he did, he spent 18 months there, and he's fluent in Nepalese. But he read documents from the terrorist side only. And almost all of the seven thousand people he interviewed were peasants. Meanwhile he saw no landlords, and didn't even bother to interview any of the native foremen we've got managing our pencil-tree farms.

HUNT: But the real problem, Phil, was that he went there with purely preconceived ideas and set out to confirm them. Like all Karlists, he assumed the peasants were pro-terrorist and against us. And that's what he proved. Really, though, how can he be so cocksure about a figure like fifty-five percent? Maybe it's only *thirty*-five percent, after all.

STANFORD: For that matter maybe it's only *twenty*-five percent. Or *two* percent. 'Cause, really, the idea that a majority of people could believe in Karlism is hopelessly absurd.

WILSON: What exacting standards! Must be pretty hard on your researchers, submitting to such skepticism.

HUNT: I'd say that skepticism is our most important product.

DR. ROBACZEK: With utmost pride I say that my own personal motto since my teens has been, "Doubt everything, believe nothing." *(Soulfully)* I can still recall how awed my young mind felt when first encountering the arguments of those great philosophers who assert that matter does not exist and the so-called real world is a fiction. These arguments came with the force of a revelation to my then-tender soul. I suddenly realized that any of the things we take for granted could very well be dreams. *Everything* is a fiction—that is an idea I still contemplate whenever I sit by my fireplace, sipping sherry. The so-called data in this young Karlist's book may be little more than phantoms of his mind. Reported bombings in Nepal may ultimately be illusions. "Doubt everything, believe nothing." History may be the greatest fiction. Perhaps what we read of wars, conquests, famines, sufferings, and other human follies is nothing more than an unverifiable fiction.

(Brief silence)

FEMALE MILITANT 2: *(Tall. Slender, taut, and tough. Dark frizzy hair. Hard manner. Black body suit, jeans. Gets up angrily and abruptly.)* Dr. Robaczek, really! People in the concentration camps did not think history was a fiction! Are you serious?

DR. ROBACZEK: *(Calmly.)* Young lady, how can we know that anything is not a fiction? How do we know if a tree falling in the woods makes a noise? Perhaps conqueror and conquered are ideas in our minds.

FEMALE MILITANT 2: *(Loud and brash)* Sir, you have yet to answer my question!

STANFORD: *(Reasonably.)* Miss, think of it, how can you be sure that you and I exist here in this room?

HUNT: *(Paternally.)* Really, young lady, how can anything be proved without the prover relying on his compromised perspective? Has any viewer special rights or privileges?

FEMALE MILITANT 2: Oh, Jesus H. Christ! *(Waves her hand dismissively, sits down in anger. Now looking at her companions, softer)* Can you believe this?

HUNT: Phil, you can see how it unsettles people when they find out about the Law of Verification. Nobody likes seeing his own little sacred cow put out to pasture. The most cherished beliefs turn out to lack all foundation. No wonder knee-jerk dogmatists see red whenever we inform them about Law Number Three.

WILSON: Law Number Four looks unsettling too. *(Four bleeps)*

HUNT: Yes, Phil, this is the one that makes you wonder if we can count on any ideas at all, and it says *(Words flash)*: ANY EXCEPTION IS AS IMPORTANT AS THE RULE IT REFUTES.

WILSON: Hmm, this is strange. Give us an example.

HUNT: Well, we applied it with amazing efficacy last year, when Dr. Robaczek's chief assistant took a second look at Dr. Kratt's classic study of low income and undernourishment. Lucy Carr was her name, and she came up with something astounding. She noted that 106 of the low income individuals interviewed by Dr. Kratt did not suffer from undernourishment. If anything, they were extremely healthy and full of pep.

DR. ROBACZEK: Yes, astounding it was. And we came to the realization that Kratt's Law had been refuted.

WILSON: Now how is that?

HUNT: Well, Dr. Kratt's conclusions just weren't valid anymore. So it was time for a change, time to replace something as old and obvious as Kratt's Law with something up-to-date. So Dr. Robaczek ordered a new study, and on page 1 then announced a new perspective saying the exact opposite of Kratt's Law. We've dubbed it Robaczek's Law, and it says *(bleep, words flash)*: LOW INCOME IS NOT THE CAUSE OF UNDERNOURISHMENT.

(Ripples of confusion in audience)

WILSON: Good grief, our old hunches just don't work anymore.

STANFORD: Yeah, well, think of it, Phil. The two people I know who're undernourished happen to be very wealthy. So I might conclude that undernourishment is caused by being rich. Who's to say?

WILSON: *(Bewildered.)* Well, then, what's the real cause?

STANFORD: Phil, see? You said "the *real* cause." But there's no such thing. That's pre-Perspectivist thinking.

HUNT: Low income's a factor, but let's face it, seeing it all as economic is Karlist dogma. Maybe it's the cell structure of the undernourished. Or sun spots.

STANFORD: You know, this reminds me of those militants who've been picketing the Ministry of Peace and criticizing our Royal Air Cavalry for alleged atrocities in Nepal. It's their view, they're entitled to express it. But things just aren't that cut 'n' dry. Our Air Cavalry is also responsible for implementing the "Lollipops for Nepalese Toddlers" program. And I might mention now that we *(points at himself)* at Perspectives Industries planned Lollipop Policy. *(Some sounds of exasperation in audience)* Why don't the militants take note of *that*? Well, I'll tell you why, It's because our Lollipops for Nepalese Toddlers program refutes all their rhetoric about bombing "atrocities," that's why.

VOICES FROM MILITANT SIDE: *(Loud, angry.)* After all that killing! Lollipops! Big deal! Rubbish! You for real?

VOICE OF MALE MILITANT 2: Do the Royal Air Cavalry give 'em land and clothing?

STANFORD: Excuse me, you're going to have to learn to speak one at a time.

MALE MILITANT 2: *(Gets up. Tall, broad-shouldered. Brown hair a bit long and wavy. Rectangular face. White shirt, gray corduroys)* The fact is the NLF give land, food, and clothing. The Royal Air Cavalry do not.

VOICE OF FEMALE MILITANT 2: They massacre 'em from the skies.

STANFORD: Well, that's off the track. I'm talking lollipops, you're talking something else. Tell me, young fella, do those

Nepalese terrorists give lollipops?

(Brief silence, followed by combined applause and catcalls)

MALE MILITANT 2: Hey, wait, that's not the point. You're—

STANFORD: Not the point! We take all this trouble airlifting lollipops to Asia, and you say it's not the point! Since when do Nepalese terrorists give away lollipops to their people? Or to *our* people?

(Applause, shouts of "That's right!" from friendly side)

HUNT: *(Calmly, soothingly)* Ted, really, what can you expect from spoiled children? They've had all the lollipops they want. They can bike right down to the Lollipop Boutique and consume them by the dozen. So they've got this racist attitude toward Asian peasants who might want them too. *(Sighs.)* They've never known what it's like not to have lollipops.

STANFORD: *(Getting more heated)* I know, Huntley, but this dogma of theirs gets to me. We're wrong, they're right, it's so simplistic. Tell me, you kids ever heard about the Air Cavalry officer who saved a drowning Nepalese girl's life? He plunged right into the river and pulled her out, and you know, she's alive and kicking now. So tell me, was that an atrocity? Would that native girl have been saved if our pilot hadn't been there? *(Breathes heavily. Brief silence)* I get angry at you young militants. *(Shouts of "Go to hell")* You just don't see individual self-sacrifice. Our Air Cavalry pilots are human beings, each one a unique world unto himself. Are they all brutes, each one, to a man? Well, in my book, if you find just one who isn't, that smashes all your glittering generalities. I don't like blanket statements. They offend common decency.

HUNT: *(Chuckling lightly, slapping him on back)* Easy does it, Ted. Calm down. Phil, you've got to understand Ted. He gets worked up over his beliefs sometimes.

(Sympathetic "Ohs" and "Ahs" from part of audience)

WILSON: Oh, that's good, there's so much lack of faith today.

STANFORD: *(Quite earnestly)* It's a matter of common decency.

HUNT: Of course, Ted, you know we agree, okay?

WILSON: How'bout a round of applause for Ted Stanford's beliefs? *(A few fast bars of jazz music. Clapping and hissing from audience.)* Well, Mr. Hunt, what's Law Number Five like?

HUNT: Law Number Five is our Democratic Law. *(Five bleeps.)* It respects all ideas, because it says *(words flash)*: ALL IDEAS ARE EQUAL, AND ANY INDIVIDUAL'S IDEA IS AS GOOD AS ANY OTHER INDIVIDUAL'S IDEA. *(Clears his throat.)* We refuse to attribute superiority or inferiority to any idea. The important thing is not to let any individual's philosophy be imposed on anybody else.

STANFORD: Here's a for instance. A slaveholder might have his own theories about slavery, and a slave has others. But you cannot say that any of these ideas is quote—better—unquote than the other. Each individual freely believes what he wants, without being entitled to a monopoly.

WILSON: So abolitionist and pro-slavery ideas are equal?

HUNT: Yes, because *all* ideas are. They're only theories anyway, so who's to say what's better or worse?

DR. ROBACZEK: Our democratic approach knows no bounds, covers all of Man's history. Ultimately the Ptolemaic theory of the cosmos is as good as the Copernican. After all they are only the individual beliefs respectively of a Greek and a Polish thinker. And there is plenty of proof to back them both. The same can be said about militarist and pacifist, Karlist and anti-Karlist, Darwi...

WILSON: Even Nazi and Jewish?

STANFORD: *Any* idea, Phil, so long as it's well argued.

WILSON: Dr. Robaczek mentioned militarist ideas.

DR. ROBACZEK: Let me explain. I find militarist and pacifist ideas equal because, to my view, both are equally wrong. It is my belief that Man fights wars due to an implacable instinct in his genes. It is human nature that drives Man to kill other men. When we send pilots to Nepal, we are driven by the war instinct. When Nepalese terrorists shoot down our planes, they are obeying the war instinct. And when demonstrators or neo-abolitionists march and shout in protest, they are obeying the war instinct. Pilots, terrorists, militants, and abolitionists are merely heeding the primeval call of our genetic pool.

WILSON: So Man fights because there's a wild beast in him.

DR. ROBACZEK: Exactly, exactly. How else to explain Hitler's policies, or those of his opponents? It was the beast in Man that killed Jews and Gypsies, not necessarily Hitler. And it was the beast in Man rearing its ugly head whenever French terrorists killed German military men. Biology is all.

WILSON: You really are a man of vision.

DR. ROBACZEK: No, please, no, Mr. Wilson. That is my perspective. There are others, though I am convinced of mine.

WILSON: Speaking of wars, Nepal keeps getting more elusive. Do you believe all ideas are equal on *that* score?

HUNT: That is just where our democratic approach comes in. We've got a very controversial theorist, General Leo Kurtz, who believes the solution to the war is to destroy absolutely everything in Nepal—houses, factories, farms, the whole works. With ironclad logic he demonstrates how killing all Nepalese will further our grim struggle against Muscovite- and Martian-inspired planetary terrorism. General Kurtz, let me say, is no opportunist. He is sincere in his beliefs, and I respect sincerity. But we've also hired a young researcher whose basic idea is that this Kingdom should call back its Air Cavalry and simply forget about Nepal. His perspective is as extremist as that of General Kurtz.

WILSON: And how do you gentlemen feel about their views?

STANFORD: Phil, I reject all extreme viewpoints. Law Number Two, right? Balance, not absolutes. Somewhere there's a middle way between atomizing Nepal and just cutting out. A golden mean.

DR. ROBACZEK: Our perspectives on the *status* of the war are also pluralistic. For example, to the pessimists who think the war a terrible loss for this Kingdom, I on the contrary pronounce it an enormous success.

WILSON: *(Eyebrows raised)* Now *that's* news to me. It's been six years now and no end in sight. How can we call it a success?

DR. ROBACZEK: Oh, but we can. Despite the implacable fanaticism of the Nepalese Karlists, we have achieved our strategic goal.

WILSON: Which is what?

DR. ROBACZEK: Our goal has been to prevent India, Muscovy, and Mars from overrunning Australia and Brazil. You yourself said so earlier; there are no Muscovite or Martian troops in any of those lands. And yes indeed, that is right, those lands are free of foreign troops precisely because we drew the line at Nepal. Had the Royal Air Cavalry not intervened in Nepal, Australia and Brazil would now be Indian, Muscovite, and Martian colonies.

(Quick, sharp cries of "Bull shit!" and "What a crock!" from parts of audience)

WILSON: *(Exhaling deeply)* Good heavens, Dr. Robaczek, you do take a planetary view of Nepal. Now Law Number Six looks interesting. How about the lowdown on that one?

(Six bleeps.)

HUNT: Yes, this is our most controversial law, the Law of Morality. It says *(words flash)*: "GOOD" AND "EVIL" ARE IRRELEVANT TO SCIENTIFIC PERSPECTIVISM.

WILSON: So it's your goal to go beyond good and evil?

HUNT: They're simply not relevant, Phil. After all, no one has been able to *measure* good and evil. Besides, when you think of it, the most quote—evil—phenomena can have redeeming features.

STANFORD: I suppose it comes down to recognizing that there's millions of equally valid interpretations for any given act.

DR. ROBACZEK: Every morality is simply a mode of conceptu-alization, neither more nor less "true" than others.

HUNT: So you see, Phil, if all modes are equally plausible, then there's no point in considering any of them. Good and evil are like our old friend the elephant.

STANFORD: A *white* elephant in this case, right, Huntley? *(Chuckles.)*

WILSON: I realize it's complicated, but does anybody of you have a definition of morals? Dr. Robaczek, got an operative notion?

DR. ROBACZEK: Yes, well, as I see it, good and evil are not concrete constants but, rather, unstable and elusive variables. They function as infinitely emergent roles within a vast series of interlocking social games. And these millions of contingent social myths are continually deploying themselves along the behavioral poles of an extended multifunctional axis.

(Brief silence)

WILSON: An interesting definition.

STANFORD: It's not just interesting, Phil. It's necessary. We've gotta be scientific, and that's why we shun any dogma that says, "This is right," or, "That's immoral." Each of us has his own ideas about abolitionism or anti-Semitism. But the Company is neutral, since all sides are equally innocent or equally guilty.

WILSON: That's intriguing. How'bout an example of your neutrality?

STANFORD: Well, take our latest anthology. Came out Monday. Title is *Studies in Comparative Genocide*. None of the scholars we hired came to the project with any preconceived judgments. 'Cause we didn't want anybody with a knee-jerk response either for or against.

WILSON: And exactly what did they do?

HUNT: The team carefully examined the various kinds of

genocide performed in Germany, Muscovy, the Caribbean Islands, Massachusetts, Indonesia, and Brazil.

WILSON: By the way, did anyone commission this study?

HUNT: Yes, the Ministry of Peace, Atomic Subdivision. So anyway, these diligent men sorted out the huge array of methods utilized in those different places. They provided a theoretical framework plus graphs, diagrams, and columns of figures showing rates of aggregate growth. A thoroughly professional job. And they didn't pursue things in a spirit of blind condemnation. That's what some dogmatic abolitionist or Karlist would have done. Our team knew that morals and science don't mix. Their job was to analyze a specific technical problem by taking into account the differing points of view of all involved.

DR. ROBACZEK: And of course balancing the good against the bad.

STANFORD: Exactly, that's our businesslike approach, a balance sheet for everything.

VOICE OF MALE MILITANT 3: Balanced for whom?

STANFORD: *(Sighs impatiently)*

WILSON: Please—

MALE MILITANT 3: *(Gets up. About 5'6", brown-skinned. Long, black hair. Olive-dark military fatigues)* I said objective for whom? The point I'm making is it's easy to be objective when you're not on the receiving end of genocide.

HUNT: Excuse me, but you militants have a nasty habit of speaking out of turn. There are rules of civilized procedure.

FEMALE MILITANT 3: *(Gets up. Tall, stocky. Short, light brown hair. Square wire-rimmed glasses. Gray blouse, green corduroys. Midwest accent.)* Excuse *me*, Mr. Hunt, but you folks aren't getting my friend's point. For the millions who've been genocided, objectivity wasn't the issue. And incidentally, why should the Ministry's Atomic Division—

HUNT: *(With subtle scorn)* Atomic Sub-division. You might get your facts straight.

FEMALE MILITANT 3: —why did those guys commission this study?

STANFORD: Oh, boy, here we go, more Karlist paranoia.

DR. ROBACZEK: That past participle "genocided" does not exist.

WILSON: Well, ladies and gentlemen, you've just heard nothing less than the basic Laws of Thought from Perspectives Industries.

FEMALE MILITANT 3: You rotten sons 'a—

WILSON: How 'bout a round of applause?

(Fast big-band jazz. Mingled applause and hisses)

□ □ □

(Three bleeps)

WILSON: Well, gentlemen, could you give us all some notion of your role in a free society?

STANFORD: Phil, I hate to sound arrogant, but we're the ones who make ideas available in this Kingdom and on much of our planet. We manage the free flow of ideas.

HUNT: How many kingdoms can boast a firm that markets every possible idea?

WILSON: Even the enemy's ideas?

HUNT: Oh, yes. *(Chuckles slightly.)* Not that anyone at Multi-facetia takes those ravings seriously. It's laughable, their self-righteous attacks on our Air Cavalry, rumblings about confiscating paper and pencil farms *we legally own*, and crackpot slogans about redistributing the land and giving everybody three bowls of rice a day.

DR. ROBACZEK: Such materialism I find terribly repellent. Animals too can feed their bellies! I cannot see land and rice as the destiny of Man. Those Nepalese terrorists are blind to the soaring greatness of Man's spirit. *(Light applause)*

STANFORD: I agree completely, Doctor. I too am of the belief that Man is primarily spirit, not matter. But we've gotta give all views a chance, so we'll sell Nepalese terrorist ideas to any consumer who wants 'em. Of course, we don't want him led astray by ideology. So before we distribute these so-called "ideas" we go to Psychomarketing for a package which we then melt down with the Nepalese Karlist stuff and pour into Robaczek's Roulette. In a few days the beautifully wrapped dogma's in the shop-windows and Multiplex Malls. Same words, of course, but the bright colors, the scholarly apparatus, and the photographs of naked girls all help put the enemy dogma into scientific perspective.

HUNT: Let *me* ask you something, Phil. How open-minded are those Nepalese terrorists?

WILSON: Well, I guess they don't show both sides, do they?

HUNT: Do they market *our* view to the Nepalese consumer?

WILSON: I don't suppose so.

STANFORD: And that's why we're fighting over there, to give the Nepalese consumer a fuller range of perspectives.

HUNT: Of course, the terrorists know that they can't compete with our firm, so they try to keep us out.

MALE MILITANT 1: *(Stands up abruptly.)* Come on, you guys. The *peasants* are pro-NLF. They've got no *need* for your Company.

DR. ROBACZEK: But naturally, the terrorists brainwash the peasants, and the peasants become pro-terrorist.

FEMALE MILITANT 3: *(Stands up.)* Damn it, you guys' re brainwashing too.

STANFORD: *(Impatiently)* Ludicrous. We do the exact opposite. We advocate openness to *all* ideas. That's brainwashing?

WILSON: Doctor, quick, give us some "perspective." *(Laughter in audience)* What's the essential function of Perspectives Industries?

DR. ROBACZEK: *(Without hesitation)* The function of Perspectives Industries is to attack and destroy all ideas.

WILSON: *(Brief pause)* All ideas?

DR. ROBACZEK: All.

WILSON: *(Bewildered)* Now that's a tough one. If Perspectives markets ideas, then why *destroy* them?

STANFORD: *(Impulsively)* Well, it's great for sales.

DR. ROBACZEK: Yet there is the deeper metaphysical reason too. Since nothing is certain, then no idea is completely adequate, and no idea should be spared. Remember the Fifth Law: ALL IDEAS ARE EQUAL *(words flash)*, that is to say, equally valid and hence equally false. And so we have the duty to prevent anyone idea from gaining too exclusive a hold over the consumer. Otherwise he becomes unbalanced, like abolitionists or anti-Semites, who believe that only their idea is the correct one.

WILSON: How do you deal with Karlism? I know it's the ideological faith preached by Muscovy and Mars. Is there much to it?

HUNT: Not really. As you know, Karlism is based on the views of Marcus Karl, the so-called thinker born up in Boston of immigrant Martian parents. He took a doctorate in New England and wrote a thesis on ancient theories of labor. After that he did some rabble-rousing at a few plantations, and then spent most of his life at the Boston Public Library writing unreadable books attacking our system, such as the three-volume monster called *Slavery*. We publish it in a handsome boxed set.

WILSON: Tell me, for somebody who'd like to understand Karl's Utopia, which book do you suggest for starters?

HUNT: Frankly, Phil, I've never bothered with Marcus Karl. It's just not worth the time. Would you read *Mein Kampf*? Poor Karl didn't know a thing about economics, despite all his tables and graphs. He just gave vent to his irrational hate for our open system. And look, agreed, in his time the slaves were overworked and badly paid. But he actually said the slaves would get worse off and poorer.

WILSON: Hasn't worked out that way, has it?

HUNT: Well, both slaveholders and slaves are richer now. And we're glad. Today's slaves own personal moviolas, electric kitchens, and tandem motorcycles. Some former slaves now drive gold-trimmed cars with velvet seats and oak panelling in them. No slaves in Marcus Karl's time had moviolas or big cars. You can see why he's dated.

STANFORD: Nothing's turned out like Karl said it would. He actually prophesied that the slaves would overthrow the system. Well, in this Kingdom, every slave revolt since Karl's time has been put down by the police or the Air Cavalry. There go Marcus Karl's predictions for you.

HUNT: Besides, Karl preached this collectivist dogma that everyone belongs to a social class. He failed to see the slave as an individual. He couldn't foresee our classless Kingdom where even slaves can go shopping in Multiplex Malls.

STANFORD: Something they couldn't do back then. Now they can.

WILSON: So what was Karl's solution?

HUNT: Abolition. He thought abolition solves everything.

STANFORD: Pretty utopian, eh? Really, there's always been individuals who're smarter than others. So why try making everybody equal? Besides, without slavery, people won't work. They get lazy.

HUNT: And who wants Karlist-type equality? People basically want to own more moviolas and tandem motorcycles and big cars with liquor cabinets in them, and maybe have a few slaves. It's human nature. But the Karlists want to deprive everybody of the right to be rich.

WILSON: What about the Karlist kingdoms? How do they manage?

STANFORD: Phil, I'll give you a classic instance. Y'see *(points at himself)*, this guy's been to Muscovy, and he knows whereof he speaks. I got sent there way back in the summer of' '45 by His Majesty's Government, on assignment from the Ministry of Exports. I stayed mostly in big cities like Stalingrad, Minsk, and Smolensk, selling farm equipment. Well, what shocked me about those places was the wretched housing. People crowded four or five to a room everywhere. And in Stalingrad I actually saw no houses! Plenty of folks in tents, though. And after beholding *that* nightmare, I said, this is Karlism! Thirty years of Karlist rule, and they can't even house their people! And in my Petrograd hotel room there wasn't a pillow, and it was hot that summer, but there were no cold drinks to be had at the hotel, let alone air conditioning! And y'know, I thought of my three-story house here in the Triple Cities, with its refrigerator chock-full of T-bone steaks and instant Martinis, and as I suffered in my deprivation, I thought, God in heaven! If this be Karlism, then I'll take our free market society anytime!

(Thunderous applause and bravos! from much of audience. Some hissing and booing from one corner)

WILSON: *(Moved, wipes his eyes)* Mr. Stanford, that's a powerful speech. I mean, I'm on the verge of tears it's so moving. From your eloquent account it's crystal clear that Karlism just doesn't work.

HUNT: *(With conviction)* It doesn't. Everywhere the Karlists get a chance they mess things up. Look at the housing problem in Nepal now. Millions of mountain people freezing without shelter. How can anyone buy Karlism when peasants lose their shacks?

DR. ROBACZEK: That is the difference between Hitlerism and Karlism. Under Hitler, the Jews lost everything. Under Karlism, everyone does. Did Hitler ever build a wall in Berlin?

WILSON: So it looks as if Karl's ideas are doomed to failure.

STANFORD: Sure. Trouble with Marcus Karl was, he didn't understand human nature. He couldn't accept the natural desire to own slaves and land. Somewhere I've come across his crackpot view that nobody should have more than two houses. Well, suppose I draw the line at three? Or three thousand? Who's to say?

DR. ROBACZEK: Quite ridiculous. It is simple human nature. I would *love* to own three thousand houses.

HUNT: Everyone would. But then those abolitionists come and say all slaveholders' lands should be doled out to the slaves, just like that. Good heavens, there's too much government meddling in our lives as is.

STANFORD: As far as I can see, there's no greater threat to our liberties than abolitionism. Try to imagine abolitionists at the Royal Court. D'you think they'd let pro-slavery ideas be sold freely in the Malls?

FEMALE MILITANT 2: *(Gets up. Emphatic)* Just one minute!

HUNT: Why, yes—

FEMALE MILITANT 2: I'm a bit unclear as to why abolitionism is a threat to liberties. After all, the slaves would be gaining their liberty.

STANFORD: A nice idea, but how does one go about it?

MALE MILITANT 1: *(Gets up.)* Easy enough. You make slavery illegal. Then you enforce the law with troops.

STANFORD: Well, y'know, that's taking away one man's freedom and giving it to somebody else. I don't buy that. I don't believe in sacrificing the individual to the group. That's collectivism, and it's the first step to the horrors of Hitlerism.

DR. ROBACZEK: Young man, what difference is there between these coercive ideas and those of Hitler toward the Jews?

STANFORD: Besides, y'know, it's a tough job, running a plantation. Some slaveholders work twelve hours a day, minding their own business, so live and let live, that's my motto.

HUNT: Let me suggest that you militants try persuading individual slaveholders instead. Coercion solves nothing.

STANFORD: Exactly. As I see it, slavery's an individual problem to be solved by individuals. If a slaveholder frees his slaves, that's his choice. If a slave buys his freedom, that's his choice. But neither of them needs somebody to tell him what's for his own good.

FEMALE MILITANT 3: *(Gets up.)* Really now, Mr. Stanford. We're not talking individuals. We're talking about the slaveocracy that rules this Kingdom. And we believe the power and property of that slaveocracy should be abolished now!

(Applause and cheers from militants' side. Confused murmurs elsewhere)

WILSON: In other words, Miss, just because a man has slaves, that makes him a member of the so-called "slaveocracy?"

FEMALE MILITANT 3: I would say so.

STANFORD: That's not right. You're not seeing the individual.

HUNT: I simply *cannot* see what is to be gained by putting people into categories. Really, that is appalling.

STANFORD: I've got slaves, and I don't see the word "slaveocrat" pasted on my forehead when I get up in the morning. I'm just me, that's all.

DR. ROBACZEK: It is racist to put people in categories.

FEMALE MILITANT 1: No, sir, no, it's *not* racist to say there's a ruling class in this Kingdom. Can't you see that?

HUNT: Well, frankly, Miss, I doubt that your alleged ruling class even exists.

MALE MILITANT 3 AND FEMALE MILITANTS 1 AND 3: What?

HUNT: Seriously, this so-called slaveocrat class. That's something dreamt up by Karlists. There's no such thing.

STANFORD: You kids've picked up some conspiracy theory. I mean, since when're slaveholders involved in some secret plot?

DR. ROBACZEK: Let me remind you students that Muscovy and Mars also believe this Kingdom is ruled by so-called slaveocrats.

MALE MILITANT 2: C'mon, old man, it's the Royal Air

Cavalry who've been bombing Nepal, not Muscovites or Martians.

HUNT: Well, so? If we withdrew, you know what would happen. Thousands would be massacred by the Karlists.

STANFORD: Is that what you people want?

FEMALE MILITANT 2: *(Snaps.)* How d'you know? Can you be so sure? How'bout Law Number Four? Be more skeptical!

DR. ROBACZEK: Young lady, it has happened. Look at France in 1945, just after Germany withdrew, where 100,000 people were imprisoned or executed by the so-called liberators. And thousands more who fled to Paraguay and Bolivia. And all because of their beliefs. Could any decent human being allow it to happen again?

FEMALE MILITANT 1: *(Quietly)* But we've killed millions of Nepalese already—

STANFORD: *(More forcefully)* Well, don't stray from the issue.

MALE MILITANT 3: Which is what?

STANFORD: Which is, what'll happen if *we* withdraw. 'Cause I'll tell you: if *one* person, *one single person* were to be killed as a result of our withdrawal, we would've failed that one person. We would've shirked our responsibility, which is to save that one life.

FEMALE MILITANT 3: The Royal Cavalry have killed millions.

DR. ROBACZEK: Such an obsession with a single issue.

HUNT: Listen, Miss—uh—what is your name?

FEMALE MILITANT 3: None a' your damn business.

HUNT: Fine, but you shouldn't get so emotional.

DR. ROBACZEK: Emotionalism is dangerous. Hitler was emotional.

STANFORD: Y'see, you kids ignore the sanctity of individual life. That's where we differ. You care about statistical man. We care about the individual.

MALE MILITANT 4: *(Long, scraggly, dirty-blond hair. Gold-rim*

glasses. Drooping moustache. Denim jacket and trousers)
Christ almighty, is this guy serious?

DR. ROBACZEK: A good point, Ted.

HUNT: If that doesn't convince them, nothing will.

MALE MILITANT 3: *(Shouts.)* That's the biggest crock I've heard.

FEMALE MILITANT 2: *(Shouts.)* It's pure dog shit.

WILSON: Please, mind your language.

HUNT: Now look here, you've the right to disagree, that's what we're fighting for, but let's not resort to verbal violence.

STANFORD: Much as I disagree with you, young lady, I'd never stoop so low as to call *your* ideas "dog shit."

VOICE OF FEMALE MILITANT 4: *(Very loud)* Oh! You guys are so damn full of it!

WILSON: Miss, please—

HUNT: I beg your pardon—

FEMALE MILITANT 4: *(Jumps onto stage. Tall, slender, attractive. Long blond wavy hair. Angular features, flushed face. Baggy blue blouse half-tucked into beige trousers, white tennis shoes, all paint stained. Earnest, insistent manner)* Jesus! You and your twisted words! It's nothing but a bunch of pretentious gobbledegook!

WILSON: Miss, please—

FEMALE MILITANT 4: Everything you say is so false, so upside down, so completely unnatural, it's incredibly sick!

DR. ROBACZEK: *(Scornfully)* What is "natural," after all?

FEMALE MILITANT 4: *(Bangs on table.)* Shut up, you jerk! *(Points.)* Look at them! *(Amazement among the men. Confusion in audience)* These goons are selling things to our children? Designing toys? Putting out films for our schools? Imagine that!

HUNT: Phil, call the police quick. *(Wilson exits.)*

FEMALE MILITANT 4: *(Louder, angrier. Waves her fist.* Millions of Nepalese are dying from round-the-clock bombing. Millions of our nation's subjects still live in slavery. And *you* talk about it all being *(her lips twist)* a matter of point of view.

VOICE OF WILSON: *(Frantically)* This way, officers. That's the one. *(Enters, followed by two policemen who jump ahead and grab her. Applause from portion of audience.)*

POLICEMAN 1: *(Burly, ruddy, redhaired)* Okay, you, move along!

(They start dragging her away. She tries to shake them off.)

POLICEMAN 2: *(Short, skinny, swarthy)* Move along, he said!

FEMALE MILITANT 4: You haven't heard the end yet, you gangsters!

(Exeunt. Shouts of "Attagirl" and "Show those zombies!" from militants. Fast big band jazz music drowns them out. Brief darkness, sudden silence)

□ □ □

(Three bleeps)

WILSON: *(Upset)* This is a—shocking experience.

HUNT: Intolerance is always shocking, Phil.

WILSON: I mean, they've no respect for other beliefs.

DR. ROBACZEK: And this incomprehensible hatred of slaveholders. Slaveholders have to eat too. They have their rights as much—

HUNT: Phil, we've just witnessed the most dangerous force on this planet. And Perspectives has got to fight it.

WILSON: What is it?

HUNT: Fanaticism.

DR. ROBACZEK: There is no greater threat to free thought.

HUNT: These kids think slaveholders are evil and abolitionists are saints!

DR. ROBACZEK: And they label German soldiers evil but Muscovite tanks and French terrorists absolutely right. Yes, we must fight this fanaticism at every opportunity.

WILSON: A noble aim, gentlemen, and yet we've got these fanatical militants among us. How come?

STANFORD: It's purely psychological, Phil. You know, youth's a tough time. And it's toughest in this most rational kingdom in history. We've got plantation management down to an exact science. Abolitionists simply have an irrational hate for our society's successes. Kids especially suffer from sexual drives, and masturbation isn't enough. A lot of 'em hate their parents too, so they find an outlet in extremism. In Germany they turned to anti-Semitism, here they resort to abolitionism. It's a ritualistic thing, like killing their fathers. Just last night my daughter informed me that slavery and the Nepal war are evil. I knew she was just getting back at me.

WILSON: So how to tackle this problem of youthful excess?

STANFORD: Well, you saw much of it already—our idea boutiques and toys, and our Roulette models. But there's also our human resources. We've got a huge troupe of first-rate artists, musicians, and poets. And we send them to the schools, farms, factories, and private parties, where they set up their musical thought shows. Armed with portable orchestras, magic lanterns, and chorus lines, they bring word of our Six Laws. They sing of slaves who've become rich slaveholders, they publicize our wares, they fight all dogmas.

DR. ROBACZEK: Very often, too, we confront them with issues of transcendence. We invoke those eternal questions that dwarf our trivial human affairs. Let us suppose that the students persist in their obsessions—abolition, Nepal, etc. And so I ask them somberly, "But, please, tell me, this abolition, will it abolish the greatest problem of them all, the problem of death? Someday we all must die—you, myself, the slaves, the slaveholders; all must die. Can your revolution free Man from this most fearful of enigmas?" It renders them speechless. Other times I point at my cup of coffee and muse profoundly, "See this cup! Is it really a cup of coffee? Why is there a cup and not no-cup? What is reality? What is coffee?" I remind them of the cosmic absurdities of life and ask whether leaving Nepal will bring much comfort to those troubled by the problem of nothingness. *(Waxing lyrical)* These potential militants thus discover the larger riddles that transcend mere Karlism or abolitionism. It dawns on them that the slavery issue is but a speck in an infinite cosmos, an age-old struggle between Self and Other. Ah, yes, they are sublime, these conundrums of old.

HUNT: We also pose a challenge to them when we detail our "Lollipops for Nepalese Toddlers" program. With our graphs we indicate the huge amounts of lollipops handed out by this Kingdom to the Nepalese these last ten years. We set up Lollipop Maps and show footage of Lollipop Distribution Camps, special areas where thousands of Nepalese families are sent lollipops. We list the top ten flavors out of 94, the broadest range of choice the Nepalese consumer has ever seen. Incidentally, Muscovite lollipops come in two flavors only. Oh, and we include a display of our gorgeous multihued wrappings.

DR. ROBACZEK: A display that speaks with eloquence. We remain aware that aesthetics is crucial, perhaps more so than food.

STANFORD: The one that really gets the militants, though, is our bright color slide of a cute little native girl, all radiant as she sucks on her lollipop. *(Slide flashes on screen)*

MALE MILITANT 4: *(Stands up.)* Great. Meanwhile you guys've made a desert out of that little girl's country.

DR. ROBACZEK: *(Concerned)* No, please, go easy on words like "desert." Such hyperbole reminds me of Herr Hitler's distortions of language. Whatever the might of this Kingdom's weapons, they cannot alter patterns of climate or the chemistry of soil. Our bombs are huge, yes, but they cannot create sand or cactus from nothing, they cannot stop the rains. Strictly speaking, a desert is an arid expanse of sand where it seldom rains, and to ignore this, in my view, is loose and dangerous thinking.

WILSON: Doctor, I do admire your tough stance toward language.

STANFORD: Besides, what's so bad about deserts? Deserts make beautiful landscapes. I've got a big wall poster of a desert in my executive suite. And look hard in any desert, you'll come across some fertile areas with ponds and date trees. Take the Sahara, the driest of them all, and yet it's got hundreds of those things, ask any safari leader, he'll tell you. So it all depends on how you view it. From one perspective a desert is a series of fresh ponds, surrounded by palm trees and connected by stretches of sand. Why, I wouldn't mind having an oasis myself.

WILSON: *(Bewildered)* Good golly, you gentlemen do make short work of our established ideas.

HUNT: Ted's view of deserts is pretty original, isn't it?

WILSON: Amazingly so.

MALE MILITANT I: *(Brusque)* It's not original, it's false.

HUNT: *(Haughtily)* And you have Truth with a capital T?

FEMALE MILITANT I: *(Reasonably)* We never said we did.

FEMALE MILITANT 3: *(Gruffly)* Talk about distorting language. Come on, guys, let's get the hell outta here.

(The militants, about thirty of them, rise up and begin filing out.)

HUNT: Ted here has his point of view. A decent human being's got to respect it. And we fight an uphill battle in order that new interpretations like his can be heard and sold. It's not easy, but what can you do if they insult you and stomp out mumbling obscenities?

(As militants leave hall, rhythmic clapping and shouts of "Out of Nepal!" are heard outside.)

STANFORD: Listen to 'em, they're at it again, these rowdies, so much in the grip of fanaticism and dogma.

FEMALE MILITANT I: *(Earnestly)* That's not fair, what you said.

DR. ROBACZEK: Miss, there are rules of fair play. Peace and harmony are in your friends' hands.

MALE MILITANT 3: No, fella, it's in *your* hands.

MALE MILITANT 2: Quit passin' the buck, will ya?

FEMALE MILITANT 2: *(Last one to leave. Points at stage)* You guys better change your ideas before it's too late. *(Slams door.)*

DR. ROBACZEK: Well, is that not ridiculous? "Change," she said. That is amusing!

(About 100 people are heard outside, chanting or shouting. From now on the noise turns gradually louder.)

HUNT: "Change." Heavens, we change our ideas every week! If anybody's the force of change on this planet, it's us.

STANFORD: It's these young militants who don't change. They harp on the same worn-out issues. No flexibility.

DR. ROBACZEK: Perspectives Industries grows constantly, and what is growth if not change?

HUNT: We aren't Number One for nothing.

(By now the crowd is larger, perhaps several thousands. Mumbles in audience)

STANFORD: It's those abolitionists spreading hate again.

HUNT: Just last week thousands of slaves went on a rampage in Salinas. You know who egged them on—some Karlists and their abolitionist mercenaries.

STANFORD: *(Angrily)* And you know, Phil? They badly beat up thirteen slaveholders and shot one dead. In cold blood.

DR. ROBACZEK: It is simply shocking. This violence rejects the very basis of civilization.

(Meanwhile explosions and gunfire in the streets. Sound of low-flying planes. The shouts become louder and more disorganized. Some action is just outside the auditorium walls. In audience,

nervous talking, an occasional cry)

HUNT: Any movement that takes an individual life can only be the sheerest barbarism.

STANFORD: Goes to show you, abolitionism's no better than any other cause.

(Explosion shakes building.)

FEMALE MILITANT 5: *(Storms in. Medium height. Smooth-brown skin, straight nose, straight black hair. Fresh, Hispanic-Indian look. Camouflage fatigues, boots. Sweaty. Points sub machine gun at stage. Voluminous alto voice)* Okay, you guys, this is it.

(Followed by Male Militant 2 with crowbar and Female Militant 3 with carbine. About a dozen others stand in back.)

WILSON: Hey, now, just what's with you people?

HUNT: How dare you storm in here like SS troops?

FEMALE MILITANT 5: We are not like SS troops. The SS wanted imperialist wars and slave labor. We don't.

STANFORD: What do you want?

MALE MILITANT 2: We demand abolition of slavery and total withdrawal from Nepal.

FEMALE MILITANT 3: And land for the slaves.

FEMALE MILITANT 5: The issue is peace and justice.

HUNT: *(Smiles.)* My dear, you must define your terms. What is "justice?" Or for that matter, what is "land?"

STANFORD: Yeah, who's to say?

DR. ROBACZEK: Let us discuss these philosophical issues.

WILSON: Seems operative. Why don't you kids join us?

FEMALE MILITANT 5: To hell with you and your idiotic discussions! We wanna end your dirty little war, not talk about it!

STANFORD: Well, who're you to impose your ideas on anybody?

(Gunfighting extends through halls of building.)

HUNT: You are like Nazis, forcing your views like this.

MALE MILITANT 2: Dammit! We're for peace, you're the Nazis!

DR. ROBACZEK: Utterly ridiculous. We tolerate all views.

STANFORD: Did Nazis let individuals say anything they want?

FEMALE MILITANT 5: *(Points her left index finger.)* Cut the irrelevant crap, old man. You guys're in favor of carpet bombing—*(mockingly)* just like Nazis! *(Normal voice)* We're against it.

HUNT: Miss, I favor the war, yes, but I'm open to other views, unlike you young fanatics. *(Militants hoot him down.)* See what I mean?

STANFORD: Phil, call the Armored Police.

(Wilson hurries out.)

DR. ROBACZEK: *(Shouts)* And the Municipal Air Cavalry.

(Gunfire just outside auditorium. Sounds of voices of people being hit. Some militants exit hurriedly.)

FEMALE MILITANT 5: Don't bother, you goons. We're not gonna waste time here. *(She sprays ceiling with submachine gunfire. A glass chandelier crashes down on stage, a few feet in front of panel.)* Let's go!

(Exeunt quickly; meanwhile Female Militant 3 takes aim at target outside and fires just before exiting last.)

WILSON: *(Enters, anxious and under stress.)* Maestro, please? *(Soft piano trio jazz in background. Meanwhile sounds of windows breaking. Continued gunfire both far and nearby. Confusion and fear among audience)* Ladies and gentlemen, please remain seated. Peace and order will soon be restored.

(Sounds of airplanes flying overhead)

DR. ROBACZEK: *(Shakes his head.)* It is most unfortunate that Royal authorities must quell Karlist violence. Sad *(sirens)* because these militants and abolitionists are merely residual beings. They are holdovers from a superstitious age of absolutes and are now desperately clinging to their religion.

HUNT: Sure it's sad, Dr. Robaczek, but it's no fault of ours if these dogmatists are history's rejects. *(Sounds of bombs whistling and detonating)* They are stubborn reactionaries doggedly opposed to our great revolution. We are individualistic, scientific, and modern. They are collectivistic, emotional, and enamored of the State, like Hitler was. Which is why their violence must be kept in check.

(A portion of the building is bombed. Noises, rumbles, shakes)

WILSON: Maestro? *(Loud, lively, brassy, big-band jazz. Outside, more sounds of bombs, gunfire, sirens, shouts, screams. Then, a lull)* Ladies and gentlemen *(drum roll)*, thank you for coming to this week's production of *(cymbals crash)* Meet the Companies! *(Trumpet calls are heard as the words appear on the screen.)* Tonight you've heard three high officials from Perspectives Industries *(words flash)* expound the secrets of their exciting enterprise. *(Continuing jazz, now soft. Combat noises flare up outside. A bomb whistles, hits a nearby corridor. Microphone goes dead. Silence outside)* They've given of their time to explain to us their multifaceted approach to our world. *(Screen goes blank. Lights go out.)* Meanwhile their struggle for new perspectives goes on, and *(The microphone and the lights are restored, now sharper and stronger than before.)* we hope you've all been inspired by the examples they've shown us. Come back next week when we'll be presenting—

(The sudden sound of a low-flying airplane drowns out his final words. He and the executives stand up and take an informal, relaxed bow. Warm applause from the audience. The band winds up with some parallel ninth-chord cadences.)

APPENDIX

Selections from the Private Notebooks
of Carlos Chadwick

1. On America, and Americans

We have generated and given unto the world a dogma uniquely our own—Dogmatism of the Center. Among its broad mental results are the countless Americans handicapped by political dyslexia: can't tell right from left.

□

The original Greek of our noun *idiot* signified anybody who is exclusively personal, individual, and private. Knowing that, we must inevitably ask ourselves if—be it by conscious intellectual choice or unreflecting practice—a good many Americans qualify as idiots or at least show a substantial idiocy quotient.

□

The time has come, however, to revise an old American adage: in certain instances it's all too easy to blame your problems on yourself.

□

Experience has demonstrated: it's often enough the case that necessity (not idleness) is the devil's workshop, while at the same time an innocuous, earned, and sanctioned idleness can be the mother of invention. Of course there is idleness and idleness, for what exotic inventions our idle but idiotic rich can fashion within

249

the devil workshops of their minds! (After which they hire designers and scribes to give public shape to those inventions!)

□

"It all depends on your point of view" say many Americans. I say: *False*, or one-tenth true (if that!). It depends far more on the points of view, and particularly on the views of *your* view, that are being held at that time by your enemies and adversaries! (Whether they be enemies public or private, actual or potential, and conscious or not, really matters little.)

2. On Forced Labor

The Soviet Russian labor camps in Siberia constitute one of the most vicious, most shocking, most appalling, and most heartrending crimes committed by Man against Man since the installment and growth of our plantation camps in Dixie.

□

Really, the spectacle of my fellow Americans (who legally sanctioned bond slavery on their national soil *for two whole centuries)*, now wailing with such horror, grief, and indignation over Soviet decades of labor camps, is nothing less than *nauseating*.

□

No doubt, there were differences between the Siberian labor camps and our Southern cottonfields. For example, the latter were hot in summer, and the former were bitter cold in winter. There is also the undeniable fact that forced labor was shipped by rail in one case, and by boat in the other. Moreover their inmates were mostly white, and sometimes brown or yellow, whereas ours were exclusively black. And while the Anglo-American system of slave labor flourished throughout the 17th, 18th, and 19th centuries, the Soviet Russian variety emerged in the 20th.

3. On Expansion and War

Hitler deported, enslaved, and murdered untold millions of white heterosexual non-Communist Europeans. His was the greatest of all human crimes.

□

Crimes notwithstanding, Hitler rescued and then aided in the unprecedented growth and enrichment of the German capitalist system. That is among the best-kept of business secrets.

□

At different times in history the Spaniards, French, and Anglo-Saxons have forcibly displaced, deported, enslaved, and murdered millions upon millions of peasants and non-whites. That process we now know as the Rise of the West.

□

In mid-century Stalin cruelly deported, enslaved, and murdered untold millions of peasants, revolutionaries, functionaries, intellectuals, and white Europeans (including, alas! many Germans). That he did so in the name of socialism gives tremendous solace to orthodox American hearts and minds today.

□

Between 1941 and 1945 the Soviet people experienced the bloodiest military battles, the longest combat frontlines, and the absolutely highest casualty figures in all human history. My fellow Americans (you, so notoriously fond of your "Biggest This" and "Highest That" statistical games), you do not know that history—though some of us know why you don't know it.

□

The Soviet push into Central Europe thoroughly whipped, destroyed and all but defeated the German Nazi war machine. Then we rushed in from the West and claimed victory for ourselves. That is one of our best-guarded, least comforting, most demoralizing of state secrets.

4. On Definitions

terrorism—an illegitimate, primitive, barbarous war practice whereby volunteer troops kill persons from a point somewhere on the ground.

strategic bombardment—a legitimate, advanced, civilized war practice whereby professional technicians kill persons from a point somewhere in the air.

enlightened self-interest—the rational and moral force that has led American financiers, entrepreneurs, and executives to their condition of civic greatness.

greed—the malevolent force driving Japanese corporations, Arab oil magnates, and American labor unions, all of whom think about nothing other than private gain.

the Bottom Line—the end that justifies the means.

collectivism—the pernicious creed of Soviet bureaucrats, who preach subordination of the individual to the group.

individualism—the enlightened creed espoused by the leading officials of large-scale, multinational, corporate conglomerate organizations in industry, finance, and sales, who preach the freedom of the individual from the group.

executive—in American Managerial Science, an individualist who sits and struggles with the Bottom Line and is paid a minimum of a few million per year.

Warsaw, Prague, Budapest—cities where live the world's most oppressed peoples. Dominated by Moscow, whom they all hate and refuse to obey.

Warsaw Pact—the world's biggest concentration of troop strength, comprising seven backward, inefficient, and hopelessly failed Marxist nations that are poised for a Blitz of Paris, London, and New York. Dominated by Moscow.

Soviet tank—a modern symbol of evil with which the Warsaw Pact nations intend to blitz Paris, London, and New York.

B-52—a modern symbol of freedom, routinely equipped with a stockpile of hydrogen bombs and thermonuclear devices.

5. On Ancient Histories

Why has the decline and fall of Rome so constantly been looked upon as a terrible, lamentable, earth-shaking tragedy? From another "perspective" the whole thing could just as well be seen as the emergence of the Franks and Visigoths. (France! Spain!)

□

Why has the rise and expansion of the juggernaut Rome never been described as the effacement of Etruria and the destruction of the Celts?

□

The Franks, the Visigoths, the Vandals *et al.* were conquering Rome throughout the 5th century A.D. Meanwhile the Romans were bulldozing into Carthage, Gaul, Spain, Britain *et aliis* during the 2nd and 1st centuries B.C. The differences, then, are chiefly chronological.

□

Alexander, the Great! Julius Caesar, the Emperor! Attila, the Hun! Three renowned conquerors, their differences again being chiefly chronological, ethnic, and linguistic. That, and the matter of subsequent historians' preferred loyalties.

6. On Empire, and Imperialists

"Your rich men are full of violence, your inhabitants speak lies, and their tongue is deceitful in their mouth." (Micah 6:12)

There is a beautiful and awesome logic to the way in which my fellow Americans (whose country steadily attains ever-greater heights in its rational endorsement and religious celebration of greed) also systematically deny to their vast global empire any economic motives whatsoever. This is that novel and uniquely American Theory of Economic Non-Determinism, or Cupidity in One Country.

"Behold—the earth shall be utterly laid waste, and utterly despoiled; for the Lord has spoken this word—Therefore a curse devours the earth, and its inhabitants suffer for their guilt." (Isaiah 24: 1, 3, 6)

When Kurtz scribbled "Exterminate the Brutes!" concerning Africans, it became a famous line in a British novel.

When someone suggested that we "Bomb Vietnam back to the Stone Age," it was the colorful campaign slogan of a respected Yankee general.

"But, O Lord of hosts, who judgest righteously—let me see thy vengeance upon them." (Jeremiah 11:20)

And when Asian or Latino or Slavic leaders arm their arsenals and fight back and say, "Death to the gringo imperialists," well . .

" 'Behold, I will punish them; the young men shall die by the sword; their sons and daughters shall die by famine; and none of them shall be left.' " (Jeremiah 11:20)

Well, why not? Maybe an honest-to-goodness nuclear war (or an accident) would be good for certain Americans. You know, experience, broadened horizons and all that sort of thing. Exterminate the brutes! I'm for nuclear war. Yeah!

"I smote you with blight and mildew. I laid waste your gardens and your vineyards, your fig trees and your olive trees." (Amos 4:9)

The 1972 floods in Pennsylvania, or any other natural disaster: it would be comforting to view them as the Lord's vengeance for our barbarous, neo-Nazi bombing overseas; it would be a joy to see and hear the fire-and-brimstone preachers telling their (my) fellow Americans that they've gotten what they deserved. As some streetcorner Isaiah or shopping-mall Micah might say, "It's God's punishment, so—zap!—take that!"

"Is not this the fast that I choose: to loose the bonds of wickedness, to let the oppressed to free . . . ? Is it not to share your bread with the hungry . . . ?" (Isaiah 58:6)

But all we have left now is our subtle, refined, learned, and guiltily perverse feeling of *Schadenfreude*.

"Woe to you, destroyer. When you have ceased to destroy, you shall be destroyed." (Ibid, 33:1)

7

In all sorts of ways I still actually believe in Perspectivism; I am a product of Perspectivism; and there are many avowed Perspectivists who remain good human beings. The trouble is, Perspectivism has become a semi-official, even right-wing ideology, and countless distortions and crimes are being committed (and probably will be committed) in its name.

8

No one knows why, but it seems to be a fundamental social law that the most enviable features and very best practices of any given nation tend to be most shrilly and aggressively trumpeted by that nation's stupidest and emptiest, most ignorant and dangerous, most banal and evil and, in sum, very worst human elements.

□□□□□

A Chicano jazz pianist falls in love with a sorority girl and reads all of Ayn Rand to get into her good graces; he ends up converted—with strange consequences.

Gene H. Bell-Villada strikes again . . .

THE PIANIST WHO LIKED AYN RAND: A NOVELLA AND 13 STORIES

. . . available in print and ebook editions

Growing up Latino, music, music criticism, and university life in the 60s are among the themes of Bell-Villada's short fiction, in styles ranging from realistic to fantastical to experimental. Shifting between wistful and satirical moods, and wholesome and sinister atmospheres, the international author's stories touch down in San Juan, Philadelphia, Cambridge MA, Manhattan, Tucson, Berkeley CA and other settings, including an imaginary isle of silence.

"Readers who appreciate wit, an offbeat perspective, and a biting look at the blind spots in U.S. culture will greatly enjoy this volume." —Rachel Kranz, Artistic Dir. Theater of Necessity, New York